UPSTAIRS AT DEREK'S

Jo Edwards

Published by Weasel Green Press

This book is a work of fiction. Names, characters, places, and incidents either are products of the author's imagination or are used fictitiously. Any resemblance to actual persons, living or dead, events, or locales is entirely coincidental.

UPSTAIRS AT DEREK'S

Cover Design by The Art of Communication www.book-design.co.uk
Edited by Mike Rose

ISBN: 978-1-908212-46-7

First Edition

DEDICATION

For my neighbours. Everybody needs good ones.

UPSTAIRS AT DEREK'S

Prologue

She's standing behind the DJ booth, watching the bride as she floats around the dance floor, her cream silk dress skimming the floor. It's exactly the sort of dress she would choose; slightly off the shoulder, scooped neckline, lace bodice – it is simple and understated but so, so beautiful, and heart-meltingly romantic. There's no one else in the room as the couple sway to Ed Sheeran. "People fall in love in mysterious ways, maybe just a touch of a hand ..." Their eyes are locked together. The groom's gaze is a little unfocused but, despite the influence of Jack Daniels, it's clear he's smitten with his bride. Glen used to look at her like that. When had he stopped; before the conference in Manchester, or after? Uh-oh, here it comes again, the green-eyed monster, rising up like bile to choke her. Sometimes, when Glen is away and she's alone in bed, the suspicion envelops her so thickly she fears it will suffocate her.

Outside, the sun is beginning to set behind the hills, the last rays falling on the silvery river, diamonds dancing on its surface. "Kiss me under the light of a thousand stars ..." She picks up a cluster of empty glasses from an abandoned table and holds them to her chest. What would her first-dance song be? 'Stuck On You', Lionel Ritchie? No, nothing from that era, too painful; she doesn't want to be reminded of *him*. Something more uplifting, perhaps. How about 'River Deep Mountain High'? She gives herself a little shake, annoyed at her weakness. She's never going to have that first dance. You need a wedding first. Glen might have asked her once, but not now, it won't happen now. Michael Bolton's 'Said I Loved You But I Lied' – that's more appropriate, the theme tune to her life. The truth might hurt for a little while but a lie hurts forever. She gives a start as someone taps her on the shoulder and she turns to find the weary-eyed receptionist behind her. "I thought you ought to know that one of the bridesmaids has passed out in the Ladies. It's the larger of the two, unfortunately. She's blocking all three cubicles and we can't shift her. Chef's gone to fetch the luggage trolley but it's going to take all of us to haul her on to it."

"Right," she sighs. "I'll come and give you a hand."

"Change your shoes first. Open-toed aren't a good idea, the place is awash with puke."

This is not my life. This can't be my life.

Chapter One

"How the hell did his teeth get under here?"

"It must have been when he sneezed. I wondered where they'd got to."

"They're grinning at me." My sister straightens up and leans against the faded pine chest of drawers. "You know, I think it's the first time I've ever seen Dad smile, apart from when I left home, of course." She looks around the small bedroom and shivers. "It feels like he's still here, what with the overpowering stench of TCP and that horrid old string vest hanging over the chair. Why on earth didn't he buy himself a new one? It's in absolute tatters."

"Um," I rub my nose awkwardly. "He didn't wear it, Cath, he used it as something to grip, when he was, er, straining."

She frowns at me uncomprehendingly. "Straining? What do you mean, why was he-" she breaks off, her face contorting in disgust. "Oh my God. And that chair I was sitting on, that was his-"

"Commode." I finish for her and then a wicked thought strikes me: "Actually, I don't think I ever got round to emptying it. Would you do it for me?"

Cath's horrified eyes dart to the chair. "Are you sure? I mean, he died over three weeks ago, and you've had so much to deal with, perhaps you've just forgotten cleaning it out."

I shake my head, gazing dejectedly down at the carpet. Unable to refuse my request when I appear so forlorn, Cath makes a valiant attempt to hide her revulsion. "Alright, I can do this." She edges hesitantly around the bed toward the chair, her face already a sickly shade of green. "I mean, you've had to do this for years, haven't you? And it's only bodily fluids, after all, just a bit of wee."

"He suffered terribly with diarrhoea near the end."

"Oh Jesus." She reaches the other side of the room and, swallowing hard, slowly lifts the seat of the chair, steeling herself to peer inside.

"BOO!" I yell. Cath whirls round, the seat slamming shut.

"Colin, you bastard!" She grabs a pillow from the bed and hurls it at my head. "You know how squeamish I am, you sod. I can't even look at my own, I have to close my eyes before I can flush the bog."

I laugh and lob the yellowing pillow back onto the bed as Cath sits down on the edge of the mattress. She pushes a stray wisp of chestnut hair from her eyes as she surveys the meagre room. "Seriously Col, what are you going to do with Dad's things? I doubt you'll be able to sell much of it, even Steptoe would turn his nose up at this old tat."

I sigh. "I'm sorry there's nothing for you to have, Sis, you know, as a memento of Dad. He didn't have any trinkets or anything, although there is his watch; do you think Louie would like it?"

"Youngsters don't wear watches anymore, Col, they just look at their phones. Anyway, I'm not at all sure I want to be reminded of Dad." Her face floods with guilt and she bites her lip. "Sorry, I didn't mean that. You did a brilliant job looking after him, and for all that time. I don't think I could have done what you did, he was always so, well, so-"

"*Enigmatic.* At least, that's how the vicar described him."

Cath emits a loud snort. "That's just a diplomatic way of saying he was a miserable git. The vicar struggled to find anything positive to say about Dad apart from his name - he didn't half bang on about that, didn't he? 'Christopher, he who holds Christ in his heart'... the only thing he held in his heart was trapped wind."

"He meant well though, Cath-"

"No, he didn't! He begrudged anyone else any happiness, he cast a shadow over everything. The *enigmatic* elephant in the room, that's what he was to me, and I can still sense him here now, a dark woeful presence in the corner."

"That's just the damp patch." My feeble attempt at humour fails to raise a smile. "We should try and keep happy memories, Sis, that's what Mum always did. She used to say Dad was a right charmer in his younger days, do you remember?"

"I assumed she was being sarcastic." Cath flicks agitatedly at her hair again, exposing streaks of white at the roots. These were normally carefully hidden beneath the glossy brown tresses. "Did he say anything to you, Col, you know, about anything? Before he passed?"

I can't bear the anxious pleading that sparks in her eyes and I have to look away. I so badly want to tell my sister that in his last moments Dad had said her name, or asked for her to be there, but it wouldn't have been true. Dad never did speak of his daughter; it was as if she didn't exist. Cath always pretended she didn't care, but I knew Dad's indifference hurt like hell. I sit down on the bed next to her and give her a hug. "His last words were, 'I'm sorry, Son'. I think that's what he said. It was barely a whisper."

"Sorry indeed," Cath scoffs, covering her vulnerability with customary bolshiness. "*Sorry* barely covers it, does it?

And for what, exactly? The way he treated Mum, how he was with us, running his business into the ground-"

"Woah! Come on, Cath, don't get all bitter and twisted. What would Mum say to you right now?"

She fiddles with the hem of her purple sweatshirt. "Mum would say there's no point in looking back, you've got to keep looking forwards."

"And?"

"Yesterday is history, tomorrow is a mystery and the present is a gift." We chant in unison and Cath chuckles. "She used to say that whenever we were upset about anything, and then she'd do her Godfather impression with the sugar cubes. It always made us laugh."

"I can do my walrus impression with a couple of chopsticks, if you like?"

"No, you're all right, there's only so much excitement I can take in one day. But I could murder a coffee if you're making one." Cath gets to her feet reluctantly and returns to the chest of drawers. "Better make it a strong one, Col, I'm going to start bagging Dad's clothes up." She shudders. "I wish I had one of those radiation suits to put on like they have at Sellafield. Right, where to begin? This pullover can go for a start, I've never seen anything quite so hideous. Someone should have told Dad that paisley went out with the Ark."

"Er, that's one of mine, actually-"

"Oh my Christ!" Cath's head jerks back violently as she pulls open a drawer. "It's his underpants. Get me a clothes peg, Col, quick as you can."

Finally, hot and sweaty, we heave the last of the bin bags down the front path and squeeze them into Cath's Lexus. I force the boot lid down on the bulging black bags with the sense that Dad is in there with them, ready to explode in fury, livid at being ejected from his home of fifty years. It didn't feel right clearing out his things so soon after his death, but Cath had been keen to get it done. "I'll take it all to the clothes bins at Asda," she says, wiping her brow with the back of her hand. "Although someone would have to be spectacularly down on their luck if they ended up wearing any of these old rags. Mind you, some of the girls in Louie's class walk around in Grandad pyjamas, so you never know, Dad might have been on trend for once in his life. Will you be able to dispose of his undies?"

"Oh yes, we're always having bonfires at work, I'll get rid of them that way."

"Well, be careful, there are laws against obnoxious fumes." She looks back at the bungalow, suddenly serious. "Are you going to be alright here, Col, on your own? You've never lived by yourself before, I'm worried you're going to be lonely."

I blink in surprise, the thought having never occurred to me. "I don't think it will feel that different, really. I mean, Dad wasn't big on communication, was he? He sometimes went weeks without speaking to me."

"God Colin, was it always so awful?" My sister's face crumples.

"No, of course not!" I do my best to sound convincing. "We had heaps of fun together - why, we watched three episodes of Antiques Roadshow back to back once! We knew how to live."

"Three hours of Fiona Bruce? I'm not sure I'd want to live. Talking of antique women, did you tell Aunt Beth that Dad had died? I noticed she wasn't at the funeral."

"Yes, I called her." My reply is hesitant. I'm unsure whether to relay the actual conversation, 'good riddance to the miserable old buzzard,' to my sister. "She's in sheltered housing now, in Essex. She wasn't well enough to travel."

"Colin!" We turn as a jowly face appears at the fence, a

jet black quiff belying the gentleman's ageing years. "Sorry to bother you, mate, but could you pop round when you've got a mo? The flush has gone on the dunny again."

"Of course, Derek, but I can't believe it's gone again."

"I can. My daughter pumps it like she's drawing water from the Earth's core. I've told her not to be so heavy-handed, but she never listens. What chance has the flush got against someone with arms like a Russian shot-putter?"

"Righto Derek, I'll be round to take a look."

"Thanks, mate. I'd do it myself but I've got a bout of bloody gout again. Jean says there's a slice of lemon drizzle in it for you."

"Smashing."

"The bloody cheek of it," Cath hisses, as Derek limps back down his driveway. "You've just suffered a bereavement and he's got you doing unpaid labour."

"It's no trouble and anyway, it's the least I can do. Derek and Jean were ever so good to Dad, especially towards the end. They took turns to look in on him during the day while I was at work. And Dad was horribly rude to them by all accounts, but it didn't put them off – they still went in every single day."

"That's all very community-spirited and shit but seriously, Col, you need to bust out of here. It's your time now, you're *free*." Cath folds her arms and I try not to flinch as her all-seeing solicitor's eyes examine my face. "Surely you don't want to stay here, in Codgers Close? The average age on this estate is about one hundred and fifty-three; you must live in permanent fear of being mown down by a mobility scooter. The village hall is advertising a talk on the different varieties of tree fungus, for crying out loud!"

I shift my feet uncomfortably. I'd already put my name down for the talk.

"At least get Wi-Fi, show some acceptance of being in the

twenty-first century. And why don't you sell up and get a nice trendy flat in town? Those new ones by the river are gorgeous and they're slap-bang in the centre of everything. You'll be living a real life for a change, not stuck in a repeat of Last of the Summer Wine."

I laugh. "I think anything trendy would be wasted on me. And I doubt any of those flats have a garden."

"No, that's true." Cath looks approvingly round at the neat borders and the lush little square patch of lawn. "You do keep the garden nice."

"I should think so, in my trade. The daffs are all finished now but I'm glad Dad saw them come up again, it was one of the few things he still took pleasure in. He rarely ventured outside, though, because of all the satellites watching him."

Cath's eyes brim with tears and she touches my arm. "Come for your tea on Monday, you need fattening up. I'll do shepherd's pie."

"Hasn't Louie turned vegetarian?"

"Yes, but that won't last more than twenty-four hours. Come round about sixish, David should be home by then. Oh, God dammit, it's starting to rain - I'm off. See you Monday."

"Ok, bye."

Cath jumps into the Lexus and fires it throatily into life. Her window slides down. "It stinks of TCP in here!" she yells, taking off with a pair of Dad's braces trailing from the window. Suddenly feeling very alone, I gaze around at the curve of bungalows that make up Cotter Close, some of them neat and trim, others unkempt, with paint peeling from the window frames and weeds growing freely in the guttering. I try to imagine how it might have been back in the sixties when the estate was new and buzzed with professional young couples and their expanding families, just like Mum and Dad. They'd had money in their pockets then, as Dad's plastering firm flourished. They must have been so happy when they moved in to number seven, *lucky number seven,* Mum used to call it. I've always thought that a cruel irony.

As the rain gets heavier, I turn swiftly on my heel and nip back inside, shaking the droplets of water from my jumper as I stand in the hallway. "Just you and me now, Mum," I say to the silver picture frame on the hall stand and she beams back at me, eternally happy, her lovely smiley face surrounded by dark brown curls. The remainder of the weekend stretches out ahead of me; no tablets to dish out, no meal routines to adhere to, no trips to the pharmacy... Cath was right, my life had been on hold caring for Dad, now it could begin again. But what did that mean, exactly? How can you begin again when your half-century is fast approaching and your salary barely covers the bills? It's not as if I have anyone to begin again with. I catch sight of my reflection in the hallway mirror and hardly recognise the face that stares back. Is that really me? My skin is grey and creased, there's so much more forehead now ... *stop, stop, look away*. There's a leaflet on the doormat inviting me to join the local bowls club, and for a second I realise I'm actually considering it. Not quite what Cath had in mind. Keep busy, that's the answer. I fetch my tool bag from the shed and hurry next door, through the rain, via the back gate.

Keen Jean from number sixteen is sitting at Derek's kitchen table, tapping her feet to Jailhouse Rock. She's wearing velour leopard print slippers. Although there's a teapot in front of her, she's clutching a small glass of cloudy liquid. "Hello Colin, this is good of you. Did Derek tell you about Miss Piggy? She ate her own body weight in fig rolls and that, as you know, is one hell of a lot of figs. It's no wonder the flush gave up the will to live." She suddenly whips up a tea cosy to reveal a sponge cake. "Ta da! The knitted safe house – little Miss Piggy Figs couldn't snout out the lemon drizzle. Fancy a slice?"

"Yes, lovely, thank you. Did you make it?"

"Did I buggery, got it in Asda. Want a drop of Derek's good stuff to go with it?" She holds up her glass. "Rhubarb, 2013. A very fine vintage."

"Er, no, I'll pass thanks," I say, trying to disguise a shudder. "My eyesight hasn't fully recovered from the Dandelion 2012. I actually thought I'd gone blind after the first sip."

Jean bellows with laughter. "That was a corker, wasn't it? Blew my nipples clean across the room. Go on, you could do with a pick-me-up, you look knackered, lad."

"I'm fine, just been clearing out Dad's stuff. He didn't have much, not really, but it still took a surprising amount of time."

"It's a tough thing to do," Jean nods, taking my hand in her wrinkled claw. "It's not just someone's things you're boxing up and sending away, it's someone's *life*. Losing a loved one, it's like being in an emotional washing machine." I quickly take a bite of lemon frosting to stop my throat constricting. "That reminds me," Jean continues. "Derek's got a box of your father's that he asked him to keep. He'd forgotten all about it until he came across it in the loft the other day. He was trying to reach the ballcock and tripped right over it."

"Really?" I'm taken aback. I turn to Derek as he hobbles into the room. "Are you sure it's Dad's stuff? He never said anything."

Derek nods. "Yes, quite sure. I've had it for years. Your father asked me to store it because he said he didn't have the space. I can't remember exactly when that was, but it was a long time ago."

"How strange, there's plenty of space in our loft."

"I assumed, at the time, it was some of your mother's belongings, you know? Things he couldn't bear to throw out, but didn't want to have around the house. Too painful."

"Oh, right." That made more sense. "Shall I take it away

with me?"

"Yes please, Col, it's too heavy for me to get down, not with my ankles. Have you seen them? Size of bloody footballs."

"That idiot bus driver does nothing to help," Jean grumbles, refilling her glass from the teapot, presumably the chosen hiding place for the Rhubarb 2013. "Waits he does, waits till he sees you almost get to a seat then steps down hard on the accelerator and shoots you right down the back of the bus like a bloody pin ball machine. Do you know what I think? That Stagecoach actually train their drivers to pull away at the exact moment, they're an absolute bunch of sadistic bastards..."

I edge out of the room, Jean still muttering, and follow Derek into the hallway. "I've got to sit down again," he pants. "I'm in agony. And Judge Rinder's about to start. Your father's box is upstairs, room on the left."

I stare at Derek in dismay. "U-upstairs? You want me to go upstairs?"

"That's right, Son, unless you're expecting it to use the Stannah stairlift all by itself. Now, don't look so worried, there's no ghosts up there. Nothing to be frightened of now Jean's removed her smalls from the radiators; they'd scare the devil himself! Ha ha!" Derek leaves me in the hallway at the bottom of the stairs. I gaze up at the rise of dark brown swirly-carpeted steps, unchanged in over three decades. I hadn't been up those stairs in over thirty years, not since that summer... oh God, how can it still feel so vivid, that same intense rush of emotion from so long ago? I shake myself, as if that will somehow knock the memories from my head. I take a deep breath and start up the stairs. One, two, three, there were thirteen from memory, *thirteen steps to heaven,* I used to say to myself. My mouth is suddenly dry and my stomach performs a little flip. *This is ridiculous.* A left turn and I'm in the room, *our room.* Nothing has changed. Every inch of the little square bedroom is occupied just as before; the wobbly MFI desk with the Easter cactus on top, still flourishing and covered in bright red flowers, the ugly Yucca plant fat and squat in the corner, bottles lining the parameter of the room, each with their own handwritten labels – 'Elderflower 2016', 'Merlot 2014' and the evil 'Dandelion 2012'. There are more bell jars than I remember, all emitting a heady, yeasty aroma. The bookcase still has the dusty radio cassette player on top but the books are gone, replaced by rows of videos. I examine the titles: The Burbs, Beverly Hills Cop, Gremlins. I force myself to look at the bed. It's exactly the same. A single wrought-iron framed bed is covered with a counterpane of vibrantly coloured crocheted squares. Rain pelts against the window pane, the familiar sound propelling me back to the August day we took shelter, the little room hot and humid. Spandau's Ballet's 'True' on the radio cassette player. I remember our laughter as Tony Hadley started to drown, the tape winding itself up in the machine, and then joviality turning to serious longing, urgent whispers, secrets exchanged, promises made. We said we were forever and I thought we'd meant it. *I'd* meant it, but she hadn't felt the same. She didn't want me, despite everything she'd said. The hurt and rejection swirl about the room, ready to pull me down into a whirlpool of remembered despair. A cruel summer indeed. Derek is wrong, there is a ghost up here; the ghost of what might have been.

There is a large cardboard box on the floor in front of the MFI desk, with 'Christopher Hector No 7' written on the side in black marker pen. I heave it into the middle of the room and sit down, straddling it with my legs. I'm apprehensive but intrigued. What had Dad squirrelled away up here? Aunt Beth had helped Cath and I clear through everything after Mum died, Dad hadn't been capable of doing anything. I open the flaps of the box and find it full of books. They are clearly a set, all bound in leather-look dark brown covers with gold embossed lettering. I lift them out one by one, their musty smell reminding me of the school library. Wuthering Heights, Jamaica Inn, Jane Eyre... I can't recall Mum reading anything quite so dark, maybe the set had been handed down by my grandparents. Or perhaps, given the stories are full of gloomy, threatening men, they could well have been a present from Aunt Beth.

At the bottom of the box is a thick layer of newspaper. I take it out, holding the Observer well away from me so I can read the date. I'm going to need longer arms soon. 2 October 1985 – Mum had died the previous summer. The picture on the front page is of a fresh-faced Neil Kinnock, mouth open in full rant as he delivers an impassioned speech in front of a packed conference. The headline reads: 'Kinnock attacks the militants'. Under the main article a paragraph is captioned 'Unemployment to remain above 3 million', and below that 'Sinclair C5 ceases production after just 7 months'. I am mystified at why Dad might have wanted Derek to store the books, but then so many of Dad's actions simply couldn't be rationalised.

I glance back into the box and see it isn't empty. Under the layer of newspaper are two bundles of envelopes, their pretty pastel colours a stark contrast to the gloomy heap of books and yellowing newsprint. I examine the top bundle in surprise. The loopy writing is addressed to 'Mr C Hector', a smiley face drawn into the 'o'. All the envelopes have been opened, the letters left inside. Each one has a little silver love heart sticker on the back sealing the flap, and each heart had been torn in two when the letter was opened. It must be Mum's letters to Dad, love-letters, written when they were dating, or courting, as she used to call it. I am touched that Dad kept the letters all this time, but sad he'd hidden them away beneath the books, abandoned in Derek's loft. Why had he done that? Ashamed of showing emotion, no doubt; he'd always viewed it as weakness. I never noticed his lack of affection when I was young, probably because Mum had enough for everyone.

I have no desire to see inside the envelopes; reading my parent's love letters would be about as excruciating as it had been watching Blue Lagoon with them. I still can't believe we thought it was a documentary on Iceland. I peer at the postmark on the top envelope and reel in shock - 8 October 1984 - but Mum had died at the end of August! Who on earth had been writing to Dad with love hearts and smiley faces? The envelopes are post marked with a blurry 'Canterbury' – who did we know there? Oh my God, hadn't Aunt Beth lived in Kent at some time? *Yes, she had*. The letters must be from her, but no, surely not. She couldn't stand Dad. Unless... A cold fist clenches in my stomach. *An affair. Was that possible?* I recall a conversation Cath and I had with Mum one Christmas. Aunt Beth had sent Dad a book entitled 'How to Win Friends and Influence People' and he'd thrown it straight onto the fire in a fit of temper. "Why does Auntie Beth hate Dad so much?" we'd asked Mum when things had calmed down. She'd murmured, "Methinks the lady doth protest too much". I wanted to ask what she meant but as Cath had nodded knowingly, I didn't want to risk a 'Derrr, *stupid,*' from my older sister, so I'd nodded too and left it at that.

I spread the envelopes over the carpet and sort them into date order. There are thirty-two letters in total, the first posted on 15 September 1984 and the last on 21 July 1985. Why had the letters stopped – because the affair had ended? I stare at the rows of little torn hearts, my fingers itching to delve inside the envelopes but terrified at what they might contain. A sickliness creeps over me at the thought of Mum being betrayed in that way. *By her own sister*. Dad's last words float over me again: "I'm sorry, Son". Was he referring to the affair, knowing I'd find the letters? Why hadn't he just burnt the cursed things? Perhaps I should throw the letters away and think no more about it. *What you don't know doesn't hurt you,* another of Mum's sayings. She's right, she was always right. Whatever secrets the letters contain there is nothing that can be changed now.

"Colin, are you ok up there? I'll need the loo soon, that rhubarb has gone right through me."

I push the letters back together into their colourful bundles. I'll put them out with the recycling tomorrow, but right now Derek's waterworks are calling.

Chapter Two

Head down, I stand up on the pedals, urging my ancient Raleigh racer to the top of the steep incline. With lungs at bursting point and my heavy rucksack doing its utmost to pull me backwards, the terra firma finally levels off and I catch my breath. I free-wheel through the large iron gates of Hogpits Heights and along the tree-lined, blue-belled driveway into the estate. When I first came to work here, a shy and green seventeen-year-old, it was the private home of an orthopaedic surgeon, and his twenty acres were tended to by just myself and one other gardener. Over time, the surgeon was replaced by a barrister and then by a mobile phone entrepreneur, Gordon Winter who, when faced with the economic downturn, opened up his gardens to the public. Hogpits Heights now boasts a plant sales centre, tearooms, petting farm and an adventure playground. It is quite some enterprise and the number of employees swells to twenty-two during the summer months, with additional staff employed at the house which, nestling in a leafy hollow and hidden away from the public, had been renamed 'Wintersdell', the new owners less than enthralled with its original title, 'Hogpits Bottom'.

The drive opens into a sun-dappled gravel car park and I pull up in front of the wooden-gated entrance, slotting my front wheel into the cycle rack. The path into the gardens is lined with red and yellow tulips and in the corner of the top lawn the Chilean fire tree is coming into bloom, a dazzling burst of orange against the brilliant blue sky. I pick my way carefully around the puddles from last night's downpour and on past the tearooms, nodding to one of the girls, a young brunette, who is having a cigarette before we open. I always nod at her, she always ignores me. Her phone is pressed to her ear. "Stop it, you're so naughty! No, I'm not telling you that, you'll just have to use your imagination, won't you?" She takes a drag. "No, stop it, you're terrible, I'm not sending you a picture! What if she sees it? Well, *you* send *me* a picture, then. Of course I won't show anyone. Go on, I dare you."

Tucked away behind the tearooms is The Hut, a large wooden shed that serves as our tool storage, staff room, refuge point and counselling centre. We'd made it as comfortable as we could amongst the pots of creosote and array of gardening implements, and a smattering of rodent traps kept the mice away from our snacks and sandwiches. Tony is leaning over the workbench, his floppy brown fringe falling into his eyes as he studiously stirs his mug of tea, into which he will have plopped four lumps of sugar. He looks up in delight as I enter. "Col, you're back!" He rushes toward me, arms outstretched, before catching himself and awkwardly stopping short, offering me a manly hand shake instead. "How is, er, how are things, with, um, with-"

"Things are fine, mate," I rescue him, putting my rucksack down and flicking the kettle back on. "And thanks for coming to the funeral, I really appreciated it." My throat tightens again and I swiftly change the subject. "How's it been here?"

"Bloody bedlam!" Tony exclaims, throwing his hands into the air dramatically. "Everything's growing so damned quickly, I don't know if I've been coming or going. The lady of the manor's been barking out orders like a demented sergeant major." He adopts a posh voice: "Mow the lawns, no, polish the pea shingle, no, trim my bush." He takes a deliberately noisy slurp of tea. "I'm so glad you're back, I'm absolutely knackered."

I grin. "And how was your weekend, another quiet one, I assume?"

"I went on a date with that girl from The Stag, you know, the one that started behind the bar a couple of weeks ago."

"Oh yes, I remember her first night – you spent the entire evening drooling into your Carling." I heap a spoonful of Gold Blend into my Head Gardener mug. "So, where did you take her?"

"Nando's, of course, but it was an utter waste of money because she totally flunked the test."

"The test?"

"Yeah, my Nando's test. You can tell if a girl's a keeper by what she orders." Tony shakes his head sadly. "A mixed leaf salad, I ask you! There's no future in that, is there? I'm looking for someone who orders the Wing Roulette with a large spicy rice and a double helping of Macho Peas. You know, a proper woman."

"Somebody call?" I give a start, almost pouring the boiling water onto my hand. We hadn't heard Natalie come into The Hut. Tall and slender with sleek black hair, she smiles her shark-eyed smile at Tony, who physically flinches. "I can eat what I like at Nando's, I never put on any weight. Of course, that's because I *exercise,* a concept some women have never heard of." She runs a bony hand over her slender stomach. "I was at the gym at six o'clock again this morning." She looks at us triumphantly, seemingly waiting for some gasps of admiration. I inadvertently stand a little taller, sucking my stomach in, aware that Tony is trying to edge behind me.

"People are always saying to me 'Ooh, Nat, why do you work out so much?' So I reply 'Well, take a look at me then take a look at you'." She laughs and puts her hands on her hips, pushing her chest out. "I'm only joking, of course. But my husband never complains, that's for sure. What do you think, Colin? We're the same age, after all. Does my figure look any different to how it was at secondary school?"

"Er," *don't look at her breasts, don't look at her breasts* "You always look very nice."

I clearly hadn't given a rapturous enough response and her eyes narrow into slits. "Oh, that's right, I forgot about your incredibly high standards. You probably had another date with one of the Kardashians this weekend, did you? Who was it this time, Kim or Khloé? Did you give them a doubler on the back of your bike to the Berni Inn?" She laughs again, presumably in an attempt to take the sting out of her words, but it still feels like someone has squirted a grapefruit into my eye. "I'm only joking, God, your face! Anyway, you two had better get a wriggle on and start the mowing, Mrs Winter said she's seen Tarzan swinging through the top lawn."

"It's a bit wet for mowing–"

"And she wants the bank in front of the house dug over today, so chop chop." Natalie looks around. "Where's Chicken Ron?"

"He's feeding the horses," I say quickly, glancing back at Tony who nods vigorously. "And then I've asked him to go down to the lake and move the heron scarer again."

"Hmmm," Natalie frowns, unconvinced. "He'd better not be slacking, Mrs Winter's made it quite clear there's no room for passengers; we're on an incredibly tight budget this year."

I smile. "Yes, we had an inkling things were tough when Mr Winter downsized to the seventy thousand pound Range Rover."

Natalie looks at me suspiciously, unsure whether I'm

being sarcastic. "I can't stand here all day chatting, I've got to go and check on a delivery of Miracle-Gro. The supplier keeps cocking up the order – honestly, how difficult can it be? It's up to me to sort everything out. Again." She swings out of the door then sticks her head back inside. "*You* haven't been at the Miracle-Gro have you, Tony? Is that what's making your stomach expand? Ha ha! See you losers later."

"Thank God she's gone," Tony gasps, letting out a whoosh of pent-up air on the back of my neck. "My arse starts to sweat whenever Nasty Nat's around, and I don't mean in a good way." I'm intrigued at how a sweaty arse can ever be in a good way, but I stop myself from asking. "You should stand up to her more," Tony grumbles, emerging from behind me. "You're the head gardener, she can't tell you what to do. She didn't even say sorry about your old man, and that evil laugh of hers! I make the exact same noise when I catch my knuckles on the cheese grater."

"Where is Chicken Ron?" I ask in trepidation.

"Sleeping it off, I should think, he had an absolute skin-full in The Stag last night. He's getting worse, you know, Mr Winter caught him napping inside the kiddie's tube slide again last week – you could hear him bawling him out right across the grounds. Shook the buds clean off the magnolia."

"We'll have to keep a closer eye on him, Tone," I say anxiously. "If he loses this job he'll never get another and Christ only knows what will become of him then."

"Righto, I'll nip round to his cottage and wake him up. Pass me the hoe, would you?"

"What do you need this for?" I ask, taking the hoe from the corner of The Hut and handing it over to him.

"I shove it through his letter box and poke him in the head until he regains consciousness. Cover for me, I might be a while."

It's days like these that make being a gardener feel like the most privileged job in the world. Forgotten are the numb fingers and the chilblained toes of winter, forgotten too, the days of downpours when the rain soaks right through to your boxers. The gardens are a riot of colour and alive with birdsong. I stop digging to watch a group of long-tailed tits buzzing in and out of the hedgerow. I catch quick glimpses of fluffy pink from their little barrel chests. The sunshine warms my upturned face but a hint of freshness in the air reminds me it isn't quite summertime yet. "Cast ne'er a clout 'til May be out," Mum always used to say. I'd ignored her advice, of course, rushing outside in shorts and a T-shirt as soon as the sun shone. It was no wonder I always caught a spring cold.

I lean on my shovel looking down on the splendour of Wintersdell, with its Roman-pillared entrance and elegant spiral topiary. I'd only ever been inside the house once, just into the hallway to deliver a weeping fig, and I'd been awestruck by the high ceiling and marble floor. A sweeping staircase curved up and around the inside of the hall; it was like being in a Jane Austin novel. I give a wry smile as I compare it to the gloomy, narrow hallway of number seven Cotter Close. Funny how it had never seemed dark when Mum was there. My mind turns again, as it had done throughout a restless night, to Dad's letters. *Who were they from?* I prod at a clump of soil with the tip of my spade. It had been the right thing to do, hadn't it, throwing the letters away? After all, there was absolutely nothing to be gained by reading–

"What are you thinking about, Col?" Tony peers up at me from his position halfway down the sloping bank, his face flushed from the exertion of turning the heavy earth.

"Just some letters I found in Dad's stuff. I didn't read them, it didn't feel right. But I'm curious about them."

"Oh, right." Tony doesn't sound very interested. His face lights up as two elderly ladies appear at the edge of the bank and, arm in arm, pick their way gingerly along the path. "Morning ladies! Isn't it a lovely day?"

"Your paths are very slippery," one says, glaring at us accusingly.

"That's because it's been raining, love," Tony answers cheerfully.

"Well, can't you put something on them? Rosemary's only just had her hip done."

"Er," Tony glances around at the grassy paths. "I'm not sure what we could put on them... have you got any studded footware? Studs are great for preventing slippage, perhaps you've got some football boots you could put on."

"*Football* boots? Of course we haven't got any football boots!"

"Oh come on, I bet you love a good kick around, that's probably how Rosemary knackered her hip. What are you, Chelsea fans? Millwall? You've got hooligan written all over you."

I hold my breath. Tony didn't always judge situations or moods correctly, but to my relief the women chuckle, call him a 'cheeky little so-and-so' and allow him to escort them back up the grassy hill toward the tearooms. I watch them go, taking the opportunity to stretch my back and give my lower spine a good rub. Persistent back pain is the gardener's curse. A door slams beneath me and I turn to see Mrs Winter striding from the grand entrance of her house. She wraps an emerald green headscarf around her pallid face in a swift, impatient motion. As she stops in front of her Mercedes and fumbles for the keys, Mr Winter looms large in the doorway and shouts something at her. I can't catch what he yells, but he sounds furious. His wife ignores him and climbs into the car, starting it up with great angry revs. As Mr Winter runs down the stone steps the car shoots past, spraying him with shingle. He roars and waves his arms, but his wife has gone. I hear the engine as it rounds the bottom of the dell and takes off up the driveway, frightening the rooks out of the Sycamore trees with indignant screeches. As a thunder-faced Mr Winter stamps back up the steps I turn quickly away and continue my digging, not wanting to be caught slacking. I'd been on the receiving end of both of his barrels once before and it wasn't an experience I ever wanted to repeat.

"They were nice old ducks." Tony bounds back down the path and skids to a halt in front of me, bending down to pick up his fork. "Invited me to go to bingo with them on Tuesday night; I might just do that, I've been thinking about trying out an older woman. They've got so much more *confidence,* haven't they, not to mention all that experience."

"Yes, but will they have their own teeth?"

"Well, Chicken Ron's missus hasn't got any teeth and it doesn't bother him, in fact he says it's quite useful, especially when she's-" He breaks off sharply. "Oh crap!"

"What's up?" I ask in alarm.

"Twat approaching, three o'clock." Tony leaps down the bank and we stab frantically at the soil, as if we're trying to reach Australia. "Don't look round, just dig, *bloody dig!*" Tony hisses urgently.

"Alright then, lads?"

Our tactics haven't worked. With a sinking heart, I look over my shoulder and tilt my head, following the navy overalls upwards until they end at the smirking moon face of the general maintenance man. "Oh, hello Wes," I say, dropping my head back down and continuing to work at the soil.

"It's all kicking off in there again." Wes nods towards the house, sucking in his breath theatrically. "Man, you should have heard it! Thought I'd better get out quick before Gordon starts chucking the Royal Doulton around again. I was almost decapitated by a china ballerina last time."

I make a sort of "Huh" noise, still gazing at the soil. It

always amused me how Wes referred to Mr Winter by his Christian name, even though I knew he wouldn't dare address him as such.

"Problems with the heating system again," Wes continues, waving an enormous ratchet at me. "Good thing I used to work in the engine room of HMS Invincible, that taught me a thing or two about rotating compressors, I can tell you."

I glance across at Tony, who rolls his eyes at me. We carry on digging but Wes is undeterred. "So, how was your weekend, Colin?"

My manners getting the better of me, I reluctantly straighten up and rest on my spade. "My weekend was fine thanks, Wes, but I had to start packing up Dad's things, which I found really difficult and–"

"Good, good, that's good. Mine was a crazy blur, of course. I had another wedding on Saturday night, a big one this time, over two hundred guests turned up in the evening and some weren't even invited; I daresay the rumour that I was performing had something to do with that."

Tony snorts loudly and manages to turn it into a cough. "Were you spinning your discs again, Wes?" I ask. "Or doing your magic circle bit?"

With a flourish, Wes produces a business card from the top pocket of his overalls and hands it over to me, the ever-present smirk intensifying. The card reads 'W.E.S - Wondrous Entertainment Services' and beneath the printing is a headshot of Wes, his beaming round features giving him the appearance of an emoji.

"*Officially,* I was there as the DJ," he says, with a wink. "But the bride and groom heard I did a bit of singing."

"And they still booked you?" I hear Tony mutter.

"*Can* you sing?" I ask Wes.

"Can I sing, he asks!" Wes laughs out loud. "Yeah, just a bit! I sang to their first dance and there wasn't a dry eye in the house."

"Probably crying to get out," Tony whispers, a little too loudly.

Wes ignores him and leans in conspiratorially. "You should see my Bublé."

"Your what?" I ask in alarm.

"It's *amazing*," he purrs and points to his forearm. "Goosebumps." He looks at me expectantly, but I'm not at all sure how I am required to respond. He taps his arm again. "*Actual* goosebumps."

"Talking of er, poultry," I stutter, "you haven't see Chicken Ron, have you?"

Wes blinks at the change in topic. "Yeah, I saw him over by the horses, in the north field."

"Ah, that's good. Was he picking up the muck?"

"Nope, he was sitting in the wheelbarrow flicking through a copy of Busty Babes and swigging from a bottle of Smirnoff."

"Jesus-"

"I'll go," Tony says, slipping on the grass in his haste to get away. "It's no trouble, no trouble at all."

"I'd better let you get on, Wes," I try, kneeling down and pretending to be absorbed with a clump of moss. "I expect you're snowed under, too." Anyone else would accept the brush-off, but I can still sense him hovering over me.

"What's that in your ear?"

God no, not this again, please not this again. "There's nothing in my ear, Wes. Now, I must get on-"

"Yeah, there is! There's definitely something in your ear. Have a look." I watch my knuckles turning white as I grip the moss, fighting the desire to plunge my head under the soil. *Just play along and get it over with.* I put my hand up to my ear. "Nope, there's nothing there, Wes."

"Oh really, nothing there, you say? So what's this, then?"

Wes flicks his wrist and after a moment of frantic flapping, produces an egg from his sleeve, waving it triumphantly in my face. "Ha ha! You're weren't eggpecting that, were you?" *Same crap joke, too.* "Well, I'd better *scramble,* don't want to *crack* you up too much!"

Fat chance. I manage a weak titter of laughter. "Good yoke, Wes." *Now, please make a hasty eggxit before I batter myself to death.*

We have an hour for lunch and make the most of every minute, resting aching limbs and refuelling grumbling stomachs with sandwiches and bars of chocolate. In The Hut, Tony and I relax in deck chairs with our mugs of tea, listening to the Time Tunnel on the radio. I'm reading Of Mice and Men while Tony sprawls in his chair, exhausted from wheeling a comatose Chicken Ron from one hiding place to another, desperately trying to keep him out of view of visitors and Mr Winter. He said he'd been very tempted to tip him into the lake but figured "there's enough slime in there as it is". Ron is currently parked up behind the compost bins.

Tony taps his knuckles on the arms of the deck chair to the radio. "Frankie Goes to Hollywood," he muses. "I reckon it's 1988, no, no wait, didn't they write it about the Gulf War? It must be 1990."

I shake my head. "You're miles out. And it was about the Cold War-"

"Don't be daft, it's never that old! When Two Tribes go to war, one is all that you can score... You up for a game of darts tonight, Col?"

"I can't, I'm afraid, I'm going to Cath's for tea. She's doing shepherd's pie."

"You lucky bugger, I wish someone would cook for me. Mum's idea of fine dining is sticking an Iceland lasagne in the microwave." He picks up a lump of putty from the workbench.

"This looks about the same texture. So, what have you got today, Col?" He nods at my sandwich as he bites into a large sausage roll. "It looks like it's bleeding."

"Brie and red currant jelly."

"Aw, gross!" Tony pretends to heave into his Greggs bag. "Brie's full of listeria. My brother bought a brie and bacon sandwich at the races and he was firing out of both ends for two weeks straight. We had to get the cesspit emptied five times."

"How is your brother, Tone?" I ask, putting my sandwich down, suddenly queasy. "Is he still working at the racecourse?"

"No, he got the push for taking bets off punters."

"What was wrong with that?"

"He was only supposed to be emptying the bins. Eh up, it's Dynamo."

Wes stomps into The Hut and slings his rucksack across the floor, reaching into the little cupboard for his lunch box before slumping, scowling, onto the pile of sacks in the corner. "What's wrong with him?" I whisper to Tony.

"He's probably seen Facebook." Tony fiddles with his phone and holds the screen up for me to see. He'd posted a picture of Wes standing outside the tearooms clutching his ratchet. The caption read: 'Massive Tool'. I bury my face in my book as Wes glares over. "What are you reading, Col?" Tony asks, massaging the lump of putty in his hands.

"I found it amongst my Dad's stuff; it's a Steinbeck, Of Mice and Men. Have you read it?"

"No, but I saw the film, with John Malkovich. He played a puppy strangler."

"Well, he didn't really mean to kill the puppy–"

"I can't finish a book, got no patience. I don't even bother reading a Facebook post if it's longer than two lines." He squeezes the putty thoughtfully. "But you, you're an intellectual, Col, that's what you are, always got your nose in a book. I've never understood why you've worked here all your life, you should be on Countdown, in Dick's Corner."

"It's Dictionary Corner." I put the book down on my lap, realising I'm not going to be allowed to read it. "I did start college, but after Mum died I had to drop out and look after Dad."

"Why?"

"He had a breakdown. At least, I think that's what it was. He always did suffer with dark moods and we thought he would eventually improve, but he never did recover, not really. He just wasn't capable of looking after himself."

"Couldn't you have put him in a home or something? I know that sounds harsh, but people are trained to deal with all that head stuff."

"We never thought about it, Tone. I looked after him and that's how it was. He was prescribed medication but getting him to take it was another matter. I gave up on college and took a job as close to home as possible, so at least we had some money coming in."

"And you got stuck here..." Tony moulds the putty into a phallic-looking column and waves it at a sulky Wes. "What was it you really wanted to do, if you'd stayed at college?"

"I wanted to be a vet."

"Oh, Jesus, you had a lucky escape if you ask me! Spending all day with your arm up a cow's arse? No thanks."

"At least I get to work with animals here."

"Yeah, Chicken Ron." There's a lull in conversation, the silence filled by Lionel Ritchie's soothing tones. Tony sings along: "Are you somewhere feeling Lonely or is Lonely feeling you?"

"1985," Wes mutters from the corner.

"You're close, but you're not right," I reply in my best Roy Walker Catchphrase impression.

"It's 1989, one hundred percent," Tony insists.

"How the hell would you know?" Wes fires back. "You weren't even born until 1991, I've got Y-fronts older than you."

"My mum plays eighties stuff all the time." Tony concentrates on remoulding. "And she tries to sing like Kate Bush; scares the shit out of the cat. Do you remember the video to this song?"

For some reason, we all look at the radio, as if we can see the video being played on it. "Hello, is it me you're looking for?"

"I don't know, Lionel, I'm blind." Tony holds up the putty. He'd sculpted a head, a sort of moon-faced Lionel Ritchie. "What year is it then, Col?"

"Ah, have you given up? It's 1984."

Nasty Nat's head appears in the doorway. "1984? That's about the same time you started this lunch break, isn't it? Come on, if the mowing's not finished by the time Mrs Winter returns you'll be searching for your dangly bits amongst the long grass, although I doubt yours are visible to the human eye, eh, Colin?"

"God, was she this evil at school?" Tony moans, having seen Nasty Nat walk safely out of earshot past the window. "How on earth did you put up with her, Col?"

"I didn't have much to do with her at school, she wasn't in my class. Although, she did ask me out once."

"WHAT?" Tony's and Wes' heads shoot up like meerkats. "You've never told us that before!"

"There's nothing much to tell," I mutter, my face getting hot. "She sent a friend to ask me if I'd go out with her and I said no."

"Why did you say no?" Wes asks, sounding astonished.

"Well," I think back. "I didn't really like her."

They laugh. "That never stopped me at school," Wes says. "In the words of the great Bachman-Turner Overdrive, I took what I could get!"

"No wonder you're so unlucky with the ladies, Col," Tony scoffs. "You're too bloody fussy!"

I give a rueful grin. Too fussy, indeed, chance would be a fine thing. In fact, it had been almost a year since there had been anyone; Janine, a quiet accountant with an amazing shock of curly red hair. There had been more regular girlfriends when I was younger, but not that many: Linda Dearden who worked in her father's cycling shop and led me out the back to the workshop for a snog whenever the shop was empty; Jackie Street, who I'd met in The Stag one Christmas and we'd dated right up until Glastonbury, when I found out she'd shared a tent with James Askew; then there was Miriam Tingley, the Morris dancer who drove a mustard Austin Allegro and kept giving me love bites which I hated because they really hurt and I'd had to wear scarves, even in August...

"What are you thinking about, Col?" Tony asks, getting up and stretching his legs. "You look all sad."

"I was thinking about the past," I tell him with a sigh. "And my disastrous history of dating. Although you could hardly call it a history, more like brief spasms."

"Wasn't there anyone you really liked?"

"There was someone special, yes. At least, I thought so. I was pretty smitten." I shrug. "I guess no one else has ever come close to Sarah."

"Sarah?"

"My first love. My only love, as it goes. Sarah Shaw."

"Didn't she win Eurovision once? She used to perform without any pants on."

"That was Sandy Shore. And it was shoes-"

"What was so great about this Sarah, then? Nice jugs?"

I take an apple from my lunch box and rub it thoughtfully on my jeans. "Sarah was just so, well, lovely. We met on the first day of college and hit it off immediately. She was always positive, never had a bad word to say about anyone; you felt like a better person just by being around her. And she was so pretty, all the boys fancied her, but she never went out with any of them."

Tony nods knowingly. "Frigid."

"No, she just wasn't into the usual boyfriend-girlfriend shenanigans that went on, she had a confidence, you know? She knew what she wanted out of life."

"But she went out with you! Did you do the deed?"

"A gentleman never tells." I hide my burning face in my sandwich box.

"That means yes, you dirty dog! But what happened to her?"

"She moved away, really suddenly. Her parents split up out of the blue and her mum took her to live with her aunt. I never saw her again."

"But, didn't she text you or nothing?"

"We didn't have mobiles back then, Tone, they were just something Yuppies used to sell their shares with. We didn't have a house phone, either."

Tony gasps in shock. "You didn't have a phone? Were you, like, seriously poor or something?"

"Yes, we were, we got cut off. Dad's company was falling apart and after Mum died he became really ill and couldn't work. We thought Mum had some life insurance, but turns out she didn't. So there wasn't any money coming in until I started working here. It was one hell of a struggle for a while; we almost lost the house."

"Wow." Tony taps his teeth, still coming to terms with the notion of life without a mobile phone. "So, what you're saying is that you and this Sarah bird get it on, then soon after she says she's moving away and you never hear from her again." He looks at me pitifully. "Have you ever thought – and don't take this the wrong way, mate – that you might just be a really crap shag?"

It was a very distinct possibility. In fact, I recalled overhearing Jackie Street the Glastonbury Cheat describing what I assumed was our sex life to one of her friends: "It isn't true what they say: you *can* get quicker than a Kwik Fit fitter." Fair enough, I had tried to hurry proceedings, but that was because I caught her looking at her Swatch while we were having sex. It hadn't been like that with Sarah. It had been a magical experience, the most amazing, wonderful thing that had ever happened to me. I thought it had been the same for Sarah but, looking back, that was probably just what I'd wanted to believe. I realise Tony is waiting for an answer. "I don't know, mate," I say to him. "I just don't know. Sarah turned up at the house one morning not long after Mum's funeral. She was in floods of tears, told me her Dad had been cheating and her Mum was leaving him. They were going to stay with her aunt and she promised to send me her new address. She kissed me, clung to me for a moment and then she was gone."

"Any idea where they went to?"

"Her aunt lived somewhere on the east coast. That's all I know."

The postmark

"Are you alright, mate?" Tony asks, looking at me in alarm. "You've gone the same shade as Morticia."

"Um," I can't think straight, my head is whirling. The letters to Dad had been posted in Canterbury; could they have been from Sarah? Why had she written so many times to Dad? Unless... My stomach lurches. The letters were in the recycling bin! What time did the bin men come? I jump up, sending my sandwich box flying across The Hut. "Got to nip out, Tony," I call, stumbling to the door. "Cover for me."

"Told you about that brie, didn't I," he yells after me. "You'll be shitting through the eye of a needle for weeks!"

I sprint up the path and wrench my bicycle out of the

stand, pushing it across the car park and straddling it in one swift motion. Head down, I pump my legs as fast as they will go. *Come on, come on!* Breath coming in short gasps, my lungs start to burn. *Keep going, faster.* I'm going to be too late, the bin would surely have been emptied by now, the letters crushed into a pulpy mess. I fly along the country lanes, swerving crazily to avoid lethal pot-holes and bewildered pheasants until finally, heart pounding in my throat, I swing into the estate of bungalows and swoop into Cotters Close, wrenching on the brakes to stop myself flying into the back of the dustcart. They're here! One of the men is emptying number five's bin – *ours is next*. I leap off my bike and, leaving it lying in the road, race around the cart reaching number seven at the same time as the bin man. "No, no, stop!"

"What the–"

"Sorry, sorry," I gasp. "I need to retrieve something." I thrust my arm into the wheelie bin and pull out the bundle of letters from beneath a crumpled Shreddies box. "Got them!" I smile at the befuddled bin man, who shrugs and shakes his head. Hands trembling, I carry the pile of letters back to my abandoned bicycle and pick it up, wheeling it down the drive and propping it against the wall. My legs weak, I sink onto the front door step, the envelopes lying in my lap like primed hand grenades. They are all addressed the same way, 'Mr C Hector'. I'd assumed the C had stood for Christopher... I am being ridiculous; if they were meant for me, why had Dad hidden them amongst his things? Of course they weren't for me, *idiot*. Feeling slightly calmer, I pick an envelope at random from the pile and prise the letter out, unfolding the sheet with fingers that are still shaking. There is an address in Herne Bay in the top right-hand corner and a telephone number. The letter is dated 22 November 1984:

Dearest Colin

Well, here I am, writing to you again, even though I know you will not reply. I don't know why I continue doing this to myself, but I guess there is still a tiny piece of my heart that cannot accept you no longer want me. Desperation on my part, I know, but I am still clinging to the smallest fragment of hope that there is some other explanation. Perhaps, in your grief, you simply haven't opened your post. Or your dog ate my letters. But I do know the truth, of course I do. You don't even have a dog. I just can't admit it to myself, not yet anyway. But soon. And then these letters will stop. If I hear 'You're a Hard Habit to Break' one more time I shall howl. You must listen to it too, it's being played all the time; don't you feel anything?

If only you would write back, just one letter, one sentence even, telling me it's over. Or call me. You could just say one word, say goodbye and hang up, I can handle it. But to hear nothing, it's utterly torturous. I can't believe someone as wonderful as you capable of cruelty. My address and telephone numbers are, as always, at the top of the letter. Please, Colin, please reply to me.

Is it better to live with hope or without it? I don't know anymore.

There is still *Only You. Forever.*
Sarah

I can't move. I am aware I'm holding my breath, but suddenly breathing doesn't seem important anymore. Thirty-two times she'd written. I never knew. I thought she'd forgotten me, met someone else, moved on. Only You. Forever. I feel as hot as I'd done on that airless summer's day upstairs at Derek's. She'd asked me then, as we lay side by side in the tiny single bed, 'Are we forever?' And I'd said we were. She must have clung to that, writing letter after letter. The pile of envelopes with their torn silver hearts burns a hole in my thighs. If I'd seen just one, I'd have called her instantly, I'd have written straight back, I'd have written every day. We'd have made it work, whatever the distance. But she'd never have known that. She thought I didn't want her. My cheeks are damp, sweat and tears mingling together, trickling into my collar. I clutch the envelopes to my chest and stare unseeingly up at the house. "How could you, Dad?" I sob. "How could you?"

Chapter Three

17 Dunes Way
Herne Bay
Kent
CT6 7HR

1 October 1984

Dearest Colin

I know you probably haven't had the chance to write or call because you are preoccupied with your father. I do hope he is beginning to turn the corner, he looked so lost and confused at the funeral. I know it is going to take a long time, but he will gradually come to terms with your mother's death, and begin to cope a little better. I hope you are looking after yourself, you need time to grieve, too. I expect Cathy has gone back to Uni now, hasn't she? You must miss her, but it won't be long before she's back for Christmas.

We are settling into life with Auntie Sheila, who has been very good to us, even though I get the feeling she and Mum don't like each other very much. I put the tension down to the circumstances we find ourselves in; Auntie Sheila's house is very small and we are all living on top of one another. Mum is still crying a lot and drinking too much gin. This makes her say some very unkind things about Dad. I can't say I blame her after what he's done (I told you what he was up to with his receptionist in my last letter, didn't I?) but it's still not nice to hear him called a ... ... and a ..... I'll leave you to fill in the dots!

Dad phoned me yesterday, but I didn't really want to speak to him and anyway, I couldn't hear what he was saying because Mum was yelling things in the background. I think he wants me to come home, but I am certainly not going to abandon Mum. She really needs me right now.

I tried to call you again but I still couldn't get through; I think you must have a fault on your line. You haven't been cut off, have you? I expect your Mum used to deal with all the bills and things; it must be so difficult, trying to keep on top of the family finances along with everything else.

I don't know how long we will be staying with Auntie Sheila. I will try and get a job. It's a shame the holiday season is over because I'm sure I could have found work on the sea front, in a little cafe perhaps, or even walking the donkeys along the sands. As it is, Herne Bay feels like the Land That Time Forgot, but I know I shall find something soon and then I'll have money for the train fare. I'm aching to see you again, I miss you so much. I want to be back in our little room and feel your arms tightening around me... I'd better stop there in case the postman is reading this! I have been listening to The Flying Pickets over and over; please don't tease me, it's the only modern record Auntie Sheila has!

Their words are true, though. There is Only You.

Forever, your Sarah

PS Even if you can't call, PLEASE PLEASE write soon. I need to know you are ok xx

I place the letter next to the pile of envelopes on the table, the silver hearts shining in the gloom of the kitchen. Clouds have been gathering all afternoon and the sky is a solid grey.

I don't want to go to Cath's for dinner, I want to stay at home and read the rest of Sarah's letters. My hand reaches for the phone but I pull it back. My sister is very difficult to say no to. I'm not sure I can summon up enough courage to call her and cry off. Besides, some human company would be good, a distraction to the ghosts in my head.

I cycle the six miles to Cath's in a trance, the leaden skies and sombre light adding to my sense of unreality. I apply the squeaky breaks of the Raleigh and steer carefully onto the gravelled drive of my sister's house. There is a figure crouching under the bay window of the dining room, the hem of a long trench coat brushing the gravel. "Hello Louie!" I call as I dismount, forcing myself into cheeriness. "What are you up to?"

Black-lined eyes blink round at me through a dark spiky fringe. "Hello Unck. I'm taking another picture of this flower for my biology media project. We have to make a short film capturing something that signifies life."

"Blimey, that's a pretty wide-ranging topic. What are you doing?"

"Well, I started to take pictures of road kill and tombstones, you know, to show the pointlessness of it all, but Mum said it was too morbid and made me delete everything. So now I'm doing this tulip. I've taken a picture of it twice a day for the last six weeks since it's come up through the earth and started to flower. When you play the sequence on rapid speed, it will show it going from bulb to bud to full bloom. You know, coming to life."

"That's brilliant, very David Attenborough. It's rather late flowering, but it's a lovely mauve colour–"

"Then I'm going to film its petals dropping away one by one so I can call it 'Bloomin' Death'."

"Oh, right. And is there a prize for the best film?"

"Yep, we post our films on the school's website and

whoever gets the most views wins a microscope and some iTunes vouchers."

"You've been extremely patient, photographing it every day. I hope you win."

"I've got no hope," Louie sighs. "Carl Longbottom shot some footage of his mum and step-dad shagging. He's called it 'My Family and Other Accidents'. It's already gone viral."

"Ah. That one might get disqualified, of course... Anyway, I'll go in and say hi to your Mum." I carefully remove the egg box from my bike rack. "I've bought some eggs for you all, from work."

"Don't expect me to eat them." Louie turns back to lining up his shot, the camera lens inches from the tulip. I notice his black nail varnish is chipped. "I couldn't possibly stomach a slaughtered chick."

"Er, no, of course not. I'll see you in a minute, then." I edge away through the open front door, wretchedly clutching my box of murdered babies. "Hello! Anyone at home?"

"In here, Col," my sister calls from the kitchen, sounding harassed. I walk along the oak-panelled hallway and follow the waft of fried onions into Cath's capacious kitchen. A blanket of hot air engulfs me. "Woah!"

Cath is backed into the open American fridge freezer, her hair sticking out and face flushed bright red. She's pressing a bag of frozen peas into the nape of her neck and rolling a glass of white wine across her flaming cheeks. "It's the bloody Aga, Col," she groans. "I just can't get the hang of it. The frigging thing takes ages to heat up, then a lifetime to cool down, by which time it's turned your kitchen into a sauna and as for actually cooking anything, well, you can forget it! The moment you lift the lid on the hotplate the oven starts getting cold - what the hell is that about? The first meal I attempted should have been simple enough, chicken and roasted vegetables. Well, after thirty minutes the vegetables were still raw but the chicken breasts looked like Magda's in 'There's Something About Mary'."

"What made you get one?" I ask, perspiration breaking out on my upper lip.

"Aga envy, pure and simple. Sheila Rudd, one of the other partners has got one and you know I can't bear to be trumped by that ghastly old trout. Her Aga has only got three ovens so, of course, I went for the model with four. Four bloody ovens! The guys from John Lewis were pissing themselves when they left, especially when I asked them how to make cheese on toast. One of them said, 'Ah, Mrs Walsh, it's not really about cooking, it's about lifestyle'. He got that right! It just happens to be a lifestyle that doesn't involve feeding your family." She pauses for breath. "God, you look awful, Col. What's wrong?"

"Oh, it's nothing-" To my horror, I feel my throat tightening. *I'm going to cry in front of Cath.* I quickly hold out the egg box. "I've bought you some eggs, from work."

"Christ, I can't even boil an egg on this bloody thing, but thank you, I'll stick them in the fridge next to this ghastly stack of cardboard."

I see a collection of Quorn ready meals on the shelves. "So, Louie's persisting with his vegetarian phase, is he? Good for him, it's great to see him sticking at something."

"Hmmm, it's only been a few days, Col, don't get carried away. Ever since he borrowed my Morrissey records all we've had is this meat is murder crap, but at least he's stopped listening to that Ozzy Osborne Bark At The Moon stuff, that was a disturbing couple of months. I do wish he'd listen to some more modern bands."

"Like?" I tease, knowing she'll struggle to name any.

"Oh, I don't know, Ned Sherrin, or whatever he's called... Stop laughing! Do you want a beer?"

"Yes please." I sit down at the table and fan myself with an A4 writing pad. There are notes and files strewn all over the table. "Interesting case, Sis?"

"No, not really." Cath ventures out of the fridge to pass me a can of Budweiser. "Just another knickers-off-the-washing-line job, your bog-standard pervert. No imagination, some people."

"Right, right." I open the ice-cold can and hold it against my cheek for a moment.

Cath looks at me quizzically. "Are you sure you're ok, Col? You don't seem yourself at all."

I take a huge gulp of beer and feel safe the tears aren't returning. "I've had a bit of a shock, that's all." Sweat trickles down my back. "It's just, I found something in amongst Dad's books."

"Oh yeah? It wasn't a copy of Mary Berry's 'Me and my Wonderful Aga' was it? If so, you can shove it right–"

"No, it was a pile of letters. Letters that had been written to me." I pause. "It looked as if Dad had deliberately hidden them."

Cath opens her mouth to speak but Louie slopes into the room. "Mum, have you seen my iPad?" He is still wearing his trench coat, seemingly unperturbed by the stifling heat of the kitchen.

"It's probably buried under that lot," Cath nods at the table. "What were you saying, Col?"

"Have you asked him yet, Mum?" Louie moves the files around listlessly. "I've got to let school know."

It is my turn to look at Cath expectantly. "Ah yes," she starts, producing a tissue from her sleeve and dabbing her glistening forehead. "I wonder if Louie could do his work experience with you at Hogpits? It's only for two weeks, at the beginning of July; he'd love to help you with a bit of digging and er, whatever else it is you do there."

"Really?" I look at my nephew in surprise. "I thought you wanted to work with Lawrence & Son, the undertakers on the High Street?"

"That's not going to happen now," Louie replies gloomily.

"Why not?"

"Because they've met me."

"He had an *informal* interview with them," Cath explains, extracting the iPad from beneath a blue plastic folder. "He did really well but in the end they decided his disposition was a little too *downbeat* for the position."

"Hello, hello." David, my brother-in-law appears in the kitchen, reeling in disbelief at the heat. "Jeeps, it's roasting in here! Must be all Cath's hot air!" He gives his wife a friendly dig in the ribs as he loosens his tie. "Hi Colin, how are you doing?"

"I'm fine, thanks. Had a good day at work?"

David pulls a face. "We've had another restructure at the bank so my role's changed again. I'm now a Strategic Sustainability Procurement Consultant."

"Impressive title! What does that involve?"

"Search me. I've just been on a three-hour teleconference about it but I'm none the wiser. Complete gobbledegook. Got a new car out of it, though, an upgrade on my BMW. It's an automatic."

"He hasn't actually worked out how to drive it yet," Cath chips in. "I've had to stick a note on the dashboard saying No Left Foot! But he still pumps it up and down trying to use an imaginary clutch."

"Yes, and I'm sorry, love but I overshot the driveway again and almost ended up in the dining room. I'm afraid I ran right over the flower bed." Louie makes a strangled noise in his throat. "You ok there, son? Right, I'm going to get out of this suit before it melts on me."

"So, will it be alright then, Col?" Cath asks again as her husband leaves the room. "For Louie to work at Hogpits with you? He's dead keen."

"I'll have to ask Mrs Winter," I reply, carefully. "Are you sure, Louie? The great outdoors doesn't seem like your sort of thing."

"It's the only option left now," he says. "Either that or Toni&Guy, but I can't face sweeping up dead hair for two weeks."

"No, I suppose not."

"I'll need to get some clothing though, Unck, I haven't really got anything tragic enough for gardening."

I nod. "We'll take a trip to Millets. It's an outdoor shop." I explain when Louie looks blank. I take another sip of cold beer. "What are you going to do about your video project? It sounds like your model's been wiped out."

"It doesn't matter," Louie shrugs. "It kinda sums life up, doesn't it? Before you have the chance to truly flourish you get cut dead by the trappings of capitalism."

Cath rolls her eyes and waggles a finger at her son. "Where the hell is all this lefty clap-trap coming from? We didn't hear you protesting about the evils of capitalism when Dad bought you a new iPhone out of his annual banker's bonus, did we?"

"That's different! Dad had to get me a replacement because he sat on my old one and smashed the screen."

"Don't remind me about that," Cath sniffs indignantly. "They were extremely rude in A&E, suggesting it was a self-inflicted injury. How dare they! I heard the nurses sniggering together behind the curtain about 'another one downloading the anus app'." She breaks off as footsteps slap down the hallway and her husband returns, dressed in just a pair of navy boxer shorts.

"Dad!" Louie hisses, mortified, as his father sits down at the kitchen table and shakes open the Telegraph.

"What?" David looks up in surprise. He folds the newspaper down and catches sight of the headline. "Ah yes, see what you mean, England all out for a hundred and twenty-one - shocking."

I'm glad I came, it's what I needed. The evening turns into typical Walsh mayhem – Cath ending up having to use the electric wok to cook the mince and, unable to get a saucepan of water to reach boiling point, gave up on the potatoes and topped the shepherd's pie with layers of Doritos. I rather like it. Louie microwaves a Quorn lasagne which he declares "very tasty", but I notice him heaping on salt and pepper, and then ketchup, and finally salad cream. Cath berates David for guzzling a whole bottle of wine, although he's only had one small glass and she's currently attempting to line up a cork screw to open another, swaying precariously in front of the Aga, or the 'beast with four stomachs' as David calls it. With all the windows and the back door wide open, the kitchen has finally cooled down and David has been persuaded to put a pair of shorts on.

"These bloody fiddle-arsed things!" Cath wrestles with the cork. "Screw tops, people, screw tops! Who the hell buys corked wine anymore?"

"You mean wine with a cork," I grin. "I don't think anyone actually sets out to buy corked wine."

"Whatever." Cath gives a final heave and the cork flies out with a satisfying pop. She pours herself a generous glass and sips it thoughtfully, watching me over the rim. "You know Col, we're orphans now." David snorts with laughter and Louie buries his head in his hands. "What's wrong with you two?" Cath demands indignantly. "I'm just stating a fact; Colin and I have lost both parents now and I don't think that's anything to snigger at, thank you very much."

"Second Bottle Syndrome, love," David chuckles good-naturedly. "You always get all teary-eyed and emotional."

"I do not!" Cath takes another sip and tries again. "So,

what are you going to do with your life now, Col? I mean, you're free from any ties, so you could travel, see the world, meet lots of new people."

"Mmm," I trace my finger down the condensation on my beer can. "I would love to travel, but I'm not going to get very far on a gardener's salary and four weeks holiday a year. I have been thinking about doing an Open University course."

"But that won't get you out and about, will it? Aren't you lonely, Col?" I jump as Cath grasps my arm and gazes into my eyes. Her own are a little glazed. "You must be lonely, you're rattling around in that house on your own, you don't have anyone to take care of you."

"He's having the time of his life, Cath!" David laughs. "He's got what every man dreams of; the beer fridge to himself, total control over the TV remote and uninterrupted viewing of the adult channels." He beams round at us, his smile fading as we all stare back at him. "Well, er, that's what *some* men would want, of course, I'm not saying that I–"

"You need to meet someone, Colin," Cath persists. "Someone to share your life with."

"I'd love to get a dog," I say, "but it will be on its own all day, so I don't think it's fair. Of course, I could go home every lunchtime..."

"Oh Col, not a bloody dog, you need a proper relationship, with a woman. You've never really had a *long-term* girlfriend, have you?"

"Mum," Louie mumbles. "You're so embarrassing."

I shift in my seat; it is getting hot again. "You know our Col likes to play the field!" David declares, trying to rescue me with a whopping great lie. "Who was that lovely red-head we met with the nice bum? Jenny, wasn't it? I liked her."

"You mean Janine?" I rub my forehead. "Yes, she was nice, but she was scared of Dad and hated coming to the house.

The final straw came when we were trying to concentrate on Springwatch, but Dad kept staring at her because he thought she had snakes coming out of her head. He became extremely agitated. I didn't hear from her again." That had been almost a year ago and there hadn't been anyone since. There hadn't really been anyone before, come to that. Brief *dalliances* you could call them, for want of a better word. I certainly couldn't class them as relationships, at least not compared to what I had with Sarah. One meaningful relationship in my whole life, then nothing more, in thirty years. That had to be some sort of record, and not one I wished to dwell on. I swallow the sudden surge of self-pity and smile ruefully. "I think I might be getting a bit long in the tooth for the dating game."

"But you've got so much to offer a girl!" Cath exclaims.

I nod. "Yes, so I have. Let's see, an ever-increasing forehead, deteriorating eyesight, Compo's wardrobe–"

"At least you're not called Louie Walsh," Louie sighs. "I've got no hope in the girlfriend department."

"We need to get you registered on some dating websites." To my horror, Cath grabs Louie's iPad and starts to tap. "It's how everyone meets their partner these days."

"No, Cath!"

"Don't worry, I won't state your correct age and I can embellish your occupation. Botanist, perhaps, that sounds alluring. I'll need a picture, not a recent one of course, perhaps that nice one of you at Louie's christening, by the font. I'll have to Photoshop the vicar out, he looks like Peter Sutcliffe."

"Stop it, Cath," I say firmly. "I am not Internet dating and anyway, I haven't even got a computer, remember? My knowledge of technology extends to a calculator."

"But I gave you my old iPhone and now Dad's gone you can get WiFi, it's not expensive." Thankfully, the phone ringing distracts Cath and she totters across the kitchen to answer it. "Hi Ally, how are you? Oh dear, what's wrong, babe? He's done *what?* Oh, I can't believe it, the swine. What an utter turd of a human being..."

With the sun setting across the sky, Louie departs to do his homework and David and I look out across the pretty garden. Cath is rocking herself on the swingy bench under the apple tree, chatting away animatedly. David opens his sloe gin. "It's a shame about that Janine sort, she really did seem very nice. Lovely bum, really very lovely indeed."

The thick purple liquid burns my stomach and makes my head swim. "I don't blame her for ending it. Dad was a lot to contend with."

"He never really recovered, did he, from your Mum passing away so suddenly?"

I shake my head. "It tipped him over the edge. Although we didn't realise he was on the edge, we had no idea his business was folding. I'm not even sure Mum knew."

"Everyone went bust in the eighties, Col." David tops up my glass before I can stop him. "When I first started at the bank they put me on the enquiries counter and every day a customer would come in to tell me they'd lost their job. I remember one man, a kitchen fitter, actually broke down and sobbed in front of me, the poor bastard. And there was a steady procession of small businesses collapsing. Not that the bank manager cared. He was making an absolute killing on the utilities privatisations; do you remember the British Gas Tell Sid campaign? Funnily enough the bank manager was actually called Sid! He paid off his mortgage with the profits he made." He rubs his nose ponderously. "That's all a little bit shit, now I come to think about it."

Cath lurches back into the kitchen and tops her glass up. "That was Alison Parker," she waves the phone handset. "Her little sister is having terrible man-trouble again and Ally calls each evening with an update; she has worse luck with her love-life than you, Col, despite spending a small fortune having her tits done. Not exactly money well spent, was it?"

I hear a tinny voice protesting. "You have disconnected the call, haven't you, Cath?"

"Bollocks." Cath punches the red button on the handset and grins. "Oops! You know Alison's sister, don't you, Col? Ginny, she was at school with you."

"Virginia Parker? Yes, but she was a few years below so I didn't really know her."

"Yes you do, she came to my birthday party last summer with Alison, remember? She was going through the divorce from hell. You chatted for ages."

"Oh, right." I can't recall either Ginny or our conversation, but possibly the sloe gin is affecting my brain function.

"You should give her a call."

"Right." I take another sip. "What for?"

"To discuss the impact of Brexit on UK trade and income... for Christ's sake, dipshit, to ask her out!" I fear Cath is about to hurl her glass at me in frustration. "Honestly Colin, you're enough to make a parson swear. I'll text you her number. Call her."

"Yeah, sure thing. I will."

We finish clearing the kitchen and I say my goodbyes, straddling my bike with a reeling head. Cath flings her arms round my neck and hangs on tight, almost choking me. "I should have done more to help with Dad," she wails, fumes of Chardonnay blasting into my face. "It was all down to you, all that respons- responib- repons, reponcey stuff, and now you're all alone, I love you, Col, you know that, don't you? Say you know that, say it-"

I unpeel myself and assure her I'm fine, waving precariously up to Louie at his bedroom window as I wobble off on my bike. My legs won't seem to co-ordinate with the pedals.

It's late and I'm slightly drunk, but I can't resist reading another letter. The next envelope feels thicker and a cassette falls out onto the kitchen table. It's an orange and black Casio tape with a faded hand-written label. I can't make out the words. When had I last played a cassette? I can't remember. I get unsteadily to my feet and carry the cassette through the kitchen and out the back door, making for my shed at the end of the garden. I flick the light on and locate my old radio cassette player on the potting table. I place the cassette inside and click the door shut, sitting down on an upturned plant tub to unfold Sarah's letter.

14 October 1984

Dearest Colin

I hope you, Cathy and your Dad are doing ok and that you are now back at college. Please say hi to all the guys for me - I miss them all, yes even the Tory Boys! The bombing in Brighton was so dreadful, have you been watching it on the news? Just awful. It feels churlish writing about my own worries while that's been going on, and please tell the TBs I am thinking of them. I don't have any sparring partners here, but I am playing referee as the tension continues to grow between Mum and Auntie Sheila. As you know, we have no money. Mum seems to expect Auntie Sheila to house and feed us for free, but of course she can't, she's only a cleaner. I thought Mum had some savings with the Pru as she paid in every month as regular as clockwork, but she says she can't get to it, as she's not prepared to pay the penalty, whatever that means.

Today, there was a huge row over a watermelon, would you believe? Auntie Sheila had purchased it from the Co-op and cut it into slices. When she found Mum had eaten some (most) of it, Auntie Sheila demanded Mum pay her 6p per slice. (She'd worked it all out on a calculator). Mum said she had no money left to pay for food, but apparently one of Sheila's neighbours saw Mum in the high street coming out of Wimpy's clutching a double cheese deluxe. Well, the row that followed was just horrible, mud flying in both directions. Mum called Sheila a 'dried up old spinster', and Sheila called Mum a 'fat tart', to which Mum responded 'how dare you! I am NOT fat!' which, I have to confess, made me laugh out loud. But, aside from that small chink of light, it was truly awful to witness. Afterwards, Mum told me that Sheila had always been jealous of her being the younger, prettier sister who got all the male attention, whereas Sheila was 'left at the altar and then on the shelf'. I am quite shocked at Mum's behaviour, it is completely out of character. It is extremely kind of Auntie Sheila to let us stay here and Mum needs to remember that.

But the fact is we are totally skint. Mum says she's not capable of getting a job, and I haven't managed to find one yet. Surely Dad should be giving us something, shouldn't he, as support? He can't just decide he wants to be with someone else and cut us off without a penny. I'll see if I can get Mum to make an appointment with one of the solicitors in town, or the Citizen's Advice Bureau, perhaps. That should be free.

So, things are not good here, my love. How I wish we were back in our room, well, Derek's room, happy and safe. Didn't everything seem so uncomplicated then, so simple? It's hard to believe that in such a short space of time both our lives have been turned upside down. As there are no signs of returning home to Trowbridge, perhaps you could visit us soon? I can't send you the train fare as I've been through all my post office savings, but perhaps you can find it from somewhere?

What a mess everything is. I don't want to put pressure on you but I hope you will write soon - please, please, please!

Yours, forever (and ever!)

Sarah

I tuck the letter back inside its envelope and press 'play' on the cassette recorder, not expecting it to work. There's a shushing sound as the tape slowly starts rolling, then Alison Moyet's velvety voice fills the shed. I'm immediately transported back to that summer, in our hiding place upstairs at Derek's. *Love Resurrection*. I can smell the heady scent of her, feel the heat radiating from our bodies as we press against each other in the narrow single bed. Those big dark eyes looking up at me, full of desire. *Pleading.* And later, arriving home on a cloud, glowing, feeling so alive as I float up the driveway.

And then Cath opens the door and tells me Mum is dead.

Chapter Four

At seventeen, I hadn't been able to comprehend how it was possible for somebody to be seemingly happy and healthy when you said goodbye to them at ten in the morning, only for them to be pronounced dead by nightfall. I was next door the whole time it was happening, oblivious to the horror, the panic, the ambulance arriving in a screaming rush and then leaving again, very slowly. A severe stroke, Cath had said. Since then, I'd done a vast amount of reading on the subject, constantly thinking back for signs that Mum might be suffering, or hiding something from us, but aside from a few headaches, I couldn't recall her complaining of anything. It hadn't helped that I'd been so preoccupied that summer. I was in love, my head was so full of Sarah Shaw I couldn't concentrate on anything else. To my shame, I wasn't able to recall a single thing Mum and I had talked about during those last months. House-sitting for Derek had created an all-consuming summer haven, and when I wasn't with Sarah, I stayed in my room listening to my LPs, discovering that the soppy love songs I'd always scoffed at had suddenly become deep and meaningful. How many times had I played 'Stuck on You'? Always with my headphones on, of course, I couldn't risk Cath overhearing, my older sister would have teased me mercilessly. Sleep had been almost impossible. As soon as my head hit the pillow my mind would re-live each look, every touch, everything Sarah had said, *had promised*. It had been so hard to accept she didn't want the same. Now I know that she did.

"Keep looking forwards, sweetheart, leave the past in the past." Mum's words wash over me. I'm nursing a nagging headache and with a determined wind blowing into my face, I fight to climb the steep hill to Hogpits Heights. It's like peddling through treacle and I curse myself for drinking on a school night. Why hadn't I said no to David's sloe gin? I was too polite. No, it wasn't politeness, it was weakness. Dad always said I was a push-over. Cath never had any problems saying no to anything or anyone, so how come I had turned out to be completely the opposite? I clearly hadn't inherited the assertiveness gene.

The sudden roar of an engine causes me to brake hard and I swerve into the hedge to avoid Mr Winter's Range Rover, its wing mirror narrowly missing my handlebars as it sweeps past. I raise a hand in apology in case he is looking out of his rear-view mirror. *Pathetic!* That's me all over, saying sorry for something when it wasn't even my fault. I seriously needed to grow some balls, as Tony would say. It was a shame you couldn't just purchase a pair in Asda.

As I carry my rucksack past the tearoom, I nod to the brunette who is trying to light a cigarette against the stiff breeze. She ignores me, her phone clamped to her ear. "Well, you'll just have to make do with that one, won't you? I'm not sending you anymore! What do you mean, you want to see the real thing? Cheeky! Whatever would your wife say?" Pause as the lighter flicks frantically. "No, I'm not going to meet you! Honestly, you're terrible, you've got a nerve even asking-"

It is duller today, but shafts of sunlight keep breaking through as the wind chases the clouds across the sky. I'm running late and The Hut is empty, although the radio has been left on. ELO's 'Horace Wimp' is playing and I give a rueful smile as I snap it off. Even Spire FM is trying to tell me something. I can hear the whine of the hedge-cutter in the distance and guess that Tony has made a start on taming the privet hedge that lines the lower lawn, embarking on a battle that will last until November. Taking a stroll around the grounds under the guise of appraising which tasks require prioritising, I wander down to the petting farm to say hello to Fred, the snowy white goat. He'd become a bag of nerves since the recent loss of his partner, Ginger, with an adverse affect on his digestive system. I lean over the fence and Fred edges towards me, letting me rub his coarse nose as he chews at the zip on my fleece before a gust of wind startles him and he jolts, with a fart, back to the protection of the apple tree. The lop-eared rabbits eye me curiously as I pass their pen, their little mouths working away to devour their breakfast. I keep a wary eye on Nasty Nat who hones into view every so often, but she is a safe distance away; I can see her ducking and weaving about the children's playground as if searching for something. With my headache beginning to ease, I make my way back to The Hut to fetch the second hedge trimmer so I can give Tony a hand. An A-line-skirted figure strides across the top lawn, a purple scarf streaming out behind. "Mrs Winter!" I call, raising my hand and breaking into a trot to catch her. "Can I have a quick word?"

"Ah, Colin." Mrs Winter turns her ghostly face toward me as she waits for me to reach her. I notice her eyes have heavy dark rings around them. "I was very sorry to hear about your father."

"Oh, thank you." I study the turf, feeling awkward. "Um, Mrs Winter, I wanted to ask if it would be possible for my nephew to do his work experience here in July. He's extremely hard-working and er, very keen to learn."

"Your nephew?" Mrs Winter purses her thin lips and frowns, fingering her pearls. "I'm not sure, Colin, we're on a very strict budget at the moment."

"No, no, you don't need to pay him, not when he's doing work experience."

The pallid face brightens, turning almost translucent in the pale sunlight. "Well, that's fine then. Excellent, in fact. We could use another pair of hands to prepare for the Open Day in July." She fixes me with her piercing stare and I try hard not to wince. "The Open Day is critical for us, Colin. We're pulling out all the stops to attract more families during the school holidays. It is, as my husband charmingly puts it, a shit or bust day – we've already spent a small fortune on advertising. The gardens have got to be at their absolute best." *Then you should be holding it in June! All the rhododendrons will have finished, the Chilean fire tree will have turned to ash...* I ignore my inner voice and nod, managing what I hope is a confident and reassuring smile. Mrs Winter looks at me anxiously. "Are you in pain, Colin?"

"Yes, careful the wind doesn't change, Colin, you'll get stuck like that!" Nasty Nat is behind us, appearing out of nowhere like a genie, as she often did. "There'll be even less chance of you attracting a woman! Ha ha ha! I'm only joking."

"Did you want something, Natalie?" Mrs Winter asks, curtly.

"I wondered if either of you have seen Ron this morning?" Nasty Nat replies innocently. "The horses don't appear to have been fed and the eggs haven't been collected from the hen house." She looks at me, eyes glinting. "Where do you think he could be, Colin?"

Oh God. No doubt Chicken Ron is either still at home or under a park bench, sleeping off another heavy session. *And* he is on a final warning. Both women are waiting for me to answer and I feel my face flaring up under their scrutiny. I flounder. "He's um, er, he's–"

"Down by the lake I expect," Mrs Winter snaps, glaring at Natalie. "It's already full of blanket weed; I mentioned it to Ron yesterday, so that's where you'll find him." She folds her arms across her chest. "Colin is responsible for the gardeners, Natalie, I'm surprised you have the time to do his job as well as your own."

"I, I, I was simply *concerned* for Ron," Nasty Nat stutters, her face turning the same colour as mine. "For his well-being."

"Hmmm," Mrs Winter considers her for a moment before turning back to me. "Perhaps you can see to the horses, Colin? And collect the eggs. Good. Now, are there any other members of staff you are *concerned* for, Natalie? No? Right, let's crack on, please." She turns on her heel and breathing a sigh of relief, I beam into Nasty Nat's crestfallen face before bounding away across the lawn. I need to fetch the hoe.

It had been a good morning, despite feeling rough around the edges. I always enjoyed tending to the horses, especially Venus, my favourite, a majestic chestnut who watched me through her beautiful brown eyes, occasionally blinking her long dark lashes. She reminded me of Betty Boop. The egg collection wasn't quite such a serene experience. The hens clucking around me were so bossy and demanding it was like being surrounded by hundreds of miniature Mrs Winters. At least Psycho the cockerel hadn't been around this morning. He was extremely unpredictable and had occasionally been known to flail at people with his horrid claws, jumping up almost to face level. He had a particular disliking for Mr Winter, which is why Chicken Ron often napped in the hen house, knowing his boss would never venture too close to the hens for fear of provoking a Psycho attack.

It's lunchtime, and entering The Hut, I'm transported to another world, ala Mr Benn. 'Beat Surrender' is playing on the Time Tunnel, and immediately I am back at the Devizes youth club disco, dressed in a blazer, drain-pipe jeans and trainers, trying to be Paul Weller. I'd even started to smoke, the desire to look as cool as he did holding a cigarette outweighing the fear of lung cancer. That desire had back-fired somewhat, with each drag resulting in a prolonged fit of coughing and spluttering. I cringe as I recall sitting in my mate's Ford Escort outside the youth club and, as a group of queuing girls looked on, I tried to casually flick my cigarette butt out of the window. I missed. The glowing stump fell back onto my thighs and leaping out of the car, I treated the queue to a frenzied dance with accompanying girly shrieks. My mate simply shook his head very sadly and drove us straight to Den's Diner, or Losers' Cafe as we called it, so we could console ourselves with cheesy chips following yet another evening of zero success with the opposite sex. I ate a lot of cheesy chips back then. I still do.

I hear squelching footsteps approaching and Tony appears on the path outside. "Alright, Col?" he utters, sitting down wearily on the steps to The Hut and removing his boots. A whoosh of water shoots out from each one as he tips them upside down.

"What happened, Tone?"

"Chicken Ron got stuck in the mud at the edge of the lake again. I tried to heave him out from the bank, but he pulled me in, the bastard. He was laughing so hard his glass eye popped out. Luckily we managed to get to it before the pike this time." He wrings out his socks one by one and lays them across the sunny window sill. "And I'm done in with that hedge cutting, Col, my arms are practically hanging off."

"I'll take over this afternoon," I tell him, feeling guilty for my leisurely morning. "You can do some light duties; the little box topiary trees by the house need clipping again."

Tony groans. "And what poncy shapes does Morticia want them sculpted into this year? I thought she'd have learnt her lesson following the leaping dolphin disasters - everyone thought they were moustaches. And do you remember when she wanted the prancing horse cut into the box hedge? I spent an entire week on it and she just sniffed and said 'It's not exactly Michelangelo standard.' Cheeky cow! I nearly said that's because I'm a hairy-arsed gardener love, not Edward flipping Scissorhands."

I chuckle, remembering my attempt to create a squirrel out of one of the bushes in front of the house. Mrs Winter referred to it as the 'devil rat' and eventually asked me to cut it down because it was giving her nightmares.

"Allo allo!" Wes enters. "Has everyone had a good *moaning*?" He flicks the kettle on and turns the radio down, much to Tony's annoyance. "Listen very carefully, I vill say this only wunce." He laughs and nudges my shoulder. "I used to love that show, didn't you, Col?"

"Um-"

"And that Vicky Michelle, she was a right sort. Not to mention sex-bomb Helga and the fallen Madonna with the big boobies! Ha ha!"

Tony, too young to know what Wes is talking about, stares at him in bewilderment. "Gotta love the eighties," Wes sighs, making himself a cup of tea. "Although it was back to the seventies for me last night." He lobs his tea bag into the bin, tapping his spoon loudly on the side of the mug, making sure he has our attention. "Mid-week burner, nice little earner. I did an Elvis set."

"Sounds good," I say politely, ignoring Tony's warning 'don't encourage him' scowl. "Did it go well?"

"Did it go well, he asks!" Wes laughs. "Yeah, just a bit! The best moment was when I did 'Loving You', which was especially requested by the bride's mother. She was in a wheelchair, poor thing and I sang every word to her. Tears were streaming down her face, and at the end of it–"

"Don't tell me!" Tony cries. "She got out of her wheelchair and walked! It's a miracle, an amazing miracle! Praise the Lord!"

I'm forced to take a bite of my cheese and pickle sandwich to stop myself laughing. A furious Wes is considering a suitable riposte, but Nasty Nat enters The Hut at that moment and Wes, like everyone else, is intimidated into silence. "It's like a morgue in here," she comments as her eyes sweep over us. "Gosh, is that *two* sausage rolls you've got there, Tony? One to feed each chin, I suppose!" She fiddles with the kettle and pushes the mugs around on the bench. We watch her uneasily out of the corner of our eyes. What is she doing here again? She usually ate her lunch in the tearooms. Prince is now playing on the radio and Nasty Nat tweaks the volume back up. "Remember this one, Colin? Although you probably party like it's 1899! Was that the last time you took a girl out?" Ah, of course, I needed to be punished for earlier. How many other grown men allowed themselves to be bullied in the workplace? No doubt she'd dismiss it as banter if I protested. "Did you have to pay for your last date, Colin? Was it in shillings?"

Tony makes a growling noise in his throat. It isn't quite loud enough for Nasty Nat to hear but I appreciate his support just the same. Nasty Nat turns to nudge the radio volume back down and Wes makes his bid for freedom, slipping silently from The Hut in a move Houdini would have been proud of.

"It's such a shame, Colin." Nasty Nat leans against the bench examining me with mock sympathy. "What's putting the ladies off, I wonder? Could it be those Asda Grandad jeans, or the sight of you engaged in conversation with an old goat?"

Oh God, she'd heard me talking to Fred; how humiliating. *Grow some.* "Oh, I wouldn't say you were an old goat, Nat."

I smile at her. "I've always thought of you as more of an old cow." Tony's sharp intake of breath causes him to choke on a pastry flake and I thump him on the back as I look up into Nasty Nat's shocked face. "Just joking, of course."

"Yes, well," Nasty Nat tosses her dark hair, trying to regain some composure. "I'd better let you get on. I daresay you need to oil your secateurs or something." She stalks out.

"That was brilliant!" Tony gasps. "You actually shut her up for once."

"I shouldn't have called her a cow." I bite my lip, mortified. "That was really rude. I should go after her and apologise."

"No bloody way, she had it coming. Anyway, what's the worst that can happen? Apart from her telling her husband, of course. He's a body builder, built like a brick shithouse."

"Oh God."

"I reckon you could take him, Col, you're wiry. You'd better have half of my apple Danish though, start bulking up."

We munch in silence for a bit. I feel so bad about my cow comment, that hadn't been at all gentlemanly, but Nasty Nat always seemed to know which wounds to twist the knife in. "Are you doing anything tonight, Col?" Tony asks hopefully. "I could do with some help finishing my application for Deal or No Deal, the bloody thing's about forty pages long."

"I thought they'd stopped making that show."

"They have, but they're still doing some one-off specials to show at bank holidays and stuff."

"Oh, right. Have you completely given up on Big Brother, then?"

"Yeah, they just want complete sideshow freaks now, don't they? Not even Chicken Ron would get a look in. I've got to make a five minute video to go with my application; will you help me with it?"

"Sure. What sort of things have you got to cover in the video?"

"Some of the made-up hobbies I put in the application. Perhaps I could film it by the lake, that would cover scuba-diving and dolphin conservation in one go."

I laugh. "Have you considered filming your actual hobbies?"

"What, Maccy D's and KFC? That's hardly going to impress the producer, is it, not unless he wants to use my film as an obesity health warning."

"You should definitely make the video here," I say. "If you get on the show it will be a great plug for the gardens and the Winters will absolutely love it. You could interview some of your wonderful colleagues for the film, although you'll have to bribe them to say nice things about you, of course."

"Ha bloody ha! You won't be taking the piss when I'm two hundred and fifty grand richer. You can buy a lot of chicken buckets with that, the birds will be queuing up." He whips out his phone. "That reminds me, I must message Laura from Nando's, she's poked me again."

With Tony ensconced in his phone, I sneak another of Sarah's letters out of my rucksack and open it up.

24 October 1984

Dearest Colin

I thought about my last letter to you and realise how boring and trivial it must have sounded. Self-indulgent, even. I can't believe I moaned about my life when you have so much to deal with right now. No wonder you haven't replied. I must try harder.

It is pretty obvious I won't be going back to college this year and I phoned Mrs Peters (you know, the lady in Registrations who has a lisp like Toyah) to tell her I was dropping out. I asked if she would pass a message on to you, but she said you'd left. She wouldn't tell me why, stating student confidentiality, so I am assuming you have to look after your father. Has he become really bad? Has Cathy had to leave university too? You poor things, I do wish there was something I could do to help you all. I hate being stuck in this Godforsaken place hundreds of miles away. I feel so utterly useless.

Things are still a little tense here following Water (Melon) Gate, as I am calling it, however the good news is that I have managed to find some work. It's only washing-up in a hotel (well, loading and unloading the dishwater) but there may be some bar work and waitressing when the Christmas functions begin. Christmas! I thought we'd have found a place back in Trowbridge long before then, but it doesn't look likely, I'm afraid. At least I hope that my financial contribution may, in some small part, help ease the tension between Mum and Sheila.

I have been looking into correspondence courses, in a vain attempt to keep my brain in gear. Maybe creative writing - what do you think? God, no, I hear you cry. That's probably why you don't reply, because my letters are so badly written!

I do wish you'd call, I jump every time the phone goes. There was a knock at the door the other day and for one magical fleeting moment I believed it was you. It wasn't of course, it was just the coalmen. I wish you'd write, wish you'd phone, wish we could come home... I'm spending my life just wishing. Flock of Seagulls - that's appropriate, there's hundreds of them round here, roaming the bay in gangs, armed with flick knives and knuckle dusters.

Yes, I think I am losing it.

I miss you. I love you.

Yours, forever
Sarah

It has grown dark in The Hut, a large black cloud shutting out the light. I fight off a wave of nausea. I don't know what I'm finding the more sickening: reading Sarah becoming increasingly hurt and bewildered as she tries to justify my lack of contact, or her heartfelt concern for Dad, the man that was the cause of her distress. He'd opened all her letters, so presumably he'd read them. How could he let her suffer like that, why had he been so cruel? If he was scared I would run off to be with Sarah leaving him to cope on his own, I would never have done that. I'd have found a way to take care of Dad and still be with Sarah. We'd be together now, I knew we would, with a little family of our own. Sarah wanted children, she talked of us living in a 'noisy, messy house of fun'. What sort of father would I have made? A big softie, no doubt, the kids would have walked all over me. I wouldn't have minded. *Ah, stop wallowing in it.* I'll never know now so it's pointless torturing myself.

I fold the letter up and tuck it away, wondering if Sarah is living the life she craved. I bet she has a wonderful, *valuable* career; perhaps she is the head of a charity, or a ground-breaking journalist, fearlessly exposing injustices and corruption. I look across at Tony, still engrossed in Facebook. I should try and find Sarah. Would it be possible? Maybe, maybe not, but I could at least try. If I succeed in tracking her down, I can explain about the letters, tell her I hadn't seen them. It was so long ago, she might not care, or even remember, but something told me she would. A rush of excitement replaces the nausea. Could our passion be re-ignited? *No, don't get carried away, that's ridiculous thinking... Isn't it?*

The room brightens as the big black cloud moves away.

"Hold it steady, Col, you're jiggling around like there's a wasp up your arse. You're gonna make the viewers sea sick! We'll have to start again."

"Sorry, sorry." I adjust my grip on the camcorder and stop recording. "It's just that it's really heavy. Why don't we use your iPhone instead?"

"No, I can't at the moment, the memory's full. It's after that night with the twins from the hair salon - there's no way

I'm deleting any of those memories. Or mammaries, I should say."

"Ah. Right." I try to hold the recorder in a more comfortable position. Wes had assured me it was 'state of the art' but it feels incredibly clunky. "Ok then, let's go again."

"Your heart's not really in this, is it? You need to give it some welly, Col - shout ACTION! when we're ready to roll. Come on, give it all you've got!"

"Right, sorry. Er, action."

Tony clears his throat, cracks his knuckles and nods at me. I press the red button and attempt to hold the camera steady, pointing it at Tony as he begins to stroll around the edge of the lake. He stops suddenly, snapping his head round to face the camera and beaming a bright, toothy grin. "Hi Noel! My name is Tony Chisholm and I'm a landscape gardener. This is where I work, the beautiful Hogpits Heights." He sweeps his arms theatrically around him. "This is the lake, which was just a muddy puddle when I first arrived here. Now, as you can see, I have transformed it into an oasis, home to one hundred carp, quite a few ducks and a nasty old pike. The gardens are open for the public to visit, and for an extremely reasonable entrance fee you can enjoy these lovely surroundings. Unless you're a real oldster, of course, in which case you'll have to stick to the upper lawn, the paths aren't really suitable for the crinklies."

I stop recording. "I don't think you should refer to the elderly as crinklies, Tone, it's not very nice."

"Isn't it? I thought it was a term of endearment? No? Bollocks. Ok, let's go again." He takes a deep breath and loosens his shoulders, looking at me expectantly.

"Action!" I call.

Tony faces the camera again, flicking the smile back on. "Not all the paths are suitable for, er, for everyone, which is a shame because I believe all people should be treated as equals." He adjusts his face into an expression of earnest sincerity. "Close up, Col!" he hisses. I don't know how to zoom in, so I step forward a few paces. "If I win the show's jackpot, I will give it, well some of it, to a poor disabled person, such as..." He flounders for a moment. "Stephen Tompkins."

I stop again. "Who?" But Tony is on a roll so I whip the camera back up and keep filming. "Hogpits Heights is owned by a super-rich telecommunications entrepreneur and his wife, Mort-, I mean Mrs Winter, who is an albino, just like the lovely rabbits we have in the children petting area."

"Er, Tone," I interject. "I'm not sure *children petting* area sounds quite right-"

"But by far and away the best thing about my job is working in such a peaceful and tranquil environment. I'm an immensely spiritual person, and I have really found myself amongst all this serenity." Tony moves right to the edge of the lake, pressing his palms together, as if in prayer. "I like to meditate each morning, just as the sun is rising over the crest of Hogpits Mount," he gestures towards a hillock in the distance. I wonder if I should tell him he's pointing west. "I can really find myself amongst the peace and solitude, and I like to think about all the important things in life; the children living in poverty in Africa and Blackpool, the old people who are lonely and– Shit!" A whoosh of water covers Tony as something heavy lands in the lake behind him. I jump backwards but Tony isn't quick enough and another loud splosh douses him again. "Ugh! What the f–" As he swings round, a clump of green gunk hits him straight in the face. I hear a cackle of laughter and turn to see a figure crouching low in the reeds. A hand appears, scoops up another fistful of blanket weed and flings it at Tony. It slaps against his neck then slides down his white T-shirt, leaving a trail of green slime. "Ron, you stupid pikey scumbag piece of shit!" Tony's roar makes the ducks rise up in alarm and they take off across the lake in a cacophony of quacking and flapping. Tony takes off too, yelling obscenities as he chases Chicken Ron out of the reeds and up the path toward the stables. An elderly couple approaching the lake stop dead in their tracks, mouths open, aghast at the foul-mouthed tirade.

I replay the footage as I stroll up to The Hut, giggling like a schoolboy as I watch it back. It is an unfamiliar sound and I wonder when I last laughed out loud at anything. I seem to have been numb for weeks, like living in a thick layer of bubble wrap. There's another unusual noise as I reach the top lawn and I realise my mobile is ringing. I pull it out of my pocket in surprise, unaccustomed to receiving calls. I don't recognise the number. "Hello?"

"Oh, hello." It's a woman's voice. "Is that Colin?"

"Yes?"

"Hello, Colin. It's Ginny."

"Who?"

"Ginny, Ginny Harris, used to be Parker. Alison's sister."

"Oh, right." *Dammit, I'd forgotten to call her.* "Hi Ginny. I'm so sorry I haven't been in touch, I've been, er, really busy lately, you see–"

"You play it cool, I must say."

I laugh. "I can assure you I have never played anything cool in my entire life, I wouldn't know how!"

She chuckles. "Well, even though you haven't called me, I'm willing to give you the chance to make it up to me. Would you like to take me to dinner on Saturday?"

I hesitate. I'm not at all sure I can face a whole evening of awkward small talk, and anyway, Tony and I were planning to go to The Stag on Saturday for a game of darts. "Blimey, Colin, don't make me beg! It's just that Cath said you weren't doing anything, but if doing nothing is preferable to having dinner with me…"

"No, no, it's not that," I say quickly. *Bloody Cath!* "It's just

I've agreed to go out with my friend on Saturday night, and I don't like letting him down."

"Bring him along, then, we can double-date if he's got a girlfriend."

"Um," I frown. Did Tony have a girlfriend at the moment? He usually has someone 'bubbling under' as he calls it. "I think so."

"Great! That's settled, then. Shall we say seven-thirty? Where do you fancy?"

Gosh, where to suggest? Nando's, Pizza Express?

"Because I love Truffles, would that be all right? I'll book a table as they get really busy."

"Lovely," I say weakly. I'd never been to Truffles, although I'd often walked past it in the High Street, glancing in through the sash windows at the pristine white tablecloths and straight-backed, poker-faced waiters. It was the sort of place my mother would call 'glitzy' and not my kind of thing at all, but I didn't like to protest at Ginny's choice of restaurant, not after she'd had the courage to call and ask me out.

As I say goodbye to Ginny, Tony arrives on the lawn panting heavily, sweat pouring off him. His face, neck and T-shirt are stained bright green. "Lost the bastard in the woods," he gasps. "Think he went down a fox hole. He'll come out as soon as it's opening time, though; I'll bloody well get him then." He wipes his sopping brow. "What are you grinning at?"

"You look like Shrek!"

"Christ." He gazes down at this T-shirt mournfully. "This is brand new. What was the footage like, can we use any of it? I bloody hope so, this is rapidly turning into the ball-ache from hell. I know we can't use the clips by the animals because Fred kept guffing, but what about the bit we filmed in front of Wintersdell with me on the steps? Can we use that? With any luck the viewers will think I own it."

"But why would a multi-millionaire be applying for Deal or No Deal? Come on, you need an injection of reality, Tone. What would you actually spend your winnings on?"

He thinks for a moment, head on one side. "I'd just like a more comfortable life, really, with a few little luxuries thrown in. I'd go to college, get myself a decent job, put a deposit down on a house and treat Mum to a holiday, she's never been anywhere other than the Mendips Caravan park. She'd love to go to a place where she doesn't have to wear three jumpers and pee into a tin potty at night."

"Then cut out all the spiritual mumbo-jumbo rubbish." I wave Wes' camcorder at him. "We'll film you sitting on a bench with a pint outside The Stag, and you can say exactly what you just said. Tell Noel how you really feel."

"What? I'll never get on the show if I describe my actual life! It's such dross."

"No, what you've said is what everyone wants, people will relate to you." I smile encouragingly at him. "And I daresay we'll need to shoot quite a few takes before we get it right, so–"

"So we'll probably get through quite a few pints!" Tony brightens up considerably. "Shall we do it tonight?"

"No time like the present, Tone." *No present like the time.* Plus, tonight will be an excellent opportunity to break the news about Truffles on Saturday night. Probably best I wait until his third pint, at the very least.

25 November 1984

Dearest Colin,

I'm sorry about my letter of the 22nd. I was very tired and emotional when I wrote it, please forgive me. I know you love me and you will write soon, I just have to be patient.

I am sure that things will be strange at Christmas

without your Mum; I hope you will still be able to celebrate and try to have a good time, she would have wanted that, wouldn't she? This is the first Christmas for my Mum and Dad being apart (I'm not counting the time Mum stormed out because Dad gave her a new saucepan set) and it all feels very strange.

Anyway, I can't write too much more as my job at The Three Keys is keeping me busy and my boss is extremely demanding. He's called Popeye, which is a rather cruel nickname as his eyes go in different directions. It can be a little disconcerting. When I first walked in he shouted "Get out! I'm not having you cocking your leg over the umbrella stand again!" but turns out he was talking to the dog. He's all right really and the natives are friendly, although they don't much care for the London weekenders, or the 'Big City Losers' as they call them. Some are a bit leery, especially after a shot of Wood's rum (it's like tar!), but I can handle them and there's certainly no need for you to be jealous, the average age of the clientele is about sixty!

I love you so much. I know you love me, but it would be nice to hear you say it again, to be reassured. Who was it said: 'A life without love is like a year without summer'?

Please write and tell me you can't wait to see me. Please make the sun come out again.

Your Sarah. Forever

Chapter Five

The bus rattles past the long stone wall that lines the race-course and hammers down the hill, stopping at the traffic lights by Halfords before taking off again with an alarming spurt of speed. It grinds to a halt in front of the Toyota garage where a small knot of passengers are waiting. The doors open with a bad-tempered hiss. An extremely plump lady is first on, fishing around in the pockets of her purple flowery dress before waving her bus pass at the whatever-looking driver. The kids sitting at the back of the bus giggle as she makes her way up the aisle and squeezes with difficulty into a seat. I catch "Nice dress," then "What's that hanging down under the hem? Oh, it's her tits," followed by hoots of laughter.

I unfold another letter from my pocket and attempt to focus on Sarah's handwriting as the bus jerkily takes off again.

5 December 1984

Dearest Colin

I was up early this morning and made it down to Woollies just as they opened so I could get the Band Aid single before it sold out. It's the most wonderful song, I can't believe they put it together so quickly. I think Boy George sounds the best, what do you think? It's a pity there are no female lead vocalists, just Bananarama in the background, but still, sometimes you just have to accept things for what they are i.e. the very best intentions.

The news report from Ethiopia was just heart-breaking, I had no idea people were suffering so terribly. The sheer scale of the tragedy is mind-blowing. I hope every single person buys the record and it makes millions of pounds, enough to end the famine. Mum made a stupid comment about not sending money abroad when people in this country need it and that caused another blow up with Auntie Sheila, who said, 'Yes, you're right, charity begins at home, you still owe me for three rolls of Andrex'.

I tentatively suggested (again) that Mum finds a job but she said her nerves are still shot to pieces and blamed Dad for destroying all her self-confidence. I overheard her on the phone last night and I was sure it was Dad she was talking too, even though she was whispering so Auntie Sheila wouldn't hear, but it just sounded like the familiar way they used to talk together, do you know what I mean? It would be great if they are back on speaking terms. She'll never forgive him, though, and why should she? I'd never forgive you if you did that to me. Not that you ever would, of course, you're simply not made that way. That's one of the (many) reasons I love you so much. Yes, I know, pass the sick bucket!

I'm starting to think about Christmas and because I haven't got a lot of money for presents, I'm knitting Mum some legwarmers, although it took me ages to find burgundy wool.... Oh God, I'm so sorry, I've just re-read that bit - how boring am I? Knitting!!! It must be working amongst all the oldies at the Three Keys, I've been infected with geriatricity! I hope there's a cure!

Yours forever, Sarah

PS. Wouldn't it be wonderful to volunteer together for a charity, do you think we could? I'll start looking into it.

PPS. I almost made it to the end of the letter without begging you to write back. Didn't quite make it.

I tuck the letter away as the bus stops again and an elderly couple step carefully on, clutching their Tesco's bags for life. Next to board is a tall thin figure in a long dark trench coat, hair teased up into short spikes like a hedgehog, a long black fringe hiding his face. He pays the driver, whose lip curls at the sight of the black nail varnish and, having counted the money, rams the bus into gear, taking off before his passenger has the chance to sit down. He is propelled forwards, falling in a heap onto the seat next to me, prompting an outburst of laughter from the back.

"Hi Louie."

"Hello Unck." Louie brushes his fringe out of his eyes, but it immediately falls back to cover them again. "Sorry you're having to spend your Saturday shopping with me; I'm sure you'd rather be at home smashing yourself in the face with a sledge-hammer or something."

I chuckle. "It's no problem, I need some new clothes myself as it goes, so it will be great to have a young person's opinion."

"You'd better see if you can find one, then. My opinion never counts for anything, not unless you're into graveyard chic, innit."

I blink at my nephew in surprise. "Louie, did you just say 'innit'?"

"Yeah. Everyone at school says it, so I thought I'd try it out."

"And? How did it sound?"

He sighs. "Tragic."

"Where's Simon, Louie?" Someone calls from the back of

the bus. "Where's Sharon? Simon, Simon! Sharon, Sharon!"

"What are they saying?" I ask Louie in confusion.

"You've never watched X Factor, have you Unck? He's one of the judges. Well, he used to be. Or is he back again? I'm not sure. Don't worry, you haven't missed anything."

An Irish accent rings out. "Ya look like a popstar, ya sound like a popstar, ya're the whole package!"

"Wes at work used to love the X Factor," I tell Louie. "He was always going on about it and even went for an audition once. I'm not sure how it went; he hasn't mentioned it since. You'll get to meet Wes when you do your work experience next week. You'll, er, you'll like him."

"I don't expect he'll like me," Louie replies. "I appear in the school's yearbook as the boy least likely to have anyone at his funeral."

"Ah." I rack my brains for a safe topic. "How are your mum and dad?"

"Mum's working on a flasher case. She reckons he'll get off because the evidence is so slight. Dad made a massive cock-up at work and cost the bank three hundred thousand. He's been moved to another role again, something to do with payment protection insurance; he says it's impossible to screw that up 'cos it's already completely buggered."

"Blimey." I rub my forehead. "I'm glad I only have a bit of bindweed and a few moles to contend with."

The bus swings into the station and we dismount, leaving to calls of "The girls at home are gonna love ya!" as we walk through the teeming town centre. Louie has never been to Millets before and gazes around in bewilderment at the unfamiliar expanse of outdoor clothing and equipment. I find him some black T-shirts, a pair of black jogging bottoms and some sturdy dark brown boots, all of which he declares "ultra tragic". He tries on the ensemble with an over-sized moss green fleece and stands miserably in the doorway of the changing cubicle, head down, his fringe drooping dejectedly. The young sales assistant ducks swiftly down behind the counter but I can still see her shoulders shaking uncontrollably. I fight hard to keep a straight face.

"Looking good, Louie! But wouldn't you prefer a smaller fleece?"

He shakes his head. "I want to be able to wear my bondage jumper under it. Retain some humanity."

Having paid for Louie's new outfit, we head to Debenhams to search for something for me. The last date I'd been on was with Janine, she of the serpent tresses. I'd worn my smartest jeans, but denim wouldn't do for the splendour of Truffles; should I wear a suit? I only owned one, in black, which I'd purchased for Dad's funeral. It didn't seem appropriate for that to double as a date outfit. I try to ignore the sharp stab in my heart as I think of Dad. I wouldn't be nervously shopping for a first date outfit if it wasn't for him, I'd be with Sarah, happily ambling around Waitrose hand-in-hand, choosing ingredients for a romantic supper, rather than another of those sad-bastard meals for one. I shake off the tidal wave of self-pity and wander into the Jasper Conran section, casually examining the price tag on a navy twill suit jacket. I gasp in shock. Three hundred and eighty-five pounds - is that just for the jacket? It is! "Can I help you, sir?"

I turn to find a dapper, slender little man examining me. He has large round spectacles and slicked back silver hair. "I'm just looking, thank you."

He purses his lips. "Looking for what, exactly, sir? Something for a special occasion?"

"Yeah, he's got a date," chips in Louie, who is examining the braces. "He's going to Truffles."

"Ah, Truffles," breathes the Silver Fox, clasping his hands together. "How marvellous. A little oasis of Mediterranean heaven right on our door step. You must try their Chateaubri-

and, it's to die for." He beams at me. I try to smile back, but all I can see are pound signs looming large in front of my eyes, growing bigger and bigger... suits, shirts, expensive steaks, cocktails. Ginny is bound to want a cocktail, if she is anything like Cath-

"And, of course, you want to impress the... lady?"

I realise it is a question. "Oh, yes, it's definitely a lady, absolutely. She's one hundred percent woman." I try to make my voice a little deeper. "But I'm not quite sure about *this* suit, I don't think it's quite…" *cheap* "…classical enough."

"I see, sir." I shift uncomfortably as the Silver Fox's eyes sweep over me, taking in my George from Asda polo shirt and comfort-fit blue jeans. I tuck one leg behind the other in a pathetic attempt to hide my aging trainers from his gaze. "Well, you could go with a suit, of course, if that's what you want, but it's really quite relaxed dining in Truffles these days."

"Is it?" I squeak, so relieved I forget to sound butch.

"Oh yes, it's all very understated and discreet." He touches my arm very lightly and steers me to The Collection section. "Why don't you have a peek at these gorgeous chinos? You can't go wrong with a casual classic. They look great with an open shirt, and lucky you! There's twenty percent off today."

I glimpse the £27.99 price tag and smile at him gratefully. "There's lots of different colours, aren't there? These mustard ones look very nice."

"That is, I'm afraid, a contradiction in terms, sir," the Silver Fox swiftly cuts in, stepping in front of me to block the mustard trousers from view. He deftly plucks a pair of navy ones from the rail and hands them to me. "These are slightly more *sartorial*, especially when teamed with a crisp, white shirt."

"Right." I nod, glancing round at the shirt racks and pointing at some white ones. "Shall I go for something like this?"

"Only if you're determined never to see the lady again. Always steer clear of polyester, sir, or sparks will fly. For all the wrong reasons."

"O-k, I'll have another look. At the cotton ones. Thanks very much for your help."

"My pleasure. I hope you have a successful evening. And do try the duck liver parfait, it's divine."

"We're going to Burger King after this," Louie informs him. "You can come too, if you like."

"That's most kind of you, young man, but I won't be visiting that particular establishment today. Maybe I'll go when..." He thinks for a moment than clicks his fingers. "When hell freezes over. Now, please excuse me, I have to save that unfortunate-looking gentlemen from another double denim disaster. Good day to you."

I hold up a white cotton shirt. It has pale blue vertical stripes running through it. "What do you think of this one, Louie?"

"Yeah, it's fine," he replies without looking. "I love these braces, they're sick."

"Er, yes. Sick." Is that a good thing? "I am going to get this one, it's nice. And it's non-iron, apparently, so that's a bonus. Then we'll go to BK, shall we, get you a veggie burger?"

"No, I've gone back to meat. I figure I need to be a bit more red-blooded to make it through the hell of a school day; at least have the strength to lift a full wheelie bin off myself. I'm going to try and build up some stamina, bulk myself up, be more manly. Ooh, can we go to Boots on the way? I'm out of moisturiser."

I feel old. Sipping at my gritty cappuccino, I try to keep up as Louie flicks and scrolls his way through his iPhone, showing me app after app, which, as far as I can make out, are designed to remove any requirement to think for yourself. "You see,

Unck? Because we're near Sainsbury's, it's reminded me to get Cherry Cola," and "If I've been in the sun for longer than four minutes, this warning alarm will sound."

I nod weakly. I know I'm woefully out of touch with technology and it's a constant source of embarrassment. I can no longer kid myself that it is considered 'quirky' not to be on any form of social media; people just think I'm weird. It hadn't helped that Dad wouldn't have a computer in the house because he believed people could watch him through it. Or had that just been a ruse, a way to prevent me connecting with others? It was difficult to know what to believe now. Dad had certainly made me paranoid about the Internet and social media scared me to death. How stressful it must be, to constantly seek the approval of others. Tony was obsessed with Facebook; the first thing he did each morning was log in to see 'what everyone is up to', but then all he did was moan about the bombardment of cat pictures and the 'annoying twats' who sent quasi-menacing chain messages threatening to unfriend him if he didn't repost. I force a smile and manage a feeble titter of laughter as Louie shows me a video clip of a baby armadillo playing with a rubber dog chew toy.

"I've just received a friend's request." Louie taps at his phone. "Someone called Lizzie Wriggler." He turns the screen and I see a picture of a semi-naked young lady, her long legs wrapped lithely around a fireman's pole.

"Blimey, she looks very, er, *grown-up*," I mutter, not entirely sure how a responsible uncle should respond. "And you say she's a friend of yours?"

"No, 'fraid not, Unck. Lizzie is probably a bald-headed sweaty bloke called Mervyn who just wants you to click on his porno site. Still, a friend is a friend..."

I shake my head in bewilderment. "I suppose you don't really know who you're talking to when you're in cyberspace, they could be anyone. And anywhere." *Ask him, go on, ask him.*

"Can you find someone on Facebook, Louie? I mean, like an old school friend, or something?"

"Of course, Unck. Who are you looking for?"

I blink rapidly. "Oh, um, I don't know really, I just wondered how you'd go about it."

"What's the name?" Louie jabs at the screen, looking up expectantly. I'm aware my mouth is flapping, but no sound is coming out. She would be married, her name would have changed...

"Sarah Shaw." I blurt, my heart suddenly thumping. "S-h-a-w."

My head swims and I grip the edge of the Formica-topped table. Can it really be this easy? Tap a name into a phone and instantly you find someone you haven't seen in thirty years - am I about to see Sarah, after all this time? Learn about her life, her family?

"Oh."

"What is it? Have you found her?" I stare at Louie anxiously

"There's loads of Sarah Shaws, Unck. Hundreds, in fact." Louie turns his phone again to show me the rows of faces, whizzing the screen up and down so that they begin to whirl, finally blurring into one.

"Right." My heart rate returns to normal, but my mind is still racing. I watch the faces flashing in front of my eyes and I know I'm going to examine every single one. I don't care how long it takes, *I will find her*.

"There's Mum." Louie raps on the window and Cath, laden with bulging Marks and Spencer's carrier bags, deftly swerves the oncoming masses and diverts into Burger King.

"Hello, hello, how's it going?" Cath flops down at our table, piling her bags onto the spare seat. "God, I'm black and blue, those evil old biddies in Marksie's have got bloody sharp elbows! It was only some cardies on reduced, not the crown jewels. Alright, Col? Oh Jesus, you don't risk the coffee in here, do you? Didn't you see Panorama the other night; survey of fast food workers - what would you never let your friends and family consume? Top of the list, cappuccino. The dirty bastards never clean their pipes." I peer down at my almost-empty cup, suddenly queasy. "Ginny's so looking forward to tonight," Cath continues. "I love Truffles, I'm so chuffed you're taking her somewhere decent. What are you planning to wear?" I open the Debenhams bag and show her my purchases. "Hmmm. Vertical stripes, really? You should have gone horizontal, given you the illusion of girth. And the chinos, well, they're *inoffensive,* I suppose." The distasteful way she said the word made it sound like 'inoffensive' was a bad thing. It felt like an excellent result to me. Cath looks at the iPhone. "What are you doing?"

"He's searching through the Sarah Shaws," Louie tells her.

Cath frowns, rummaging around in her handbag for her purse. "Sarah Shaw, who's she? Go and get me a Texas Crunchy Whopper will you, Louie? I missed breakfast; tried to fry a bit of bacon on the Aga, but gave up after half an hour. On the plus side, the shower was scalding hot."

Louie takes the proffered fiver. "Do you want another cup of typhoid, Unck?"

"No, I'll pass, thanks."

As Louie joins the scrum of people waiting to order at the tills, Cath considers me inquiringly. "Who are you looking for, Col?"

I hesitate, unsure whether to tell my sister about Sarah's letters or not. She really doesn't need another reason to think badly of Dad, and she's bound to fly off the handle if I tell her. I play safe. "I don't know if you remember Sarah, my girlfriend at college? No reason why you should, it was decades ago. Anyway, I found some letters from her amongst Dad's stuff and I was curious, that's all. Wondered what she was up to now." I glance out of the window in an attempt to appear nonchalant.

"So, I fix you up on a date with Ginny tonight and here you are searching the Internet for another woman? Honestly Col, I don't know why I bother."

"Oh no, it's not like that."

"It's exactly like that! I'm surprised at you Colin Hector, I really am, I thought *you* were one of the nice guys, not like the rest of those idiots that can't keep it in their trousers for five minutes." She points a scarlet-nailed finger at me, her voice growing loud and indignant. "Ginny's had quite enough of being messed around by men, thank you very much, she's been to hell and back. I only set her up with you because I thought you'd treat her decently, show her some respect. But you're proving yourself to be quite the Ryan Giggs, aren't you?"

"You've got it wrong, Sis," I mutter miserably, as heads swivel to stare at the love rat. "I never got to see Sarah's letters till now. She wrote me dozens of letters after she moved away but she didn't get a single reply. I'll be able to explain if I can contact her."

Cath stares at me incredulously. "But that must have been thirty years ago! She won't remember."

"I don't care," I say stubbornly, filled with a determination that takes us both by surprise. "She believed I abandoned her and she has probably hated me ever since. I need to put that right."

"For God's sake, Col!" Cath is beyond frustrated. "You're so terrified of upsetting people! She won't care, she'll have moved on with her life, probably married with a string of rug rats. She might even be a granny, it's not inconceivable. Just let it go, what's it matter after all this time?"

"It matters to me," I insist, my face flaring up at the effort of standing up to Cath. "You didn't read the letters; I broke her heart."

"But, if she's married her name will have changed."

"There are still ways. Louie can help me with the social media searches, I'll recognise her immediately."

"Oh, really? She won't look like she did in nineteen-eighty-whatever, you know, all hot lips and perky bits. She's probably fat and flabby now, with jowls like a basset hound."

"I don't care."

"She might have moved to Australia, for all you know. Or she could be dead, have you thought of that? Come on, Col, you know what Mum would say, leave the past in the past."

"No." I shake my head. "Mum would tell me to put things right, you know she would."

Cath opens her mouth to protest but Louie returns, placing her Whopper in front of her. "Sorry, it's got a few bites out of it. Some kids from school grabbed it off me and passed it around."

"Little shits!" Cath bursts out. I look at her in alarm and she catches herself, forcing a smile. "I suppose I should be grateful really, I'll never be short of work; they're next generation legal aid. Is that them, Lou?"

"Yeah, they're just leaving." A group of grinning teenagers is heading out of the door, clutching their polystyrene burger cartons. One calls out in an Irish accent: "Ya made that song your own! Ya're like a little Gary Barlow!"

Louie sighs. "I've so got to change my name." He nods at his phone. "Any luck, Unck?"

"I haven't had the chance," I tell him. "I'll have a proper look on the bus on the way back, if that's ok?"

Cath snorts. "Ridiculous. Raking up the past, you're going to do more harm than good." She frowns at me. "You *are* going to get your eye brows threaded before tonight, aren't you? Nothing turns a girl off more than their date howling at the moon."

12 December 1984

Dearest Colin

The most exciting news ever! I am coming home for Christmas!!!!! One of the regulars, Postman Pat, is going to his sister's in Bristol and has offered to take me to and from Dad's - isn't that sweet of him? It's only for a couple of days because Pat said that's all he can stand of his sister per annum, but it's still brilliant! We shall set off after Pat has finished his round on the 23rd, and then he will pick me up again on Boxing Day. I thought Mum would be upset that I'm spending Christmas Day with Dad and not her, but she was surprisingly calm about it. I don't know how I feel about Dad, given what he's done, but I really miss him and I guess I have to give him a chance to explain.

I know you need to spend time with your family, this year more than ever, but could we meet up on Christmas Eve? How about midday outside the Cathedral? Don't panic, I haven't gone all religious, but Dad's taking me shopping in the morning so I will be in town, and it does seems a suitably romantic venue, don't you think? I have got you a few little gifts, but I have sent what I would normally spend on presents to the miners' families Christmas fund - it's not much, but it's a gesture. Please don't worry if you haven't got me anything, it doesn't matter, I just want you. And don't be embarrassed because you haven't been in contact, I understand. At least, I think I do.... No, actually, I lied. I don't understand. But I'll know you'll explain it to me.

I can't wait to see you, I know I'm not going to be able to sleep one single wink for the next 11 nights - I'll be the zombie lurking outside the cathedral!

Your (stupidly excited) Sarah

Sarah had arranged to meet me. How long had she waited at the Cathedral before she realised I wasn't coming? So, where had I been that Christmas Eve... *The cemetery.* Cath and I had gone there with a red poinsettia for Mum's grave, and then we'd had cheese on toast for lunch at the little tea rooms in Wilton before Cath suggested we went to the cinema to 'escape from all the depressing festive shit'. That ghastly Christmas might have been bearable if I'd known Sarah was waiting for me, that she still wanted me. *I've got to find her.*

Chapter Six

"Did you see that?" Tony disrupts my thoughts as he plonks his pint in front of me and sits down heavily on the stool. "Crafty Courtney beat me again *and* she gave me a three dart head start." He chucks his arrows disconsolately on the table. "You give her a game, Col."

I panic. My new chinos are far too loose, despite having taken the same waist size for the last twenty years. I hadn't had time to make another notch in my belt, and now my trousers are in grave danger of sliding down my backside Snoop Doggy Dog style.

"I'm a bit tired actually, mate. I'll sit this one out."

"*Tired?* It's six-thirty on a Saturday night! How can you possibly be tired, you old fart?"

"I was helping one of the neighbours turn his compost this afternoon, it was pretty hard work."

"You crafty sod! No wonder you can afford to dine out at fancy-pants restaurants, you're moonlighting!"

"I think, technically, money has to change hands for it to be classed as moonlighting."

"You do it for free?" Tony splutters into his pint. "Bugger

that! You're too nice, Col, that's your trouble, people take advantage."

"I like to help, and anyway, I do get payment in kind."

"O-M-G, there's a word for people like you - necrophiliac!"

"No, no! I mean they pay me back in other ways, like Olive who always makes me a carrot cake, or old Reg, who lets me–"

"Suck on his Werther's Original? Seriously, mate, you've got to get away from there, you're in danger of disappearing into your own anorak. You're a free spirit now, it's time to live a little."

I study my pint. Tony sounded just like Cath and I wonder if the two of them have been comparing notes. I rub my eyes, sore from the hours spent peering at several hundred Sarah Shaws. One picture had caused my heart to lurch, but when I looked more closely I could see it wasn't her, which was just as well given she lived in Salt Lake City and her occupation described her as a 'mainstream Mormon'.

"There's Stickle Jack," Tony stood up again. "I need to speak to him, Mum wants some more trout. God knows why, she's no idea how to cook the bloody things. The last one stuck its own head in the gas oven when Mum started twerking in the kitchen. Back in a mo."

I sneak an envelope from my pocket and take a massive gulp of beer, steeling myself to read Sarah's next letter: I'd been putting it off all day. I was almost at the end of Sarah's letters, there were only four left after this one. In trepidation, I extract the letter and smooth it out on the table. Here goes.

30 December 1984

Colin

I wasn't going to write again. Or I was just going to write 'you bastard' in massive capital letters and send that to you. However, I decided to write instead and try to make you feel as awful as I do.

What a Christmas. For some reason, I'd convinced myself you'd show up to Dad's on the evening of the 23rd, knowing I would be there. Never mind, I figured I'd see you the next day, at the cathedral. I didn't, of course, because as you know, you didn't turn up. What you don't know is that I stayed there until it was almost dark, praying to a God that I don't believe in that: 1. each approaching figure was you and 2. I wouldn't die of hypothermia. I didn't even know I was crying until a homeless guy stopped to see if I was ok and offered me ten pence from his tin. If ten pence could mend a broken heart, I would have taken it. Instead, I gave him your presents. He's now the proud owner of a silver rope chain necklace, the Hatful of Hollow album and a huge Care Bare (the brown one with the red heart). I bet you're thinking 'Phew, I'm glad I didn't show up!' See, I can still laugh at myself even though I'm dying inside.

On Christmas Day, I tried to help Dad with the cooking, but our hearts weren't in it and Dad had drunk two bottles of Black Tower before we'd even sat down to eat, and then I had to endure the most self-pitying drivel about how empty his life was and how he was so alone in the world. I finally snapped and told him he only had himself to blame as it was his decision to screw around with his receptionist. He gave a hollow laugh and slurred "Is that what your mother told you? I think you'll find it was the other way round, love." When I'd finished choking on a (concrete) Brussel sprout, I tried to get him to elaborate but all he would say was "Ask the man from the Pru" then he passed out on the sofa in front of Mary Poppins. I didn't know if it was the drink talking or whether he'd been serious. My head is in such a whirl. The two people I trusted most in my life, with my life, both show themselves to be fake. I don't know what's real anymore.

Couldn't you just have written or phoned to say you wouldn't be at the cathedral? Why couldn't you do that, or sent someone with a message? Why did you just leave me there in the freezing cold? It's Christmas. I can't believe you capable of such cruelty; and yet it must be true.

'Tis better to have loved and lost than never to have loved at all'. I can tell you that's complete rot.

Goodbye. You won't hear from me again.

Sarah

I feel sick. Poor Sarah, stuck there in the bitter cold, heart pounding at every approaching figure, waiting and hoping. I remembered that pitiful Christmas Day, the first without Mum, when Cath and I had tried our best to replicate Mum's magical traditions, preparing stockings for each other with silly little gifts and making a just-about-edible Christmas lunch from Mum's heavily stained Delia Smith cookery book. Dad, morose and monosyllabic, had shown no interest in proceedings. Yes, Cath and I had feigned cheerfulness, but it felt desperate, *desperate*. How different would it have been if I'd known Sarah still loved me, still wanted me? Cath went skiing the following year, in fact she never spent another Christmas Day at number seven. I didn't blame her. It sounded as if Sarah's Christmas had been just as wretched. But, despite how she'd ended her letter, she *had* written again. There are still four letters post-marked after this one.

I quickly shove the letter back into my pocket as Tony returns, rubbing his nose. "Jees, that man stinks. He hasn't got any trout at the moment but he has got a ton of tight-lipped mussels he's trying to offload."

"Don't you mean green-lipped?"

"That's what I said but apparently 'there's no opening these fuckers'."

"Oh. Right." I examine my pint for a moment then glance up to find Tony studying me.

"What's up, Col? You've been ever so quiet lately. I mean, you are pretty quiet in general, but you seem uber-quiet, like your mind's elsewhere. Is it this bird you're seeing tonight?

She's not a tranny or anything, is she? Not that it's a problem, I'm not one to judge."

"I don't think Ginny's a transvestite, but knowing my luck with women... Her sister is Cath's best friend and Ginny was a couple of years below me at school. Apparently, I met her quite recently but I'm ashamed to say I can't recall." I want to tell Tony about Sarah but I'm worried he'll be just as dismissive of the search as Cath. "Who are you bringing?"

"Letitia, the girl from the Odeon, she kept flashing me during the Bond movie, do you remember? Flashing me with her torch, I mean. We're meeting her there because her shift doesn't finish until six-thirty, so she said she'll get changed in theatre three when the lights have gone down." He narrows his eyes. "Quit stalling, Hector, you haven't answered my question. What's up?"

Shall I tell him? "I have had something on my mind, as it goes."

Tony stares at me in concern. "Shit, I knew it, I thought you were losing weight. You're ill, aren't you? What is it, mate, your prostate, can't stop weeing?" I shake my head. "It's not an enlarged testicle, is it? Oh God, which one, left or right? Christ, I don't think I can help, mate. I mean, I'd do anything for you and all that, but I draw the line at fondling your ball bag. Perhaps you should ask Wes to have a look? He could magic you up a new bollock from behind your ear."

I lower my head, pretending to look forlorn. "That's all right, Tone, I understand, it's too much to ask of you. I'm sure it's nothing serious, I'll be fine." I take a sip of lager. "Probably."

"Bloody hell." Tony squirms in his seat, beads of perspiration breaking out above his top lip. "Right, well, we can't take any chances, I'd better take a look. I'm not touching them, mind." He slides his phone across the table. "Go and take a picture of them on this, get a close-up. Just remind me to

delete the bloody thing, my mum's got a habit of scrolling through my pics and I don't want her coming face to face with your scrotum selfie. A screlfie, not something you want trending on Instagram. Anyway, hurry up, the taxi will be here any minute."

"No, you're all right." I put him out of his misery, grinning broadly. "There's nothing wrong with my bits. They might be extremely rusty, of course, but generally in good working order."

"You bugger!" Tony punches my arm, relief flooding through him. "That's not funny! The last thing I wanted before an evening of romance was the image of your flesh chandeliers dangling in front of my eyes. So, what is wrong with you, still coming to terms with your old man passing away?"

I hesitate before answering. "In a way, yes, I suppose I am. When I was clearing through his things I came across some letters from that girl I told you about, do you remember? My first love, Sarah, she left very suddenly to live with her aunt on the east coast, in Herne Bay. She wrote lots of letters."

Tony's mouth falls open. "No way! She was having it away with your old man?"

"No, Tone," I say quickly. "The letters were meant for me, not Dad. Sarah wrote at least thirty-two times after she left but I never saw any of her letters." I swallow. "I think my father hid them from me."

Tony stares at me incredulously. "The old *bastard*, what the hell did he do that for?"

"I don't know." I take a huge gulp of beer, horrified to feel my throat constricting again. *Man up, for God's sake*. Poor Tony will be mortified if I start blubbing in front of him. "Dad wasn't a well man–"

"Bullshit!" Tony spits, his eyes blazing. "He was well enough to intercept the postman thirty-two times, wasn't he? Well enough to hide them away out of sight, he knew exactly what he was doing, the evil old git. How could he do that to his own son? I'm going to go and take a shit on his grave."

"He was cremated."

"Then take his ashes, chuck 'em down the bog and park a massive great turd on them!"

"Taxi for Hector!" the landlord calls, with fortuitous timing. "Where are you two losers off to this evening? Grab-a-granny night, is it, or speed-dating for the blind?"

"Ha flippin' ha." Tony flicks a beer mat in his direction. "For your information, *Kenneth*, we are taking a couple of extremely classy ladies out to dinner at Truffles."

"Ooh get you, Mr La-di-da! Truffles, eh? You'd better have some of these, then." He tosses a packet of Scratchings at us. "That poncey nouvelle cuisine won't be enough to keep an ant alive."

We hurry along the High Street having stopped the taxi on the outskirts of town when we could no longer bear to watch the luminous figures on the taxi meter racking up an extortionate fare. I am grasping the waistband of my chinos as I run to keep from tripping over the hems. I did have my thumbs hooked through the belt loops to keep my trousers up, but Tony told me that was a 'homo signal', so I thought better of it, especially as we were passing the Pink Olive. We finally reach Truffles just before eight, panting heavily and sweating profusely, screeching to a halt outside to quickly run hands through hair and tuck shirts in. A dirty hand appears from a bundle of rags on the pavement. "Have you got any spare change?"

"How do we know?" Tony gives his customary answer. "We haven't finished living our lives yet." He tips his head back. "Are my nostrils clean, Col? No straggly hairs poking out? Eyebrows, mate, slick 'em down. Bit more. Bit more. Great, let's go."

As we barge in through the frosted glass doors the diners

nearest the entrance look up in alarm and a white-jacketed waiter steps deftly in front of us, blocking our path into the restaurant.

"May I help you, gentlemen?"

"Booking," I gasp. "Hector."

"I see." The waiter examines a book that is propped open on a music stand. "Yes, I have your reservation, four diners at *seven-thirty*. The other members of your party are waiting for you in the bar. This way, please."

Tony rolls his eyes at me as we quick-march after the waiter and through to the bar area. I blink at the dazzling white of the wall and floor. Black marble-topped tables are dotted about, tea-lights flickering from each one. A woman with long auburn hair is sitting at the bar chatting to a swarthy-looking barman who is pouring what looks like cream from a silver cocktail shaker into a Martini glass. "The other members of your party have arrived," the waiter introduces us and the woman turns round on her stool, rather reluctantly, I notice. She is very young, her huge bosom set to burst out of a skin-tight red dress. "Colin, this is Letitia, from the Odeon." Tony pushes me forward and I fight hard to keep looking at her face, desperate not to glance down at her chest.

"Hello Letitia from the Odeon," I shake her hand and she giggles.

"Call me Letty, everyone does." She gives Tony an accusing prod. "You're late. I've already had two cocktails and Theo's just made me another." The barman flashes a Colgate smile, the small rows of teeth giving him the appearance of a wolf. "I have to look after my ladies," he purrs as Letitia swoons.

"It's called a Baileys White Russian but I got Theo to add some crème de menthe to this one so it's gone a bit green."

"Yeah, well, me and Col will have a beer," Tony is put out. "I don't fancy the Kermit cum."

"I will bring them to your table," the waiter is hovering.

"Follow me, please."

"Oh, we're waiting for one more," I tell him. "That's if she turns up, of course!" I give a nervous laugh. A fair-haired woman sitting at the bar catches my eye and smiles sympathetically. She's probably been stood up too.

"Who else are we waiting for?" Letitia asks in surprise.

"For Ginny."

"But, this is Ginny," Letitia leans back and points at the fair-haired woman. "We found each other at the bar. We were both tut-tutting because our dates hadn't turned up and then we realised we were waiting for you two!"

The woman at the bar smiles at me again. She is about forty-ish, very slim with shoulder-length hair and a long straight face. She is also wearing a red dress, although it is a darker shade than Letitia's and she is more conservatively covered. I didn't expect to recognise her from school but I thought I might remember her from Cath's party. I don't.

Letitia remarks "I didn't know this was a blind date," at exactly the same time as Ginny says "It's nice to see you again, Colin."

"Hello Ginny," I shake her hand. "I'm sorry we're so late."

"We're not!" Letitia exclaims before Ginny can answer, shooting a sly grin at the barman. Sensing the waiter is becoming impatient, I awkwardly try to help Ginny down from the bar stool, not sure where to touch her and ending up tugging listlessly at her arm.

"Sorry, sorry."

"That's alright, it's impossible to get off these things in a ladylike manner. It really is lovely to see you again, Colin. Is, er, your stomach ok? I notice you're clutching at it."

God, these bloody chinos. I smile ruefully as we sit down at the table. "My stomach's fine, I'm just too scared to let go of my trousers. I'm afraid I didn't try them on when I bought them today and found out too late that they don't quite fit."

She gives a tinkly little laugh that, I observe, she manages to do without actually smiling. "At least you'll have room to grow after a big meal!" She shoots me a coy glance from her blue, almond-shaped eyes. They remind me of a Siamese cat. "It's sweet that you bought new clothes for our date."

"You might not think that when my trousers end up round my ankles. Oh, sorry." It's unfortunate the waiter overhears that particular part of our conversation. He hands a menu to me with a pained look on his face, before turning to Ginny with a little bow.

"Would you care for an apéritif, some champagne, perhaps?"

"We've ordered two beers," Tony cuts in quickly. "But you might as well bring two more. What are you having, girls, gin and tonics? Or going straight for some wine?"

"We'll have some wine, shall we, Ginny?" Letitia is examining the wine list. "Oh no, you don't drink, do you? Woo hoo, all the more for me! I like the Italian stuff, but this is all French... What about this one, is this any good?"

Tony glances at the list and does a double-take. "Bottle of house white," he tells the waiter, swiftly closing the wine list on Letitia's fingers and whipping it away. "And we'll have some bread to be going on with, please." The waiter purses his lips.

"Very good, sir. Would you like me to explain anything on the menu to you?"

"Why, are there lots of big words? I think we'll manage, thanks very much." Tony shakes his head as the waiter leaves to fetch our drinks. "Why do they have to be so snooty? You're only waiting on tables in Salisbury High Street, mate, not feeding grapes to the Holy Roman Emperor." He reads the menu out loud. "Rag-out, I wonder what that is? And what the hell is 'roo ill'? Something that makes kangaroos puke? Thank Christ for Google." He takes his phone out of his pocket. "Scuse me, guys," he beckons to a couple on the next table. "Do you know what the WiFi code is?"

"No," the man glares at him. "People actually *talk* to each other in this establishment."

"Jeeeesus," Tony mutters under his breath. "I only asked."

"Never mind, Babe," Letitia giggles. "Just have a steak, you know where you are with a nice bit of rump."

"Don't you like chicken, Letty?" Tony asks her.

"Ooh yes, I love chicken."

"Then suck this, it's foul!"

I want to hide under the table with embarrassment as they both roar with laughter and disapproving glares shoot like angry laser beams in our direction.

"Is there anything you fancy?" I ask Ginny.

"Colin, you can't ask her that on your first date!" Letitia squeals.

"Yeah, at least let her eat something first," Tony chips in. Ginny laughs good-naturedly as I hide my burning face behind the menu. "I think I'll have the bourguignon," Ginny decides. "But I'm not sure about the starter. Maybe the camembert."

I haven't thought about starters, so I flick back to have a look. I wonder if Tony has clocked the prices... "Bugger me!" *Yes he has.* "Twenty-eight quid for a frigging steak?" Tony is horrified. "I expect the whole bloody cow for that! And it doesn't even come with vegetables - no, you've got to pay another four ninety-five for that privilege."

"I shouldn't have suggested here," Ginny whispers to me as other diners glance round at our table again. "It is quite pricey."

"No, it's a great choice, it's really lovely," I smile at her, hoping I sound convincing. "I've always wanted to try it but never had the right..." *salary* "...occasion."

"Aw, that's so sweet," Letitia buts in. "You're so nice, Colin, how come you're still single?"

"Probably because women always describe me as nice!"

"Have you never been married, then?"

"No, sadly not."

"What about you, Ginny? Have you ever been married?"

Ginny's right arm gives a violent twitch and she grabs it with her left hand, her knuckles turning white. "Yes. But thankfully not anymore." She takes a deep breath before slowly releasing her grip. "Shall we skip the starters and go straight for the main? That way we might have some room left for a dessert; they look scrummy."

I smile at her gratefully as the waiter returns with our drinks. "Are you ready to order?"

"Hell, yes." Letitia is first. "Can I have the sirloin steak, please, medium rare."

"You sure about the steak, Hun?" Tony quizzes her, his face a little pale. "Chicken would be better with white wine, you know, or one of these veggie dishes-"

"I want the steak, Babe! With peppercorn sauce."

"Is it extra for the peppercorn sauce?" Tony glances at the waiter who confirms with a curt nod. "Really? Twenty-eight quid and you couldn't chuck in a bit of giz? Will it be any cheaper if she doesn't have a plate?" He gestures at Letitia's chest. "She can eat off those."

The waiter doesn't smile. "For you, madam?"

"I'll have the bourguignon." Ginny tells him. "What does it come with?"

"Boulettes."

"What's that?" Tony asks.

"Dumplings," I say, inadvertently looking straight at Letitia's breasts. *Oh God.* "I'll have the same," I say quickly. "What are you having, Tone?"

"I'll just have the steak tartare," he replies, closing the menu decisively and handing it back to the waiter. "And make sure it's well done."

The waiter's lips twitch and he manages a strangled, "Very good, sir," before heading back through the swing doors into the kitchen.

"I need the loo," Letitia announces, getting up. "Kermit's gone right through me. You might as well order another bottle of wine, Tone, this one won't last long." A loud burst of laughter from the kitchen makes her jump. "Jees, I nearly peed my pants! You coming, Ginny?"

The women head across the restaurant toward the toilets, Letitia already a little unsteady on her feet. A grinning waiter stands back to let her pass. "You and Letitia seem to be getting on well," I say to Tony. He sighs.

"Letty's great. Just not my type."

"Really? But she's so bubbly and loads of fun; I thought she'd be exactly your type."

"No way, mate, haven't you noticed the false everything - nails, tan, tits, eyelashes? Not even her hair's real. Nope, she's too high maintenance, she'll never pass the shower test."

"The shower test?"

"You know, when they step out of the shower in the morning *au naturel* and they either look terrific, or like an extra from Shaun of the Dead."

"Isn't that a bit, well, *shallow,* Tone? Having a nice personality is far more important."

"Only ugly people say that, Col." He takes a small sip of beer and scratches his nose. "Yeah, I know you're right, but I don't want to be with someone who spends all their time and money trying to change how they look, I want someone who's happy with themselves. And she's got that bloody dress on back to front, did you see? It's supposed to be backless, no wonder her baps are hanging out for all the world to see. Anyone would think she got dressed in the dark."

"Well, she did, didn't she? Theatre three."

"No, it's back to the drawing board for me, I'm afraid.

Yours seems ok, though, classy but not up herself. She doesn't drink, mind, so alarm bells are ringing; she's probably a recovering alky."

"I'm surprised I didn't recognise her," I say, still feeling embarrassed. "Apparently, we have met before, at Cath's, but I simply can't recall her."

"Well, you wouldn't, would you?" Tony takes a larger glug of beer. "Not with all that Botox and shite she's shoved in her face."

"You think she's had Botox?"

"Bloody hell, mate, I know the lighting's bad in here, but are you completely blind? She's got more filler than B&Q."

"Blimey." It's my turn to gulp at my beer. "I did notice her forehead was lovely and smooth. But why on earth would she waste her money on that sort of stuff? She doesn't need it."

"You never really know a person until you stand in their shoes and walk around in them," Tony muses.

"To Kill A Mockingbird?"

"Shawshank Redemption. Anyway, I bet your Sarah's a looker, isn't she? Or have you been pining over a munter with a nice personality for all these years?" He shakes his head. "I keep thinking about what your Dad did to you, mate, I still can't believe it. And why the hell did he keep the letters, why didn't he just burn them?"

"I don't know." *I'm sorry, Son.* "Perhaps he always intended to show them to me, and, well, forgot. Maybe." I quickly drop my eyes to avoid Tony's scornful expression. "I'm going to try and trace Sarah," I tell him. "I know it was years ago, but I want to explain and apologise. We couldn't find her on Facebook, so Louie's been looking online at the census records and so on. Although, Cath thinks it's a bad idea."

"It's a great idea!" Tony's face brightens. "That's actually really exciting, tracking down your first love; you never know, she might have been waiting for you all this time, trapped in a loveless marriage or imprisoned in a tower, Rapunzel-stylee. It would make a great film - The Shaw-shag Redemption! I wish I'd used that for my Deal or No Deal video."

"Well, if she has thought of me at all it won't be fond memories, I can assure you of that. More like which bit she'd like to cut off first. She's probably happily married with a family, and that's why Cath thinks it'll do more harm than good. But, for me, it feels the right thing to do. At least, to try."

"Well, if Louie can't trace her online we'll go to... where did you say? Hernia Bay? We can have a lad's weekend."

"Oh, boys, you need to try them bogs, they're well lush!" The girls are back. Letitia sticks the palm of her hand in my face and wiggles her fingers. "Smell that? Pomegranate and ginger, proper gorgeous. Lucky Ginny was there to stop me licking it, I thought it was cream you actually ate!" She shrieks with laughter at the same time as attempting to take a sip of wine and slops half the glass down her front.

"Are you ok?" I ask Ginny quietly as Tony makes a great show of mopping the wine up with his napkin, sending Letitia into further hysterics. "I'm sure this is not the sort of evening you had in mind."

"I'm fine," she assures me, showing her teeth again. I'm suddenly put in mind of Bruce, the shark in Finding Nemo. Damn Tony, now I'm examining her face for signs of surgery or needle marks. Her lips are very plump, are they full of something? If you kissed them passionately would they burst, leaving bits behind in your mouth- "Ooh great, our food is here!" Ginny claps her hands together in delight as a large white plate is placed in front of her.

"Oh, did you go for a starter?" I ask, peering at the tiny dark mass gently steaming away in the middle of the plate.

"No, no, it's the bourguignon," Ginny replies. "Look, here's yours. It's very rich, so you really don't need much to be full."

Just as well. I catch Tony's incredulous expression as Letitia's minute steak appears. "Twenty eight frigging quid!" he mouths at me.

The waiter gives a little bow as he places the last dish in front of us. "Can I get you anything else at all?"

"A magnifying glass?" Tony suggests.

"It looks wonderful," Ginny says and I admire her enthusiasm.

"Do you eat here very often?" I ask her, unsure whether to pick up a fork or a spoon and waiting to see which she uses.

"Not as often as I'd like. I used to come here with–" her right arm twitches again, just missing her glass of water. "With friends. It is lovely for a treat, I think, and for first dates. The atmosphere is so muted, if that's the right word; you can actually have a proper conversation with one another."

"My dinner's got grass on it!" Letitia booms, holding up a piece of cress. "Get my phone out would you Babe, I've got to take a picture of this, no one's going to believe me otherwise. There's grass growing on my dinner!"

"Oh, er, do you go on lots of first dates, then?" I'm crushed. "I mean, sorry, it's none of my business, of course."

"That's ok," Ginny doesn't seem to mind my clumsy question. "I tried Internet dating for a time, so yes, there were quite a few first dates, but I've given up on that now. It wasn't for me."

"Selfie, Tone, take a selfie!" We squeeze together obediently as Tony all but breaks his neck trying to fit us into the frame on Letitia's phone.

"Still," Ginny continues, as we resume eating. "The one good thing about Internet dating is that your picture is on your profile." She glances at me from beneath her eyelashes. "So when you do meet, you're recognised."

"I'm so sorry about that," I mumble, but although she isn't smiling I can tell she is teasing me. "I don't think I'm very good at face recognition, there was something on the radio about it the other day, it's how information is processed in the brain," I stop myself and give an embarrassed grin. "Sorry. If you want to bury your face into your bourguignon, I quite understand. I have that effect on women."

"Don't be silly!" She pokes me playfully. "There's no reason why you should remember me. We only spoke very briefly at Cathy's party; we were outside on the patio admiring the roses and you gave me some advice on my climbers."

"Oh yes!" I *did* remember her. "You were worried about the state of your clematis, you'd let it get too dry."

"Colin, you total perv!" Letitia roars across the table. "You can't discuss Ginny's clematis on a first date! At least give her a kiss first!"

"Will anyone fancy a dessert?" I ask swiftly.

"Something warm, moist and sticky," Tony chips in, enjoying my discomfort.

"Flapjacks!" Letitia squeals.

Oh God. A waiter catches my desperate stare and comes over to clear the plates and take our dessert orders. I can't continue my conversation with Ginny as Letitia is showing her pictures of her holiday in Mykonos. I had to admire the way Ginny was able to chat away with the younger, drunker girl without patronising her or seeming in any way judgmental. She did seem a very nice lady.

"You got enough cash left for a kebab?" Tony whispers disconsolately. "I'm hungry like the wolf."

"So am I. I've ordered myself a hot chocolate for pudding, I thought it might stop my stomach rumbling for a bit."

"Oh Christ, what new hell is this?" Tony screws up his face in disgust as Letitia's cheese dessert is placed on the table.

"Gorgonzola with honey and walnuts," the waiter advises us.

"And all for just ten ninety-five," Tony nods at Letitia.

"Each walnut equates to about two quid, I reckon. And what's this?"

"I ordered the brownie, too," Letitia slurs. "In case I didn't like the cheese. Oh my God!" She pushes the Gorgonzola plate away. "It stinks of feet!"

"If it's a mouthful of blue veins you want–"

"Stop it," I hiss at Tony, embarrassed and fed up with the crudeness. "Please let's just get this evening over with. And for Christ's sake don't give her any more to drink, she's plastered."

"Anyone want the cheese?" Tony, realising Letitia is not going to eat it, offers the plate around the table. Ginny and I shake our heads. "Well, there's no point wasting it, I'm going to give it to that poor homeless guy outside. At least he'll appreciate it."

As Tony leaves the table, a tray of eight loaded shot glasses appears. "Yay, Tequila!" Letitia bursts into song. "It makes me happy!"

"I can't do Tequila," Ginny says in alarm.

"It's Sambucca," the waiter advises, making a hasty retreat.

"We didn't order these!" I call lamely after him but he's vanished.

"I ordered them." Letitia is lining them up. "We'll do Tequila suicides."

"What, with Sambucca?"

Tony re-appears, slinging the cheese plate back down on the table, the Gorgonzola still intact. "Can you believe it? I offered the plate to the homeless geezer and he turned his bloody nose up at it; 'Oh, I'm not a lover of the Italian blue-veined'. He took the walnuts, though and when I asked him if he wanted a glass of water, the cheeky sod said; 'A dessert wine would complement these better, perhaps a Muscat?' Honestly! Even their tramps are pretentious twa–" He breaks off as he catches sight of the shot glasses. "Oh Jesus."

I stand at the kitchen sink, rubbing a stick of Vanish over the splashes of vomit on my new shirt. This isn't quite the way I had imagined the evening ending, but then I could say that for most of my first dates. We'd finally managed to get Letitia out of the restaurant by grabbing her as she rose for the Mexican wave she'd been attempting to get going amongst the few remaining diners. I had to hold her upright, pinned against the side of the Marmaris van, as Tony got himself a kebab. At one point, Letitia had slipped from my grip and, clutching at my waistband, slid to the ground, pulling my trousers all the way down to my ankles. One woman in the queue had laughed so much she'd wet herself.

The taxi had to stop twice for Letitia to be sick, an unsympathetic Tony berating her for the waste of money, and once we reached her house, she'd been unable to locate her door key, turning her handbag out on the lawn. Tony propped her up against the front door with her nose pressed against the doorbell so that it rang continuously and we backed away, waiting by the gate until Letitia's mum finally opened the door. Dressed in a pink velour dressing gown, she hurled abuse at us as we fled, before turning her wrath on her daughter. As Tony put it in the cab on the way home: "It wasn't the worst evening ever. But it was pretty fucking close."

Leaving my shirt to soak in a bowl of warm soapy water, I pour myself a glass of milk and open a packet of Oreos. Comfort dunking has become a ritual following an evening of disappointment. Poor Ginny, what must she be thinking? She'd indulged Letitia's performance for most of the evening, smiling benignly, but I could see her teeth were gritted towards the end. I walked her to the taxi rank and saw her safely into a cab, but unsurprisingly, she climbed straight in, not pausing for a kiss goodnight, not even offering a cheek to peck. Nor did she mention meeting up again.

The answer phone is flashing and I press 'play'. "Hello Unck, it's Louie. No luck on the Sarah Shaw search, I'm afraid. I've tried the electoral records and the last census records and stuff and there's lots of them, but no one with that birth date. I think she's probably dead, but she's definitely not buried in Herne Bay, I searched the online cemetery records. You'll have to go to Canterbury, I think, check the local records. What's that, Mum? She says needle in a sodding haystack. Sorry, Unck, speak soon. Bye."

I dip my Oreo thoughtfully into my glass. Why couldn't Sarah be traced? A marriage, a death – wouldn't that show up somewhere? Possibly her mother had remarried and Sarah had changed her surname. How on earth could you find that out? Perhaps this is hopeless, a waste of time... but no, no, my resolve isn't going to crumble as quickly as my Oreo. I will go to Herne Bay, I'll go next weekend, start the search. I have the address, so it isn't a needle in a haystack. Not quite.

Chapter Seven

9 February 1985

Dear Colin

Well, just as you thought it was safe to approach the doormat (!) here I am, writing to you again.

The miners might be caving in, but I am not. I've thought about it over and over and have come to the conclusion there is a valid reason for your silence.

I believe you are still grieving for your mother and I remind you of her death. It makes you feel guilty because we were next door loving each other while she was dying. I am sorry to be blunt, but I think it needs to be said. And faced.

So, I have convinced myself that's why you won't write, but I'm not going to keep speculating anymore and driving myself insane. I know you are not cold and cruel, nor would you deliberately humiliate me. I shall keep writing to you, but not nearly as often, just now and again so you know I am still thinking of you. I know you will not reply but maybe one day you will and then I shall finally understand.

January was a horrible month; I had the most dreadful cold and behaved (literally) like a complete drip, nose permanently running, eyes constantly weeping, listening to 'I'm All Cried Out' over and over. Eventually, I pulled myself together. I'm not a starving Ethiopian, neither am I rotting away in a cesspool in Cambodia (have you seen The Killing Fields yet? You really must). Anyway, by comparison, I am amongst the luckiest people on this planet.

So, with my new-found Super Girl powers, I confronted Mum about what Dad had said on Christmas Day, you know, about the affair being 'the other way round'. She denied it at first but I finally wore her down and she admitted it had been her: she'd had the affair, not Dad. The Man from the Pru would call round on the last Wednesday of each month and Mum gave him £5 which he entered into a savings book before, apparently, entering her (sorry, that was really crude, but I'm *so* angry with her). Dad found out what had been going on when he discovered a Prudential compliment slip in their bed. In a fit of temper he told Mum to get out.

How could she let me think that about Dad when all the time it was her? She hasn't even said sorry, not really, even trying to suggest it was Dad's fault for not giving her enough attention. What is she, 6 years old? As if that excuses her behaviour!

Things are really bad in the house with Auntie Sheila and Mum. Sheila got her quarterly phone bill and it seems there's lots of out-of-area calls on it. Mum denied it was her, but I know it's not me, as I always use the phone box on the corner. I don't know what we're going to do, but we can't stay in this toxic atmosphere much longer. I've been to the Citizen's Advice Bureau to see what they could suggest housing-wise. They think we can apply to go on the waiting list for a council house but how long will that take, now Thatcher's selling them all off? Where, exactly, are people like us supposed to live?

I dreamt about you (again) last night. We were renting Derek's upstairs rooms and we'd converted them into a flat of sorts. It was all very twee with Eternal Beau dinner plates and Laura Ashley bedding, not very 'us' at all! But we were so very content, sitting together on the floor, listening to

Songs from the Big Chair (I bet you love it too, don't you?), not doing anything, just snuggled together in the half-light, listening. I was furious when Mum dropped a jar on the kitchen floor and woke me up. Honestly, who eats Nutella at three in the morning? I tried so hard to get back into the dream but you never can, can you? Oh well. (Heaves big sigh). It was lovely while it lasted.

So, there you have it, my January Tales Of The Unexpected. Like I said, I know you will not write back, but I want you to know that I have not given up on you. And I never will. I don't know if that's strength or weakness on my part, but anyway, there you have it.

Yours, forever

Sarah aka Super (Non-Drip) Girl

PS. In my dream Derek's horrid yucca plant was still lurking there in the corner!

I fold the letter away into my pocket as Cath's Lexus sweeps into the gravel car park. As it pulls to a halt, Louie climbs out, almost unrecognisable bundled up in his oversized green fleece and with his hair flattened. He clumps over to me in his new workman boots, Cath following, trying to brush some dust from his jogging bottoms.

"Ugh, Mum! Leave off."

"I just want you to look your best, darling, this is such an emotional moment for me." Cath clutches at her son, eyes welling up. "You'll understand when you have children of your own. My baby boy's all grown-up now; I can't believe you're starting your first ever job."

"It's only work experience, Mum and anyway, it's not my first *ever* job, I had that paper-round, remember?"

"Yes, but that hardly counts, you only lasted one weekend."

"It wasn't my fault, those Sunday papers are massively heavy! The bag slid off my shoulder when Mrs Green's Chihuahua bit my ankle."

"I know, darling, it was very unfortunate, but just do your best not to maim anything today, that's all anyone can ask." She grips the front of Louie's fleece. "Oh dear, maybe this is a bad idea after all. You're not used to all this fresh air, it's so *heady,* I'm not sure you're ready for such an excess of vitamin D. Perhaps you should go to work at the bank with Dad, like I suggested. I know he doesn't really know what he's doing but perhaps you could explain it to him."

"He'll be absolutely fine, Cath." I tug at Louie's sleeve in an attempt to peel him away from his mother. "Look, here's Tony come to welcome you. Why don't you go and say hello to him?" I manage to propel Louie through the gates as Cath releases her grip to wave at Tony.

"Look after him for me, Tony, and make sure he eats all his lunch, it's his favourite, Dairylea Dunkers. And put factor fifty on him, I know it's cloudy but he's extremely light-sensitive. And Colin, don't let him spout any of that lefty claptrap around the Winters, I expect they shoot socialists, don't they?"

"No, they just set the dogs on them," I grin, stepping in front of Cath to stop her following Louie through the gates. I suddenly feel awkward, but know I have to ask. "Er, have you heard from Ginny at all?

"Hmmm." Cath shoots me an exasperated look. "I phoned her yesterday to see how Saturday evening had gone. I don't know what on earth possessed you to drag Tony along with one of his desperados, you know they're genetically programmed to self-destruct."

"Letitia was a bit of a nightmare."

"A bit! I heard she had everyone rushing around for a fire extinguisher when she set fire to Sambucca *in her mouth.* And

Ginny told me about the spot thing, that sounded absolutely disgusting."

"It was." Letitia had treated us to her spot impression which involved placing a marshmallow into her mouth, blowing her cheeks out as far as they would go then slapping her hands hard against them. The half-chewed marshmallow shot out onto the tablecloth with a pus-like *splot.*

Cath sighed. "You should call Ginny, see if you can salvage anything."

"I don't think she'll want to hear from me again."

"You don't know until you try! And anyway, it's not like you've got anything to lose." She catches herself. "Sorry, I didn't mean it to come out quite like that, but you know what I'm saying."

Yes, I did know. I had nothing to lose but pride in another of those cringe-worthy first date follow-up calls: 'I really do like you, Colin, but just as a friend...'

I should have got it out of the way yesterday and called Ginny to apologise but I'd put it off, choosing instead to turn Derek's compost for him again.

"Oh Christ, there's that ghastly Natalie Brady," Cath hisses under her breath. "How you can stand working with her, I don't know. Oh, hi Nat! How are you, alright? Yeah? Great, brilliant, see you then, Hun. Bye." She turns back to me with a shudder. "Ye Gods, she's enough to scare the crap out of the toilet. Look, why don't you give Ginny a call and tell her I've asked you both to dinner at the weekend? That way, there's no pressure and you can relax together over a lovely meal with nice normal people. Well, David and Louie can't technically be classed as normal, of course, and it won't be a lovely meal, not on that bloody ogre thing, but I could cheat and get us all a take-away. What do you think?"

I hesitate. "That's very kind of you, Sis, but I might be away next weekend."

She stares at me in astonishment. "*You,* away? Where?"

I examine my left boot, dragging my toe in the gravel. "I thought I might take a trip to the coast. To Kent, perhaps." I thought she might not make the connection but she immediately throws her hands into the air.

"You're not persisting with this ridiculous search for Sarah bloody Ra Ra skirt? Why are you doing this to yourself, she won't have given you a thought in over thirty years!" She rubs her forehead in agitation then takes a deep breath. Her tone softens. "Look, I do know how you feel, Col, but some things are better left alone. Trust me, I know. When I was at uni I fell for one of the second year students, Darren Barnes his name was, and we got together at the end of term party, if you know what I mean. We couldn't see each other over the summer break but I thought about nothing else for the entire holidays; I absolutely ached to see him again and I assumed it was the same for him. When I returned the following term I was so excited I could scarcely breathe, and there he was, the love of my life, standing in the doorway to the common room. I said 'Hi! How are you?' He just looked at me blankly; he didn't have the first clue who I was! I knew at that moment he hadn't given me a single thought. Ten weeks of sleepless nights yearning for him, crossing each day off on a calendar, daydreaming about our future together and I was nothing to him, absolutely nothing. Just another conquest." I glance up from my boot to find her eyes fixed earnestly on me. "Can you imagine how that felt? It made a massive dent in my self-confidence, in my *self-worth.* I don't want that to happen to you."

"Luckily I don't have any self-confidence to dent!" I try to make light of it but Cath still looks serious.

"Just because you have strong feelings for someone doesn't mean they feel the same way, no matter how desperately you want them to."

"But this is different, Cath. I told you, I'm not tracking Sarah down to rekindle the old flame." Although, the thought of her being unattached and forgiving is flickering hopefully in my sub-conscious. "I just want to tell her that I didn't see her letters. I need to tell her."

"Well, you're going to make a great big steaming plonker of yourself." Cath flaps her hand dismissively and catches sight of her watch. "Oh, buggery bollocks, I'm due in court. Shoplifter, Damien Whicker the Haribo nicker." She runs back to the Lexus and wrenches the door open. "Look after my baby boy and call Ginny – you know, a real woman, not the ghost of girlfriends past."

Ominous black clouds are gathering overhead and I hurry along the path to catch up with Tony and Louie. Cafe Girl is on her phone outside the tearooms. I nod to her. She ignores me. "I don't know what I'm doing tonight, I might be busy. Why don't you ask *your wife* to come and watch you? .... So, why do you want me to come? ... Stop it, you're terrible! Hmmm, I'll think about it, I'll consult my diary ... What? Well, that's all you will be pulling tonight! ... I said I'll think about it, you cheeky–"

I find the others outside The Hut with Nasty Nat, Tony looking petulant.

"Hi Colin," Nasty Nat greets me with her dead-eyed shark smile. "I knew straight away this was a relative of yours, he's got the same fashion sense. Ha ha! But I'm afraid he's about to get those shiny new boots dirty, Mrs Winter wants all the muck picked up from the top paddock."

"Oh. I thought Louie could help us with the mowing." I attempt to save my nephew. Muck-picking was a horrid, smelly, back-breaking job. "We need to get as much grass cut as possible before the rain comes."

"Well, as head gardener it's your decision, of course. Only Mrs Winter's furious that it wasn't finished on Friday; I told her you'd asked Ron to do it, but he doesn't seem to have made much headway. I wonder what he was doing?"

"Right, right," I swiftly admit defeat. "It's not the nicest task for your first day, Louie, but it's really important for the welfare of the horses. If you make a start I'll get Chicken Ron to come and join you."

"Why do you call him Chicken Ron?" Louie asks.

"Never mind about that now," I say quickly. "I'll give you a tour of the gardens then take you down to the paddock."

"No need," Nasty Nat steps in. "I'll take him around, it's a good work out for me, you don't get a booty like this sitting around on your arse all day watching Loose Women." She slaps her back pocket and laughs. Behind her, Tony pretends to vomit into the geraniums. We watch Louie traipsing after Nasty Nat, his arms dangling dejectedly, hands hidden under the over-long sleeves.

"Never mind Lou Lou!" Tony calls after him. "You're a working man now, might as well get used to shit-munching."

"I don't suppose many kids spend their work experience knee-deep in manure and with Chicken Ron for company," I sigh. "Poor sod."

"Chicken Ron is a complete liability," Tony grumbles as we enter The Hut to collect our tools. "He does nothing to help himself; just how long are we supposed to go on covering for him?"

"Until he can collect his pension."

"When will that be? How old is he?"

"No idea," I shrug. "I don't think he's completely sure himself."

"Hmmm." Tony peers out at the dark sky. "It's looking like Armageddon out there." He slaps his hands together, ready for action. "Holy Hailstorms, Batman, we've only got one hour to save the universe."

"To the twin cut, Robin, this city needs us."

By some miracle, the rain holds off until just before lunch, and then the spits and spots turn into persistent drizzle. The few visitors still braving the gardens scurry for the tearooms. I follow the greasy path down to the lake and out to the paddock beyond. A green-fleeced figure is wrestling a wheelbarrow full of manure across the uneven ground towards the large compost heap. "Louie!" I yell. "Lunchtime!"

"Alright, Unck, I'll just empty this last load."

I watch Louie reach the compost and attempt to push the heavy wheelbarrow up the ramp. On the final shove, he loses his footing on the wet grass and falls, his face plunging into the wheelbarrow. It tips up, emptying the contents all over him. "Louie!" A snort of laughter catches in my throat and I rush to help my nephew as he lies prone beneath the barrow. I try to lift it off him but I'm laughing so much I have to sit down. Louie slowly emerges from the mound, shaking the brown clumps from his hair and fleece. "Can I have my Dairylea Dunkers now, Uncle Colin?"

The rain is really coming down and it hammers on the wooden roof of The Hut, rendering conversation impossible. Tony is sitting in one of the deckchairs watching with fascination as Louie records his latest sneeze in a notebook. His favourite is 'No. 63: Cafe, Devon. V Strong. Looking at scone.' While they're occupied, I take the opportunity to unfold another of Sarah's letters I'd secreted in my copy of Wuthering Heights. I smooth it out surreptitiously.

10 March 1985

Dear Colin

Well, it's finally happened. Auntie Sheila has told Mum to get out. The last straw began innocuously enough with a small flare-up over a missing Marathon bar and somehow this evolved into full-on warfare. Auntie Sheila branded

Mum a 'demented hippo, wallowing through everyone's lives wreaking havoc' prompting Mum to cruelly goad 'barren and wort-ridden' Sheila for being jilted on her wedding day. And then:

Auntie Sheila: 'Do you know why he couldn't go through with it?'

Mum: 'Because he obviously came to his senses!'

Auntie Sheila: 'He told me he'd slept with another woman the night before and was too wracked with guilt to marry me.'

Mum: 'That was probably just an excuse to get out of it.'

Auntie Sheila: 'I've always wanted to know who that other woman was.'

Mum: 'He didn't say?'

Auntie Sheila: 'No, he didn't say, he said he was too ashamed to tell me. I assumed that was because she was some disgusting fat slag. I thought, who do I know who's a disgusting fat slag?'

Mum: 'Why are you looking at me like that? It wasn't me!'

Auntie Sheila: 'If the cap fits...'

This went on for some time. I've no idea if it's true – Mum continued to deny it, of course, but she would, wouldn't she? Auntie Sheila's clearly suspected it all these years and somehow, given Mum's track record (and her goldfish impression when confronted) I believe this could be the real reason for the ever-present tension between them. But I feel ashamed of myself for believing something so awful of Mum; that probably says way more about me than it does her.

Anyway, Auntie Sheila said I was welcome to stay, but how could I abandon Mum? She's still my Mum, whatever she's done. I won't bore you with the tale of our trip to the women's refuge (shudder), but we are now (unhappily) ensconced in Bedroom 11 at The Three Keys while we sort ourselves out. I'm working for free to cover the cost of the room and Popeye is trying to get Mum to work as well (to pull her considerable weight, as he puts it), but she says she can't, her nerves are in tatters. If Popeye catches her at the Monster Munch again I fear the rest of her will be in shreds soon, too.

How on earth has my life got to this? Here I am gazing out over a car park from the tiny room I live in with my mother, writing to my imaginary boyfriend, and all my worldly possessions stuffed into a luggage room in the basement. Mum constantly mutters in her sleep and calls out names; who the heck is Scott??? The only Scott I know is the one who works at Wimpy's on the High Street. And I seem to be shrinking; I think it's all the manual work. I simply don't stop and before you know it lunchtime has been and gone and in the lull between that and re-opening time, I'm too knackered to eat.

I'm sorry to moan. I'm not sure where Super Girl's gone, but I hope she's back soon. I need her more than ever.

Popeye did give me the afternoon off on Wednesday 'back by 4 o'clock mind, three hundred spuds won't peel themselves' and I went to see The Breakfast Club with Anna, the girl who helps me change the rooms. Have you seen it yet? I'm not sure it's your sort of film but I enjoyed it, at least up until they played 'Don't you Forget About Me' and suddenly tears were rolling down my cheeks. Thank goodness it was dark in there; hopefully Anna didn't notice she was sitting next to a lunatic.

Tell me your troubles and doubts
Giving me everything inside and out
Love's strange, so real in the dark
Think of the tender things that we were working on
Slow change may pull us apart
But when the light gets into your heart
Don't you, forget about me.

Because I will never forget about you.

Your (not so super) girl
Sarah

I will never forget about you. Was that true, would Sarah remember me? She might not want to be reminded of such an unhappy time in her life. Perhaps it was selfish of me to try to find her, opening up old wounds, raking up the hurt and the heartache all over again. I tuck the letter back inside my book. I can just about hear 'Don't You Want Me' playing on The Time Tunnel over the rain and I'm reminded I need to call Ginny. I don't want to do it in front of the others so I move to the doorway. Perhaps I could get away with a text instead. *God, I'm such a coward.* But what to write? I gaze across at the steamy windows of the tearooms as if to find some inspiration there. Huge raindrops bounce against the A-board that reads 'Try our delicious Hogpits home-made range, all freshly prepared today.' *Get on with it Hector*. Dear Ginny... no, not dear, too formal. Hi Ginny, hope you are well.

"Who's that you're texting, Colin, your girlfriend?" Mrs Winter zooms up the path toward me like an Exocet missile, sleek and shiny in her black raincoat. I blink in surprise at the beaming smile radiating from beneath the wide-brimmed rain hat.

"No, no, er, I mean, I suppose, sort of, it's a girl that's a friend..."

"Honestly, you boys, always playing the field!" Mrs Winter gives me a playful tap on the arm and I stare at her in alarm. She'd made physical contact! It obviously can't be sunstroke; is she drunk? "Now, you've heard the exciting news about Wiltshire Life coming to the Open Day to write a feature on us?" I hadn't, but I nod enthusiastically. "Well, it gets even better, Colin: they're bringing Brian Beardmore *MBE* with them!" She rubs her hands together with glee, almost breaking into a little dance. "This is the most wonderful exposure for us, Colin, simply tremendous, Brian's become massively popular on Gardeners' World. And we've never had an actual Member of the British Empire visit Hogpits, aside from that MP, but we don't count him, not since the prison sentence. Now, they're arriving at three o'clock. Mr Winter and I shall do the tour of the gardens with Brian, so I need you to come along too, walking just behind us but within ear shot to answer any questions Brian may have about the..." she flaps her hand around dismissively, "shrubbery and things. We're going to have a trial run tomorrow, so there's no need to be nervous."

"It will be a real privilege to meet Brian," I tell Mrs Winter. "Dad used to listen to his radio show, it was one of the few things he tolerated."

"Just don't mention his latest novel, the reviews have been shocking." She looks me up and down. "Outfit-wise, obviously Brian won't expect you to be suited and booted, but I think your best jeans and a white shirt, if you have one? I mean pure white, Colin, not a greyie-white, or one that's been through the wash with a red sock. And I've ordered you a personalised Hogpits fleece to set it all off."

A fleece, in July? "Um, thank you."

"Isn't it simply terrific?" I think for one terrifying moment she is about to hug me, but she is distracted by a figure over at the tearooms. "You there!" she yells at Cafe Girl who has edged outside for a fag. "Tart!" The cigarette drops from a pair of horrified lips. "Brian loves his treacle tart, so get Reeves the bakers to deliver one. None of our home-made rubbish for an MBE."

Having stretched lunchtime out for as long as possible, Louie's clothes are dry enough for us to scrape off the worst of the manure with a pallet knife. The heavy downpour has finally subsided and a timid sun is peeping out from behind the dark clouds. Too wet to continue mowing, we have the ideal opportunity to hoe the loosened soil, and deciding to weed the hosta bed, we stroll together past the plant shop where visitors are slowly re-appearing. An elderly gentlemen is attempting to take a ceramic plant pot down from the top shelf, stretching up to reach it with great difficulty. "Let us give you a hand there, sir," Tony calls, winking at me as he pushes Louie forward. "You're the tallest Lou Lou, get it down for him." Louie obediently trots over and reaches up to the pot. He pulls on the lip. The pot tips over, covering Louie in a sudden whoosh of icy rainwater.

"Oh my goodness!" The old man steps swiftly backwards, brushing droplets of water from his jacket and glaring at Louie accusingly. "You splashed me."

"S-s-sorry." Louie is rooted to the spot in shock, his T-shirt soaking under his open fleece.

"That wasn't very kind, Tone," I reprimand, fighting hard to keep a straight face as Tony roars with laughter.

"Oh, come on! The tricks you used to play on me when I first started. You sent me to Chicken Ron to ask for a long-weight, do you remember? He was gone over an hour before I cottoned on."

As the visitor is clearly unamused, I pull Louie quickly away. We duck down along the lower path and under the trees to the shaded hosta bed. We've only just made a start turning the heavy soil when Tony hisses, "Stand by your beds lads, it's the Lord of the Manor." We turn as the red-faced Mr Winter strides towards us along the wet path. He doesn't even stop as he booms, "Got something for you lot down at the lake. Come on." We look at each other quizzically before setting off after him. The paths are greasy from the rain and we slip and slide in the hurry to keep up with our boss. As we reach the lake, we see what looks like a giant rake lying on the bank. Huge spikes grin at us as we approach and I can see it has two long rusty chains attached to each side. *What on Earth is it?* "There you go," Mr Winter stops in front of it. "Got it from a pal of mine at the Rotary club. He owns a dredging company."

"Are we going to dredge the lake?" I ask weakly.

"Got it in one, Einstein. I'm not having that bloody blanket weed causing a stink on Open Day. I wish I could sell the stuff, the amount we pull out each year. I reckon we should dry it out and flog it to the Peking Palace as seaweed." To my alarm, he actually appears to be considering it.

"How does it work?" Tony tries to lift the monstrosity, testing the weight.

Mr Winter stares at him incredulously. "How d'ya think? You chuck it in and drag it back. It's not rocket science."

"But, I don't reckon we'll be able to chuck it very far-"

"No, so you'll have to take it out in the dingy to do the middle of the lake, won't you?" He glances at his watch. "I've got to go, there's a town planner's meeting at the Masonic lodge. Right, Colin, we've only got a fortnight to Open Day so you'd better have these gardens looking shit-hot." He puts his hands on his hips and looks around the lake, nodding approvingly. "Set up some trips in the dingy, kids love that sort of stuff. Charge them ten quid a ride. No, make it twenty. We need to maximise revenue, the whole day's costing a frigging fortune the amount my wife's chucking away on it. You've got a delivery of six hundred begonias coming later."

I feel my eyes widen in amazement. "*Six hundred?* For the shop?"

"Nope. The wife wants some fancy display or other. Christ knows, you'll have to ask her." He notices Louie for the first time. "What's that?"

"This is my nephew, Mr Winter. He's here on work experience."

"Don't tell me I'm paying for him on top of everything else?"

"No, you don't have to pay him–"

"Good, good." He turns on his heel and begins to stride

away, calling over his shoulder, "Crack on, I want the lake finished by close of play. And get that lazy half-wit to do some work before I kick his sorry arse to kingdom come."

"That was a bit harsh," Louie protests, when Mr Winter is out of earshot. "I cleared that whole field this morning. I worked as fast as I could."

"I think he meant Chicken Ron." Tony is examining the dredger with trepidation. "This thing weighs a frigging ton, how the hell are we supposed to get it in the dingy? It's only an inflatable, the bloody thing will sink."

"We'll have to drag it through the water rather than put it in the dingy." I prod the dredger with my foot. "But we're definitely going to need another pair of hands. Two in the dingy and then two on the shore to drag it back."

"Well, it will have to be Twat Man," Tony sighs. "Chicken Ron was last seen heading for the stables with a bottle of Jack."

"Who's Twat Man?" Louie asks.

"You obviously haven't met Wes, or you wouldn't need to ask. Come on, let's go and find him. And whatever you do, don't make eye contact or laugh at his jokes. Oh, er, Lou Lou, have you ever seen these plants before? They smell absolutely amazing; go on, have a good sniff."

Louie obligingly leans forward and sticks his head into a skunk cabbage, inhaling deeply. "Oh my Christ!"

We finally manage to get a system going. Tony lies at the front of the dingy gamely holding on to the dredger as it cuts through the water like a grotesque figure head, and Louie perches at the back, paddling slowly out to the middle of the lake. Wes and I stand on the bank in the brace position, clutching a chain each and ready to pull. Once the dingy is in position, Tony lets go of the dredger so it sinks to the bottom of the lake. Louie then paddles the dingy clear, and Wes and I haul on the chains until the dredger finally appears back on shore. It's exhausting work, but I have to admit it's extremely effective. The spikes trap a thick mass of blanket weed each time, far more than we'd ever managed to clear out previously. The effort of heaving the dredger in on the chains is preventing Wes from talking, which is an added bonus, however he's making up for it between tugs: "Just found out my mate Gavin has passed away after some serious heartburn."

"Gosh, I'm so sorry to hear that-"

"I can't believe Gavisgon."

Please kill me.

"Why can't Dracula's wife get to sleep?"

"I don't know, Wes."

"Because of the coffin."

"Make this the last one, guys," I call in desperation. I note Louie's drained face as he steers the dingy in behind the dredger. "I think we could all do with a break, and it's getting close to home time anyway."

"Thank Christ," Tony mutters, massaging his aching biceps. "I think my arms are about to drop off. *And* I'm losing feeling in my hands which is the last thing I need; I'm going on a date with Denise Double Ds tonight."

"Did I tell you what I'm doing this evening?" Wes starts.

"Right, come on Lou Lou." Tony is suddenly in a hurry to get going again. "Last one, let's make it a good 'un."

"I'm performing at the Red Lion."

"Get paddling, Louie. Quick as you can."

"I'm going to start my set with my Enrique medley, the ladies love that, then moving on to my Bublé…"

I try to zone out of Wes' constant babble, watching Louie paddling away with Tony at full stretch in the dingy. I flick away the annoying flies that are increasing in number around the huge pile of stinking blanket weed. I feel like plunging my head into it as Wes starts to croon, 'I can be your hero baby...'

This is worse than the jokes. "Hurry up," I mutter under my breath as Louie and Tony make painstakingly slow progress out into the lake.

"I can take away your pain, oh yeah yeah..."

This is not my life. This can't be my life.

"I will stand by you forever..."

The dingy has stopped. Whatever are they playing at? "It's stuck!" Tony bellows, his voice ringing out around the lake. "The teeth are caught on something."

"Shall we give it a tug?" I call back. Tony shouts something but he is looking down into the water and we can't catch what he's saying.

"Tony!" I try again. "Shall we give it a tug?" Another muffled response drifts back. I look at Wes. "What did he say?"

Wes shrugs. "I'm not sure. I think I caught the word jerk, so he's probably asking us to give it a swift one, I expect that will do the trick. Are you ready? We'll go on three."

We grip the chains with our blistering hands and bend our knees, bracing to protect what's left of our spines. "One, two, *three.*" Wes and I pull back sharply on the chains. The dredger doesn't budge. Both Tony and Louie shout something but we still can't hear. "Go again," Wes urges. "Hard as you can. One, two, *three.*"

We heave on the chains but the dredger holds firm. "This time!" Wes cries. "The guys are yelling their heads off, it must be nearly loose. Give it everything you've got. Ready? One. Two. *Three!*" We give it one final almighty heave and the dredger shoots upwards, cannoning into the dingy. This time there's no mistaking Tony's cry of "FUUUUCK!" as he flies backwards. There's a hideous ripping noise as the spiked teeth plunge into the front of the orange dingy, which immediately starts to deflate. "Paddle, frigging paddle!" Tony shrieks at Louie, and they both flail wildly at the water with their hands. The dingy is contracting around them as they claw at the surface of the lake, desperately trying to get back to shore. The dinghy shrinking rapidly, they quickly find themselves encased in an orange rubber ring. Wes tries to shout "Swim for it!" but he's laughing so hard he can't get the words out. As the last piece of dingy disappears beneath the surface, Tony and Louie strike out for shore, a churning messy dog paddle, chins uplifted to avoid inhaling lake water. "Why don't they just stand up?" I ask Wes, but this just makes him worse, his annoying hoots of laughter echoing around the lake.

I wade into the water to help as Tony and Louie emerge coughing and spluttering. Tony is enraged. "What the hell did you do that for? You nearly bloody drowned us, you stupid dicks!"

"I'm sorry mate. We thought you wanted us to give it a jerk."

"NO! I said don't, whatever you do, pull on it, you jerk."

"We couldn't hear you properly." I look at Louie anxiously, a squelchy sodden mess with tendrils of blanket weed in his hair. Muddy water streams down his face as he wipes his hands across his eyes. "Are you ok, Louie?"

"What about me?" Tony snaps, spreading his arms out in dismay. "I'm supposed to picking Denise up in a couple of hours and I smell like the last jockstrap in Davy Jones's locker."

"I shouldn't worry," Wes gasps. "She'll be used to dating pond life!"

"We'd better get you back to The Hut before you catch pneumonia," I say to Louie. "God, your mum's going to be furious with me when she sees you; work experience really isn't supposed to be like this. You've had the day from hell."

"It's alright, Unck." Louie makes an attempt to wring out the bottom of his fleece, but only succeeds in adding more water to his overflowing boots. "I figured that anyone who has to work with me would attempt to kill me. Or themselves."

I look around at our sorry group. What would Sarah think if she could see me now, a reeking, sweaty, bedraggled mess, surrounded by flies like Pig-Pen? Stuck in a dead-end job with a fifty-pence an hour pay rise once every three years. My resolve to find Sarah intensifies. She deserves to know what a lucky escape she's had.

"How was your first day, darling?"

"Wet."

"What on Earth are you wearing? You look like a scarecrow."

Cath had it spot on. We'd been forced to take the clothes off the scarecrow just so Louie had something to go home in. He turns to me, clutching his work clothes in a Morrison's bag-for-life. I can see a piece of blanket weed poking through a hole. "No offence, Unck, but I might go to work with Dad tomorrow, at the bank. I'm not sure there's enough insurance to cover me here."

"Oh God, what did you kill?" Cath clutches at him. "They didn't let you handle the guinea pigs, did they, not after what happened when you bought the one home from school for the weekend?"

"That wasn't my fault, Mum, I didn't know Dad had lit the chiminea."

"He did really well, Cath, he's worked like a trooper." I clap Louie on the shoulder. "Thank you Louie, you've been brilliant."

"Cheers, Unck, see you Saturday."

"Saturday?" Cath glares at me. "Seriously? You're involving my son in your mid-life crisis wild goose chase?"

"Lad's day out," I say breezily, trying to make light of it. "Bit of sea air, if nothing else." I flinch under my sister's stony stare. "Well, I must away, I'm absolutely shattered. Home for a shower and a beer. Although probably not in that order!"

We all look round as a vast delivery lorry rolls into the car park. The driver shouts down from the window. "Six hundred begonias for you, mate."

Oh crap.

Chapter Eight

13 July 1985

Dear Colin

I had to write and tell you about the most wonderful day today, the one and only day I've felt real happiness since leaving you. The bar was packed from midday, the TV volume cranked up to the max and from the very first note of Rocking All Over The World, the place was absolutely jumping. It was such an electric atmosphere, people were dancing on tables, the locals holding hands with the Big City Losers, everyone doing the Radio Gaga clap (weren't Queen PHENOMENAL?), grown men sobbing at the video clips from Ethiopia, the charity boxes were stuffed full... I've never worked so hard in my entire life, the till didn't stop ringing. Popeye was grinning from ear to ear all day, he even said I could help myself to a Bacardi and coke, albeit 'just a single mind, don't go taking the piss'.

The only bum note was Simon Le Bon's bum note - the whole bar howled with laughter, but I felt sorry for him. I knew you would do, too. It's funny, but I felt closer to you today than ever before because I knew that somewhere, you were watching too. I did think you might even be there and I scanned the crowds, just in case I spotted you being squirted with water. Boy, it was hot today but hardly anyone was on the beach. It felt as if the whole world reunited in front of their tellies to bring about the end of famine in Africa. After this day, how can governments grant funds for space exploration and sporting events when the world has seen people dying of hunger? (Did you know Birmingham intend to spend £66 million on a new stadium if they win their Olympic bid? £66 million!!!!). People are going to come first from now on and it feels fantastic. NO MORE FAMINE.

I know I'm gushing, but I'm not going to apologise for it. Today has made me realise that life is real and precious and should be lived in the moment, appreciating what you've got, not yearning and pining and weeping for you've lost.

I can't spend my life just wishing.

So, I've made a momentous decision - I am going to stop writing to you. I am letting you go.

I can't stand long drawn out goodbyes, so I'm going to sign off now. I'll never understand why you gave up on us, but who knows, maybe one day I shall.

Your Sarah.

This is the fifth time I've read this letter. *My Sarah* had finally given up on me. After ten months of hope, she wasn't prepared to put herself through it anymore. Only it wasn't the last letter she wrote, there is one more. My hand hovers over the final envelope, but I withdraw it. I can imagine what the very last letter might contain; an almighty change of tone after the euphoria of Live Aid had worn off. Sarah wouldn't have let me off that lightly and the last letter probably contained a massive outpouring of anger and vitriol. I couldn't bear it and I didn't want anything to make me change my mind about finding her. No, I wouldn't read that last letter.

It's seven-thirty in the morning and several blasts of a car horn tell me Tony has arrived. I open the front door to find him leaning against the bonnet of his brother's Renault Clio, his eyes hidden behind a massive pair of square sunglasses. "Morning Col!" He reaches inside the window and peeps the horn again. "I bet you've got the horn! All set to track down the love of your life? I reckon we'll find her imprisoned in some back street sweat-shop and you'll swoop in, chuck her over your shoulder and bring her back here. To bungalow-land." His beam fades a little as he takes in my jeans and polo shirt. "Is that what you're wearing? It's not exactly Richard Gere standards."

"Well, I'm not changing into a sailor suit. And anyway, I doubt very much if we're actually going to find Sarah today." I'd been telling myself that all night, each time I turned to look at the alarm clock to see if morning was any nearer. But my blood surges as I say her name. I *might* see her today, it isn't completely unthinkable. "New sunglasses?"

"Yeah, they're really cool, aren't they? Oakleys, got them off Fleabay. Bit scratched, but what do you expect for fifteen quid?" Tony pulls at the door handle of the Clio. "Come on then Casanova, your carriage awaits."

"Do you think it will get us there?" I ask, looking at the vehicle doubtfully. Although the Clio is mainly maroon in colour, there are several large splodges of white across the bodywork. The back bumper is, bizarrely, a sickly yellow and the wheels all look decidedly depressed, as if they don't want to be seen holding up such a monstrosity.

"Of course it will get us there! Ronnie B's never let me down."

"Ronnie B?"

"Yeah, you know, Ron Burgundy. Can't you smell the air freshener?" He sniffs the air. "Rich mahogany! Right, come on, come on, we've a long journey ahead of us. Let's get this show on the road!"

I clear a space in the footwell, pushing aside packets of

crisps and cans of Red Bull, and with a throaty roar Tony fires us out of Cotter Close and across town. It's too early in the morning for any traffic to hinder us and the sun is already high in the sky, promising a lovely summer's day. Louie is waiting on the front step, hair sculpted into a freshly-shaven Mohican, long spikes running along his head like the showy crest of a cockatoo. He's holding his arms up defensively as Cath, dressed in a long green dressing gown attempts to dab something on his face. She's momentarily distracted by the sight and sound of Ron Burgundy bumping up the gravel drive, and Louie takes his opportunity to duck out of her reach. I climb out and hold the seat forwards as Louie dives, spikes first, into the back seat. "Everything alright, sis?" I ask apprehensively.

"Oh Col, make him put some sun screen on, for goodness sake." Cathy sounds exasperated. "You know he gets third degree burns standing next to a candle. I've tried to make him take a baseball cap, but he refused, saying he doesn't want to squash his mohawk. Who does he think he is, Hiawatha?" She sighs then looks me up and down. "So, you're still going ahead with this ridiculous nonsense? Desperately Seeking Sarah?"

I give a firm nod. "Yes. I know you think it's a waste of time, Cath, but I need to do it for my own sanity, if nothing else. I've not slept properly since I found those letters."

"Well, I doubt you'll get as far as Basingstoke in that piece of junk." She gestures at the car, its engine turning over raggedly, the exhaust pipe billowing dark smoke into her hydrangeas. "Anyway, I called Ginny and she's up for dinner, so I said to come to mine next weekend. She's really looking forward to seeing you again."

"Is she?" I find that very hard to believe. Tony beeps the horn impatiently and I turn to go, but Cath grabs my arm. "Col-"

"What?"

Her anxious eyes search my face and she seems to be struggling to find words. This is a first for Cath. She gives a little shrug and relaxes her grip. "Nothing. Have a safe journey."

I see her pulling her dressing gown tightly around her as she watches Tony take three attempts to turn the car around. She grows smaller in the wing mirror as we exit the driveway. Tony cranks up the radio and The Killers blare out. "Right lads, we've got a stack of Red Bull, we've got our cheesy Doritos, and we've got Mr Brightside. Kent, lock up your daughters, we're coming to get ya!" He puts his foot down hard on the accelerator and we shoot off down the lane, only making two hundred yards before an electronic voice tells us to 'Perform a U-Turn where possible'.

"Shit."

When we'd set out, Doris the sat-nav lady had informed us it would take two hours and fifty-three minutes to get to Herne Bay. After four hours, we still had forty minutes to go. The M25 had been horrific and having finally got away from it, we realised Tony's attempt at a short cut was, in fact, taking us towards Tilbury Docks. I lost count of the number of times we crossed the Medway. It didn't help that his new sunglasses impeded Tony's vision and he had difficulty reading the road signs, ducking and swerving at the very last heart-stopping moment.

I took a turn at driving, although as I drive so infrequently, I wasn't the most confident behind the wheel. Tony enjoyed his rest, being able to look out the window at all the 'honeys' the lovely weather had bought out. As I took us through Maidstone, we stopped at the traffic lights in the middle of the bustling town, windows down and music blaring. A group of giggling young girls crossed the road in front of us and as Tony smiled and waved at them, a One Direction song came on the radio. In his desperate scrabble to turn it down, Tony only succeeded in turning it up and as the lights went green, I stalled Ron Burgundy. A clamour of horns blasted us from behind and everyone turned to stare. Louie slid as far down in his seat as he could go. "This is *ultra* tragic."

Hot, sticky and exhausted we finally arrive in Herne Bay. As we turn the corner of Canterbury Road, there's the sea, a shimmering blue mirage in front of us. Our spirits lift and Tony pulls into a space on Central Parade. I climb out gratefully, turning my face into the refreshing sea breeze. Louie emerges, blinking in the strong sunlight, his spikes drooping in the heat. Tony groans loudly as he unfolds himself from the driver's seat, stretching his arms up to the sky. "That was the journey from hell. I feel absolutely disgusting. I'm sweating in crevices I didn't even know I had." He peels his damp shirt away from his back. "I'm going straight into the sea to cool off."

Louie and I stare at him. "The sea will be freezing, Tone," I say.

"Good." Tony tugs his shirt off and starts unbuttoning his jeans.

"You have bought your swimmers with you, haven't you?" Louie asks anxiously.

"Nope." Tony kicks off his shoes and drops his trousers, revealing black Calvin Klein underpants. "Come on you pair of wimps, I'm going to count to ten and the last one in buys lunch. One-"

I look at Louie. "Two-"

"Shit." Louie bends down to untie his laces.

"Three-"

"Oh crap." I pull my polo shirt over my head.

"Four-"

"My spikes, they took me forever!" Louie cries, attempting to remove his T-shirt without dislodging his hair.

"Five-"

A seagull rises up, squawking in alarm as Louie reveals his torso, a stark white against the azure sky. "Six-"

I fumble with my belt. What pants am I wearing? Are they relatively new, or one of my prehistoric pairs, grey with holes in-

"Seven-"

I rip off my socks and throw them into the car. Louie is struggling to find his fly amongst all the other zips on his bondage trousers. "Eight-"

"Come on, Louie," I urge. "Get them off."

"Nine-"

"Got it." Louie whips his trousers down. He has Minions boxer shorts on.

"Ten!"

We run along the concrete parkway and leap onto the sand below. Each trying to hold the other back, we streak across the beach, only vaguely aware of the blur of shocked onlookers who had, up until this point, been enjoying a peaceful day at the seaside. We race into the sea, jumping over the shallow waves and shrieking in shock as the icy water splashes up our legs. "Global warming my arse!" Tony screams. "Come on!" He surges ahead, the water up to his thighs. A wave rolls in towards him. "Oh my God, my todger!" His voice is an octave higher.

"Ugh!" The water slaps against my underpants and behind me, I hear Louie cry out in pain.

"It's f-f-f-f-freezing, Unk! I can't do it."

"Geronimo!" Tony throws himself into the water with a massive splash. I brace myself to do the same but not wanting Louie to come last, I turn back to him.

"Come on, Louie, you can do it!"

"I can't, it's too cold!"

"We'll go in together! Ready, steady-"

"No! I'm going back before I die of, of, toxic shock, or something." Louie swings round, but loses his balance and falls, completely disappearing under the water. He surfaces coughing and spluttering, salty droplets streaming from his black spikes.

"Hector, you chicken shit!" Tony scoops a handful of glacial water over me. "In, in, in!"

"No point now," I call, my teeth chattering. "I've already lost." I start to wade back towards the shore, but Tony pounces, and I gasp as the icy sea swallows me up. Louie hauls me to my feet and we all wade into shore, suddenly very conscious of our sagging underpants and the audience of families on the beach.

"Cover the crown jewels, lads," Tony hisses and we place our hands strategically in front of us as we trot up the sand and back along the parkway. The car looks as if it should have a 'Police Aware' sticker in the window. The doors are wide open, our garments scattered over the seats and window frames. A seagull is pecking at Louie's bondage trousers as they lie across the roof. As the loser, I'm ordered to fetch the burgers and cokes, so I have no option but to pull my jeans on over my wet legs and soggy pants. I squelch to the kiosk as Tony and Louie stretch out on the bonnet to dry off. Even though I'm only gone a few minutes, Louie's chest is already turning pink by the time I return, and he retreats into the car to eat his lunch.

I lean back against the hot windscreen and gaze out over the bay. It really is a beautiful spot, and rather comforting to know Sarah had come to live in a place like this. Is she still living here? Could she be amongst the families on the beach, enjoying a day out with her children? Or had we passed her in the town, seated at one of the cafes? It is a long-shot, I know that, but my heart skips a beat knowing I could bump into her at any moment; I would definitely recognise her, I'd know her anywhere. Tony interrupts my daydream. "The seaside never looked like this when I went on holiday as a youngster. Golden sand and blue sea? No, everything was always grey. Mum actually thought Fifty Shades of Grey was about Mendips caravan park. She got quite a shock when she went to see the film." He takes a swig from his bottle of coke. "When's the last time you went on holiday, Col?"

I cringe at the memory. "I had a weekend away with Miriam in Dorset, but we had to take Dad with us because I couldn't leave him on his own."

"Miriam?"

"Yes, she was the Morris dancer, with the mustard Austin Allegro. She wanted us to go to the annual folk festival in Swanage, but Dad totally freaked out as soon as he got there and saw all the people in their costumes, you know, bells and sticks and things – he was convinced he'd died and gone straight to hell."

"I think he had a point, mate." Tony screws up his burger wrapper purposefully. "So, where are we off to next? What's Sarah's old address?"

My stomach lurches again at the mention of her name. "Dunes Way. It's just a few roads back from the coast. I think we should try there first rather than the hotel."

"Cool beans. Right, my pants are still soaking, so I'm going to have to go commando. Close your eyes back there, Lou Lou, I'm about to drop my cacks."

My heart is pounding in my mouth as we follow the Sat Nav directions to Dunes Way and I take deep breaths to calm myself down. *Don't be so stupid, she won't be there now.* A forwarding address is the best we can hope for, unless… She might be there, she *might* still be living with her aunt, it's not inconceivable. My pulse quickens again as we enter Dunes Way, a small circular terrace of around twenty houses, and not too dissimilar to Cotter Close with some properties smart and well-kept, others in various sad states of disrepair. We pull up outside number seventeen, a mid-terrace two-up two-down, with a pale blue front door and lavender bushes lining the path. We climb out of the car, the old guy at number fifteen eyeing us warily as he cuts his hedge. You can't really blame him. As if the car isn't enough of an eye sore, I'm walking like a toddler with a very full nappy, my pants still sopping wet. Tony's doing lunges against the pavement kerb before announcing, very loudly, that he is "flapping about like an elephant's trunk in a gale" and Louie, his guy-liner having run, looking like a cross between Alice Cooper and Sitting Bull. "This is it, Col," Tony gestures at the blue door. "Go on, mate, we're right behind you."

I make a futile attempt to smooth down my stiff, salty hair, and then walk up the path with as much confidence as I can muster. *This is where Sarah had lived, she'd have walked up and down this path many times.* I jab the bell and wait, Tony and Louie close behind. Nothing. "Ring it again," Tony urges impatiently. I press the doorbell a second time, leaving my finger on it for a little longer. Still nothing. "Sod it," Tony groans, "they're not at home, the ungrateful bastards. Don't they know how far we've travelled just to knock on their poxy front door?"

"That's ok, we've got all the graveyards to go round yet," Louie says, looking more cheerful. "We can come back here a bit later."

We turn to leave but the sudden rattle of a chain stops us and the front door swings opens. A woman stands in the doorway and for one ghastly second I think she's naked, but I realise she's wearing an orange bikini that is exactly the same colour as her skin. Her piercing dark eyes sweep over us. "Can't you read?" She points at a sticker on the glass panel. "I don't buy anything from the door and I'm sick of you immigrants disturbing my peace trying to sell me your old bits of tat." She jabs an accusing finger in my face. "*Stolen* bits of tat, I'll bet. And don't you even think of coming back and doing a poo on my doorstep like that other bastard did, I'll set my husband on you."

"Um, s-sorry," I stutter. "We're not immigrants, we've travelled from Wiltshire to look for someone who used to live at this address. Sheila, her name was."

She glares at me suspiciously. "Sheila?"

"Y-yes." Is this Sheila? Sarah's aunt would be well into her seventies by now, is this woman old enough to be her? I'm hopeless with ages; her leathery skin is extremely wrinkled, it could be her–

"Never heard of any Sheila."

"Oh, come on, love," Tony launches his charm offensive, treating her to his cheeky-chappy grin. "Throw us a bone here. We're sorry to have disturbed your sunbathing, although your tan already looks pretty good to me." He removes his sunglasses and gives a start. "Ugh! Cripes alive. Er, look, we've driven a long way to knock you up, s-sorry, I mean, look you up. Please help us."

"I'm not giving you any money. I don't care if you're disabled, just out of the looney bin or riddled with rabies. You can get a bloody job, or better still, go back to where you came from."

"Well, we come from Devizes, so yes, in a way we are seriously disadvantaged." Tony's attempt at humour falls on very stony ground. "But contrary to popular belief, we're not all two-headed inbreds, we're just perfectly normal lads, as you can see."

Louie lets out a sudden shriek and starts dancing around in a circle, flapping his hands wildly at his head. "A bee, a bee! It's stuck in my hair putty." He careers blindly down the path and out of the gate, arms flailing maniacally as Tony rushes after him. I try to reason with the open-mouthed woman.

"I'm sorry we've disturbed you. We're just trying to trace Sheila and her family, the Shaws. Could they have lived here before you?"

"I told you, I've never heard of any Sheila. I don't know what your game is but you can clear off. Go on, get off my property." The door slams shut. I stare at the peeling blue paintwork but don't have the nerve to ring the doorbell again. What now? I can't believe the trail has gone cold already. I trudge despondently past the buzzing lavender bushes and lean against Ron's bonnet, watching Tony holding Louie in a vice-like grip as he attempts to flick the bee out of its waxy trap.

"You there!" The old man at number fifteen calls over to me.

"We're just leaving," I say wearily.

"Did I hear you say you're looking for Sheila? Sheila Kremer?"

I swing round to face him. "I don't know her surname, but she lived here in the eighties. Do you know her?"

"I'm afraid Sheila died, quite some time ago now. Cancer, it was. That bloody disease; it took my wife, too, and my brother, just last year."

"I'm so sorry." I move closer to the hedge. The old guy has a weather-beaten face but it is open and kindly, and there is a friendly twinkle in his eyes. "Did you know Sheila well?"

"Oh yes, everyone in the close looked out for each other in those days; all good friends we were, you always had someone you could turn to for help. Not like nowadays." He gestures next door with a shudder. "She can't even say good morning, that one. Got a face that would make an onion cry."

I smile. "I'm really looking for Sheila's family, her sister and her niece, Sarah. They moved in with Sheila in 1984 and I was hoping to track them down. I was, I mean, I am an old friend of Sarah's."

"Oh yes?" He gives me a knowing smile. "An old friend of Sarah's, eh?"

I feel my face turning red. "That's right. Do you remember her?"

He nods. "She was a corker, wasn't she? Probably still is, I shouldn't wonder. She was friendly with it, mind, never gave herself any airs and graces. Her mother was another kettle of fish altogether. Rowena, her name was. She was as strange as her name." I wait, but he doesn't elaborate, eyes gazing up into the blue sky as he thinks back.

"Did they stay here for very long?" I prompt.

"They did stay with Sheila for a while, I couldn't tell you exactly how long. They left after the sisters fell out." He smiles wistfully. "Over money, probably, that's what it often is with families. Sheila never really spoke of it, but I know it upset her greatly."

"They moved into The Three Keys for a while, didn't they? I thought they might have come back here, when things had calmed down."

"No, Son, they never came back here. They moved on."

"Oh." So they weren't still living here in Herne Bay. My heart sinks. "Any idea where they went?"

"Let me see," the old man rubs his stubbly chin thoughtfully and I hold my breath. "Where did Sheila say..." *Please think! Please remember!* "What was the town called, now..." Time stands still. I'm conscious of Tony and Louie wandering over, and I hold up a hand to stop them breaking his concentration. "It began with a P, I think. Or was it a T?" My fingernails are digging into the palms of my hands. "It might have been Tonbridge."

"Where's Tonbridge?" Tony asked.

"Kent."

"Alright, I only asked-"

"No, I'm not sure it was Tonbridge." The old chap shakes

his head. "Nope, I can't recall. You could try at The Three Keys, Popeye still owns the hotel and he would have been there when Sarah was. You could ask him if he remembers." The neighbour picks up his shears again, ready to resume the hedge-trimming.

"That's great, thank you very much for your help." I try to sound upbeat but my heart is back in my trainers. It is too much of a long-shot. Staff turnover in the hotel industry is notoriously high, there is no way the owner will remember someone from thirty years ago.

"Cheer up, mate." Tony gives my arm a light punch. "We're not throwing in the towel just yet." He looks at his watch. "Right lads, back in the motor, quick burger stop, then we'll find this hotel. Give my pants a feel would you, Louie? They must be dry by now."

Crawling slowly back along the packed sea front, another burger resting heavy in our stomachs, we finally locate The Three Keys Hotel right at the end of the bay. Perching high on a corner facing the sea, we can immediately tell it is the favoured place of the locals. The picnic tables are taken over by tattooed, vest-topped, denim-shorted young men, not the brightly coloured garments worn by the holiday-makers thronging the other establishments along the front. Someone exclaims, "Hey up, it's the three wise monkeys!" which we all pretend not to hear, not fancying our chances against the sinewy locals. Inside smells of damp dog and bleach, and as we walk over the red and brown swirly carpet, I feel a pang of anguish at the thought of my lovely, fragrant Sarah working in a place like this. Perhaps it had been different in the eighties, but somehow I doubted it. The bar is dark and our eyes don't immediately adjust to the gloom after the bright sunlight. There is a loud yelp as Tony treads on a brown Labrador lying almost invisible on the floor. There is nobody serving, but a thin-faced man sitting at the bar nursing a pint of Guinness calls out, "Popeye! Punters."

A bald, elderly man appears from a door behind the bar. His left eye settles on Tony, his right on Louie. "Yes, lads?"

"Coke, please," "Pint of Stella," they say in unison. Popeye shakes his head.

"You'll have to speak up, lads, I'm a bit Mutt 'n Jeff."

"Two cokes and a pint of Stella please!" Tony booms.

"Righto. Do you want ice?"

"What, in my lager?"

"No, I was talking to him." As he appears to be looking at the thin-faced man at the bar, we wait for him to answer. "Well?"

"Um, yes please," I say hesitantly.

"What?"

"YES PLEASE!"

"Righto." He stabs a miniature shovel into the ice barrel. "Been for a swim, have you?"

"Briefly," I say. "It was freezing."

"What? Not many go in the sea now, they say it's too polluted. But I've taken a dip every single morning since I was a nipper, come rain, come shine; it's never done me any harm."

"You sure about that?" Tony mutters under his breath.

"Just down for the day, are you? Or here on holiday?"

"We're looking for someone called Sarah Shaw," Louie tells him, very loudly. "She's from the past. Like on one of those long-lost family programs."

"Ah." Popeye squirts cola into two half-pint glasses. "She's a bit of alright, that one. And happy, with it, always smiling. I do love a cheerful woman."

We gape at each other. "Y-you know her?" I stammer, my heart racing. "But, I thought she hadn't worked here in years?"

Popeye stares at Louie and at me. "She's never worked here, what made you think that? She's based in London, I should think, that's where most of them end up."

"Most of who end up?" Tony is confused. "Prostitutes?"

"That's harsh," Popeye frowns. "I mean, she's a bit flighty, I give you that, but there's no way she's on the game. I mean, the show's on before the watershed, for goodness sake."

"The show?" I ask weakly.

"Yes, Long Lost Family." Popeye places our drinks on the bar. "The wife loves it, not that you'd know it. She spends the entire hour sobbing into a bar towel."

"So, you were talking about Davina McColl?" Tony asks.

"Of course. Who did you think?"

I sigh. "We're looking for a woman called Sarah Shaw. She used to work here, but I don't suppose you'll remember her. It was back in the eighties."

"Crikey." Popeye rubs his forehead. "That's a lifetime ago, son. Sarah Shaw, you say? Doesn't ring any bells, I'm afraid. What did she look like?"

Like an angel. Perfect. Wonderful. My face reddens. "She was young, eighteen, brown hair, curly and er, very soft. She was nice. In nature, I mean."

The man at the bar snorts. "In our dreams! Doesn't sound like anyone who's ever worked here. Burping Brenda hardly fits that description!"

"She lived with her auntie in Dunes Way," Louie chips in. "Sheila Creamer. She's dead now."

"It's Sheila Kremer," I correct.

Popeye and the man at the bar shake their heads. "Sarah stayed here for a while, with her mother." I try. "She's called Rowena."

"Oh, Christ alive!" Popeye throws his hands into the air, making us jump. "I remember Rowena, I'll never bloody well forget her. She was an absolute nightmare. We threw a party when she left, do you remember, Pat? All the locals stood outside and cheered her off. I felt sorry for the daughter, mind, she didn't deserve a mother like that. No one does."

"Can you remember where they were going?" I ask eagerly.

Popeye scratches his head. "No, I can't recall the name of the place."

"Was it Tonbridge?"

"Yes, it was something like that. I do know they were clean out of money, so Rowena had no choice but to go back to her husband. That's where they were headed when we saw them off." He beams round at us. "I remember feeling sorry for the husband, he'd only just got rid of her, the poor sod. There he is, living the life of Riley and suddenly the She Devil descends on him again." His smile fades as three incredulous faces gawp back at him. "What's up, lads?"

"They went back home?" I ask feebly. "To, to Trowbridge?"

"Jesus Col, you mean she's been living up the bloody road?" Tony bursts out. He and Louie are waiting for a response, but my jaw just flaps. *Sarah had moved back home.* I grip the bar, my head reeling from the revelation. She'd been so close, but she'd never come round, not made contact, not ever. But why would she? I hadn't responded to her letters, why would she want to face further rejection?

"Thank you for your help," I mutter to Popeye as we move away from the bar and sit down at a table.

"Are you alright, Uncle Colin?" Louie looks at me anxiously. "Did you think they'd still be living round here?"

"Yes, I suppose I did. It never occurred to me that Sarah's mum and dad would get back together."

"Do you remember their old address?" Tony, matter-of-fact as always, taps into the sat-nav app on his phone.

"Um," I pretend to hesitate. Of course I remembered Sarah's address; I'd performed a two-hour round trip to cycle past it every Sunday for months on the off-chance Sarah might be there visiting her father. "I think it's Penton Avenue. Number 127. I think."

Tony prods away at his iPhone and then Doris tells us to "take a left turn." He holds the screen up for us to see. "Penton Avenue. Only one hundred and thirty-three miles back the way we came."

"I'm really sorry, lads."

"It last changed hands in January 2008. For £395,000," Louie informs us, looking at Zoopla. "So she won't be there now."

"Didn't you ever go round there?" Tony asks me, not unreasonably. "Not even to ask Sarah's old man how she was, or where she'd moved to?"

Why hadn't I ever stopped and knocked on the door? Why hadn't I been more persistent, more rigorous? Sarah had written thirty-two letters before she'd given up on me; all I'd done was cycle around in circles like a love-sick Bradley Wiggins. I'm so pathetic, so *weak*. I realise Tony and Louie are expecting an answer.

"When she left, Sarah said she'd contact me. But she never did, and finally I had to accept that she was moving on with her life without me. I thought she'd met someone else."

"It's like a storyline from a movie," Tony comments, peeling a bar mat. "Boy meets girl, boy shags girl, then circumstances force them apart and they each end up believing the other doesn't love them anymore."

"Super tragic." Louie shakes his spikes sadly.

"Mind you, not even the most far-fetched plot would have them living a short bus ride apart." Tony takes a swig of Stella and grimaces. "Flat as a frigging pancake. Come on, let's get the hell out of here. Quick pit-stop at that arcade on the front and then we'll head off."

"Home?"

"No, Lou Lou, I thought we'd drive another one hundred and thirty-three miles in the wrong direction for no apparent reason. Of course bloody home."

The room is quiet and dark, just the sound of the kitchen clock ticking. If only I'd had the courage to open Sarah's last letter we'd have saved ourselves a torturous journey. It had gone four o'clock before we finally left Herne Bay, Louie sprawled across the back seat, his nose sun burnt and his right hand heavily bandaged after an Alsatian-sized seagull had snatched his burger from him. It had been a nightmare prising Tony out of the arcade as he'd been determined to win a Pooh Bear on the grabbers for his new girlfriend, Denise; I reckoned he'd spent the best part of twenty quid trying, the expletives worsening each time Winnie dropped from the grabbers. I'm sure it hadn't helped that he'd kept his sunglasses on throughout. I'd thought the revelations of the day would have kept me alert, but my head nodded, chin touching my chest. When I woke at one stage we were crossing a bridge. It was the bloody Medway again.

I'm clutching Sarah's last letter, its envelope on the kitchen table, the torn silver heart shining in the gloom. I hadn't been able to face reading the last one, believing it full of remorse and recrimination. I was wrong.

20 July 1985

Dearest Colin

I know I said I wouldn't write again but I had to tell you our news – we are coming HOME! Yes, it's really true! Mum and Dad are going to give it another go. Inspired by Live Aid, Mum likened their relationship to the Bob Geldof/Midge Ure partnership: one simply doesn't work without the other. So, we are coming back! Our house is going to seem like a mansion compared to room 11 at The Three Keys! I'll be able to start back at college in September and Dad has promised me driving lessons. It's all too fabulous for words, my life is beginning again! Sorry, too many exclamation marks, I know.... but I'm excited, so there!!!!!!!!!!!!!

I have to admit to a little voice inside my head which questions Mum when she asserts 'I do still love your father, I can't wait to be back in his arms'. Does she really mean this or is it because she's run out of options? After all, Popeye had just about reached the end of his tether with her, having received his latest phone bill. The Little Voice is driving me mad and I hope it goes away, I don't want to turn into one of those bitter and twisted sorts who are cynical about everything and suspicious of everyone – that's not the girl you fell in love with, is it? I shall do my utmost to believe the best in people again, just like I always used to; after all, what else is there?

Mum and I arrive back home on the 29th and I thought I would let you know that I'm going to come and see you. I'm not angry, I promise, so you can answer the door without fear of me flying at you like a banshee. I know it's all over between us, but I just want to hear you say it. I need to hear you say it. Then I'll go and get on with my life and never bother you again.

Whatever happens, I can't wait to see you again. Like I said, I do still want to believe the best in everyone.

Your (massively excited!) Sarah

Instead of the expected sorrow and bitterness, it was a letter full of joy and excitement, *of anticipation* - so, why then, hadn't Sarah been round like she'd said? Had her mother changed her mind and they'd not come home after all? Perhaps they'd moved in with the man from the Pru instead. The only thing I know for sure is that this really is the final letter. There are no more after this one.

God, what a day. I'm no closer, not really. I'm never going to find her.

Chapter Nine

It was fortuitous that the entire week had been focused on the preparations for Open Day, so I had little time to dwell on the futile trip to Kent. Tony and I had worked from dawn until dusk each day with Mrs Winter constantly on our backs, barking out orders until she was satisfied there was not a single blade of grass out of place nor the merest hint of a weed, nothing that might offend the eyes of Brian Beardmore MBE. Every nerve, muscle and sinew ached from our efforts, with Tony almost morphing into Gromit as he single-handedly planted six hundred begonias on the steep bank opposite the house, spelling out 'Wintersdell' in vibrant pink. At one point his back seized up and he'd had to crawl up the path on all fours until some visitors spotted him and bought him back to The Hut in a wheelbarrow.

The morning of the big day arrived a little overcast, but the forecast predicted a mainly dry day with just the chance of a passing shower if we were extremely unlucky. Hogpits Heights had been transformed. Colourful triangles of bunting fluttered over the hedges, the top lawn littered with stalls and white tents, from which plants and homemade goodies were to be sold. The hot dog stand and burger van were primed and ready, the waft of frying onions making me realise how long it had been since breakfast. There was a plethora of garden activities set out for the children with hoop-la, skittles and giant Jenga, and over in the face-painting tent, Nasty Nat had set out her brushes. Her husband, the bodybuilder, biceps bulging beneath a tight black lyrca top, was in the process of erecting a highstriker. The A-board read 'Strong Man Challenge! Ring the bell, win a prize'. A massive mallet lay in the grass beside the board and I'd skirted past, hoping I wouldn't be forced into what would undoubtedly be a humiliating attempt to make the puck hiccup all of six inches.

The main lawn had been converted into a makeshift circus ring by bales of straw, ready for the midday magic show, the bales to double up as seating. The horses, watching inquisitively from their paddocks had been beautifully groomed, their coats shining as a feeble shaft of sunlight appeared. Chicken Ron had been dispatched to trap Psycho Sid in his coop and Fred's nervous farting was interspersed with loud bangs as Mr Winter shot into the sky, shocking the noisy rooks from the trees. He'd told me he didn't want the 'noisy bastards flapping and shitting' on an MBE. I am looking forward to meeting Brian Beardmore immensely; he seems such a lovely man on the telly.

As I arrive back at the top lawn, I see Mrs Winter speaking animatedly to Cafe Girl who is seated behind a long trestle table and looking bewildered. There are piles of forms and stacks of blue baseball caps in front of her. Mrs Winter waves me over. "Colin, you do know about this, don't you? We want at least two hundred membership sign-ups today, is that clear? That's the target and failure is not an option. Try and persuade people to take the three year membership, but if they won't, at least make sure you get the annual sign-up, I don't want any of this 'I'll have a think about things' namby-pamby crap, they don't leave until they've signed. And paid. Emma here has the card machine, but we'll take cash and cheques too, if anyone still uses such things. Everyone who signs up today gets a free hat, so I want you to wear one and promote membership to every single person you come across. Keep sending them over to Emma. No, better still walk them over to the stall and stay with them, make sure they don't get away. Here's your hat." Mrs Winter hands me a blue baseball cap. It has a picture of a grinning cartoon wild boar with 'I'm a Hog' emblazoned underneath.

"Er, right. Thanks." I place the cap on my head, noticing on the stall that the children's version has a picture of a beaming piglet with 'I'm a Hoglet' printed above the peak of the cap.

"What's wrong?" Mrs Winter snaps, glaring into my eyes. "I saw your face fall Colin Hector, you can't hide anything from me. What is it?"

I glance at Emma who stares back up at me in alarm and I feel myself getting hot. "W-well, it's nothing really, probably just me being pedantic, or pernickety, you might say –"

"For God's sake man, spit it out."

"Well, a hoglet is a baby hedgehog, isn't it? A baby hog is a piglet."

There is a short silence. "You cretin!" Mrs Winter screams. I step back in shock before realising she is addressing her husband as he stalks past behind me. Mrs Winter brandishes a Hoglet cap at him. "Got a good deal on these, did you? I bet you used those dodgy printers from Rotary ... *pricks.* Hoglets have pricks, which, incidentally, is exactly what we're going to look like. Whatever is Brian Beardmore going to think of us? A fine bloody advert for the countryside we are!"

I can't hear Mr Winter's rumbling response but I see his shot-gun jerk up and I side-step swiftly away, shooting an apologetic look at the wide-eyed Cafe Girl before ducking into the cake tent to escape the ensuing ferocious argument.

Tony is inside, his blue cap on back to front, chatting up the cup-cake lady in the hope of some free samples. It seems to be working, given the number of empty cake cases surrounding him. He turns at my approach, his eyes shining. "Colin! There you are. You'll never guess what!"

"They do a piri-piri flavour?"

"What? No, I've only got an audition for Deal or No Deal! That boring-bastard video worked, they loved it, bloody loved it. Hardly anyone gets called for an audition, you know, not according to Noel's online forum."

"That's brilliant news, Tone, well done you!"

"It's actually going to happen, Col, this is it! I'm going to win big, maybe not the jackpot, but I reckon a hundred grand at least. Enough to change my shitty little existence for ever. I knew something awesome was going to happen, I had that tingle in my loins, did I tell you?"

"Yes, but I thought that was from one of the twins at the hair salon... When is the audition?"

"Next month, starts on the fifteenth, and you have to commit to at least two weeks because you never know when you're going to be selected. It's at the TV studios in Bristol. Will you come with me?"

I hesitate. "I don't think we'll both be able to get the time off, mate. Not in the middle of summer."

"No, no, I s'pose not." Tony scratches his head. "Will you help me with some interview practice, then? You're great with words. Actually, it's a shame you can't go and pretend to be me." He looks me up and down and I realise he is actually serious. "Quick squirt of man tan, dab of Just For Men-"

"No way," I swiftly close him down. "It's not going to happen. Anyway, talking of, er, disguises, have you seen Wes this morning? He's dressed like Willy Wonker, and he's dragging a huge trunk around with Wes the Wonder printed on it."

"Wes the Wanker, more like." Tony rolls his eyes. "He's performing at the midday show, God knows how he talked Morticia into that one. I thought the idea of today was to attract people to the gardens, not send them screaming into the traffic. Oh great, here comes someone else to piss on the parade."

Nasty Nat had sidled in. "So, this is where you're both hiding, is it? I should have known you'd be in the vicinity of cakes, Tony, that cap was made for you! And with a stomach that size you look like you're expecting hoglets! Ha ha ha!" Cornered in the tent, I wonder if it's possible to squeeze under the canvas. I take an involuntarily step backwards as Nasty Nat comes a little nearer, her beady eyes focusing on me. "You're not hiding from my husband, are you, Colin? I can't say I blame you, I don't suppose you want to be seen anywhere near him in case people compare you. Just joking, of course. He is much admired, though, he's got over two thousand followers on Instagram - have you even heard of Instagram, Colin?"

"No, Colin has real friends, not pretend cyber loons," Tony suddenly snaps, making us all jump. "I think any man who poses around in his pants on social media has some serious insecurity issues." He waggles his little finger at her. "I expect it's a size thing, they say it shrivels to the size of a peanut when you overdo the steroids." There is a stunned silence. Tony had stood up to Nasty Nat! Just how many cupcakes had he eaten? Nat swiftly recovers from her shock. "I'll pass that message on to my husband, shall I?" She edges to the entrance of the tent. "It's been nice knowing you, I wonder who'll tear you apart first, my husband or Mr Winter? When I heard all that shooting I assumed he was aiming at you two."

"Why would he want to shoot us?" I ask in trepidation.

"I should think he'd want to kill whoever planted those begonias."

"Are you actually serious?" Tony is incredulous. "Do you know how long that took? What's wrong with them?"

Nasty Nat's lips part in a deadly sneer-smile. "Well, if you're happy with them looking like that, then who am I to say anything? I mean, Colin's the head gardener, it's his responsibility, not mine. I'll just mind my own business...." She slides from the tent, still smirking.

"Blimey, Tone, thanks for your support and all that, but you shouldn't take on Nasty Nat, it's not worth it. She'll make your life a misery."

"Don't care mate," Tony is blasé, leaning back casually against the cake table. "I'll be out of here soon, so stuff her. People don't take the piss so easily when you've got a hundred grand sitting in your Santander 123 account. And stuff the Winters, too, the money-grabbing vultures." He pauses, bravado beginning to seep away. "We'd better check on the begonias, though, she's got me worried now. I did run out of slug pellets, I hope those slimy little gits haven't chomped the lot."

We leave the tent and scuttle around the side of the lawn, heading down into the woods on the lower path before reaching Wintersdell nestling in the hollow at the bottom of the slope. There, on the bank opposite the splendour of the mansion, six hundred bright pink begonias spell MINGERSDELL. *"Jesus,* Tone," I hiss, horrified. "That's not funny, that's not funny *at all.* This is a massive day for the Winters and the place is going to be heaving with visitors any minute. What the hell were you thinking?"

"I didn't plant it like that!" Tony cries. "It must be Chicken Ron, the bastard. He's sabotaged it!"

I panic. "We're going to have to re-plant it, pronto."

"But there isn't time, we're about to open."

"Colin!" A purple-faced Mr Winter yells up from the steps of the house. "I need you in the car park before there's a bloody riot. Get the morons to park in a straight line, can you, and make sure no one tries to get in through the hedge, I'm not having anyone duck the entrance fee."

"Ok, Mr Winter, I'm on my way." I turn back to Tony. "Thank Christ for that, he didn't notice. I'm going to have to go, mate, but we can't leave it like this. Just rip the plants out of the M and the G, quick as you can."

"You must be frigging joking!"

"Just do it, Tone, now. Before that sugar rush wears off."

With Tony's expletives ringing in my ears, I run through the grounds of the house and along the private driveway before carefully tip-toe-ing across the cattle grid into the car park. There is indeed some chaotic parking, with space filling rapidly and a crocodile of vehicles backed up along the drive. I manage to gain some semblance of control, directing drivers into orderly rows and guiding pedestrians to the entrance, where I hear protesting cries of "How much?" at the £9.50 entrance fee. As I help a woman with three young children (one balanced on her hip, one clinging to her leg, one face down on the ground screaming) unfold a zebra-print baby buggy, my mind wanders again to Sarah. She might be here today with her own family. What would her children be like? They wouldn't be screaming brats, I was sure of that, they'd be happy, funny, intelligent kids. Her husband would be a handsome heart-surgeon or a human-rights lawyer; they'd work together on worthy causes that made a real difference to people's lives. What would she think of me, working here at Hogpits ever since I dropped out of college? Thank Christ he didn't reply to my letters, that's what she'd think. She wouldn't be wrong.

"Here, you, what sort of sick bullshit is this?" An angry-faced man in a vest top accosts me. "An entrance fee as well as a parking fee? You lot are taking the complete piss."

I stare at him in confusion. "You don't have to pay for

parking, just to enter the gardens."

"Then why is there a guy at the top of the driveway taking money off all the cars as they come in? I've just given him a fiver."

Oh God. I can guess who that is.

The gardens are teeming with visitors. There are little knots of people at every stall and long queues have formed at the hot food vans. It's a magnificent turnout. Children keep emerging from the face-painting tent with their faces elaborately painted, the girls as lions or tigers and the boys as superheroes. I have to admit Nasty Nat is a brilliant artist and her husband is proving to be just as popular, with the highstriker attracting quite a crowd. Testosterone-filled roars of approval break out each time the bell rings.

Tony, having done his best to scrub a ton of deeply embedded soil from his fingernails, joins me in the queue for the hot dog van. Wearing our blue caps pulled right down, we hope to grab a quick bite to eat before being spotted by the Winters and given more tasks to perform. We don't want to be seen by Nasty Nat's husband either, but we wouldn't admit that to each other. Mrs Winter emerges from the throng by the coconut shy and spots us immediately. I can see her eyes shining icily from her translucent face. *Tough it out, there's a hot dog at stake.* I greet her with a beaming smile. "Wow, it's going really well, isn't it? And I can see lots of blue caps, so we must be doing a roaring trade in memberships."

"What happened at the home produce stall, Colin?

"I, er, I don't know. Is there something wrong?"

"You tell me." She fixes me with her benevolent smile that always signalled trouble. "Would you normally promote *skunk cabbage* as one of our delicious home-grown vegetables?"

"Skunk cabbage? Good God, no."

"So how did it get onto the stall? That's hardly going to

impress Brian, is it? Poor Mrs Heppenshaw retched her false teeth out when she smelled it."

I glance at Tony but he is staring straight ahead, willing us to reach the front of the queue before we are dispatched on another lunch-delaying task. "It's difficult to say how it could have got mixed up with the other produce, we never touch the stuff unless it's absolutely necessary. It must have been added accidentally. Somehow. Or other."

"I see." Mrs Winter considers me for a moment. "Where, exactly, is Ron?"

It is best to be honest. "I'm afraid I don't know."

"This is extremely disappointing, Colin, I specifically asked you to keep a close eye on him. What was the golden rule?"

"He mustn't be where people are."

"Precisely. You need to find him, the magic show's on shortly and I can't risk him appearing out of a hat like Alice in Wonderland's worst nightmare."

"I'm so sorry, I really don't know where's he got to. I'll go and look for him." I break off as a small boy runs past, his left cheek emblazoned with a bright red swastika.

"Oh my God, the face-painting tent!" Mrs Winter turns even whiter. "What the hell is Natalie thinking, leaving her paints unattended? She knows he'll drink anything."

I watch her stride back through the crowd, a blue Hogpits Heights scarf trailing out behind her. "Why didn't Morticia just pay Chicken Ron to take the day off?" Tony grumbles. He's made it to the front of the queue and orders our hot dogs. "She's such a bloody tight-arse. What is it with her and Chicken Ron, why the hell doesn't she just let Herr Winter deal with him? He's itching to sack him. Or shoot him."

"I honestly don't know why she's so protective of Ron, I've never fathomed it. He's having a very busy morning, that's for sure. But anyway, we're free for the time being so shove some ketchup on your dog and let's get to the magic show. Give Wes the Wonder some moral support."

Clutching our hot dogs, we make our way down to the main lawn where a large circle of visitors has gathered. All the hay bales are occupied and there is a row of people standing behind. Tony and I sit down on the grass next to a little boy who has 'Gobshite' painted on his forehead. I look warily at his parents, but they are engrossed in their phones and don't appear to have noticed. In the middle of the lawn there are two bar stools, placed about ten feet apart. Both have a bucket placed upside down on them. "He's pinched those stools from The Stag," Tony hisses. "Kenneth will have his guts for garters."

A voice booms out from behind the thatched folly. "Ladies and gentlemen! The magic show is about to begin!" There are 'oohs' and 'ahs' and 'shusshes'. "You are about to witness the unbelievable! You will not believe what you are about to see. Prepare to be dazzled!"

"He sounds like Bart Simpson," Tony mutters.

"Are you ready?"

"Yes!"

"Those who don't believe in magic will never find it. I ask again, are you ready?"

"YES!"

"Wes the Wonder can't hear you! Are-you-ready?"

"YEEESSS!"

Wes strides from behind the folly dressed in a black tuxedo and a long red cape. He marches purposefully around the ring, before stopping in front of a little girl, her face painted as a cat. Her parents beam back at Wes, delighted their daughter has been chosen. Wes clears his throat. "Now then, what is your name – Pussy Galore?"

"Jesus, that's inappropriate," Tony groans.

"No, it's Olivia."

"Ah. And what have you got behind your ear, Olivia?"

Wes asks.

The little girl blinks her slanty cat's eyes in surprise. "Nothing."

"Yes, you have got something there," Wes insists. "What on earth is it?" The little girl feels behind her ears, looking up at Wes in confusion. "Can't you feel it? Really? There's a massive growth on the side your head!" Olivia looks scared now, as do her parents, their smiles frozen to their faces.

Wes reaches behind Olivia's ear and produces an egg with a flourish. He holds it aloft and everyone cheers, not without some relief. Wes moves on down the line, stopping in front of a thick-set man, his arms covered in tattooed sleeves, an empty bottle of Becks at his feet. "Ah. Hello, my good man. Now, what's this I see behind your ear?"

Dark sarcastic eyes glare back. "I expect it's an egg, innit?"

"Right, right," Wes moves quickly on. He spins on his heel dramatically, the cape twirling around him. He stops dead and points to a young boy who blinks back at him through very thick spectacles. The little boy's face lights up as Wes whips a deck of playing cards out of his pocket. "Hello there, what's your name – Mr Magoo?"

"Blimey, he needs to work on his rapport-building," I mutter, as I see the boy's mother scowling at Wes.

"Edward, is it? Now, pick a card, Edward. Actually, you'd better let Mummy do it, I doubt you can see much out of those milk bottles. Pick a card, Mum, but don't tell me what it is. Ok? Right, now put it back in the deck."

Edward's stern-faced mother slaps the card back in the pack but Wes is oblivious to her annoyance, focusing instead on the pack of cards and adopting a wide-legged stance. He places his left hand on his forehead, pretending to think, then produces the Queen of spades from the deck. He holds it out to the woman. "Is this your card?"

"No."

"Oh. Er," Wes flicks through the pack and plucks out the ten of clubs. "Is this the card?"

"No."

"Are you sure? What was it, then?"

"The eight of diamonds."

"Really?" Wes shuffles deftly through the deck. "That's very odd, because the eight of diamond's not even in the deck. Where on earth can it be?" He pats himself down, then smiles at the woman. "Tell me something, how impressed would you be if your card was in my pocket?"

"Very!"

"Yeah, so would I," mutters Tony.

Grinning broadly, Wes fumbles in his trouser pocket. His smile begins to fade as he feels frantically about himself.

"It's on the ground," Edward says solemnly

"S-sorry?"

"I saw it fall out of your hand when you were trying to hide it in your pocket."

"Um, er... Gosh! What's that behind your ear?"

"Pass me one of those plastic knives," Tony moans. "I want to slash my wrists."

Wes' moon face looms up in front of us. "My, my, what have we here? A couple of garden gnomes, by the look of it!" Everyone laughs. "What's the collective noun for this, then, a retardation of gnomes?" *Cringe.* "There's no place like gnome, is there, lads?" We smile at him weakly. "Ok. Colin, have you finished with your napkin?"

I hand Wes the greasy paper napkin that had been my hot dog wrapper. Wes straightens it out and holds it up for everyone to see. "Behold, a napkin. A whole napkin." He tears it in half and holds up the two pieces. "Behold! The napkin is completely torn in two." He makes a fist with his left hand and stuffs the two pieces into it. "Now, ladies and gentlemen, with a little bit of Wes the Wonder magic..." He fiddles about a bit, then blows into his fist, uncurling it to reveal a whole napkin. "Ta da!" Everyone whoops and applauds; even Tony looks impressed.

"Thank you everyone, you are a wonderful audience. And now, you are about to witness another *wonder*-ful spectacle." Wes moves into the centre of the ring with the bar stools and the upside-down buckets. "This is something truly amazing - the incredible Bun-sporter." Wes slowly lifts the first bucket to reveal one of the brown lop-eared rabbits from the petting farm. There is a collective 'Aaawww' from the crowd as Wes holds the little creature up, its back legs peddling furiously in the air. "Through the magic of the Bun-sporter, you will see this real live bunny, Loppy, disappear in front of your very eyes. He will be transported through space and will reappear under that bucket over there." Wes points to the second bar stool. Tony and I glance at each other, unconvinced. Wes places Loppy back on the first stool and after a bit of a tussle, puts the bucket back over him. He raises his arms to the sky and closes his eyes. "Wes the Wonder commands the great and powerful Bun-sporter to work its special magic and transport little Loppy through time." He taps the top of the bucket and lifts it to reveal an empty stool.

Collective gasps fly around the ring. "As you can see, Loppy has completely vanished. He is now moving through time. We can help the transporting process by saying the magic words. *Avacado kedavro.*" Wes begins to walk slowly towards the second bar stool, arms stretching skywards. *"Salivio hexico–"*

"Why does he have to sound like such a dickhead?" Tony whispers.

"Expelliarmus"

"Expelli-anus, more like. That sausage was well dodgy."

"Inbetigo totalo–"

"What the–"

"*Ala kazam!*" Wes reaches the second bucket and whips it up, flinging it behind him. There is Loppy, sitting on the second barstool, nose twitching.

Incredulous cries of 'No way!' ring round the audience, followed by thunderous applause. Tony's mouth falls open. "What the hell was that?" he gasps. "Some sort of voodoo shit?"

I might have been impressed too, but I can make out a writhing bulge under Wes' cape as he stoops to take a bow. "I think, maybe, he ought to make a quick exit."

Too late. As Wes bends for another sweeping bow, the original Loppy slips from his cape and scampers across the grass. The second rabbit jumps from the barstool and the two identical bunnies hop around the ring together. Wes, totally engrossed in receiving his accolades, only realises something is wrong when the applause is drowned out by loud booing. He turns to find the rabbits behind him as they try to nibble the hem of his cape. "Oh, er, ha ha! Rabbits, eh? What are they like, multiplying already." The audience starts to get up, some flapping their hands dismissively in Wes' direction, others muttering and moaning about fraudsters and trickery. "No, no, don't go, I've got other tricks, I'll fetch the hedge-cutter ... who wants to see someone sawn in half?"

More groans and catcalls. The crowd drifts away as Wes slumps onto one of the barstools. Tony and I hurry forward to chase the rabbits around the ring, being led a merry dance before finally managing to scoop them up. We carry them over to Wes who nods at us gloomily. "Cheers, lads. What an absolute bloody disaster that was."

"You did really well, Wes," I try to cheer him. "Didn't he, Tone?"

"Er, yeah, yeah, brilliant." Tony claps Wes awkwardly on the back, trying to keep hold of the wriggling rabbit with one hand. "At least, the bits that worked were brilliant. Tough crowd, that's all."

"And I really don't know what they're complaining about," I say, "I mean what do they think, that the tricks are actual magic?"

"Oh, I don't blame them," Wes sighs dejectedly. "It's the first rule of the magic circle – never disclose your secrets. Nope, that's it for me, I can't do anything right." He looks woefully around at the empty hay bales. "All I want to do is entertain people, hear them gasp, make them cheer, I love that. People always remember a great performance, don't they? It stays with you, even if you can't recall the event itself, you remember the performer and how they made you feel. I like to think I did that, I made that happen. I create a brilliant memory for someone, like a photograph." He shrugs. "No one's going to remember this, are they? Not for the right reasons, anyway. And it's not as if the DJ-ing is going well either, I can't keep up with the competition; people want Bose systems, fancy lighting and 3D projections and I can't afford any of that, not on my earnings. The Winters aren't even paying me for this performance, they said I'd get the benefits of exposure." He gives a hollow laugh then brightens a little. "Thank God I've still got my singing. Perhaps I should just stick to that, it's obviously my true vocation."

Tony shoots me a look of mock-horror. "Come on mate, it's all about resilience in show business, isn't it? Do you think Jeremy Clarkson let little setbacks stop him fulfilling his dreams? Of course not. He's risen from the ashes like a violent racist Phoenix and now he's more popular than ever. Look, here's someone come to say well done."

Edward's mother approaches, face like thunder, dragging her son along by his arm. "Look at this." She brandishes two halves of a twenty-pound note in Wes' face. "Edward did this. He said not to worry, Wes *the Wonder* will make it whole again."

Tony and I back quickly away, muttering about putting the rabbits back, and perform a quick march to the petting farm, depositing the bunnies back into their run. Over in the paddock, we can see Nasty Nat as she leads a pony around, a chubby little girl sitting astride. Presumably the face-painting has been abandoned. Fred is under the chestnut tree, studiously chewing on what looks suspiciously like the remnants of a hoglet hat. As Tony and I wearily ascend the grassy path to the top lawn, a familiar figure bounds down toward us, spikes of hair sticking straight up, a long black raincoat billowing out around him.

"Hey up, it's Bondage Batman," Tony exclaims.

"Is that Louie? He's, he's running," I half-whisper in astonishment.

"What's he shouting?"

"I don't know."

Louie skids to an abrupt halt in front of us. "I've found her, Unck! I've found her!"

I feel the ground shift under me. *Did I dare to hope?* "Do you mean Sarah?"

"No, not Sarah, but the next best thing, her mother Rowena. Look, I've found her on Facebook."

Louie holds up his phone and a Facebook profile is in front of me: Rowena Kremer. "I'd only searched under her married name before, but I suddenly thought what if the marriage failed again and she's gone back to her maiden name? And she has!"

"Great work Sherlock!" Tony thumps him on the back. He peers at the picture on Louie's phone. "Do you recognise her, Col?"

"I'm not sure," I frown, examining the photograph. I see a full-faced, dark-haired woman, aged around fifty. "I only met her a couple of times and I can't really recall her face. This woman looks too young to be Sarah's mother."

Tony snorts. "That's because it's a bloody old photo! You can see Blockbuster Video in the background, for Christ's sake; how long has that been closed? Come on, there can't be many Rowena Kremers in the world."

"Her profiles states she lives in Wilton," Louie chips in. "So she's local. It must her."

"Have you sent her a Friend's request?" Tony asks.

Louie shakes his head sadly. "Nobody accepts a Friend's request from Louie Walsh."

"Fair point. Not to worry, I'll send one." Tony whips his phone out of his trouser pocket.

"Now, hang on a minute," I panic. "I need to give this some thought. And anyway, you can't just link up with anyone you like on Facebook, can you, I mean, make friends with a total stranger?"

"Well, yeah, that's kind of the point. You can send a request to anyone, just like this, see?"

"No, no! I need to think how to approach her, I mean, what to say, how to word it–"

"Sorry, Col, I've already sent it."

I stare at him in horror. "But she doesn't know who you are! Don't you think she'll find that bizarre, or creepy? You can't just randomly befriend someone, she'll think you're a stalker, she might report you. Oh God, this is a disaster."

"She's accepted it."

"What, already? Just like that?"

"Yep, in the words of the great Tommy Cooper, just like that. Not many women can resist the Tony Chisholm profile pic. Thank Christ for Photoshop. Come on, let's go grab a cuppa in The Hut and have a proper snoop through her life." Tony grips my shoulder. "This is a massive breakthrough, mate, we're so close now. We're about to find Sarah!"

They both beam at me, their faces shining with excitement, but my stomach churns. I'm not ready to see inside Sarah's life;

to suddenly go from knowing nothing to seeing everything, it's too much, I'm not prepared for it. "I'll catch up with you later, lads," I say, feeling terrible as their expressions fall. "I must find Chicken Ron, I promised Mrs Winter I'd keep an eye on him. I can't risk any more mishaps – Brian Beardmore and the reporter from Wiltshire Life will be here soon and there'll be hell to pay if anything goes wrong." I feel their disappointed gaze as I walk swiftly away, taking the lower path down to the lake. Chicken Ron often hides in the reeds, popping up to lob stones into the water by the bridge, hoping to soak visitors as they peer down looking for fish. I know I am being a coward, but I'm scared at what I might find in Sarah's life. What if the heart-surgeon husband and the beautiful gifted children don't exist? What if she's sad and alone, a recluse, scarred for life by my supposed rejection? No, I'm not ready to face it.

Chicken Ron isn't in the reeds so I set about scouring the usual places for him – under the wheel barrow, inside the hen house, behind the compost bins – but to no avail. There are still plenty of visitors in the gardens and quite a queue for the horse-riding. The tube slide in the playground is full of kids, so Chicken Ron obviously isn't hiding in there. A little boy passes me, exclaiming to his green-faced father, "That roundabout was brilliant, Dad! Can we do it again?" As I round the sheds that contain the animal feed, I see two figures entwined in the small alleyway between the sheds. I reel in shock – it's Cafe Girl and Nasty Nat's husband! Locked together in a passionate embrace, they don't see me. I take a step backwards but catch a shovel as it leans against the shed, sending it to the ground with an angry clatter. The couple spring apart, guilty faces swivelling in my direction. I turn and run. Head down, I pump my legs as fast as I can, shooting back past the playground and the paddocks, startling the line of visitors at the horse-riding who stare at me in astonishment. Did the pair of them see it was me? They must have. They probably thought I'd been watching them for ages, rubbing my hands up and down my thighs like some sweaty-palmed pervert. I dart through the petting farm and plunge into the shaded shelter of the lower path. Lungs at bursting point, I slow to a jog then to walking pace. My heart begins to calm and rational thoughts return. Just hold on a minute, why am I so worried about what they think of *me?* I haven't done anything wrong, I wasn't the one snogging the face off a teenager while my wife was less than a hundred yards away. I feel a pang of sympathy for Nasty Nat, traipsing the horses up and down the paddock, completely unaware of her husband's treachery. I didn't like Nat, but surely I should tell her what I'd just seen. That had to be the right thing to do, didn't it? My bowels protest at the thought. Maybe it's better to keep out of it. *Easier,* I mean. *Coward. Wimp. Weed.*

I reach the sanctuary of The Hut and step thankfully inside. Two gloomy faces meet my arrival. "We've been doing some research on Rowena," Louie informs me. "She's got two hundred and seventy three friends. There are three Sarah's, but none of them are your Sarah."

The wave of disappointment is tinged with relief. "How do you know they're not my Sarah?"

"They're ancient. Relics, in fact."

"She's got the most boring profile I've ever had the misfortune to snoop through," Tony groans, flicking the kettle on. "Tedious check in after tedious bloody check in: 'Look at me, I'm in Costa Coffee, now I'm at the petrol station, ooh, I just blinked!' Give it a rest, love, nobody gives the shiniest shit."

"Does she mention being with her daughter in any of them?" I ask, tentatively. "Or with her grandchildren, perhaps?"

"No, 'fraid not, there's no mention of Sarah at all."

"I reckon she must be dead," Louie says.

"Are there any photos?"

"Yeah, loads, but they're mainly of food. Is she a chef or something? Here, have a look." Tony passes his phone to me and I scroll through the pictures. There are photographs of roast dinners, plates piled high, massive slices of chocolate cake, Costa gingerbread men... I scroll right through to the end but there don't appear to be any people photos at all. There are a few pictures of possessions dotted in amongst the food shots; a Michael Kors bag, a gleaming black Mazda MX5, a dubious-looking Rolex watch, but no family photos whatsoever. Was this Sarah's mother? If so, what had happened to Sarah; were they no longer in touch with one another?

"It's not a dead end, mate," Tony asserts, reading my mind. "Not by a long road. We can send Rowena a message and explain all about Sarah. I'm sure she'll reply, she was quick enough to respond to my Friend request, wasn't she?"

"Yes, but I'd like to have a think about it first, Tone, so hold fire." I rub my forehead. "It's been a bizarre day, all in all. My head's spinning."

"And don't forget to reply to Mum," Louie reminds me. "She's messaged you again about dinner tomorrow night. She says you're to bring Ginny."

I sigh, not relishing the prospect. I didn't know how Cath had persuaded Ginny to see me again, but then my sister was always so forceful perhaps poor Ginny hadn't been given much of a choice.

We jump as the door to The Hut flies open. Mrs Winter stands in the doorway. Backlit against the pale grey sky, her eyes blaze from her head, and I'm reminded of The Iron Man, the Ted Hughes creation that terrified me as a boy. I feel much the same now.

"Ah, Mrs Winter, there you are." Tony attempts nonchalance. "We were just monitoring social media and marvelling at all the great comments flooding in on the Hogpits Facebook page."

"Really." The way Mrs Winter spits the word makes it sound more like 'bullshit'. "That's quite a coincidence because I've been looking at Facebook too." She waves an iPad at us. "I've been particularly enjoying the photographs our visitors have been posting. Oh yes, some are really very interesting indeed." I have the horrible feeling a hair-dryer moment is imminent. "This picture, as an example, taken during the tour of Wintersdell this morning. It's the view from the drawing room. Perhaps you could explain something to me, Tony, about the view?"

We take a hesitant step forwards and peer at the picture on the iPad. Someone had posted a picture of the bank of begonias, only they hadn't photographed the whole word. Just the first half. There, in bold pink letters, is the word 'MINGE'.

I fidget nervously at the gate to the gardens, sweltering in my new Hogpits fleece. The Wiltshire Life reporter bringing Brian Beardmore has got lost and everyone is on edge as we're running so late. Nasty Nat is standing uncomfortably close to me but I can't look her in the eye, my secret lying heavily in my lower intestine. My buttocks clench involuntarily as she edges closer still. "Looking good, Colin," she hisses in my ear. "I love what you've done with your hair; how do you get it to come out of one nostril like that?"

I quickly rub my nose as Mrs Winter's ghostly face looms in front of mine again. "Have you shaved, Colin?" She sniffs me like a bloodhound. "Is that TCP, did you cut yourself? Your hair could do with a comb, it's got very long."

"I went to the hairdressers yesterday."

"Really? Perhaps you should ask for your money back." I hear Nasty Nat snort and Mrs Winter rounds on her. "Why are you here, Natalie? You're not part of the welcoming party, you should be down with the horses. Off you go, and make sure to clean up any duck poo on the paths as you go. I don't want Brian slipping over and breaking a hip, he sues at the drop of a hat. Chop chop."

I let out a sigh of relief as Nat slinks furiously away. "Colin, for goodness sake do something with your eyebrows, they're extremely unwieldy, Brian will think he's being pursued around the gardens by Odd Job." I wipe a hand across my forehead feeling beads of perspiration break out on my upper lip. "There's no need to be nervous," Mrs Winter snaps. "Just remember what we rehearsed, and don't speak unless you're spoken to." *I'm not nervous, it's the damned fleece, I'm being roasted alive.* "Where's Ron?"

"Tony's taken him to the..." *Stag* "...Wholesalers. They won't be back until closing."

"Good, good." Mrs Winter is all twitchy, unable to keep still. "God, where have they got to? Seriously, how can anyone get lost these days, it's not difficult to follow a sat-nav, is it? All the visitors are leaving and the fizz has gone right out of the Cava." The ladies from the tea room are lined up along the path, smart in their new blue aprons, waiting to greet the guests with miniature Eccles cakes and scones. "For goodness sake, Pauline, stop slouching!" Mrs Winter yells. Pauline, hunched over with osteoporosis, does her best to pull herself upright on the handrail. At least Cafe Girl isn't amongst them, I'm dreading having to face her again. What will she do – ignore me as she usually does, pretend nothing happened? I feel even hotter as I watch Mr Winter pacing up and down the path, barking directions into his mobile phone. He gestures from the gate.

"They're here! Oh my God, they're here!" Mrs Winter is beside herself. "First positions everyone, NOW!"

Heads crane to catch the first glimpse of Brian Beardmore MBE, who arrives dressed in wellies and jeans, looking just like he does on the telly, smiley and genial, his calm and soothing voice so familiar. There are two other men with him, a reporter with a notebook and a bored-looking photographer. The Winters flutter and titter around the threesome, pressing flutes of Cava into their hands. I see Wes hovering by the tea rooms, hopeful of an introduction, but the Winters have a tight rein over their guests, with carefully orchestrated greetings only. I wait for the tour of the gardens to begin, my face aching from smiling, sweat trickling freely down my back. As the little party walk past me, I fall into line behind. Brian turns back with a friendly smile. "Hello there, I'm Brian."

"Hi, Brian, it's lovely to meet you." I shake his outstretched hand, cringing as I know how sticky mine is. "I'm Colin, the head gardener."

"Colin's worked here for many years," Mrs Winter tells him, gently guiding him back to within earshot of the reporter. "Our staff are extremely loyal and they tend to stay with us for ages. Take Ronald, for example, his family has been here for twelve generations."

The reporter's ears prick up. "Really? Could we meet Ronald?"

"Oh, alas, he's taking a sabbatical. Fully funded by us, of course, people come first, that's our motto here at Hogpits. If you take care of your people they will take care of your, er, land. We'll go down to the Family Farm first, shall we? You'll find Hogpits has something for everyone." *Even a giant minge.*

I can tell Brian isn't too enamoured with the rabbits and guinea pigs, but he has a cuddle with Loppy as the photographer takes some snaps, smiling indulgently even when the wriggling rabbit kicks him right in the face with a big podgy foot. Fred is a mere white speck in the distance as he has been tethered right at the end of the far field, but I sense him watching on apprehensively.

As we move over to the paddocks, Brian is rather taken

with the meadow orchids, pointing them out to the reporter and asking the photographer to take some close-up shots while the Winters fidget impatiently. "Over here are some of our beautiful horses," says Mrs Winter, finally managing to regain their attention. She purses her lips, looking around for Nasty Nat, annoyed she isn't standing to attention in the agreed position. "Where has Natalie got to? The ponies have been extremely popular with the children today, Hogpits is such a family-friendly environment."

A blood-curling scream stops us in our tracks, the horses jolting away in alarm. "What the?" Mr Winter stops himself. "What was that?"

Another shriek rings out from the direction of the stables. "Arghhhhh!"

"Colin, go and check please." Mrs Winter tries to move the group on, but the reporter and photographer make a break for the stable yard so we have no choice but to follow them. The yard is empty, save for a massive pile of manure in the corner. "Nothing to see here," Mrs Winter declares. "Let's move on." Suddenly, the stable door flies open and Nasty Nat's backside appears. She's tugging something out of the stables and it appears to be resisting ... Oh my God - it's Cafe Girl.

"Get off me, you're hurting me! Get off! Get off!"

"I'm going to kill you, you fat bitch!" Her hands full of brown hair, Nasty Nat drags a wailing Cafe Girl out of the stables and into the yard. "I saw you, slag! I saw you - you're fucking dead!" Bent over double they tussle in the yard, moving each other around sideways like a grotesque crab. Nat tries to throw some punches but Cafe Girl is gripping her arms. Wrestling her victim to the corner of the yard, Nasty Nat shakes free and shoves Cafe Girl head first into the pile of manure. There's a revolting squelch. Nasty Nat scoops up a handful of muck as Cafe Girl scrambles to her feet and makes a bid for freedom, but she slips in the mud and falls flat, just as a furious Nasty Nat heaves the glutinous clot of manure as hard as she can. It catapults through the air and hits Mrs Winter full in the face.

There is a sudden silence. I am sure I hear Fred fart. As the brown sludge slides down Mrs Winter's face onto her cream linen jacket, we are like Mannequins, frozen in time: Nasty Nat stock-still, Mr Winter open-mouthed, reporter grinning fixedly. The only motion is the photographer's finger on the camera shutter. Cafe Girl moves first. Picking herself up she runs from the yard, sobbing loudly.

"I'm s-so sorry, Mrs Winter," Nasty Nat stammers. "I didn't mean to."

"Get out," Mrs Winter hisses, so quietly that I shiver, despite the fleece.

"But you don't understand, she–"

"GET OUT!" Mr Winter roars. "And don't come back. You're fired."

Nasty Nat turns white. "No, please, you can't fire me, please-"

"OUT! And don't even think about asking for this month's pay because you can whistle for it. Get out of my sight."

"But please-"

"GO!"

I feel awful for Nasty Nat as she trudges, head down, out of the yard. In the distance, I catch sight of a bulky figure as it slinks away into the trees behind the stables. "Look, maybe it's best not to be too hasty."

"When I want advice on staff management from a pansy-pushing poofter, I'll bloody well ask for it." Mr Winter shoves his beetroot face right up to mine.

The reporter, pen poised, pretends to flick back through his notes. "What was that Hogpits motto again, Gordon? If you take care of your people–"

"Shut your face, you jumped-up back-street hack. And if you print one word of this I'll tell the Grand Master what you get up to with his wife every Tuesday evening. You won't be so much black-balled as no-balled by the time he's finished with you."

There is a short exclamatory squeak from behind us. A pale-faced Brian Beardmore MBE is looking on, his eyes as big as saucers. Mrs Winter scrapes the muck from her face with both hands and flicks it to the ground. She gives Brian a bright smile. "Who's for some tart?"

Chapter Ten

I stretch my aching back before making another attempt to draft a message to Rowena. Tony had already texted me his suggested approach: 'Yo Ro! im messaging you for my mate cos hes not on Facebook himself due to his work in under cover ops (he'd inserted a wink face). He needs to speak to your daughter asap. PM her deets'.

My efforts were a little different, the latest reading: 'Dear Ms Kremer, I am sorry to approach you in this manner. My friend used to know your daughter Sarah and would love to catch up with her again. They are old college friends. Would you be kind enough to pass Sarah's contact details on to me? Kind regards Tony Chisholm'.

I screw the piece of paper up into a tight ball and fling it in the direction of the bin. It misses and falls to the floor, where it joins ten others. This is impossible. I can't say who I am because she might well remember the Colin Hector who broke her daughter's heart, so I am trying to be as neutral as possible. If I get it wrong she might 'unfriend' Tony and that could be the end of that.

I don't have time to start another draft as I am due at

Cath's for dinner. She has invited Ginny too, and a couple of David's friends who I hadn't met before. I don't want to go; I'd have preferred to stay in and re-read Sarah's letters from start to finish, but it was too late to back out now. I stand up with a groan; I'd given my muscles several good soakings in Radox, but they still throb from the exertions of Open Day. Despite the many mishaps, the day had actually been a tremendous success, commercially speaking. Mrs Winter, having recovered from her unexpected mud bath, had been delightedly counting the completed membership forms as I left. She'd pressed a five-pound note into my hand to 'get yourself and Tony a drink'.

I pick up the balls of messages and drop them into the waste paper bin on top of the letter from the crematorium. It was another reminder to collect Dad's ashes: if I didn't do so within the next four weeks they were to be scattered around the crematorium gardens. I must go and get them, but what am I going to do with them? I had intended scattering them amongst the daffodil bulbs in the front garden, but somehow it didn't feel right now, as if he'd betrayed the house when he'd betrayed me. I'll have to ask Cath. She'll know what to do for the best, she always does.

I carefully iron the creases from my non-iron shirt, embarrassed to be putting on exactly the same outfit as the last time I saw Ginny. The lighting had been pretty dim in Truffles, perhaps she wouldn't remember. I examine my face in the hallway mirror. I look tired, the dark circles under my eyes aging me well beyond my years. Oh, for goodness sake, is that another Dennis Healey? It is! A randomly long eyebrow hair is sticking out. It hadn't been there this morning, how the hell had it grown an entire inch during the day? *Ridiculous.* I look down at Mum, beaming up at me from her gilded surround. "I wish you were here, Mum," I whisper, even though I don't know why I'm whispering,

Dad no longer around to mock me. "I feel a bit lost. Cath thinks I'm having a mid-life crisis, what do you think? Why am I dwelling on the past so much, why can't I move on?" One of Mum's quotes floats down the hallway, as clear as if she were here with me. "Sometimes you just have to dare to do it, darling. Life's too short to wonder what might have been."

I pluck the last message from the bin and straighten out the ball, texting the message to Tony to send to Rowena. *Just do it.* I haven't even left the house when he replies: 'Done!' I marvel, as I often do, at how quickly Tony is able to text, but then feel a stab of anxiety as I remember some of his auto-correct fails, such as the time I sent him a message asking how a date had gone and his reply had been: 'We went to Nandos and then i killed her in the woods on the way home.' When I pointed out that killing her seemed a little extreme, I received: 'Shit man i meant KISSED!!!!'

There isn't time to worry about it now. Cath doesn't tolerate lateness. I pedal at a moderate speed so as not to arrive all hot and sweaty, and cycle into Cath's drive just a few minutes after seven. *Be charming, be chatty, don't make too many faux pas, just the six or seven, try and keep it below your usual foot-in-mouth average.* I check my phone but there's nothing from Tony. Rowena clearly hasn't replied yet.

Hearing laughter from the patio, I duck under the honeysuckle archway into the back garden. Cath and David are sitting at the wooden patio table with another couple, a huge jug of Pimms accompanying an empty bottle of Chardonnay. "Colin!" Cath jumps up somewhat unsteadily and waves me over. "There you are." She looks at me expectantly. "Where's Ginny?"

My stomach lurches. "Isn't she here?"

"You what?" Cath's jovial mood instantly evaporates. "For God's sake, Colin, you were supposed to pick her up!"

Oh crap. Cath had arranged for me to cycle to hers so we could get a taxi together. "Honestly, I give up, I really do. Poor Ginny, she was looking forward to arriving at a dinner party with an escort for a change, she hates having to turn up on her own. Well done you."

"I'm sorry, I forgot," I mumble pathetically. "I'll cycle round there now." I pause as the others look away in embarrassment. "Um, where did you say she lives?"

"Jesus H bloody Christ, don't bother, I'll go and call her." Cath flounces towards the French windows, calling over her shoulder "This is Helen and Harry. Helen and Harry, this is Colin, a gormless twerp."

Harry grins and holds out his hand. "How do you do?" He has thinning ginger hair and an open freckly face. Helen is short and petite, with dark pixie-cropped hair.

I sit down next to David as he plucks a can of Budweiser from a bucket of ice and hands it to me. "There you go, lover boy."

I smile ruefully. "I think gormless twerp is the more accurate description."

"Oh, I shouldn't worry about it," Harry remarks jovially. "On our first date I took Helen to see Salisbury playing at home, but I bumped into an old friend in the toilets at half time and we got chatting. We ended up leaving the game and going for a beer. It was several hours before I remembered Helen was up in the stands."

"I was still sitting there," Helen chuckles. "With a very numb bum. When he returned, completely pissed, he tried to tell me he'd been abducted by aliens. I should have known then what I was letting myself in for."

"Do you both work with David?" I ask.

"Yes," Helen confirms, "we both work in banking, but please don't judge us."

"You're with a bunch of bankers, Col!" David roars,

then quickly composes himself as Cath returns, her face like thunder.

"Ginny's already on her way," she sniffs. "When it became obvious you weren't coming she called a cab. I told her your bike was knackered, so you came straight here. I hated lying to her, but I wanted to spare her any more pain, especially after everything's she's been through."

There is an awkward silence. I glance at Harry and Helen and see they are trying not to laugh. "Where's Louie?" I ask brightly.

"Up in his room." Cath helps herself to a glass of Pimms. "He's Skyping his friend in Transylvania." Her face brightens. "Did he tell you he won a prize at school for his video? We were so proud, I think it's the first thing he's ever won anything, isn't it, David?"

Her husband nods. "We had an inkling Louie wasn't going to be one of life's winners during his first sports day. He entered the sack race, but tripped over on the start line and got all tangled up in the sack. Try as he might, he just couldn't find his way out. Everyone was pointing and laughing at the twitching brown sack in the middle of the playing field. It looked like it contained an epileptic ferret."

This is too much for Helen who snorts loudly, Pimms escaping from the side of her mouth. It sets us all off, even Cath, and the tension dissipates. As I relax into the chatter with my beer, I'm aware someone is hovering just over my shoulder. "Oh, hello." I turn round in my chair. "Er, Ginny?" I peer at the figure against the low evening sun. She is dressed in a pair of baggy jeans, a white hooded sweatshirt and a blue 'I'm a Hog' baseball cap pulled down so low it almost covers her eyes.

"Yes, hello Colin." It *is* Ginny. She steps forward and I rise, unsure how to greet her. I go to kiss her cheek but the rim of her cap catches me in the eye and half-blinded, I jerk back, my teeth grazing her nose. *Gormless twerp.* Why am I so socially awkward, *why?* "I thought we might be coming on your bike," she tells me, rubbing the bridge of her nose. "That's why I'm dressed like this."

Helen excuses herself and flees into the house. "Now that would have been romantic, wouldn't it, Col?" David slaps me on the back, saving me from having to lie. He hands Ginny a glass of orange juice. "A bicycle made for two! Never mind, next time maybe."

"It's such a coincidence," I blab, for something to say. "About your cap, I mean. We were giving the same ones out at our Open Day at Hogpits yesterday."

"Yes, I know, I was there."

"Were you?" I stare at her in surprise. "I didn't see you."

"No. You didn't notice me."

"Grub's up!" Cath announces. "Let's go inside, it's getting chilly out here."

We follow Cath into the dining room and take our places at the polished oak table. I sit opposite Ginny but she doesn't remove the baseball cap, making it virtually impossible to see her eyes. As the others chat and roar with laughter together, I make pitiful attempts to start a conversation. Ginny is monosyllabic. Is a date supposed to be this excruciating? It's my fault, of course; she's upset because I hadn't called round for her as planned. What a total buffoon I am, I could have driven us here if I'd borrowed Ron Burgundy from Tony's brother. Well OK, perhaps that wasn't the best idea but I could have gone round in a taxi to collect her, at least made some effort to make her feel special. Instead, I'd humiliated her. At least she'd still turned up, although she really looks as if she wishes she hadn't. Think of something interesting to say. "Er, how's your clematis doing?"

"Fine."

"Keeping it, er, moist enough?"

"Yes."

Cath also tried to engage her in chat but soon gave up as the wine continued to flow. Dinner was blackened chicken wings with hot chilli dip and salad, followed by blackened cod with cauliflower rice. According to David, none of it was supposed to be blackened. I do my best to eat but I'm too tired to be hungry and Ginny pushes her food listlessly around the plate. As everyone tucks into a dessert of cheese and biscuits, I check my phone under the table. There is still nothing from Tony. "Who's that, Colin?" Cath is on to me straight away. "Who are you texting?"

Cornered, I fumble for a reason to be using my phone at the dinner table. "It's just a friend, who's, er, having some issues."

"Oh, really, a friend you say?"

Deflect attention, think of something interesting. "Yes, he's uncovered an affair, between two work colleagues, a woman and a married man. My friend doesn't know whether he should tell the married man's wife, or just keep quiet about it."

"Ooh, that's a tough one," David says, pressing a chunk of brie onto a TUC biscuit. "People tend to shoot the messenger, don't they? I'd mind my own business."

"I'd tell the poor cow," Helen slurs. "I can't be doing with that kind of stuff, she deserves to know what a piece of shit she's married to. It's not fair to keep quiet about it, I bet everyone knows apart from her. I'd definitely tell her."

"Send her an anonymous message, you mean?" Harry grins.

"Yep."

"We've got Scruples somewhere." Cath rummages around in the sideboard and pulls out a box with 'The game of moral dilemmas' printed on the lid. I groan inwardly. What have I started? Every time Cath makes us play this it ends in tears. "Right, here's a question for you bankers." She reads from a yellow card. "Harry, six months after moving into your new home you find a large stash of money under the floorboards. The previous owner had died. Do you report the find to his heirs?"

"Cripes," Harry strokes his chin. "How much is it, do you reckon?"

"I don't know! Shit-loads, say."

"Well, um, my first thought is sod it, finders keepers, and no one knows it's there, but what if one of his heirs is really badly off, or sick, or disabled ... No, I don't deserve it, the money belongs to the dead guy's family. I'd give it up. Although, I might keep some of it. No, I'd give it up. Most of it, anyway."

He is rewarded with a generous round of applause. "Spoken like a true banker." Cath turns to her husband. "Right then, Hubbins, here's your question: You have a clear view of a neighbour who does yoga in the nude. Do you ask them to close the curtains?"

"Good God no, not if it's some supple young thing like the Robinson's au pair across the way at number seventeen. She never pulls the curtains in her room and when their lights are on you can pretty much see everything from the window at the top of our stairs." He beams around the table, oblivious to his wife's sour expression.

"Assume it's a hairy-arsed brickie called Trevor," Cath says, icily.

"Well, it would depend if Trevor's wife was joining in, and how bendy she was." David breaks off, finally registering Cath's displeasure. "I would look away," he says firmly. "No, no, I mean, I would ask them to close the curtains. Definitely. No question."

"Colin." *Please no, not me, why did I start this?* "If you could choose to have either one true friend or one good lover for the rest of your life, which would you choose?"

There are 'ooohs' and chuckles around the table. "That's a bloody easy one!" David roars, then quickly buries his face in his wine glass as he realises it isn't.

I shift uncomfortably from one buttock to the other. My eyes flick inadvertently at Ginny, but she is studiously rolling a grape around her plate and does not look up. "Um, well, having a true friend is really something very special, whereas a lover –"

"A good lover," David asserts.

"A good lover would be very nice." *Not to mention a bloody miracle.* "But would that be as important as friendship, in the long run? I mean, er, what does everybody else think?"

"You're right, Colin," Helen nods vigorously. "Once the heady excitement of the knicker-ripping, crash-bang-wallop sex wears off, and it always does, you don't want to be left with some dickwad you can't stand the sight of. You see couples like that all the time, squabbling and bickering their way around the aisles in Sainsbury's; they obviously despise one another. Who wants to live like that? Give me a real friend anytime."

"When have we ever had knicker-ripping, crash-bang-wallop sex?" Harry asks, genuinely intrigued.

"Oh, I didn't mean with you."

"*What?* Who with, then?"

"There may be trouble ahead!" Cath sings.

"I think I'll see how Louie is." I jump up, eager to get away from the game. "I feel bad I've been here all this time and not said hello. Do excuse me."

I nip out of the dining room before anyone can protest and take the stairs two at a time, pausing on the landing to check my phone. There is a message from Tony! I open it, fingers trembling with excitement. 'Nothing yet'. God dammit. Why hadn't Rowena responded? She'd been quick enough with the Friend request. Patience, I had to be patient. After all, it had taken me an entire day to draft the message, she was entitled to take her time in answering it. Maybe she is unsure how to answer it. Perhaps the simple answer is that she's not in contact with Sarah anymore, so she can't pass on her details.

I knock on Louie's bedroom door and go in. He is seated in front of his desk, a complex-looking excel spreadsheet on the PC screen in front of him. "Hiya Louie, it's only me, thought I'd come and say hello. What are you up to?"

"Oh, hi Unck." Louie turns his head, a pair of blood shot eyes meeting mine. "I'm just updating my sneeze log."

"Uh huh." I wonder if there were any other fifteen-year-old lads in the world who would have given that answer. "Er, had any good ones?"

"Yesterday's was quite interesting." He points at entry number 161 on the spreadsheet and I peer over his shoulder to read: 'Hogpits. Standing with goat. Just let one go.'

"Your eyes look sore, Louie, are you ok?"

"I tried those black contact lenses again, but I'm not sure about the website I got them from; China's always a bit dodgy, isn't it?"

I'm not sure how to respond to that. I remember the video. "I hear congratulations are in order!"

"Eh?"

"The school project! Your video - it won a prize!"

"Oh, yeah, I shot it when I went to work with Dad at the bank. Would you like to see it?"

"I certainly would! What's it called?"

"Life on Earth."

"O-k. So, the same as the Attenborough series?"

"No, it's a question, you know, Life on Earth? So, completely different."

"Right, right. Well, let's see it, then."

Louie taps into his keyboard and a video appears on the screen. He clicks the 'play' arrow and the film begins with a shot of a closed pair of double doors. The camera hovers in front of them for several seconds before Louie's voice cuts in. He's speaking in the hushed tones of an excellent David Attenborough impression. "Here we are, about to enter the most arid, desolate and soulless corner of the world. This is the last place on Earth you'd choose to live. It is known as ... The Call Centre."

The doors open and the camera moves forward to reveal a large open-plan office, horizontally lined with rows of desks and divided into little cubicles by blue soundboards. The camera slowly pans around to show the occupants of the cubicles, each talking into a headset as a PC screen flickers in front of them.

"There are over three hundred inhabitants in this group alone." The camera focuses in on the closest member of staff, a young lad in a black and white striped shirt. He holds up his middle finger to the camera as he lounges back in his chair, yawning into his mouthpiece. "This creature has a tough life ahead of it," Louie continues. "In order to survive here, it has to surrender any emotional and intellectual thoughts it might once have had." The film zooms in on a piece of paper on the desk, upon which a stick man with a giant penis has been doodled.

"A big male can dominate the group," the camera picks out a large, burly guy, who stands, hands on hips, speaking aggressively into his mouthpiece. "While small flies pester the colony." Switch to a short, pinch-faced woman hovering over an employee, gesticulating at her watch.

"Social interaction is brief." The view moves up to show a black wallboard with red neon digits flashing 'calls queuing 23'. "This species is running out of time."

Sweeping across the office, the camera stops in front of a glass-windowed room and then closes in on the sign on the door: 'Training Room'.

"Here," the commentary continues, "more babies are hatching." Inside the room a small group of staff sit in a semi-circle in front of a drop-down screen that has several lines of text projected onto it. "The babies have their first glimpse of a dangerous world. Many are taken right at the beginning of their lives, an affliction known as Death by Powerpoint." The camera zooms in on a girl with long black hair and a pierced lip, her eyelids heavy as her chin droops to her chest.

"Some do make it out alive." Louie swings back to the main room and to the first lad he had filmed, as he sidles furtively down the office. "But, as they begin their perilous journey, others are waiting to ambush them." As the lad stops at the water cooler, surreptitiously peeking at his phone as it pokes from his pocket, the film hones in on the eyes of the pinch-faced woman as she watches the lad intently. "Snakes' eyes aren't very good, but they can detect movement."

The next shot is of a white board, marked out in a grid with black tape. It is headed 'Today's target 225'. The team names are listed down the left-hand side, their individual figures displayed in either red or green, the latter accompanied by a laminated sticker of a smiley face, the former by that of a crying baby.

"And there you have it," Louie finished, withdrawing slowly from the office. "A hostile world only the strongest creatures can endure." The double doors close slowly on the camera and the last shot is of a sign someone has stuck on the doors: 'Please don't feed the staff'.

"Louie, that was bloody brilliant!" I'm genuinely impressed. "Such a clever indictment of modern working life - well done you! And your Attenborough voice is fantastic."

"Glad you like it, Unck."

"I really do! What prize did it win?"

"Film most likely to induce self-harm."

"Oh." I frown as a sudden rush of irritation consumes me. "That's complete horse shit, Louie, if you don't mind me saying."

My nephew stares at me in concern. "You've gone all blotchy, Unck. You didn't eat Mum's chilli dip, did you? Dad reckons she makes it with drain cleaner."

I shake my head. "I'm just hacked off at people constantly sneering at the efforts of others. Tony showed me his Facebook feed yesterday and someone had posted a picture of an overweight person for everyone to snigger at and add their vile comments. We might be living in a modern era but it's like the Victorian freak show never went away. And the trouble is, if you end up taking notice of these idiots, you'll never do anything, ever, just to avoid being criticised."

Louie shrugs. "But my film got the most thumbs down. What if they're right?"

"They're not. You don't need other people to validate you, Louie, you're already good enough, smart enough, *valuable* enough. It's a great video and you're very talented. Don't let anyone under-estimate you, not ever. Sometimes it's the people no one can imagine anything of who do the things no one can imagine. Alan Turing said that, and look what he achieved."

"Didn't he kill himself?"

"Well, er, that's not the point." What was the point? *Do as I say, don't do as I do*. Fighting talk was all very fine but rather hypocritical coming from me, my life spent cowering under the shadow of Dad's illness, always assuming I had nothing to offer anyone. Why would anyone want to be with me? "We're not born with limitations, we put them on ourselves. Or we let others put them on us. If I could give you the gift of self-esteem, I would. I just don't want you to –" *Become like me* "Live with regrets, that's all."

There is a polite cough behind us and we turn to see

Ginny standing in the doorway. "I'm sorry to interrupt you, but I wanted to let you know that I'm going."

"Ginny, I'm so sorry," I get up, feeling wretched. "We've hardly spoken this evening. Are you really going so soon?"

"Yes, I've called a cab, it should be here any minute." She keeps her chin lowered but looks up at me from beneath the rim of her cap. "You can share it with me, if you like, as you've got problems with your bike."

"Oh, yes." There is nothing wrong with my bloody bike! Now I am going to have to fork out for a taxi fare. *It's called Karma.* "That's kind of you. I'll just go and say thank you to Cath and David." I make to move past Ginny, but she reaches out, grasping my arm intently.

"Can we just go, Colin? I don't want to see anyone and I hate drawn-out goodbyes, couldn't we just slip away?"

I hesitate, startled by the strength of her grip.

"It's not like they'll even notice, they're all so drunk."

I consider it the very height of rudeness to just up and leave but Ginny's voice is tinged with such desperation I reluctantly agree. "Perhaps Louie can say our goodbyes for us."

Louie nods his spikes and Ginny smiles at me gratefully. We creep down the stairs into the hallway and I open the front door as quietly as I can. Scruples is still in full flow, but deteriorating rapidly. We hear Cath asking: "So, Helen, how much money would it take for you to go down on a Shetland pony?"

We duck under the dining room bay window and skirt around the side of the evergreens to the back gate just as the taxi arrives. Ginny says "Dunbridge, please, River Street," to the driver as we climb in. Buggerations, we are dropping her off first even though I live much closer. It doesn't seem terribly chivalrous to protest, so I keep quiet, but watch with concern as the red digital numbers of the fare keep climbing. I didn't want to appear tight, but money *was* tight, especially since Dad died. His state pension hadn't been much, but it had helped greatly towards the household bills. Now, there is even less money left at the end of the month and my current account still has a massive dent from the evening at Truffles, or Shite Night, as Tony called it.

Baseball cap pulled down low, Ginny stares out of the window into the dusk. We travel in an uncomfortable silence and I'm racking my brains again for a topic of conversation, but nothing will come. It's a surprise when Ginny suddenly speaks out of the gloom.

"I like what you said to Louie, I thought it was very sweet. You really care about him, don't you?"

"Of course, he's my nephew. I just wish he had a bit more confidence in himself, and it makes me angry when others put him down."

"I let others put me down," Ginny turns her head to look at me. "I tell myself I don't care what people think, but I do care, I care very much. It all stems from him, you see, he's damaged me. You said people put limitations on you, and they do. He certainly did."

"He?"

"My ex-husband." I give a start as she twitches violently, her right hand shooting up in air and whacking the roof of the cab. She pulls it down with her left hand and grasps her wrist firmly. "Sorry about that, I'm told it's a nervous reaction." I catch the taxi driver's eye in the rear-view mirror. "It's hard to believe that one person can affect another so badly, isn't it?" Ginny rubs her arm. "Especially when that one person is supposed to love you and care for you, and keep you safe. Yet they wilfully and deliberately screw up your life." I think about Dad and Sarah's letters and I nod sympathetically.

"Some things make you wonder how well you actually know a person," I say carefully, wanting to give a safe response.

"He laughed at me all the time," Ginny continues. "Called me stupid, told me I was ugly and that I made him physically sick. He made me feel like I was nothing. I think I *became* nothing. I was invisible, like Mr Cellophane from Chicago; I'm convinced that song was written about me. Do you know it?" I shake my head and Ginny sings in a cracked voice: "Mrs Cellophane should have been my name, 'cause you can look right through me, walk right by me and never know I'm there." She starts to cry. The taxi driver looks at me again; it is a 'do something you useless git' look. I fumble in my pockets for a non-existent tissue and then pat Ginny awkwardly on the shoulder. "There there." *I sound like her mother!* This makes her sob even harder.

"River Street," the driver announces, not without some considerable relief.

"Are you going to be alright?" I ask Ginny anxiously. She shakes her head. "Do you want me to come in with you?" She nods. Oh heck, I am no good with tears; I become an even more hopeless, embarrassed lump of lard. I help Ginny from the cab and pay the driver, who takes off before I can ask him to wait. Ginny half-stumbles up the path of her modern little mews house and, tears blurring her vision, I help her to insert the door key, noting a bedraggled clematis struggling to climb over the doorframe. *She's over-watered that*. A narrow hallway leads to a tiny square kitchen and I sit Ginny down at a semi-circle of a table as I fill a kettle. Tea and toast, that's what Mum always made us if we were ever upset. I open the cupboard above the kettle. Bloody hell, I've never seen so many different varieties of tea; green, peppermint, mango and lychee, rooibos - where is the bloody PG Tips? I finally locate something I recognise, Earl Grey, and pour a steaming mug for Ginny, popping a slice of bread into the stainless-steel toaster. The sobbing has subsided, so hopefully I can get this down her and go. I might be able to order a cab at the pub we'd driven past just up the road, that will save having to hang around here.

"Would you like marmalade on your toast?" I ask, peering into a cupboard. "Or," *shudder* "Marmite?"

"Marmite, please." *Oh boy.* I hold the knife at arm's length as I spread the tar-like substance onto the toast, breathing through my mouth as I do so.

"Here you are," I say brightly, placing my pathetic offerings in front of her. "Tea and toast." I hover uneasily, trying to gauge if it is too soon to leave. I reluctantly decide it is and slide into the chair opposite Ginny. Anyone of a more substantive build might have struggled to fit into the confined space.

"It's like a coffin, isn't it?" Ginny says sadly, as if reading my thoughts. "I have nightmares where my hips get wedged in the hallway and I can't move. I'm stuck fast and I wake up screaming." *Jesus, try and lift the conversation, think of something positive.* "I could be trapped and nobody would know I was here, nobody would come, not for weeks."

"It's not that bad, surely."

"I'm irrelevant. But you already know that, of course." She takes a bite of toast and I do my best not to grimace. "There's nothing wrong with your bike, is there? I saw it by Cath's garage and it looked perfectly ok. You forgot to pick me up, didn't you?" I open my mouth to protest, but she continues on. "It's alright, everybody forgets about me and like I said before, I'm Mrs Cellophane. Anyway, if it makes you feel any better, I lied as well."

"Oh, really? What about?"

Ginny manages a sad smile. "I'm not wearing this awful outfit because I thought I would be sitting astride your cross-bar. I had to wear something that went with a baseball cap."

"Why?"

She looks across at me for a moment with her pitiful tear-stained face then very slowly lifts her 'I'm A Hog' baseball cap. *Holy crap!* Her hair is completely green. Not just a tinge or a sheen, but violently green, like pea soup. And I'd been worried about one stray eyebrow hair! "Good grief, that's an original colour."

"It happened this afternoon at the new hair salon in town. Six hours I was there, but they couldn't put it right."

Bloody hell. I make a gargantuan effort to be positive. "Well, at least you still had the guts to come out this evening. You could have hidden yourself away here and yet you didn't, you managed to, to socialise, which was a tremendous effort. It shows great strength of character." *God, I'm in full babble-mode.*

"I dread to think how much I've spent lately, I'm terrified to work it all out. When my parents left me their legacy they thought I would use it to better myself, you know, travel, see a bit of the world, perhaps set up my own business. But my idea of bettering myself has all been cosmetic – anti-wrinkle injections, skin rejuvenation, fillers ... all that money to look this ridiculous. I've become the laughing stock my Ex always said I was." Her right arm twitches again and I instinctively make a grab for the mug. She slumps back in her chair dejectedly. "I'm sorry, I'm making you uncomfortable. You can go if you want, I do understand."

"No, it's fine." As I don't even convince myself, I try again. "You really are terribly hard on yourself, Ginny, as if life isn't tough enough! You're a lovely person inside and out."

She twists the cap around in her hands. "I'm a Hog," she reads from the peak. "Suits me, doesn't it? He always said I was a fat pig."

"Don't be ridiculous, you've got a fabulous figure."

"Have I?"

"Yes! And you honestly don't need all that ..." *Polyfilla*

"cosmetic stuff."

"You're just saying that."

"No, no, absolutely not. You're a very naturally beautiful woman."

To my delight, her face breaks into a genuine smile. "Do you really think so?"

"Yes, I do. You're a very nice person, inside and out."

"You like me, then?"

"Of course I do."

"So, you'll stay? Here, with me, tonight?"

No no no no no I blink rapidly as her big hopeful eyes hold mine. 'Please don't crush me,' they beg, 'don't reject me, don't turn me down.'

"Y-yes, I'll s-stay. If you want me to."

"I do."

Gulp.

It's five past five in the morning. The room is filled with an eerie grey light and as I look out through lead-lined windows, I see tall dark trees lining the pallid sky, a silvery river behind them. Accompanied by the first chirps of birdsong and a sick feeling in my stomach, I watch dawn break on a new low, the taste of marmite a bitter reminder that last night had actually happened. It had not been a bad dream.

I step carefully into my chinos and slowly pull them up, wincing as loose change rattles in the pockets. The sleeping figure in the bed stirs but doesn't wake, green tendrils of hair splayed out across the white pillow. I pick up my phone from the floor and there's a message from Tony: 'No reply from Rowena. BUT she checked into the waterboys last night and guess wot? Its near Trowbridge!!! Suggest stake out. Over a pint. Or 2.'

Despite itself, my heavy heart attempts a little leap. *Trowbridge.* Perhaps The Waterboys is where Rowena and

Sarah meet, maybe they are still in touch. A shaft of light appears through the trees.

Chapter Eleven

"Are you quite sure you wouldn't like to purchase a different urn?" The well-meaning, tweed-suited woman gazes at me pityingly. "I'm afraid these polyurns are a little utilitarian. The biodegradable ones start at one hundred and sixty four pounds and we can transfer your father's ashes into it for you, if that's what you're worried about. It's all handled with extreme care."

I look down at the ugly brown polyurn. "No, it's fine, thank you. It actually reminds me of Dad." I see her shocked expression and quickly add, "He wasn't one for frills."

I leave the crematorium office and bungee-rope Dad onto my pannier rack, making sure to cycle over any bumpy bits in the road to annoy him. For some reason, he always complained bitterly about pot-holes even though, being virtually house-bound, he'd hardly ever encountered any. I could have had his ashes scattered around the pretty garden of remembrance, but I wanted to hold the last physical earthly elements of Dad. I couldn't even explain to myself why, it wasn't as if his ashes could provide the answers I desperately needed.

At home, I place the polyurn on the mantel piece but I can't bear the way it dominates the room, its silent ugliness a stark reminder of the living being. I try placing it under the mirror in the hallway with the family photos, but again it is too contrasting next to Mum's beautiful smile. I flick the kettle on and sit with the urn on the kitchen table. "You're even more difficult dead than you were alive," I tell it, then instantly feel guilty for saying such a thing out loud. I shut the urn in the cupboard so I can't feel Dad's wrath exuding from it. I should be getting to work but decide there's time for a quick cuppa and I phone Cath while waiting for the kettle to boil. She answers in her dying-swan voice. "Ugh, Colin, I feel absolutely rank. My head's about to explode, I think Iron Maiden are living in it. You should see the state of the house, it looks like a bomb has gone off. How David managed to get up for work, I'll never know. He had three sachets of Resolve for breakfast. He didn't even dissolve them in water, he just tipped them straight down his throat." She pauses for breath and I hear the fizz of a ring pull. Red Bull would be my guess. "Anyway, what happened to you last night?"

"Don't you remember me saying goodbye?" I reply innocently.

"No," Cath groans. "I'm sorry, it's all a blur after the chicken wings and that bloody chilli dip. I had to drink a vat of wine just to cool my mouth down. So, what about Ginny?"

"I saw her home," I say, carefully. "She wasn't feeling great."

"No," Cath sighs. "I knew she was having an off day when she arrived in that get up. I ask you, who wears a 'I'm a Hog' baseball cap to a romantic dinner date? Not even Gwen Stefani could pull that one off."

"I've picked up Dad's ashes," I tell her, swiftly changing the subject. "He's currently residing next to the custard creams. The urn, that is."

"Does it smell of TCP?"

"Where do you think we should scatter him?"

"Blimey Col, that's a heavy one to lay on a girl first thing in the morning, especially when she's hanging out of her you-know-what. I mean, this is the last act of love we can perform for him, it's such a massive decision, and not one that should be made when you're still pissed from last night. What about in the gardens at Hogpits? Then he'd always be close to you."

"No."

"Oh." Cath is taken aback at my bluntness. "Ok then, um, what about Stourhead? He liked it there, didn't he? I mean, it bored the crap out of us when we were kids, but he seemed happy, well, less miserable, when he was there."

She's right. A late autumn visit to Stourhead was possibly the last time I ever recalled Dad smiling; Mum was throwing handfuls of flaming red leaves up into a brilliant blue sky and we were all squealing as they showered down over us. "That's a really good call, Sis, but we'll probably need permission to scatter Dad's ashes on National Trust land; there's a danger of soil sterilisation, people's ashes can contain high levels of minerals."

"Jesus, Col, Dad was one hundred per cent white Hovis, there's not a bloody mineral in him. No, we'll throw him from the top of that hill, no one will see if we're quick. Make sure it's not a windy day, though, I don't want to be picking him out of my hair for ever more."

"Euch."

"And Col?"

"Yes?"

"Can you phone Ginny, check she's ok? I can't face it."

You can't face it? "Yes, of course I'll call her, I'll do it straight away. In a minute."

I free-wheel down the driveway at Hogpits, deep in thought. What am I going to say to Ginny? This is unchartered territory for me, I'd never had to tell anyone I didn't want to see them again, they'd always finished with me first. I am going to look like a right bastard, a complete cad, as Mum would say, sleeping with someone then dumping them straight afterwards. Although it hadn't been an act of bastardry, if such a word existed, it had been an act of politeness. It might have been two acts of politeness if Ginny had had her way, but I'd been unable to manage it a second time, despite her encouragement. A cold rush of shame floods through me at the sudden flashback: Ginny looking up at me from halfway down the bed, mouth busy, eyes pleading, fringe green... I groan out loud. Who does that? Who sleeps with someone because they're too polite to refuse? Only it wasn't politeness, of course, it was weakness. I was so terrified of causing offence, I'd actually had sex with someone I didn't want to have sex with. Why am I so gutless, *why?*

I reach the gravel car park and squeeze on the brakes, slotting the front wheel into the cycle rack. Enough is enough, I have to toughen up, I have to take control of my life, reinvent myself. Starting from now, from this very moment, I am Mr Gutsy. Not the morbidly obese one from the Mister Men, but someone with substance, someone who can say 'no, that's not for me, thanks' rather than do something they don't want to. As I walk, head up, along the path and past the tearooms, I see Cafe Girl peering out of the window. She pushes open the fire exit door and waves at me. "Morning Colin! You're late today." She bounds down the path to greet me, a big friendly smile on her face. As she approaches I see she has a patch of hair missing above her left ear.

"I'm not late. I had an appointment."

"Oh dear, have you been to the doctor's? Nothing wrong, I hope?"

I consider her for a moment. "Emma, isn't it? It's nice of you to ask after my health, but it's rather unexpected given that you've never spoken to me before."

Her cheeks redden and she gives a false little laugh. "Rubbish! Of course we've spoken before, we had a chat at the Open Day on Saturday."

I shake my head. "No, we didn't. In fact, you don't even acknowledge me when I look your way, not even to say good morning. I've always thought you extremely rude." Woah! Where the hell had that come from? Suddenly it's a pretty thin line between Mr Gutsy and Mr Arsehole.

Her eyes narrow and she takes a step closer to me. "Oh, I get it, just because I'm not interested in you that way, you think you've got the right to speak to me like a piece of shit." I open my mouth to protest but she carries on. "I saw you perving on me when I was with Clive on Saturday. Get a good look, did you? I'm surprised you weren't filming us." She pauses. "Did you film us? Or take any pictures? I've a right to know."

I take a deep breath. "Let's get a couple of things straight, shall we? I am not interested in you *that way,* or any other way. Nor was I perving on you and what's his name, Clive? Seriously, that's his name? I was searching for Ron and you'd chosen one of his favourite places to have your grope with a married man. I'd rather not have seen what I did, and I think it's really unfair that Natalie's got the sack because of you."

She sticks her chin out defiantly. "So, Mr Holier-than-thou, I suppose you're going to tell Mrs Winter? If you do, I shall tell her that you're a pervert, that you follow me around and watch me. And I'll say you shouldn't be working near children. Or animals."

I shake my head in disbelief. "You really are a charmer, aren't you? I hadn't planned on telling Mrs Winter, as it goes, but now I think I might just do that. People deserve to know the truth, don't they?"

I turn on my heel and march trembly-legged away. I'd stood my ground for once, shouldn't I be feeling euphoric? So why did I want to throw up? I hate confrontation and now I've made an enemy of Cafe Girl - Mr Gutsy has already become Mr Tummy Turmoil.

Down at Wintersdell, Tony is kneeling against the side of the bank rubbing his back. He's surrounded by begonias and has only replanted the W so far. He looks up wearily at my approach. "Bloody Groundhog Day," he groans.

"Groundhogpits day!" My lame joke receives the response it deserves as a well-aimed begonia thuds into my groin.

"I can't stand much more of this shite, I'm seeing these bloody flowers in my sleep. This audition can't come soon enough. Deal or No Deal: that just about sums up my life."

"Have you spoken with Mrs Winter? About taking the time off, I mean."

"Sod that, I'll throw a sickie. I know you don't approve but Morticia will never grant me that amount of holiday in the middle of the summer."

I stare at him incredulously. "But the Winters will know you're lying when they see you on the telly! You'll get the sack, Tone."

He shrugs. "I don't care. This is it, mate, I know it is. I don't believe in fate or any of that mumbo-jumbo stuff, but I really feel this is my ticket out of here."

"Out of where?"

"Here! Look at me, grovelling around on all fours, covered in crap. You spend your whole life poncing around with pansies and before you know it you're pushing up the daisies. No, this is a chance to turn my shitty life around; I'm going to fund my way through college, get some real qualifications, then a proper profession and earn a decent wage. It's the only way I'll be able to get my own place. I'm sick of being at home amongst the packets of Tena Lady and tubes of Vagisil, always living in fear of my girlfriends needing the bog because of the flotilla of grey baggy knickers hanging over the bath."

I nod understandingly. "I guess, sometimes in life, you just have to take a chance."

"Exactly." He stabs his trowel into the ground like a stake and pulls himself up on it. "And anyway, there's no way my back's going to last the summer." He peers at me. "You look pale. Not enough iron, I reckon. Fancy a Guinness or two at this Waterboys place in Trowbridge on Saturday, see if the search-for-a-Shaw leads us anywhere? I've got custody of Ron Burgundy at the moment, just while my brother's serving his ban."

"Rowena still hasn't replied?"

"Nope, I can't understand how she's not fallen for the Tony Chisholm charm. I've sent her a couple of chasers and poked her, but nothing. Reckon she must sup from the furry cup. I thought we could go round to Sarah's old address; I know the family's not there anymore, but they might have left a forwarding address. It's a long-shot, but you never know."

"Sure, let's do it." I feel cheered. "Can we take Louie? He was a bit down last night."

"Really, what's wrong with our Lou Lou? Hey up, talking of the walking dead... Alright Wes?" The maintenance man has emerged from Wintersdell and is wandering in our direction. "Alright, lads?" His face is grey and creased. He pokes at a clump of soil with the toe of his boot.

Tony and I look at each other. "Got any good *yokes* for us, Wes?" I ask against my better judgment, but I am disturbed by Wes' uncharacteristic demeanour.

"No, not really."

"Why do nurses give their male patients Viagra?" Tony grins. "To stop them rolling out of bed!" We both roar with forced laughter, but Wes only manages a tight little smile.

"What's the generic form of Viagra?" Tony asks, sounding somewhat desperate.

Wes shrugs. "I don't know."

"Mycoxaflopin."

"Right. Good one." He scuffs at the earth. "Well, I'd better get on. See you later."

"See you at lunchtime, in The Hut?" Tony calls after him. "We can have a game of Heads Up if you fancy it?"

He's gone. "Bloody hell," I rub my chin anxiously. "Do you think he's still dwelling on the magic show? It wasn't that bad."

"Yeah, it was," Tony sighs. "I know he's a nob, but I feel for him. I bet he thought his wizardry was his ticket out of here. Now he has to come to terms with the fact that he's stuck here, a general dogsbody with no real purpose in life other than wiping the arse crevice of Mr Winter."

"You paint a very bleak picture."

"It is fecking bleak! But not for me, no way siree, I'm not on a one-way ticket to Palookaville."

"Marlon Brando?"

"Noel Edmonds."

Lunchtime in The Hut proves to be extremely peaceful. There's no sign of Wes and Tony has his face in his phone, busy Snapchatting the new girl at Greggs. I am flicking through a copy of Private Eye, but I feel exhausted and my eyelids keep drooping. It isn't until Alison Moyet's 'Invisible' plays on the Time Tunnel that I remember I still haven't called Ginny. *This is going to be one hell of a difficult conversation*. I leave The Hut and stand staring into space, trying to summon up the courage to make the call. On the fence near the entrance two pigeons are trying to mate, the male's attempts to mount his partner cumbersome and unwieldy. I cringe at another flashback. I can't do it, I can't call her. Yes you can, Mr Gutsy, do it, just do it, don't be a dick. Just dial the bloody number. Ok, here goes. Don't answer, please don't answer, go to voicemail, I'll leave a casual but caring message–

"Hello?"

"Oh, hello, Ginny? It's Colin. How are you?"

"I'm ok, thanks. You?"

"Yes, fine, thanks." Awkward silence. "Um, sorry I had to leave so early this morning, I had to, er, be somewhere and I didn't want to wake you."

"That's ok." The way she said it didn't make it sound like it was ok.

Even more butt-clenching silence. "So, what have you got planned for today?"

"I'm going into town."

"Oh, that's nice."

"To have a colonic."

"Ugh, er, right." *Just tell her.* "Um, Ginny, I've been thinking about last night and that maybe it shouldn't have happened, you know, given you seemed so fragile. It might not have been the best idea to do what we did."

"I wanted you to stay, Colin, I didn't want to spend the night alone."

"No, but–"

"You didn't take advantage, if that's what you're worried about. But it's nice that you care enough to say that, most men wouldn't give two hoots. They're only interested in one thing and once they've had that, you never hear from them again."

"No, right." *Oh Christ.*

"I think we should talk about it, though, that's what my therapist would say to do. It's important to be open about what happened, why we connected as we did. Express how we feel about one another, and where we see our relationship going. Don't you agree?"

"Um..."

"So, when shall we meet up again, Saturday or Sunday?" *Come on Mr Gutsy, where have you gone*? Mr Flacid was back. Shrivelled like the other parts of me. "Saturday?" I say, limply.

"Great, there's a lovely organic coffee shop just opened up in Cathedral Street, I'll text you the link. Shall we say eleven?"

"Lovely. See you there." I terminate the call. "Bollocks."

"Language, Colin, there are visitors around." Mrs Winter sweeps past me.

"Sorry Mrs Winter. Actually, could I speak to you?"

"No, you can't, Colin. I've got to re-jig all the staff rotas to cover Natalie's duties and then I've got a meeting with the accountant. Following that, I have an urgent appointment with an enormous bucket of Bombay Sapphire."

"It's just that, it wasn't all Natalie's fault, you know."

I can see Mrs Winter wrestling with herself and as irritation flashes in her eyes, I brace myself for an explosion. When she finally manages to speak, it's with low, deliberate tones. "Colin, when planning this visit, which, incidentally, had the potential to be the most lucrative event in Hogpits' history, I thought the worse that Brian Beardmore might be exposed to was a flatulent goat. I did not envisage subjecting him to a spot of staff mud-wrestling, obscene language, a dismissal... I don't need to go on, do I?"

"But, things aren't always what they seem."

"What are you talking about, Colin?" Mrs Winter snaps, losing her composure. "And why on earth are you defending Natalie's behaviour? I would have thought you'd be relieved to see the back of her. What she did to Emma was completely unacceptable, the poor girl's got such a massive patch of hair missing you can see her scalp. I'm surprised at you, Colin."

As she moves off I blurt: "She'd been sleeping with Nat's husband!"

Mrs Winter stops dead then turns slowly back to look at me. "What?"

"I saw them together at the Open Day. Cafe Girl, I mean Emma, and what's-his-name-"

"Clive?"

"Yes, Clive. I saw them behind the sheds, they were, er-" Snogging? Groping? "Canoodling." Who uses words like that? No one, not since 1932. "I guess, well, I assume Natalie found out about it, or she saw them, they weren't exactly discreet. That's why she lost it."

"I see." The pale eyes flick over me. "Even so, I can't condone violence in the workplace-"

"No, I know," my face flushes red as I interrupt her. "But Nat might have become temporarily *unhinged*, given the shock of her discovery, and we don't know the manner in which she found out. It's possible Emma might have–"

"Rubbed Natalie's nose in it?" It is Mrs Winter's turn to talk over me. I can almost hear her mind whirring as the narrowed-eyed stare bores into me.

"Emma's keen that you don't find out," I say, uneasily. "She's going to tell you I'm a pervert. Which I'm not," I quickly add.

"Uh-huh." Mrs Winter appears to make up her mind and her stony gaze switches to the tearooms. "Thank you, Colin."

I watch her stride away, unsure of what she's intending to do. I realise I don't much care anymore, I'm so drained I just want to curl up in the hen house next to Chicken Ron and sleep for a thousand years. I jump in fright as Tony leaps out of The Hut.

"You're a twitchy fucker Hector, what's wrong with you? Don't you want the good news?"

"I could do with some."

"Rowena's latest update." He shows me Rowena's Facebook page on his phone.

My heart swoops then falls. "A picture of a cream horn?"

"No, dummy, the post underneath."

I take the phone and hold it out to a distance where my eyes can focus. I read: 'Feeling excited. Can't wait to hit the high street tomorrow, find those finishing touches for my outfit.'

"She's going to be in town on Saturday!" Tony says excitedly. "We can stake out the High Street."

"It's a big place, how will we possibly find her?"

"Because, Mr Negative, she won't be able to resist one of her dreary bloody check-ins. We'll know exactly where she is, how she's feeling, what she's eating, when she's going for a crap... This is it mate, I can feel it in my water. We're going to find her!"

It's a cloudy Saturday morning and we've been in McDonalds for well over an hour. I'm queasy after my second Egg McMuffin, although being so nervous isn't helping my stomach acids either. Even if we find Rowena and she agrees to speak to us rather than calling Crimestoppers, what might she tell us about Sarah? Married, divorced, emigrated, dead... I'm trying to mentally prepare myself for every possible scenario, but it's hard to think straight when I'm with Tony and Louie. My nephew has dyed his hair even blacker, resulting in his face being even paler; Tony has labelled him 'son of Morticia' and they've been playing clips of the Addams family very loudly on their phones, much to everyone's annoyance. An overweight traffic warden sits behind us, sucking noisily on a straw, hoovering up every last drop of his chocolate milkshake. "I can't stand much more of this," I groan, my head in my hands. "I'm going insane."

Tony checks Facebook again. "Nothing. Come on, Rowena old girl, throw us a bone. Your timeline's chock full of meaningless bollocks and yet when we actually want you to post something, you don't bloody oblige." He sighs. "Are you enjoying your summer holiday, Lou Lou? What have you been doing with yourself, looking at graves and shit?"

"Yes."

"Are you off to Brittany again this year?" I ask him. "The same gite as last time?"

"Hmmm, I'm not sure, not after what happened to the neighbour's tortoise. I had *told* Dad to cover the swimming pool."

Tony snatches his phone up. "Code red, it's a code red!"

"What?"

"Rowena's just checked into Holland and Barrett's, she's stocking up on chewable calcium tablets – come on, let's go!"

We leap up, the other diners wincing at the cacophony of squealing steel as our chairs scrape back. "Where's Holland and Barrett's?" Louie asks. We all look at each other. Tony rounds on the traffic warden.

"Where's Holland and Barrett's?"

"Do I look like I know where Holland and Barrett's is?"

"No, fair play." Tony pounces on a bespectacled woman as she enters through the double doors "Help us, please! Which way's Holland and Barrett's? Come on love, it's an emergency! I've got Louie Walsh here and if he doesn't get his iron supplements right now he's a gonner."

"Oh, the poor thing." The woman blinks owlishly at Louie, who does indeed look on the verge of an anaemic collapse. "It's next to Superdrug, opposite where BHS used to be."

"I know it!" Tony yells. "It's in the precinct. Go lads, go go go!"

We perform a demented quick step along the crowded high street, dodging and swerving around the tide of shoppers. My heart is hammering by the time we reach Holland and Barrett; we can't just accost a woman in a shop! What will I say to her, and what if Sarah is actually with her? I needn't have worried. The shop is empty, save for a furtive-looking guy examining

Ultra Man caplets. "Where is everyone?" Tony glances all around then approaches the man at the counter. "Was an old lady just in here, buying chewy calcium tablets?"

He folds his arms defensively. "Maybe there was, maybe there wasn't. Our customer's purchases are confidential, I don't betray their trust."

"You're a shopkeeper mate, not the Pope. We just want to know which way she went."

Furtive Guy slips out and the man at the counter scowls at Tony. "You're losing us customers. Are you intending to buy anything?"

"Like what?" Tony waves his hands at the rows of organic almonds and sunflower seeds. "I'm not a flippin' budgerigar."

We leave the shop despondently and gaze around the crowded precinct. There is no option other than to watch Facebook and wait. "Which shops would an old woman frequent?" I ponder, as we squeeze together on a bench.

"We could phone Wes and ask him," Tony suggests.

"Charity shops?" Louie says. "Somewhere that sells lavender?"

"She put on Facebook about finding the finishing touches to her outfit. Is there a sewing shop or something?"

"Costa!" Tony yells. "Come on, she's checked into Costa! She's posted a picture, she's right by the window - she's having a latte and a gingerbread man."

"How long has she been there?" Louie asks as we jump up and rush after Tony.

"The head's gone. It's bitten clean off! We're running out of time lads, got to be quick!"

We fight our way to the end of the precinct, cross the High Street and burst into Costa, the long queue of people at the counter turning in surprise at our noisy entrance. There, on the empty table by the window, is a drained glass latte mug and the foot of a gingerbread man. "Which way did she go?" Tony barks at the room in general. Everyone ignores him. "Did you see her?" He grabs hold of a young man at the end of the queue, almost shaking him in his frustration. "The old lady in the corner, did you see her?"

"N-no."

"Did anyone see her?" He pleads with the queue. "She was over there, someone must have seen her?" Everyone looks away from the madman and I tug at Tony's sleeve.

"It's no use, mate, she's gone." I drag him back outside and we stand at the window, looking in at Rowena's empty coffee cup. *So close.*

Louie's phone rings. "Oh hi, Mum. What are we doing? We're outside Costa, stalking a relative of one of Uncle Colin's ex-girlfriends. Why?" He winces and holds out his phone to me. "She wants to speak to you."

I take the phone reluctantly. "Hi Sis."

"Don't 'hi Sis' me, you're no brother of mine."

Ouch. "Is something wrong?"

"Nothing gets passed you, does it, Sherlock? Yes, there is something bloody well wrong, as it goes. Take your brain, for example, it doesn't seem to be functioning. Probably because it's the size of a pea."

I shake my head in confusion. "What are you on about, Cath?"

"What am I on about? Er, let me think... Ginny, that's what!" Holy crap, I'd forgotten all about her. "She's given up waiting, just so you know." Cath's voice is ice-cold. "Humiliated by a man, *again.* I cannot believe you did that to her. And all because you're chasing around after your long-lost erection, *and* getting my son mixed up in it all."

"I'm really sorry, I didn't mean to do that to Ginny. I'll call her straight away."

"Oh, don't bother yourself. I mean, what could you possibly say to her that will make her feel any better? 'Thanks very much for the shag, Ginny, but I'd much rather chase around after the ghost of someone I haven't seen for thirty years than have a coffee with you'?"

Clearly, Ginny had told Cath we'd slept together. *How embarrassing*. I don't know how to respond, and anyway, it's always best to keep quiet when Cath is in full rant-mode. I say nothing and my silence works; when she speaks again, her tone is softer. "What is it you're looking for, Col? Tell me, please, because I just don't understand."

I feel a stab of frustration. "I don't understand either. I'm really sorry about Ginny, I did genuinely forget that we'd arranged to meet. But I don't understand why you're so against me trying to find Sarah. I loved her and it's clear from her letters that she loved me. Why wouldn't I want to find her, to explain what happened?"

I know my face has gone crimson; I never stand up to Cath and the others look on in concern. "I, I just don't want you wasting your time on the past." I've thrown her momentarily. "I'm sorry, Col, but it needs to be said. You're not getting any younger and you could be enjoying getting to know someone like Ginny, who's here for you now. You know what Mum used to say – if you persist in raking up the past, you'll only destroy the future." She pauses. "That's what I think, anyway." The line goes dead.

I hand the phone back to Louie. "Let's call it a day, lads. I've had enough."

"One last try," Tony urges. "We haven't been to The Waterboys yet, let's give it a whirl. You can drown your sorrows, if nothing else."

Ron Burgundy takes us out on the A36 towards Trowbridge before Doris the sat-nav lady directs us through a maze of narrow lanes. We delve deeper and deeper into the countryside and along past a sparkling river, before we're eventually forced to stop in a layby as the route constantly recalculates. "This can't be right," I say, peering through a five-bar gate into a meadow of buttercups. "Surely there isn't a hotel right out here?"

"Turn left." Doris instructs us.

"You're off your tits, love!" Tony yells, losing his patience. "That's into the bloody river!"

"No, it's there, look!" Louie spots a sign over the hedgerow. *'The Waterboys, idyllic village hideaway'.*

"Hooray!"

The Waterboys is a delightful boutique hotel, set in glorious rural tranquillity on the banks of the river Biss. The car park is full but Tony manages to squeeze Ron Burgundy onto the grass verge in the lane outside. There is a wedding in progress and when we finally manage to get served by the stressed bar staff, we carry our drinks outside to the garden, sitting down at a picnic table. The lush green lawn slopes gently down to the river and little knots of smartly dressed guests chat together on the patio, a photographer doing her best to round up family members for photos.

Tony takes a swig of lager, his sunglasses perching on his head. He still has white rings around his eyes from our day at the seaside. They suddenly widen in horror. "Oh, sweet Jesus, would you look at that!" One of the bridesmaids has fallen over on the lawn. Her legs kick high in the air, her knickers on display for the entire world to see. One of the groomsmen tries to pull her up, but she is a heavy lady and each abortive attempt just renders her more helpless with laughter. Phone covers flip open, instantly sharing the moment with several hundred others across Facebook.

"Duck shit!" The bridesmaid shrieks. "I'm in the duck shit!"

"She's so gonna regret that tomorrow," Louie comments, shaking his spikes sadly. "Why do women love wine so much? Mum gave me a sip of hers the other night and it tasted just like vinegar."

"She may have opened the red wine vinegar by mistake, I've seen her do it before."

"Well, what are you going to do now, Col?" Tony asks, wincing as the bridesmaid's crotch hones into view but seemingly unable to take his eyes away from it. "You could take a day off and go to the town hall, search the records for Sarah, see if you can trace her that way?"

"Yes, I guess that would be the next move." I hesitate, tapping my pint glass.

"But what?"

"I'm, well, not so sure now. I mean, Sarah moved back home but didn't make any further attempt to contact me. She said in her last letter that she was going to come round, and yet she chose not to. Not even to confront me. I guess she decided to move on with her life. I don't blame her, of course, but I can't help thinking that Cath might be right about leaving things alone. It was all so long ago."

"And you're scared that if Sarah claps eyes on you again she's going to smack you right in the chops?" Tony nods knowingly. "Yep, she probably will. In fact, I reckon she'll aim a bit lower. But that's chicken shit thinking, my friend, pure bloody chicken shit. You can't let this go. What your old man did to you both was wrong, frigging wrong. You must tell her he hid her letters, you've got to heal the wounds. At least refund her for the stamps."

"I know you're right Tone, but it all seems a bit hopeless at the moment."

"She's here!" Louie's sudden exclamation makes us jump. "She's just checked in!"

"You're shitting me!" Tony snatches his phone from Louie, examining Rowena's Facebook post. "She is, look!" He shows me his phone: Rowena had posted 'checking final preparations #gettingexcited at The Waterboys Country Hotel'.

"Preparations for what?" I ask as we all rise to our feet, looking round like meerkats. "Does she mean for the wedding?" A cold hand clutches at my heart. Could this possibly be *Sarah's* wedding? No, no way, surely it would be too awful a coincidence; after all this time I track Sarah down on the very day she's getting married?

"Flippin' heck, she could be anywhere," Tony groans in frustration, looking around at the guests dotted about the gardens. "Ok, I'll start in the bar, Louie, you go round these groups and ask people if they know Rowena. Col, you go to the front desk and get them to do a bing-bong shout-out message for her."

"What will I say?"

"I don't know! You'll think of something. Here, 'scuse me, mate," Tony accosts a young barman at the next picnic table as he wearily stacks empty glasses into a crate. "Have you seen this woman?" He shows him Rowena's Facebook profile. "She's my Gran, gone a bit doolally, so we're all out looking for her. We know she's here because she's just checked in."

The young man peers at the picture. "I dunno, she looks a bit familiar."

"She's much older now, so think of that face but with more wrinkles. And without teeth."

"Oh God yeah, it's her." He spits it out before he can stop himself. "Sorry, I know she's your Gran and all, but Jesus Christ..." He leaves that to hang and we all look at each other.

"Is she one of the wedding guests?" I ask him.

"No, she's not, but that didn't stop her helping herself to the canapés. The groom's mother sussed her and there was a bit of a dust-up. I think she left."

"Bugger!" The force of Tony's expletive almost makes him drop the crate. "When did she leave?"

"J-just now, I think."

"Car park!" We take off, running at top speed around the

side of the hotel and into the car park. Just as we get there a black Mazda MX5 shoots past, spraying us with shingle. I chase it to the end of the car park waving like mad, but it turns left out of the gates and I hear its throaty roar as it speeds away up the lane.

"Are you sure that was her?" Tony gasps as he catches up with me. "I didn't see her face."

"Yes, I'm sure. That was the car in her Facebook pictures."

"Dammit all to hell." Tony's had enough. "How has that old duck managed to give us the slip all day long? She's a geriatric Scarlet Pimpernel."

Louie trots up to us, an uncharacteristic smile lighting up his pale face. "Are you alright, Louie?"

"You need to see what's on Facebook, Unck, it's the most awesome news!"

Tony examines his phone then punches the air in delight. "Bingo! Bing-bloody-go!"

"What is it?" I ask excitedly. "Tell me!"

"There's some comments on her check-in post. Look! This one says: 'Really looking forward to your party' and here's another, it says 'Woo hoo! Just one week to go - bet you can't wait, Material Girl!'" Tony looks up at me, his eyes shining. "She's only having a bloody party! Who do you think is bound to be there?"

Sarah. Sarah is bound to be there.

I have a spring in my step as I head into work on Monday morning. A lovely show of marigolds and geraniums lines the path to The Hut and I nip the dead heads off as I make my way along. There is no sign of Cafe Girl outside the tearooms and The Hut is empty, so I pick up the hedge cutter, ready to wrestle with the privet again. I take the long way round so I can wander through the wild flower garden, which has burst alive with poppies and cornflowers, then down around the lake before heading up again to the middle lawn and my nemesis, the rapidly-spurting privet hedge.

I feel someone watching me as I prepare to strike up the hedge cutter. Nasty Nat is standing on the lawn, pale and gaunt, her hair scraped back into a greasy ponytail. She is clutching a pink-sugared donut.

"Colin."

"Hello Nat." I instinctively glance around for an escape route, but she is blocking the path. "Bit early for lunch, isn't it?"

She shrugs. "If you can't beat 'em... I haven't eaten a Krispy Creme for about twenty years. Starving myself all this time and for what? To look good for my husband." She gives a hollow laugh and I shift uncomfortably, not knowing what to say. Nasty Nat looks down at her feet, studiously examining her trainers before mumbling, "I should say thank you. For speaking up for me."

"That's ok." I eye her apprehensively. "You've got your job back, then?"

"Yes. Mrs Winter got rid of the cafe skank and told me I could come back."

"That's good," I lie. "Well, best crack on-"

"I can't really blame my husband, he didn't have much of a choice. No man's going to say no when it's offered on a plate, are they? She threw herself at him."

"Who, Mrs Winter?" I try to make a joke but she doesn't laugh.

"You work your hardest to look your best, hitting the gym every morning, Pilates in the evenings, counting calories religiously each day, and then some chubby little slapper comes along and takes it all away from you." Her eyes glisten. "She's just a fat little tart, pig-ugly too. No wonder she's so keen to drop her knickers, it's the only way she can get a man to look twice at her." She's waiting for me to respond but I know I need to tread carefully, not wishing to be lured into saying something she can hold against me. Then, suddenly, I don't care. Sarah would simply speak her mind, not wimp around like I did. I sit on the fence so often my arse is full of splinters.

"Why do you always set so much store by what someone looks like, Nat? It's superficial. There'll always be someone prettier, thinner, fitter – who cares? People judge you by how you make them feel, not what you look like."

She's quiet for a moment, looking at me inscrutably. "How do I make you feel, Colin?"

"How do you think?"

She shrugs. "Uncomfortable, I suppose. You and Tony go out of your way to avoid me, don't think I haven't noticed. You didn't like me at school and you don't like me now."

I stare at her. "Good Lord, Nat, that was a lifetime ago!"

"Why didn't you fancy me?"

"I can't remember!" Was that why she always had it in for me, because I hadn't wanted to go out with her at school? "Surely you don't still dwell on that, what does it matter now?

A single tear rolls down her cheek. "I liked you, I liked you a lot."

"I-I didn't know that."

Nat wipes the tear from her face with the back of her hand. "I tried to make you like me, I'm always making little jokes around you, fooling around. But I just seem to alienate you, and everyone else around me. Mrs Winter's never liked me, she told me that to my face." She gives a sad little sniff. "Why do people take an instant dislike to me?"

"Because it saves time! Ha Ha! Sorry, sorry, that was meant as a joke," I quickly add as her face crumples. "Just trying to cheer you up." *You buffoon.* I clear my throat. "Look, I'm not very good at this sort of thing, as you can tell, but I do know that when the chips are down you have to try and stay positive and think of all the good things you do have in your life. Focus on those. If you can be happy with who you are, you'll eventually attract the right sort of person. Someone with a bit more, well, depth."

In the distance some ducks quack noisily, sounding as if they're laughing at us. I can see Tony lurking on the lower path, obviously watching on. Natalie looks across at him sullenly. "I suppose everyone knows."

"Well, I've not told anyone and I'm pretty sure Mrs Winter hasn't." I can't help grinning at the muck-flinging memory. "It was a bloody good shot, Nat, you got her right in the chops! You couldn't do that again if you tried."

She gives a tiny giggle, despite herself. "At least it wasn't another boring old garden visit for Brian Beardmore. It's not one he'll forget in a hurry."

"Oh, sorry." My phone is ringing and I take it out of my pocket. Bugger, it's Ginny. I guiltily press the decline button, hearing the ducks laughing again. They're mocking me. Am I really trying to give relationship advice to someone else? What a joke.

Tony creeps up the path as he sees Nasty Nat walking away. "What was all that about?" he asks suspiciously. "I thought she'd been given the chop. Why was she crying?"

"It's nothing, just the usual Nat stuff," I tell him. "So, how is your prep for Deal or No Deal coming along? Not long to go now! Have you decided on a number sequence system yet?"

"Yeah, sort of, but then I think maybe it's better to go with the vibe on the day, if you know what I mean." He shakes his head in confusion. "It's all a bit of a ball-ache, to be honest. Anyway, how are you feeling about Rowena's party on Saturday? Excited, I bet."

"We're not invited, Tone, the best we can hope for is that the hotel let us have a drink at the bar and I can try and talk to Sarah if she's there."

"We've got some shopping to do first, for our outfits."

I'm confused. "I'm just going to wear my chinos, Tone."

"Didn't I tell you? It's an 80's party."

"Strange, I wouldn't have thought that was Rowena's era. But anyway, we're not actual guests so we don't need to dress up."

"Yeah we do, it's perfect, don't you see? We'll be in disguise, so no one will know we're gatecrashers. We can mingle undetected amongst the guests while you flush Sarah out. If she's turned into a munter, you can stay incognito and we'll just slip away. If, however, she's as foxy as you remember, you can go for the big reveal, you know, rip off your mask, ta da, it's me, your first love. It will be just like Clark Kent and Lois Lame."

"Lane."

"Whatever."

"You two!" A piercing voice startles the ducks from the lake.

"Shit, it's Skeletor," Tony grimaces as Mrs Winter approaches. "I'd better look like I'm coming down with something." He leans his head against my shoulder, rubbing his stomach.

"Stop slacking, Tony." Mrs Winter is upon us. "It's not lunchtime yet. So, a productive morning in the gardens, then?"

Uh-oh, what had gone wrong now? "Absolutely," I reply cautiously.

"It's just that Mr Winter called me from the Land Rover dealership. He had to take the Range in because it kept stalling on him. Do you know what could have caused that?" We exchange an anxious glance before shaking our heads. "Really, no ideas? Well, after a thorough *two-hundred-pound* inspection, they discovered the exhaust pipes were stuffed full of blanket weed."

"How bizarre!" I give a nervous snort of laughter.

"Yes, bizarre indeed, Colin, and also most impressive according to the mechanic, he said it must have taken considerable effort. What exactly have you been doing all morning, apart from NOT being in control of the gardening staff?"

Tony, emboldened by his forthcoming, life-changing audition, protests. "It's all very well to criticise us, Mrs Winter, but our jobs are really difficult, you know. We've got enough to do in the gardens without trying to keep a psychotic vagabond under control. It's not like we can keep Ron on a lead; I did suggest it, but you said it wasn't ethical. And I'm not feeling well as it is." He remembers to add.

Mrs Winter looks at him coldly. "If the job's getting too much for you, Tony, you only have to say. I get hundreds of enquiries each week from people eager to join the team at Hogpits, so just give me six weeks' notice and you are free to go and find something less taxing."

For a moment, I believe Tony is going to do just that, but his bravado stalls. "I don't understand why we have to pander to Ron, that's all," he says sulkily. "He gets away with murder, it's not as if Hogpits owes him anything."

"Well, in a way it does." Mrs Winter fingers the little cameo brooch on her dark green neck scarf, her stare switching to the fields in the distance. "Ron's family used to own all this land."

I feel my eyes widening in astonishment. "Did they really? I never knew that."

"Oh yes, it's been in Ron's family for twelve generations, but they fell on hard times and slid from landed gentry to, well, Ron. He came with the sale, his job did, I mean. It was one of the conditions." She looks at me. "He's the only link to the past, to the history of Hogpits. Mr Winter dismisses it as sentimentality, but he would, wouldn't he? Personally, I think some sentiments are more important than making a quick buck. And if those sentiments happen to irritate the hell out of my husband, well, that's an added bonus, of course." She gives me a broad wink before turning and striding away.

Chapter Twelve

The doorbell rings but when I open the front door I find the doorstep empty. Ron Burgundy is fuming noisily on the road outside and as I move tentatively forward a jump-suited figure in huge dark glasses springs out from the side of the house. "I feel the need, the need for speed!"

"T-Tony? Is that you?" I stare into his face but can only see my own reflection in the mirrored shades.

"Of course it's me, you wally, who were you expecting, Donald Trump?" He takes off his massive glasses and looks me up and down. "Blimey Col, you haven't made much of an effort, have you? You're supposed to be the King of the Wild Frontier, not Colin from the cul-de-sac."

"I feel ridiculous." I gaze dejectedly down at my rear admiral's jacket and ill-fitting PVC trousers. "Come on, Tone, let's forget this, it's hopeless, the whole thing. Even if we do get into the party and meet Sarah, what the hell is she going to think? It's her Mum's birthday, a family celebration. This isn't fair on her, we can't do it."

"Calm down dear." Tony pats me on the shoulder. "This is exactly what happened to Goose before he took on the MiGs;

he lost his bottle and the next thing you know he's crashed and burned. That's not going to happen to you Mister, not on my watch."

"This isn't Top Gun, Tony, this is real life. Sarah's life, to be correct. And she may be about to come face to face with the guy who broke her heart, although the chances are she won't recognise him because A, she hasn't clapped eyes on him in nearly thirty years and B, he's dressed like a twat."

"Colin Hector!" Tony reels in shock. "I've never heard you use that word before. You can cut that out immediately, Potty-Mouth. That's not the silver-tongued charmer Sarah fell in love with all those years ago. You're just nervous, that's all. Come on, get it together. Have you got any Tippex?"

"Tippex?" I blink at the sudden change in subject. "Er, yes, I think so."

"Great. Hair gel?"

"Um, yes, somewhere."

"Cool, go and grab them. Add a smidge of guy-liner and it's goodbye Twatman and hello Prince Charming! Goose, it's time to buzz the tower."

Oh God.

It is almost seven o'clock by the time we splutter into Cath's drive. Ron Burgundy had stalled at a T-junction and had not been at all keen to start again. I'd thought for twenty glorious minutes that we wouldn't be able to go, but Tony had eventually 'coaxed' the engine into life Basil Fawlty style and we were on our way.

Cath and Louie are waiting by the front door, but there isn't time to linger, Tony simply shouting, "We can't stop, or we'll never start again!" before bundling Louie into the back seat. I wave at Cath but she doesn't wave back, watching us leave with her disapproving face of stone. She's right, I know she's right, and I can't help thinking that had we stopped, I might have been persuaded not to go. It wouldn't have taken much.

I turn to Louie. He is dressed in a black onesie that he's zipped up to his nose, and a large wooden crucifix hangs from his neck. A pointed black hat that has 'D' printed on the front in gold lettering covers his spikes. "Who have you come as, Louie?"

"The Aids virus."

"*Jesus!* That's a bit inappropriate-"

"Why? It's iconic of the 80s."

"Iconic? A Yuppie, that's iconic, Max Headroom even, but not a disease that's killed millions. That's horrendous!"

"Ignore old wet pants," Tony addresses Louie through the rear-view mirror. "He's been clucking away like an old hen since I picked him up, not to mention swearing like a trooper. Don't worry, I reckon we can pass you off as Madonna, you know, from the Like A Prayer video."

"Oh yes, that's iconic 80s," I snap. "Only, I can't seem to recall her prancing around in a dunce's cap."

Both Tony and Louie emit a loud 'Ooooh!' at my sarcastic tone. I didn't mean to sound so disagreeable but I am sick with worry.

"This isn't the way."

"I know, but I've got to pick up Wes. I thought I told you? He's coming too."

I sigh defeatedly. "And why, exactly, is Wes coming?"

"I thought it might cheer him up a bit, put some purpose back in his life."

"What purpose?"

"It suddenly occurred to me that if we're all disguised in fancy dress, Sarah will be too, and you'll never pick her out from the crowd. Wes is going to go round and do his table magic. As he's doing his tricks, he'll ask people their names. If anyone questions him, he's going to say someone booked him as a birthday surprise for Rowena. Brilliant, eh?"

"Terrific. What can possibly go wrong?"

Wes' house is set at the end of a small row of dated railway cottages, his home easily identifiable by the large 'W.E.S - Wondrous Entertainment Services' transfer on the back of his Renault Mégane. Tony beeps the horn and the front door opens to reveal a white-sheeted figure in a floppy, purple velour hat. It skips up the drive, the features unrecognisable under a face full of intricate make-up. "Do you really want to hurt me?" The moon face beams into the car.

"You look fantastic, mate!" Tony gasps. "That make-up is amazing."

"Yeah, Nat did it. Took her the best part of two hours."

"Nat?" Tony and I look at each in astonishment. "You mean, Nasty Nat?"

"Yeah, she said she wanted to do something to help. She wishes you luck, Col, and I've promised to text her later to let her know how it goes. She's alright really, when you get to know her." He looks slightly embarrassed and I sense he has gone pink under his white mask of face paint.

"Jump in the back, Col," Tony instructs. "Louie needs to do some work on the Dandy Highwayman, your Tippex is cracking. Wes, you're now my wingman, which means you have to feed me Doritos every ten seconds. And read the sat-nav."

"Cool." Wes nods to Louie. "Don't die of ignorance. Nice one."

"I'm Madonna."

"Oh, right. Well, she died on the Brit Awards, didn't she?"

"Ok, 80s funksters, let's get this show on the road! We're doing it for Col." Tony whacks up the radio for Kenny Loggins' Danger Zone. "Tower, this is Maverick requesting a fly by. Let's rock!"

The car park of The Waterboys is packed. Having driven

around it four times, Tony eventually has to park Ron Burgundy on the grass verge again. I climb from the car praying there are no mirrors in the hotel. My eyes are watering from the eyeliner, the left particularly sore after Louie jabbed his eye pencil into it when Tony hit a pot-hole. The line of Tippex is tight across my face and although my legs are heavy, my nerves are dissipating. I think I have gone beyond caring. Disaster is written all over this evening; nothing that happens now can possibly be worse than my imaginings. We'll probably get thrown out. That's if we get in. And Sarah might not even be here, she could be ill, or have found an excuse to get out of the party; this isn't her idea of a good night, I know it isn't. Looking into the foyer, I see a more authentic Madonna in lace gloves and legwarmers chatting to a Blues Brother, and two men larking around in tight white shorts – Wham, perhaps? Yep, those definitely look like strategically placed shuttle cocks. A man in tennis whites and an enormous curly wig strolls past. He adjusts his red headband as he speaks into his mobile: "Of course I'd rather be there with you, honey, but it's a family occasion, what can I do? Aw, don't be like that, I'll make it up to you, I promise. When? Well, let's see, she's working on Tuesday night, so I could get away then."

"What a *deuce* bag," Wes giggles. "He's going to need new balls if he carries on like that!"

"Right, boys." Tony is ready for action. "Everything's going to be fine, we've just got to style it out. We walk in like we own the place and make straight for the bar. Once we're safely in position we can survey our surroundings and see if Colin can spot the target."

"What will you do Unk, when you see her?" Louie looks at me anxiously. "What are you going to say to her?"

Tony whacks me on the back. "Tell him, Goose!"

"I'm not sure about that line, Tone."

"Come on, say it! Like we rehearsed."

"Take me to bed or lose me forever," I mumble, into the tarmac.

Tony punches the air and whoops. "Way to go! Just need to sound a bit more manly, mate, you know, butch it up a bit. Unless her husband's within earshot, in which case you might have to improvise. Now, when you've spotted the target, you must give the sign." He raises both arms and crosses them above his head. "That's the international signal for distress. If we can't see her, Wes will start working his magic on the table guests and we'll try and flush her out that way. Ok? Good luck everyone. Follow me."

Head up, Tony strides confidently into the hotel and we are forced to break into a trot to keep up with him, Wes lifting the end of his bed sheet so as not to trip over it. As Tony has no idea where he is going, he comes to an abrupt halt in the middle of the foyer and we almost cannon into the back of each other. Fortunately, the doors to the function room swing open in front of us and we stand aside to let an aging Bananarama pass. I just have time to observe a large rectangular room lined with tables as Tony marches us inside and makes straight for the densely packed bar at the far end of the room. We swiftly plunge into the throng, burying ourselves amongst the neon headbands, rah-rah skirts and shell suits. The DJ booth has 'Vinyl Richie' emblazoned across it and he is playing 'I Wanna Dance With Somebody' to an empty dance floor as red and blue lights flicker around the walls. There are gold helium balloons dotted around the room, some with a large '70' on them. That can't be right, Rowena must be older than that, surely? My heart sinks still further at the thought of it not even being the right person. That's probably why Rowena hasn't replied to Tony – she has no idea who Sarah is.

We wait behind Tina Turner and Prince before reaching

the bar and Tony orders three pints of lager and a coke for Louie. Another Boy George glares across the bar at Wes, but aside from some curious glances at Louie, no one takes much notice of us. As we relax into the scrum at the bar, I allow myself a sweeping look around the room. *Is she here?* Am I finally in the same room as Sarah Shaw again? It feels surreal but that's hardly surprising as all the faces are either swathed in darkness or weirdly illuminated with flashes of red and blue. Had Sarah seen me come in? She used to love Adam Ant, but that would soon change if she saw me in this get-up.

"Have you got a positive eyeball on the target yet?" Tony hisses at my side, his voice muffled. I glance round at him.

"Do you mean, can I see Sarah? That's a negative. And why are you speaking into your collar?"

"Target not sighted," Tony informs Wes and Louie. "Repeat, we have not marked the target."

"What about the Rubik's Cube?" Louie asks. "It's trying to sit down on that chair over there. That could be anyone."

"Christ, I'm glad I missed the 80s," Tony remarks with a shudder, nodding at a group of middle-aged ladies in leotards and leg-warmers. "That's not a good look, is it? Reminds me of that song: Do your boobs hang low, can they touch your camel toe?"

"The DJ's not much cop," Wes scoffs. "Trying to do it all with a Magma? Basic. It sounds crap. And he needs to get a bit of Dancing Queen on, pronto."

"But that was the 70s, Wes."

"Doesn't matter, mate, that's just a technicality. He needs to get everyone on their feet because at the moment he's dying on his arse. I mean, where's his audience participation? These jokers are quite happy to take the money but they don't give two hoots about the actual entertainment."

"He's getting a right ear-bashing from that pissed up old duck," Tony laughs. "What the hell has she come as, Worzel

Gummidge's deranged granny?" We watch as the old lady gesticulates angrily at Vinyl Richie. She is wearing a bizarre ginger wig with bits of rag tied into it and she has squeezed herself into a baby pink strapless dress, the bodice stretched to bursting point above a full skirt, the ends of which have been cut into shreds.

"She's not exactly Saucy Nancy," Wes comments. "I mean, a strapless dress, at her age."

"I think she's being ironic," Louie comments. "Because the 80s were so tragic, she's come as a tragedy. See, look how's she's dancing. Everyone's suffering."

The song has changed to 'Girls Just Want To Have Fun' and Saucy Nancy is swirling unsteadily around the dance floor. Bananarama take pity on her and get to their feet to join in. Could Sarah be one of them? Madly crimped hair and shapeless dungarees, it's impossible to say. "This is hopeless, lads," I sigh despondently. "We'll never spot anyone here. Let's just finish our pints and go."

"You can't give up, Col, not now we're so close." Wes whacks his empty pint glass down on the bar and waggles his fingers at me. "Time for some trickery, methinks! And look at these," he flaps the arms of the bed sheet around. "Proper wizard's sleeves." A woman in a skin-tight leotard swings round to glare furiously at him. "Sorry love, I didn't mean you. Gosh, look, what's that behind your ear?"

A young girl dressed as a brilliant Siouxsie Sioux, complete with studded dog collar and leather jump suit, pushes past me to get to the bar. I notice her looking at Louie and when he finally realises she's eyeballing him and not someone over his shoulder, they exchange a shy smile. Tony elbows me in the ribs, grinning inanely. "She'd better watch herself or she'll be going home with a deadly disease!" He nods at a woman on the other side of the bar. "That's not Sarah, is it? She looks like the pretty girl-next-door type you describe." With a sudden surge of excitement, I peer across at the attractive woman. She has lovely long brown hair and is dressed in a bright yellow blaser. "Hi de hi!" Tony calls over to her.

"Ho de ho!" she booms back, her voice as deep as Paul Robeson's.

"Shit, it's a fella." Tony buries his face in his pint. "Look away, mate, look away. Don't make eye contact."

Vinyl Ritchie picks up his microphone with a wince-inducing squeak. "Girls just want to have fun. That one was for the birthday girl!" Some weak cheers around the room as Saucy Nancy takes a bow, dangerous in a strapless dress.

So that must be Rowena! She doesn't look like her Facebook pictures, but then she wouldn't, not in that garb. "That's Rowena," I say to Tony.

"You what?"

"I said, that's her, Rowena."

"Still can't hear you."

"THAT'S HER!"

Suddenly a wrinkled hand shoots through the crowd and latches onto my jacket. I just have time to thrust my pint at Tony as Rowena pulls me through the packed bar. Jesus, she's strong! I tug at her hand but she has my lapels in a vice-like grip. To my horror, she drags me right out onto the dance floor. Oh my God, she's recognised me, the man who broke her daughter's heart! What is she about to do, unmask me in front of all their friends and family? Have me thrown out then roughed up in the car park? Those Blues Brothers look like they could be actual bouncers. I am aware of people clapping and cheering as the strains of Prince Charming 'Don't you ever, don't you ever' strike up. Rowena's face is in mine, electric blue eyelids, startling purple neon lips. I blink as red wine fumes blast at me. "Come on, Sonny, nobody's dancing! The party's a disaster - come on, dance!"

I begin to move my hips a little, shooting desperate

glances towards the others. They appear rooted to the spot in horror.

"Prince Charming, Prince Charming…"

Rowena starts doing the Prince Charming dance, one arm up, then the second arm up to make a cross, then both arms down... "Come on, do the moves!" she urges, and I follow her across the dance floor doing the same with my arms. I remember doing this at the school disco and thinking I looked cool. Now, I want to die.

'Ridicule is nothing to be scared of…'

Blood is pounding in my ears and I can't hear a thing, but as I reach the other side of the dance floor I can see the tonsils of the people at the table in front of me as they howl with laughter. Vinyl Ritchie has tears running down his face and Bananarama are clutching the side of the DJ booth to stop themselves collapsing. Is Sarah here, is she watching this spectacle? We perform the dance back the other way, then Rowena grabs me round the waist and grinds against me. "Go for it, mate," one of the Blues Brothers shouts, "it's Grab-a-Granny night!"

"Mind her teeth don't fly out!"

"Don't tread on her tits!"

As Rowena attempts to spin me round, I manage to twist out of her grip, speed-mincing around the dance floor as she chases after me. "Prince Charming, Prince Charming..." I'd forgotten how bloody repetitive this song is. "Don't you ever, don't you ever, lower yourself, forgetting all your standards..."

I think my whole life has flashed before me by the time the song comes to an end. Everyone claps as Rowena takes another bow and as she's lining up her next victim for 'Wake Me Up Before You Go-Go', I flee the dance floor, slinking back through the grinning crowd to Louie and Tony at the bar. Tony silently hands me my pint and I gulp the whole lot down in one, only aware of them glaring at me accusingly when I come up for air.

"It wasn't my fault," I gasp. "She was very insistent, I didn't have any choice."

"She recognised you, then, Unk? Even under all that Tippex?"

"Sorry?"

They look at each other. "I suppose we're just a bit taken aback," Tony says, coldly. "We were expecting Sarah to be roughly the same age as you, seeing as you told us you were at college together."

I am surprised. "We were."

"What was she, then, the bloody headmistress?"

"What?"

"I'm not being funny, Col, but had I known, I wouldn't have gone to all this effort for t*hat*." Tony nods at Rowena, who is trying to grab George's shuttlecock. "I mean, I'm sure she's a lovely lady and all, but even if you did get back together, you're not going to have that long, are you? She's a coffin-dodger."

I stare at them incredulously. "You, you think that's Sarah?"

"You said so, Unk," asserts Louie. "You yelled 'that's her' and shot off to dance with her. And you gave us the signal, you know, the international distress code. Lots of times, in fact."

"Oh, for Christ's sake!" I can't believe what I'm hearing. "That's Sarah's mother, Rowena, not Sarah. How could you possibly have thought - Oh, what does it matter, this is ridiculous, absolutely ridiculous; especially now, after that exhibition. Even if Sarah *is* here, there's no way she'll admit to knowing me. *I* don't want to admit to knowing me. Let's just go."

"We can't, mate." Tony points across the room to where Wes is entertaining a table of Greenham Common women.

"Wes has only just started working the room."

I see Wes hold up a 'No More Cruise' sign and tear it in half in front of the women. This isn't going to end well.

Sarah's not here, I know she isn't here. Even amongst the crazy outfits and peculiar lighting I am convinced I would know her anywhere. She's dodged it and I didn't blame her. The music has been turned down low while the buffet is served and the queue for food snakes around the room. Returning from the toilets, I come across a table in the corridor loaded with gifts, mainly bottle bags, and behind the presents are two large picture boards. There are dozens of photos plastered across the boards, and I stop to look at them. Most of them are of a very young Rowena – bronzed, skinny, smiling, on the beach, in the sea, lying on a sun bed... I scan the rows but I can't see Sarah in any of them.

"That's a rubbish one of me." I haven't noticed a small boy at my elbow. He is wearing a Ghostbuster jumpsuit and clutching a can of Tizer. He points at a picture of Rowena relaxing in a deck chair, a little boy building a sandcastle at her feet. "I'm a lot older than that now. I'm twelve and my name's Tom."

"I think it's a very nice picture." I smile down at him. "Pleased to meet you, Tom. And what a great outfit, I love Ghostbusters. Are you, um, related to Rowena?"

"Yes, she's a sort of step-granny. But we're not allowed to call her Granny because she doesn't like it, so we call her Ro-Ro."

My head whirls. "Right, right. So, are there any pictures of your mum on here, I mean, your step-mum?"

"She's only my sort-of-step-mum," Tom corrects as he stares earnestly at the boards. I hold my breath. "Yes, there she is, but she's a bit blurry." I follow his index finger to a photo of Rowena standing next to a white pony. They are in focus, but the figure next to them is a little fuzzy, and my eyes are sore. I blink and bend lower, moving my face right up to the picture and suddenly there she is. It is Sarah. Standing slightly away from her mother, that gentle smile, the soft brown hair framing her face, the cheeks a little fuller than I remember but the eyes... those eyes, that familiar earnest gaze. I hear myself groan.

"I've got a secret." Tom, now the same height as me, clamps a hand over my ear and whispers into in. "It's not really Ro-Ro's 70th birthday, she's been 70 for ages. She's a great big fibber."

"So, is your sort-of-step-mum here tonight?" My voice doesn't sound like it belongs to me, more like Larry the Lamb's.

"Yes, she's always here, she works here," Tom tells me. I blink in shock. *Sarah is here, she is feet away...* but, she's working in a hotel? Why isn't she a human rights lawyer or head of Unicef? "She's not in fancy dress, though, just a normal red dress and she's not very happy 'cos she has to stay right to the end to clear up. And then she's got to drive Ro-Ro home."

"Doesn't she like parties?" I croak.

"She doesn't like anything from the eighties." Tom's words strike like daggers at my heart. "It makes her all sad."

"Um, I, I–" the words wouldn't come out.

"But Ro-Ro loves the eighties because she says that's when her life actually started." Tom is blurring in front of me. "Your eyes are running," he says.

"It's the eye-liner," I mutter, fumbling for a handkerchief. These bloody stupid trousers, of course I don't have anything in the pockets, they are too tight to get even a sheet of paper in them.

"Here," a black-finger-nailed hand passes me a napkin. I dab it gratefully to my eyes and look up to find the teenage Siouxsie Sioux in front of me, her face intricately made up with black-lined eyes and dark red lipstick.

"Dear Prudence," I smile at her.

"No, this is Sophie, my sister," Tom introduces us. "She's not in fancy dress either."

"Oh, right."

"Who are you?" The girl demands, a pair of shrewd eyes looking accusingly into mine. "You came in with that dreadful magician, didn't you? He's rubbish, asked me to pick a card but went through half the pack before he guessed the right one. Ro-Ro didn't order a magician, I just asked her."

"I'm an old friend of Sarah's," I say truthfully. "And it's lovely to meet you both. Is Sarah at the party, or working somewhere, in the kitchens, perhaps?"

"Why are you all asking questions about Sarah?" Sophie won't be put off. "If you were a real friend you'd know where she is."

"I haven't seen her for a few years."

"Why are you here, who sent you to spy on Sarah?"

"No, no, we're not spying on her!"

"I'm telling Dad!" She grabs a wide-eyed Tom and they disappear through the double-doors back into the function room. I hurry in after them, returning quickly to the lads at the bar. "Are you ok, Unck?" Louie asks in alarm. "You look like you've been crying."

"No, no, it's-"

"This is wonderful, Col, absolutely amazing!" A beaming Wes cuts across me. "It's just what I needed. I can't believe that for a while I thought I was losing it, you know, my magic touch, but tonight all the old confidence has come flooding back."

"She's here!" I blurt, scared we're running out of time. "She's here!"

"What?" They gape at me. "You've seen her?" Tony cries.

"No, I met her children, her sort-of-stepchildren, but she's definitely here, she works here! But she's not in a costume, just a red dress."

"So she's working here tonight?"

"Yes, I think so. Have you seen any of the staff in a red dress?"

"One of the waitresses is in red," Louie tells me excitedly. "She helped bring out the buffet and I heard her telling Rowena off for scoffing all the cheese straws before her guests got a look in."

We stare anxiously around the room, and I see Tom and Sophie talking earnestly to John McEnroe. They point in our direction and he frowns across in concern. The lights are up for the buffet and we are standing right under a spotlight at the bar. "We've been rumbled," I groan.

"Shit, what are we going to do?" Tony hisses. "He's not that big, do you reckon you can take him, Col?"

"You cannot be serious."

John McEnroe is on his feet. He looks furious. "Right, there's nothing for it." Wes downs his pint and clears his throat. "It's time to buzz the tower!"

"Wes, what are you doing?" I make a grab for the bed sheet, but it's too late, he is striding across the dance floor to the DJ booth and snatches up the microphone before Vinyl Richie can stop him. There is a dreadful howl-round and everyone flinches. Wes steps deftly into the path of John McEnroe, stopping him in his tracks and waving him back to his seat. "Hi everyone," Wes moves to the middle of the dance floor. "If I could just have your attention for a few moments."

"What is he doing?" Tony grimaces. "My toes have only just uncurled from watching Col's performance."

"I'm Boy George and I'm your class act for this evening. Or should I say, class A act! Ha ha ha!"

"Class A clown," Tony mumbles.

"Thanks everyone for coming to celebrate Rowena's

seventieth birthday. Well, as near as dammit, anyway – what's a year or six between friends?" Everyone laughs and Wes is buoyed. "So, where is our pretty-in-pink birthday girl?" Heads swivel around the room but Rowena doesn't come forward. "Ah, I expect you all think I've made her disappear!" Wes chuckles. "I hope you've enjoyed watching me perform my tricks." Expectant smile. Silence. Move swiftly on. "Yes, so, er, I think the staff here at The Waterboys have done an amazing job for Rowena this evening, and putting on such a delicious buffet. Would you all like to thank the catering staff?"

"Yes!"

"Let's get them out here, shall we?"

"Yes!"

Tina Turner pushes open a door at the back of the room and yells into the kitchen. Someone begins a slow hand-clap until finally four staff reluctantly emerge. Is one of them Sarah? My eyes sting again and my vision blurs. Bugger, I'm struggling to see clearly. There's a young man all in black, another figure in chef's whites and two women, one in black the other... I close my eyes tightly as pain surges again. I give them a rub and attempt to peer out.

"Is that her, Unck?" Louie asks excitedly. "The lady in red?"

I can sense Wes looking over at me but I can't see properly and I have to spread my hands in a 'I don't know gesture'. Wes takes control. "Thanks guys for coming out. Not in a Boy George, sort of way, of course! Ha ha! All the guests here tonight have requested a song, just for you. So come on forward guys, onto the dance floor, don't be shy." Encouraging cheers ring out as the staff edge slowly towards Wes, who clears his throat. "They've requested this song because one of you has lost that loving feeling."

"Oh no," Tony groans. "Please God, if you exist, stop this from happening."

There is a moment of hush in the function room. "You never close your eyes anymore when I kiss your lips," Wes sings, deep and low. "And there's no tenderness like before in your fingertips."

"Hey, he's quite good," Louie says in surprise.

"You're trying hard not to show it…"

"BABY!" Everyone sings.

"But baby I know it!" I feel Tony taking my arm and steering me forwards. "You've lost that lovin' feeling, whoa that lovin' feeling." I sense we're on the dance floor next to Wes, I can make out his sleeves flapping as he holds up the microphone, but my eyes are watering very badly. I try again to focus; Wes has succeeded in getting the kitchen staff out on the dance floor, but they've also been joined by lots of the guests, who are swaying, arms aloft, from side to side. "It makes me just feel like crying…"

"BABY!"

"Cause baby, something beautiful's dyin'..."

Tony is trying to push me somewhere but I can only make out under water images between painful blinks; a sour-faced Vinyl Richie looms into view, then my face is in Madonna's armpit, and then all of sudden, everything turns red. I cry out at the flash of intense pain and stagger blindly backwards, a thousand needles stabbing into my eyes. I tread down heavily on someone's white stiletto and they shove me angrily away. As I double up in pain, I hear a soothing voice, "Come with me," and someone has my arm. I allow myself to be led across the dance floor and through a swing door that closes behind me shutting out the singing. There is a pungent smell of burnt cheese and I am propped against something hard as I hear the sound of running water. A warm, wet cloth is pressed to my eyes. "Here, wash your face and eyes in the sink." A hand steers me firmly forwards, and feeling the warm water in the bowl, I gratefully splash it into my eyes. "I think you got some of that white stuff in your eyes. It's not Tippex, is it? Try and get it all out, you don't want to be going to A&E, not on a Saturday night." The pain begins to subside, and I wipe away the water with a soft cloth that is pressed into my hand. "Can you open your eyes?" the voice asks anxiously.

Straightening up, I gingerly raise an eyelid. I wince in pain, but it isn't too bad, and my vision is clearing. I open the other eyelid and stainless-steel kitchen tops glide into view. There is a large birthday cake in the shape of a cassette tape with 'Rowena's 80s Mix' in pink icing, and a slim figure is standing in front of me. I see red velvet crinkles.

"We're in the kitchens," the familiar voice is firm but gentle. "How is your vision?" I squeeze my eyes shut then open them again. My eyes clear slowly and a concerned, round face slides into focus. It's framed by soft, brown hair, a few strands of grey showing in the parting above a pair of worried dark eyes. "Can you see me properly?"

"Sarah."

She blinks rapidly and I see the start of recognition in her eyes. She takes a step backwards, her voice barely a whisper. "*Colin?* Colin Hector?"

"Yes, it's me, I've been trying to find you." I beam at her in delight, overjoyed to be standing face to face with Sarah once more. My rapture is not returned. She shakes her head in bewilderment and there is no mistaking the look of pain and anger that flickers across her face.

I half-stretch out a hand towards her, then draw it back. "I'm here to explain. About the letters."

For a moment, I think she is going to say "What letters?", to pretend she can't remember writing them, that it was a completely insignificant chapter in her life, but she stays silent, staring at me with wide accusing eyes.

"You wrote to me, from Herne Bay, when you had to

move there. I wanted to track you down, so we found your mother on Facebook, and that's how we found out about her party. I'm sorry to gate-crash it, but it's the only way I could get to see you."

"Really?" Recovering from the shock, she folds her arms defensively across her chest. "Do you know, I've always wondered what I'd say to you if our paths ever crossed again."

That didn't sound good. "But you don't understand, Sarah, I never got your letters. Not until recently, that is."

She gives a hollow laugh. "Royal Mail really are slow these days."

"No, Dad hid them from me. I don't know why he did, he just did."

"Oh, he hid them, did he? What, all of them? I wrote quite a few, as I recall."

"Thirty-two. Maybe more. I found them amongst Dad's things when he passed away in April."

"I'm sorry to hear that." Her voice softens a little but her eyes are still hard and disbelieving. The waitress in black bursts into the kitchen.

"Oh, Sarah, there you are. Have you seen your mother? They want us to bring the cake out, but she's gone missing."

"No, I haven't seen her for a while. Is Uncle Terry missing too, by any chance?"

"Right, gotcha, I'll try the disabled loos."

Sarah turns back to me. "Well, it's been nice *reminiscing* with you, Colin, but I must get back to the party."

"Please Sarah, I just–"

"What the bloody hell was all that shite about?" The Chef strides angrily into the kitchen. "A half-arsed karoke, why is he singing stuff from the sixties? He's doing 'In The Ghetto' now, there's going to be a mass suicide. Elvis in a fucking bed sheet." He breaks off, looking from me to Sarah before snatching up a meat cleaver and whacking it with tremendous force into a wooden chopping board. "Need help with anything, boss?" he growls, glowering at me.

"No, thank you, Chef, I'm fine. Colin is just leaving." I stare at her in dismay and she looks at me sharply. "Was that you? Are you still in pain?"

"But, I didn't say anything." I hear it then, a low groan, like a wounded animal.

"It's coming from over here." Chef peers under one of the stainless-steel surfaces. A pair of purple stilettos is sticking out.

"Mum? Mum, is that you?" Sarah gets down on her hands and knees to see under the cabinet. She pulls out a baking tray that has a solitary sausage roll sticking to it. She looks up at the Chef, her face draining of colour. "It's another Filo overdose, Gary. What are we going to do?"

"I'll fetch the luggage trolley," he says, resignedly.

"No, no, we can't wheel her out past all her guests, I don't want them to see her like this. Couldn't we carry her out the back?"

"You must be bloody joking!" Chef's eyebrows shoot up in disbelief. "Didn't you see how much quiche she put away? I reckon there's a ton of gruyère lying right there. My back's not up to it."

"I'll help," I offer and they turn to look at me. "We should be able to get her up between the three of us, shouldn't we?"

There is no option other than for Chef and I to grab an ankle each and drag Rowena out from under the table in a most undignified manner. She lies on her back on the kitchen floor chuckling "The Earth's moving!" as Chef puts the fire blanket under her shoulders, using it as a hoist to make her sit up. With Sarah squatting behind her to stop her falling backwards again, we tug Rowena to her feet. With an arm over each of our shoulders, we make our painstaking way out of the back entrance to the kitchen and around to the staff car park. Sarah opens the rear door of a Volkswagon Golf and we fold Rowena onto the back seat. "Girls just wanna have fun," she mutters.

Chef stomps back to the kitchens and I hover by the car as Sarah opens the driver's door. "Thank you for your help," she says without looking at me.

"Are you going to be alright?" I ask anxiously as she climbs in. "How will you get her out the other end?"

"I won't have to," Sarah replies wearily. "She can sleep in the car, she's used to it." I clutch at the doorframe before she can pull it shut.

"Please, Sarah, you do believe me about the letters, don't you? I need you to know that I never saw them, not one. If I had I would have called you straight away, I would have gone to see you. But, when you didn't get in touch, I thought you didn't want me anymore. You do believe me, don't you?"

She looks up at me, her tired eyes sad and mistrustful. "No, I don't believe you, Colin. It wasn't just the letters, was it?"

I'm confused. "What do you mean?"

"When we came back home I went round to your house. It was the first thing I did."

"I didn't know, Dad never told me!"

"I didn't see your father." She puts her car key into the ignition. "It was Cath who answered the door."

I recoil in shock. "You saw Cath?"

"She told me you were at work."

A cold sickliness creeps over me. "Yes, I would have been working at Hogpits by then. But Cath would have told me if she'd seen you, she knew I was desperate to hear from you. It couldn't have been Cath you saw. Are you sure you got the right house?"

"Don't be stupid Colin; I didn't go back to Derek's by mistake." Sarah tugs the door from my grip, slamming it shut. She turns the key in the ignition and the Golf roars into life. I see my stunned reflection briefly in the window before it slides down, emitting a waft of stale sausage meat.

"You must have made a mistake," I say limply.

"No, Colin, I didn't." Sarah pushes the gear stick fiercely into reverse. "In fact, I remember it particularly well because while I was stood on your doorstep, Cath tore me off a strip for pestering you. She likened me to an annoying fly. She said you weren't interested in me anymore and you were seeing her friend's sister."

"What?" No, no, surely it isn't possible, it can't be true. "There must have been a misunderstanding, I wasn't seeing anyone."

"Really? Does Virginia Parker ring any bells?"

"No. Well, yes, that's Ginny, but I wasn't seeing her, I hardly knew her. Why on earth would Cath say something like that?"

I stare at Sarah, searching her face for signs that she realised she'd got things wrong, or that she was lying about the conversation with Cath. But the earnest brown eyes look steadfastly back into mine and I know; Sarah isn't mistaken, she has no reason to lie, she never tells lies. She'd seen Cath and Cath had warned her off. I have the sensation of everything falling away. I am aware of Sarah releasing the handbrake and the car reversing. I want to run after her but my legs won't move. Cath has betrayed me too.

I'm walking blindly up a lane, I don't know where I'm going. I am dimly aware of a spluttering engine, then lights behind me casting my long-legged shadow onto the road in front. A horn blasts. "There he is! Col! *Col!* Where are you going, you daft bastard?"

A car door opens. Running footsteps behind me. "Bloody hell, Col, how pissed are you? You can't walk all the way home, it's twenty bloody miles, what the hell is wrong with you?" Tony catches my arm, tugging me round. Even in the twilight I don't miss his flinch of shock when he looks into my face. "Right, er, right, let's get you into the car, then. Come on, mate." He leads me gently towards Ron Burgundy, its headlights almost blacked out by the vast amount of exhaust smoke. "Get in the back, Wes," Tony orders, "Col's going in the front."

"Why didn't you tell us you were leaving?" Wes demands, holding onto the passenger door. "We've been searching bloody everywhere."

"Shut it, Wes," Tony snaps. "Just get in the back."

Wes looks from one of us to the other then quickly gathers up the ends of his sheet and climbs silently into the back. "Are you alright, Unk?" Louie asks anxiously as I slump heavily into the passenger seat. "Your eyes are very red still."

"He's fine," Tony tells him. "Just too much to drink, that's all." He gives Ron a few ear-splitting revs. "We'll drop you home first, Col, assuming we make it that far. Actually, you might have been quicker walking."

"Do you want to talk about it?"

"No. Thank you, mate, but no."

"Righto. I'll drop the others off and come back and stay with you tonight. Not *with* you as in a Brokeback way, but I could sleep on the sofa, or in the bath; I quite like sleeping in the bath actually, I have to do it at home when Mum has one of her Earth sisters staying over. I like the smell of the towels-"

"No thanks, I'll be fine." I open the car door and look back at the anxious faces. "Thanks, lads. For tonight, and for all your support. And, well, for everything."

"Blimey, you're talking like we'll never see you again!" Tony gives a nervous laugh. "Col? Game of darts at The Stag tomorrow night?"

"Bye guys."

The house is dark and silent. I sit down on the floor in the hallway. Ron Burgundy is outside for a long time, but finally I hear it pull away, its lights briefly illuminating a picture of a young Cath and I on the steps of a beach hut at Cowes, the summer we both learnt to swim, arms wrapped round each other's shoulders, clutching dripping chocolate cornets as we beam at Mum behind the camera. I can't see it now in the gloom, but in the daylight it is possible to make out a shadowy figure lurking inside the darkness of the beach hut. *Who were you, Dad?* Just out of sight in photos as you were in real life. No one could quite get to you. Another car pulls in to Cotter Close and passes number seven, its headlights flashing over another frame: Cath in a square mortar board hat, her robe a stark black against the photographer's blue background. She's holding her certificate, smiling, proud. Was that why she'd done it? Had she been scared I'd run off to be with Sarah, leaving her to look after Dad? No degree, no career, no social life... Instead, she'd condemned *me* to that fate. No wonder she'd been dead against me tracking down Sarah. Did she feel any guilt? She must have lived with the knowledge of what she'd done all these years. I don't feel sorry for her; I don't feel anything apart from a cold, white nothing. I'll never feel anything ever again.

Chapter Thirteen

The morning sunshine is dazzling. I screw up my sore and gritty eyes to protect them from the glare that bounces from the road. Light-headed after a sleepless night, I know I should have eaten something before setting off, but the ever-increasing waves of nausea has rendered that impossible. Cath's Lexus is in the drive but David's car is missing; I know he has taken Louie into town to buy him a new iPad, my brother-in-law somehow managing to bake the previous one in the Aga. I leave my bike by the porch and duck under the honeysuckle archway into the back garden, shrugging my rucksack from my shoulders as I walk across the lawn. Cath is sitting in the garden under the shade of the apple tree. The Sunday papers are scattered across the table but she is staring straight ahead, and I feel her eyes boring into me as I walk towards her. As I come close, I see she has large dark rings under her eyes, her face pasty beneath the tan.

"Hello Colin." Her tone is light and cheery, but a wobble in her voice betrays her. "Coffee?"

"No." I remove the polyurn from my rucksack and place it heavily onto the table on top of a picture of Boris Johnson.

Cath looks at it in alarm.

"Whatever's that monstrosity?"

"It's Dad."

Cath shoots backwards in her chair, aghast at my callousness. "Colin, what are you doing?"

"He's all yours now, Cath, I've done my bit. In fact," I pause, pretending to think, "you never really did anything, did you? Not for Dad, I mean."

Cath stands up, her wide eyes lifting from the urn to meet mine. "Why are you saying that, Col, what the hell's got into you?"

"You never once offered to stay with him, or look after him, not for any length of time, anyway. You left it all to me."

"But, he didn't want me around, you know he didn't! He hated me, he couldn't stand being in the same room."

"He didn't like being with anyone! He was ill, Cath, ill, but he was still your father and you did nothing to help him. To help us. It was more convenient to say he hated you so you could wash your hands of it all."

Beginning to recover, Cath places her hands on her hips and looks me square in the face. Typical Cath defiance, just as I'd expected. "I don't know why you're bringing this up out of the blue, it's so unfair. We agreed you'd look after Dad while I finished university because it made sense. You agreed to it."

"I agreed to everything you told me to do, you knew I was a pushover. So, when you finished uni, what about then; why was it all still left to me, why didn't you do more?"

"Because I'd joined a firm of solicitors, I was in training! Bloody hell Col, where's all this coming from? You know I've always been very grateful, I've always been there for you."

I give a hollow laugh. "Like you were there for me when you sent my girlfriend packing?" I see Cath wince. She sinks back down into her chair, her eyes lowering. "You never told me Sarah had called round, or that she'd moved home."

"I don't remember." Her face tells a different story. She fights back, her chin jutting upwards again. "Are you serious, Colin, a silly crush you had decades ago? Is that what this is all about?"

"No, this is about you. What you did. To me." Cath says nothing so I continue. "You told Sarah I no longer cared for her. You said I was going out with Ginny Parker." Cath remains silent, but her head lowers as she fiddles with a corner of the Sunday supplement. "Did you know about the letters, too?" My voice catches and she looks up at me, her eyes suddenly full of tears. "No, I didn't know about the letters, Col, I swear. It was Dad."

"Liar!" This comes out in such an animalistic hiss, Cath flinches away in fear. "You told Sarah to stop *pestering* me, didn't you? Didn't you? So you did know about the letters!" She looks down at the papers, tears falling onto the newsprint. "Did you read them all? I bet you did. You would have seen Sarah was in torment and you let her carry on suffering, thinking the worst of me. You knew how I felt about her, you knew. How could you have done that to me?" She doesn't answer. "What's the matter, Sis, how come you're suddenly short of words for once in your life?"

"You don't understand, Col. Dad told me to do it. I'm sorry."

"Yeah? So am I. Remember that awful Christmas we had, the first without Mum? You knew Sarah was waiting for me at the Cathedral on Christmas Eve, but still you didn't tell me - I'd have given anything to have seen her, anything. And you just left her there in the cold while you took me to the cemetery, to lunch, to the bloody pictures, anywhere to keep me from seeing her." I watch her rocking backwards and forwards, her hands covering her face. I don't feel any pity, I just want an answer. "Why did you do it? I deserve to know the truth."

She rubs her face, speaking through her fingers. "You

don't understand what I went through, Col, you've no idea. I had to deal with Mum's death, I had to arrange everything, cope with all that endless paperwork, try and sort the financial mess we were in. I took on everyone else's grief, I never had time for my own."

"But that doesn't explain what you did!" I jam my hands into my pockets to stop myself from shaking her. "Are you blaming your behaviour on Mum's death? Hardly her fault, was it?"

"Wasn't it?" Cath's head shoots up, her watery eyes glinting angrily. "Mum left us, she left us. I was so angry with her."

"You were angry at Mum for having a stroke?"

"A stroke! Really? Yes, I know that's what we told you, that's what we told everyone, but surely you've never believed that? She killed herself, Col, she bloody well killed herself! You know it as well as I do."

I don't recognise the intense feeling welling up inside me as I consider my sister, and then I realise what it is: hatred. I surprise myself by speaking calmly. "Wow, Sis, you really are a piece of work. You'll say anything to deflect responsibility from yourself, won't you? Even tarnishing Mum's memory."

"It's true, Colin. There were pills ... surely you guessed? Haven't you ever wondered why the life assurance company wouldn't pay out? And Dad bloody well knew he'd driven her to it, that's why he went downhill so fast. He knew I knew and that I blamed him, that's why he hated me. He couldn't bear to even look at me because I made him feel so guilt-ridden."

I shake my head. "You're pathetic. Do you know, I actually feel sorry for you. As if I'd believe such a thing of Mum. She was the last person on Earth who'd take her own life."

"How would you know? You were always with that girl, you were joined at the bloody hip! I was at university and

Mum knew she was losing us. She didn't want to be left alone with Dad, day after awful bloody day. Well, I wasn't going to be left with him either, and no, I didn't care about you at the time, I hated you too. I blamed you for Mum's death almost as much as I did Dad. I thought you should have seen what was happening to Mum; didn't you notice anything, didn't you see? And while she did it, while she was dying, you were next door in bed with that, that *slapper*." Bile rises in my mouth and I swallow hard. I can't speak. Cath's hands clench around the urn, her knuckles stark white against the dark brown. "Yes, I blamed Sarah too, but the truth is, this is all his fault. Everything bad that's ever happened to us is his fault. I hope hell exists and he's rotting away in it, the bastard. I didn't know he'd kept the stupid letters, this must have been what he wanted, us, at each other's throats. Look what he's done to us!"

I gaze pointedly round at my sister's five-bedroomed house, the landscaped garden, the beautiful roses over the back door. "You haven't done too badly, though, have you? Achieved everything you wanted to in life, despite your evil monster of a father. My life, however, well, we shall never know what it might have been. The wife I might have loved, the family I might have raised, what I might have achieved. So, who shall I blame for my sad little existence with all its crushed hopes and dreams? It wasn't Mum's fault, she died. From a stroke. And it wasn't Dad's fault, he was mentally unwell." I look coldly into her tear-stained face. "That just leaves you."

"Colin, please."

"Here's a Scruples question for you, Cath: when someone betrays you, how long before you can trust them again? Answer: never."

I turn on my heel and walk away from her.

The abrasive whine of the chain saw sounds good, filling my head with noise and blocking out everything else. I cut savagely through the branches, watching them drop to the ground, a pyre building beneath me. I had made it into work on Monday morning, but Mrs Winter had taken one look at me and sent me straight home again: "When someone has less colour than me, they really need to get themselves to a doctor. Or a mortuary." I probably should have sought medical advice but I hadn't been to my GP in years, and anyway, there was nothing physically wrong with me. Instead, I had been self-medicating all week, existing on a diet of Rennie tablets in an attempt to keep the horrid acid reflux at bay, and Panadol Night capsules so that some sleep was possible, albeit fractious and fragmented. It had been one hell of a struggle to get out of bed each morning, and the sheer effort required to shower and dress would wipe me out for the rest of the day.

Cath had not been in touch; I hadn't expected her to be. What was there to say? I'd spent hours searching the house for Mum's death certificate, but without success. The kitchen table was covered in old photographs of Mum, and every single one of them showed her happy and smiling, glad to be alive. I'd examined each photo over and over, searching for something behind the smile, perhaps a flicker of pain or anguish in her eyes, but there was nothing but joy. Mum hadn't killed herself, Cath was lying. *Such a wicked lie.* I couldn't see any way back for us now; my sister had gone too far.

Poor Louie had sent several messages but I wasn't sure how much his mother had told him. He wanted me to know he was in contact with Sophie from the party and they'd met up one evening, at a natural burial site in Cholderton. I'd replayed his last voicemail several times: "Sophie understands about the party now, Unck, I explained why we were there and about the letters. She's offered to speak to Sarah if you want her to? She says her dad has an over-inflated sense of self-worth compounded by low intelligence i.e. a dickhead. She says you can't possibly be any worse, so let me know if you want her to put in a good word with Sarah for you. Hope you're ok, Unck. Are you ok? Let me know. See you, then. Bye."

There was little point anyone putting in a good word for me, it was over now, done with. Sarah hadn't believed me and I couldn't see that help from a teenager would change that, especially one motivated by an opportunity to wind up her father. Tony had bombarded me with text messages. I hadn't read them all but I knew he was concerned for me. He had been keeping me updated with the gossip from Hogpits: 'saw nasty nat and wes the wally walking in the woods. He has been eating her out a lot', followed by, 'oops * taking* her out a lot!'

This morning I knew I had to make the concerted effort to get myself together in preparation for returning to work tomorrow. Tony's Deal or No Deal audition is next week and he's intending to take sick leave; if Chicken Ron is left in charge of the gardens there's a good chance we'll be closed down. I'd forced myself out of bed at seven-thirty to tackle a job I'd been promising to do for Derek, and now, balancing precariously in the apple tree at the back of his garden, I wield the chain-saw at the overhanging elderberry branches, enjoying seeing them fall away and the light flooding in.

It's hard work and I'm not match-fit. I stop to catch my breath, leaning against the trunk, sweat trickling freely down my back. I look across at Derek's bungalow where, directly opposite, is the room in the roof, *our room*. All the dark thoughts come flooding back. It's overwhelming and I clutch at a branch to steady myself. As I take several deep breaths, a sudden movement in the room below catches my eye. Jean is in the downstairs bedroom, her back to the window. In one swift movement her dressing gown falls to the floor and, completely naked, she bends over to pull her knickers on. Look away, look away ... too late, oh God no, it's a thong, she's putting on a thong. Ugh! Black lace cutting through doughy white flesh.

"Colin!" I nearly fall out of the tree. Derek is standing on the patio looking agitated.

"I wasn't looking, I didn't see anythong, I mean, anything."

"You what? Now look, we've got an emergency – can you help us?"

Relief washes over me. "Of course, Derek. What's up?"

"We're absolutely desperate, mate, or we wouldn't be asking. We need you to make up a threesome."

"Sorry?"

"Len's let us down, he's done his wrist in. Doesn't think he can grip his wood."

"Oh my days–"

"There could be fifty quid in it for you."

"Even so."

"Please Col, it's the Bert Garfield triples today and we've got a really good shot at the prize money. We can't let those smug bastards from Lyme Regis win again, they've been rubbing our noses in it all year."

Bloody bowling. A threesome might have been the lesser of two evils. *Stall, play for time.* "What's happened to poor old Len, did he have a fall?"

"No, son, he's got that RSI thingie, you know, Repetitive Stroking Injury. Spending too long on the Internet, if you know what I mean."

"Euch."

"So, can you make up our three? I know it's not really your thing, but there's a hundred and fifty quid for the winning team. It starts at ten-thirty."

No is the answer you are looking for, no bloody way, absolutely not... "Yes, of course I'll play." Weak, lily-livered, spineless clot. "I haven't got any whites, though."

"Ta da!" Derek holds up a pile of clothing. "I've got Jean's old set here, reckon they should fit you a treat. Now, flat shoes, remember, don't turn up in your high heels - ha ha ha! Bus leaves at 9.45. Cheers Col, we owe you one."

I clamber down from the tree to inspect the pile of clothes Derek has left on the patio table. I unfold the white bundle to reveal an old pair of drawstring polyester trousers and a faded polo shirt, size 16. Jean had embroidered 'Woodley Ladies Do It On The Grass' in emerald green on the chest pocket. Perfect.

I sit in the shade of the Stella Artois umbrella, nursing a flat pint of Pepsi and keeping my feet tucked under my chair and out of sight, embarrassed to be exposing so much ankle. My legs are clearly a good deal longer than Jean's. Our mat had finished early after we'd been resoundingly trounced by the Lyme Regis third team. Derek and Jean, soon realising they had precious little chance of winning the prize money, had been spending longer and longer in the bar between each end, occasionally emerging onto the terrace for a despondent smoke before disappearing back into the gloom of the club house. I watch the little knots of white figures as they huddle together at either end of the green, their muted 'oohs and ahs' mingling with the thwacks of wood on wood. I don't understand why anyone plays bowls, it is such an annoying game. You can release a wood and watch it curve around beautifully to kiss the jack. You give yourself an imaginary high-five and do a little fist pump. Then you take the next shot and even though you play it in exactly the same way, the wood veers off in the direction of Cornwall. It's not as if you can jump off the mat and scurry away to hide. The rules dictate you must stand on the mat and watch the wood until it stops rolling, thus ensuring you stand out as the prize plum. Aside from the frustration of the game, members have to endure the ever-present club politics, the terrace filled with whispered grievances: "That's the trouble with our chairman, he couldn't organise a two-car parade", "If that Limey goes any slower he'll be lined in chalk", "Black knickers under white trousers? Trollop."

The throaty roar of an engine causes disapproving heads to swivel in the direction of the car park. Ron Burgundy shudders to a halt before Tony has the chance to manoeuvre into a parking space, so the car is abandoned in the middle of the car park. Tony jumps out and makes his way to the terrace, removing his sunglasses so he can see where he's going. His mouth falls open as he spots me. "Holy shit balls! What are you wearing?"

"Jean's bowling whites."

"You look like you should be in the care of the community." Tony stares at me anxiously. "Are you having a breakdown?"

I shrug. "Perhaps."

"Well, stop having one. And check your messages once in a while."

"How did you know I was here?"

"Elementary, my dear Watson. That and iPhone tracker." He waves his mobile at me accusingly. "This is the first time you've left the house in one hundred and forty-seven hours. And why haven't you been talking to Lou Lou? He's worried sick about you." I shift uncomfortably. I don't want to tell him about Cath, it's too raw. "Louie's befriended that gothic chick from the party, you know, that Siouxsie-Sophie banshee thing. Sarah's not married to her old man, you know, Sophie says he's a cheating arsehole."

"So?"

"So ... Come on, Col, she's at The Waterboys. Right now.

Go and see her."

I look at him wearily. "I suppose you mean Sarah?"

"No, Desmond fucking Tutu. Of course Sarah. You do remember her, right? The love of your life, the one you've been pining away for all these years."

"It's over, Tone, I should have left it well alone. Now things are, well, they're just so ... putrid."

"Rubbish. I know she mugged you off at the party but she was probably in shock. You can't give up, not after all these years."

I look away. "It's no good."

Tony grabs my shoulders and shakes me so vigorously my teeth rattle in my head. "What are you, clinically dead? Take a look at yourself, Colin Hector, just take a frigging look. Is this your life now, is it? Crown green bowling on a Sunday, quick splash of TCP then a nice game of cribbage on a Wednesday? You're dying a deathless death and you don't even know it! Your old man's looking up at you right now and he's laughing his evil arse off. He trapped you into spending your life waiting on him hand and foot and now, even though he's gone, here you still are, imprisoned amongst the coffin-dodgers."

Some of the players are beginning to look round at us.

"They're nice people," I say feebly.

"But they're not exactly marriage material, mate, are they? Come on, don't *flatline.* You've still one last shot at happiness before brewer's droop sets in; bloody well take it."

I examine my Pepsi. "Get busy living or get busy dying?"

"Exactly."

"But Sarah's with someone."

"She's not married to him, though, is she? There's got to be a reason for that. And he's a nobhead by all accounts, probably hasn't even got a nob. What more do you want? Go and rescue her, she's at the hotel now. There's a wedding on."

"She'll be busy."

"Christ, Hector, is that what Richard Gere said before he swooped in on that Debra bird to liberate her from the factory? 'Ooh, I don't know, maybe I should wait until she's finished her shift' No!" Tony chucks his car keys into my lap with slightly more force than could be deemed necessary. "Go on! Go get her. I'll take over here." He rolls his shoulders and shakes his head from side to side, loosening his neck. "How difficult can it be? Just like a massive game of marbles."

I don't do spontaneous. Never have. But maybe now, maybe I should. With a rush of blood, I leap up, startling Derek and Jean who are just returning to the green clutching pints of Strongbow. "I'm sorry, guys, but there's something I have to do." I slam my pint glass down on the table. "I'm going to see the girl I used to love."

As I stride across the green. Jean's whites flapping above my ankles, they burst into applause. "Way to go Col, way to go!" Tony yells. Ron Burgundy starts at the first time of asking and I'm off, kangarooing out of the car park, heading towards Trowbridge, A34 all the way, Joe Cocker and Jennifer Warnes on the radio.

The photographer sounds exasperated: "So, are we ready? Well, what's wrong now? We're still waiting for the other bridesmaid? She's what, looking for Uncle Nick? But I thought someone had gone to the bar to get him? No, no, don't you go, I don't want to lose you, too, no, please stay where you are!" I skirt around the clucking group and into the hotel's foyer. I ask the flustered girl on reception where Sarah is. "Don't know, she's around here somewhere."

"Couldn't you page her or something?"

She shrugs helplessly as the phone on reception rings and she picks it up, her face draining as an angry voice yells down the line at her. Accepting she's going to be a while, I make my way outside to the car park and around to the back entrance to the kitchens. I enter through the open doors into a heat-haze, the kitchens alive with activity as the waiting staff mingle with the kitchen workers, frantically finalising the last-minute preparations for the wedding breakfast.

Sarah, dressed in black, is standing in the middle of proceedings talking earnestly to an angry-looking Chef. "I *did* tell you, Gary, and it's in the running order too, look. Speeches first, then the meal."

Chef throws his arms dramatically into the air. "And to hell with the kitchen, as usual, eh? We'll just have to put everything miraculously on hold again: a whole day's work turning to rat shit."

God, I choose my moments. My courage failing, I consider turning to leave but Chef has spotted me. "And now, just random people walking into my kitchen. Oh, it's you again, is it? Adam the anaemic ant. What have you come as this time, John Revolter?"

I ignore him, my eyes on Sarah. She doesn't seem surprised to see me. "Colin. What are you doing here?"

"I need to talk to you." I hold my hand up as her face clouds over. "Please. I know you're working but I have to speak with you."

She shakes her head. "I'm too busy."

"Please. I know my timing's really bad, but after all this time... Spare me a few minutes." Both she and Chef stare at me and I hold my breath. *Don't make me beg, don't make me beg.*

"Alright." Sarah hands what appears to be a timings schedule back to Chef. "This won't take long." *Ouch.* She nods toward the doors. "We'll go through to the function room, the guests aren't in there yet."

"I'll just go and boil my head, shall I?" Chef yells after us. "Unbelievable!"

The rectangular function room looks completely different

from Rowena's party, garishly festooned with scarlet bunting and cerise balloons, the vibrantly pink gerbera centrepieces surrounded by flashing LED tealights. I hope none of the guests are migraine-sufferers. A waitress pours champagne into little glass flutes and we sit down at the table furthest away from her. My name plate reads 'Dottie Slocombe' but all I care is that I am sitting next to Sarah Shaw. It's not a dream this time, she is really here, right in front of me. She hasn't changed a bit; maybe a few more lines around the eyes, her waist a little thicker. "This feels surreal," I say nervously. "I can't believe you've been so close all this time; how have we never bumped into each other in Salisbury?"

"I shop in Bath, mainly."

"Right. That's nice." I wrack my brains to fill the uncomfortable silence. "This is unusual, isn't it? A Sunday wedding?"

"Not really, every Saturday is booked for the next two years." She glances at her watch. "I haven't got long, Colin. And it looks as though you need to be back in the home soon."

"Sorry?"

"I'm assuming you have just escaped from somewhere?"

I give an embarrassed grin. "I got suckered into a three-way with Derek and Jean. That's bowls by the way, nothing more disturbing."

"Keen Jean, from number sixteen?"

"That's right, she and Derek are an item now." I'm thrilled she remembers. "The room upstairs is just as it was, although I'm afraid the ghastly yucca plant is still thriving." That was stupid, the mention of Derek's room, *our room*; it was over-familiar and her half-smile abruptly switches off. Sarah is not letting her guard down. I try a different tack. "Has your mother recovered from her party?"

"It took her two full days to get over the pastry hangover. I had to cut her out of her outfit in the end, otherwise she'd still be walking round dressed as Cyndy Lauper."

Ah, that's who she was! "Look, I know it was a stupid idea to turn up at her party; we shouldn't have done it."

"No."

"It must have been a shock for you, seeing me again after all these years." *God, that sounded arrogant!* "I mean, well, I didn't mean to presume that you even remembered me or anything, I don't suppose you've thought about me much..." I wait for her to say something but she doesn't speak. "I had to find you. After I discovered your letters in Dad's things, I just had to track you down and explain why I'd never written back." The narrowing of her eyes convey their mistrust. "I didn't see any of your letters, Sarah, really I didn't. I waited and waited for you to send me your new address and phone number, but when nothing came I assumed you'd found a better life for yourself, or you thought the distance between us too much. Or something."

The waitress arrives at our table and begins pouring champagne, glancing at us curiously as she moves around the table. It takes an excruciating amount of time for the bubbles to die down enough for each glass to be topped up again and we sit in silence, Sarah examining her fingernails as I twiddle with a napkin.

"So," Sarah looks me squarely in the face as the waitress reluctantly moves on to the next table. "You really didn't get any of my letters? You never found any on the doormat, or met the postman."

"I left for work at seven-thirty each morning, I never saw the postman."

"What about Saturdays? Some might have arrived on a Saturday."

I blush. "I did a paper round on Saturday mornings." The 'oldest paperboy in town' jeers still ring in my ears. "We needed the money."

She considers me with a frown. "And you weren't seeing Virginia Parker?"

"No, I wasn't."

"Why did Cathy say you were?"

I begin to tear the napkin into strips as I try to find an answer to this question. I still can't understand it myself. Shaking my head I mumble, "She was angry. With the world, with Mum. Partly she blamed me for it all, maybe she wanted to punish me. But I still can't grasp why she would do what she did; what she ended up doing to us."

"What I'm finding a little difficult to believe, Colin, is that you couldn't track me down. It was only Kent, not Timbuktu. Why didn't you go round to see my Dad?"

"Your Dad?"

"Yes, you knew where we lived, you knew he would have my contact details. Why didn't you go and ask him? Or phone him, at least."

Why hadn't I? "I can't recall... I guess it felt too awkward after what he'd done, or what I thought he'd done. I did cycle past his house a few times." By few, I mean several hundred.

"Wow, cycling past his house. You really were hot on my trail, weren't you?"

She is right to be incredulous. "It was all a bit of a blur after Mum died. My priority was Dad, and then when we uncovered the extent of his debts, I had to leave college and find a job. Yes, I could have been more rigorous, but I was scared."

"Scared?"

"Because you hadn't been in touch I thought you weren't interested in me anymore. I figured you'd met someone else and I couldn't bear to have it confirmed."

"You gave up on me pretty quickly."

I feel a stab of irritation. "That's not fair. My mother had just passed away, my father was a mess, we had no money, and the love of my life had moved a hundred and fifty miles away. So yes, I should have fought harder for you, but possibly there wasn't any fight left in me." I am aware my voice has taken on an unattractive high-pitched whine, but I can't stop it. "And now, having cared for my father all those years, I discover that not only did he keep your letters from me, but the person I trusted most in the world betrayed me too. My own bloody sister!" I can't continue my self-pitying rant as I feel the tears rising up again, ready to humiliate me. I snatch up the nearest glass of champagne and take several large gulps. The bubbles catch in my tightening throat and I choke, gasping for breath as fizzing foam spurts from my mouth and runs from my nose.

I feel a napkin being pressed gently into my hands and I splutter into it. I try to say sorry but soft fingertips on my lips stop me. "I can't keep mopping you up like this, Colin Hector." I try to smile but have to gasp for air. How unattractive I must look, like a hooked trout, desperate to get back in the water. To my relief, Sarah takes over the conversation. "You've been through a lot, Colin, I think I'd lost sight of that. When Mum and I moved back to Wiltshire I was so excited despite the fact you hadn't been in contact because I knew there had to be an explanation, I just knew. But then I saw Cath and when she told me you were seeing someone else, the pain was unbearable. It never occurred to me that she might be lying; why would she? I was so angry with you, so hurt, I told myself I'd never forgive you, ever." I cough again, unable to speak. The waitress approaches, ready to refill my glass but Sarah waves her away. "I always meant to confront you, tell you exactly what I thought of you, I rehearsed over and over in front of the mirror, but I never could face going through with it. I got a place at university and the years passed by." She shrugs. "The pain dulls, of course, but it's still there, deep in you, ready to surface the moment someone gets too close.

It's been so hard to trust anyone, well, any man, ever since you. If someone so seemingly sincere and lovely can treat you like that then men really are capable of anything." That was horrible to hear. *Cath has done this. Cath and my father, between them.* "Although it wasn't just you, of course, there was my mother and her duplicitous web of a life. Sometimes the only thing I know to be true is that everyone lies."

Her name badge reads 'Sarah Kremer'. I manage to clear my throat. "You use your mother's maiden name? You've never married?" A wary shadow crosses her face and for a moment I think she's going to tell me to mind my own business. I quickly add, "I've never married, not even been close. Never even been a bridesmaid, let alone a bride."

Her expression relaxes and she gives a sad smile. "No, I've never married. I had a habit of pushing people away if they got too close. Self-preservation, I suppose. And it's not always easy forming relationships in the hotel industry, not with all the long hours and shift work. But I have been with Glen for over nine years now. I did think he would propose at one time, but I've had to accept that he's never going to now."

"You're happy, though?" I'm not sure if I want to hear yes or no.

She pauses, eyes flicking to the waitress, calculating if she is within earshot or not, before deciding not to answer. "I used to be on tenterhooks waiting for Glen to propose, my heart would race if he so much as reached into a pocket during a meal, or if he went down on one knee to tie a shoelace. But now I'm on edge each day waiting for –" She stops mid-sentence, giving herself a little shake. "It doesn't matter, I don't know why I'm telling you this. I sound like a regular Miss Havisham."

"What does Glen do?"

"He's a consultant, for a marketing company."

Oh. Not a heart surgeon. Nor a ground-breaking journalist. "Was he dressed as John McEnroe at the party?"

She looks at me sharply. "Yes. Why do you ask?"

"Er, no reason." *He's the deuce-bag*. "His kids seem nice."

Her face brightens. "The kids are great. We have them every other weekend, although it's not always plain sailing. Tom's been bullied at school and Sophie's always had a difficult relationship with her father. It's particularly bad at the moment, they're constantly at each other's throats. I try not to interfere too much, their real mum does enough of that."

"Life's a bit unfair sometimes, isn't it?" I offer, quietly.

She emits an unexpected snort of laughter. "Oh, Colin, you always were the master of understatement. Life's 'a bit unfair' – I should bloody well say so, just look at us! You haven't changed a bit. I do believe that if the world were falling down around your ears you'd sit there and say, 'Hey ho, mustn't grumble'."

I smile ruefully. "Meek and mild, that's me. A real-life Horace Wimp."

"Someone's meek and mild is someone else's kind and considerate. Trust me, those are strengths, not weaknesses." She flushes, embarrassed at having paid me a compliment. Her eyes hold mine and my stomach performs a little flip. "What do you think would have happened to us, if things had been different? Would we have made it?"

"Yes," I say immediately, surprising us both with such an assertive note.

"How can you be so sure?"

"I just know. At least, speaking for myself, I didn't mean to sound like... No one else has ever come close to you. And they never will."

The waitress is back within earshot at the next table, staring at us open-mouthed as the champagne flute overflows. The doors to the function room fly open and a man in a crumpled blue suit stumbles in, staring blindly around him. "Uncle Nick!" One of the bridesmaid rushes in after him. "This way! The toilets are this way!" Guests begin streaming into the room, and Sarah rises to her feet. I'm running out of time. "I've no right to ask, I know you're with someone, but can we meet again? For coffee, or something, or anything, just to talk."

"I'm not sure Glen would be very comfortable with that... God, who told them to come in? I've got to go."

I grab her hand but let go immediately as she flinches away. "Please, Sarah, just a coffee, there's so much still to say."

She wavers. "I don't know.... Woah! Madam, your child has just necked that champagne. Well, who's he with, then? At least stop him drinking another glass! Mind the cake, can you keep the children away from the cake, please? I've got to go, Colin."

"Meet me. There's a cafe where I work at Hogpits, I'm always there. At work, I mean."

"I don't know-"

"Please come. Please."

"Alright, I've got Thursday off, I'll come to ... where is it?"

"Hogpits Heights."

"Sounds delightful. I'll see you there. At ten."

I can hardly believe it, I have secured a definite date to see Sarah again! I realise I'm grinning from ear to ear as I help Doris into her seat before forcing my way against the tide of guests and out of the function room. As I leave the hotel I see I have a text from Tony that he'd sent over an hour ago. 'FFS get changed first!'

Chapter Fourteen

I sink gratefully into a deck chair in The Hut and take a cheese sandwich out of my rucksack. The Time Tunnel is playing 'Relax' which is very timely following a morning of fighting with the privet hedge. The next few weeks were set to be a constant battle without Tony around, but Chicken Ron had at least poo-picked the top paddock this morning before he'd disappeared into the neighbouring wheat field with the latest edition of Woman's Weekly.

I take a bite of cheese and pickle as I switch my phone on. My stomach lurches as I see a missed call from Cath and my appetite instantly vanishes. I'm not ready to speak to her, I don't know if I'll ever be ready. There are three texts from Tony:

'Help! Got on the wrong train where is exeter st davids?'

'Why do i always get the nutter? bloke next to me is eating his fingers'

'Made it! Waiting to meet production team totally shitting my pants!'

I jump as my phone buzzes in my hand. It's a Skype call. Tony had set it up on my phone before he left for Bristol and

I'd not used it before. I gingerly dab the accept button and a bright orange face appears on the screen. "Is that you, Tone?"

"Of course it's me! You can see me, can't you? I can see you."

"It doesn't look like you, I think the screen is making you a funny colour."

"Oh, yeah, I was a bit heavy-handed with the Man Tan. Anyway, never mind about that now, take a look around my humble abode." My eyes swim about in my head as Tony whirls his phone around the purple and grey patterned hotel room, stopping to rest on the open door of a small fridge. "We can actually have whatever we like from the mini-bar, it's all paid for. There's even a bottle of that fizzy Prosaic stuff in here, it's well-posh."

"Take it easy mate," I warn, eyeing the two empty bottles of Becks and several crumpled packets of Highland Shorties as Tony lays his phone down to answer a knock at the door. "You've got a long day ahead of you tomorrow." There's no answer. I can hear muffled voices in the background before the phone is snatched back up, and I find myself looking into a pair of knowing green eyes.

"This is Sasha," Tony calls, pushing his face into the picture. "She's the show's producer. Say hello to Colin, Sasha, he's the one I told you about."

"Hello Colin," Sasha smiles at me. I notice the smile doesn't reach her eyes. "I've heard so much about you."

"Oh, er, really? Don't believe a word of it!"

"Tony says you're the Dad he never had. He's spoken so movingly about how his father abandoned him when he was a little boy, the whole of the production team was in tears. I've emailed it to Noel and he can't wait to have Tony on the show tomorrow, he's *exactly* the kind of misfortuned contestant we love."

Is misfortuned even a word? I make a mental note to look

it up. "So, Tony's audition went well, then?"

"Oh yeah, totes. It's such a shame you can't be here in the audience but of course you've got to stay with your little dog after its operation. Is the poor thing adjusting to just having the three legs now?"

"Got to dash, Col," Tony's guilty-looking face suddenly replaces Sasha's. "We're meeting up with the other contestants for a drink, you know, a get-to-know-you sort of luncheon."

"Ok, have a great time." I grin into the screen. "You know, there's a great bar near your hotel. What's it called, now? Ah yes, The Tortured Soul."

"Righto, bye then." Tony speaks quickly into his phone. "Um, love you."

"That's so sweet!" I hear Sasha exclaim just before the screen goes blank.

"Love you too, son," I chuckle, dabbing my phone off. "Love you too."

Tuesday lunchtime:

'OMG just met noel!!!! short and bit speaky lol but v nice'

'Not selected. andrea from anglesea won £75k! Talk about the luck of the Irish.'

'Not selected. So close! BO Bob got on. Least havent got to stand next to him anymore needed a bloody peg on my nose'

'Bob won £13k. lets hope he invests in some lynx. off to drown my sorrows with Sash.'

Wednesday morning:

I am about to leave the house when other Skype call comes in. Tony's blotchy face appears mournfully before me. "Blimey mate, what's happened to you?" I exclaim in horror.

"Dis-as-ter. Night out in Bristol with Sasha. Christ alive, that woman can drink! We got absolutely hammered and for some reason I agreed she could pluck my eyebrows. Look."

Tony pushes his face right up the camera and I wince at the painful looking red rash over his eyes.

"She over-plucked the left so she tried to match the right, and they just got thinner and thinner. They look like two keyboard dashes."

I peer at his forehead. "Are they even straight?"

"Crooked as shit. I've tried keeping my head tilted to one side, but it's making me dizzy. Why did I have that last slammer, *why?* I've got to be in the studio in ten minutes and all I want to do is chuck."

"What are you going to do?"

"Sasha's just had the brilliant idea of hiding them with glasses and as luck would have it, my sunglasses are big enough to cover my forehead almost completely. Look."

He places a huge pair of mirrored sunglasses over his eyes. They were the Top Gun aviators. "Weren't you supposed to give those back to the fancy dress shop?"

Tony looks off to the left and I can hear him speaking to someone.

"Is Sasha with you now, then?" I ask. "She's there, in your room?"

"Er, yeah, yeah, she just swung by to see if I was ok after we'd been, um-"

"Plucking?"

"*Exactly.* She's going to tell the production crew I've got an eye infection. It might even help get me selected, you know, having a sort-of disability. I should have thought of it before. Can't you come down to the studios today, Col? *Please.* I need my wingman with me. I've put a ticket for you at reception, just in case."

"I can't, mate, you know I can't. There's just too much to do at work, what with you being off sick and all. Anyway, I've got to go. Good luck today mate, I'll keep everything crossed that you get selected today."

Lunchtime texts:

'Jeez my guts are all over the place. just farted and it smelt of tequila'

'Not selected. Kim from tamworth only won £1500 poor cow. noel very kind about my eye infection but heard camera man make a stevie wonder comment. asshole'

Wednesday evening Skype call:

"Col, Col! This is it - I'm going to be selected tomorrow!"

"Really? But, how can you possibly know that?"

"I just do! This is it mate, this is it. Can you believe this is actually happening? It feels unreal, like a dream!"

There's a movement in the background. "Who's that?"

"Never mind. Please come down, Colin, please. I'm going to be on the afternoon session, so if you catch the 10.39 you'll be here in good time. Get a taxi from the station to the studio and to hell with the cost, I'll cover it from my winnings. You can tell Morticia you've caught the virus off me."

"The thing is, Tone, I'm seeing Sarah tomorrow, she's coming to the gardens to meet me for coffee."

"That's brilliant news! Bring her along, too. Sash, Sash! Can you get me another ticket? She says no problem."

"No, I can't, Tone, I'm really sorry. Tone? Tone, you still there?" The call has been disconnected, but at least I've been reminded that I have my own eyebrows to tame before tomorrow.

I jump up, scraping my chair back with such a horrid screech that Pauline on the till jolts awake. She clutches at her chest, glaring at me accusingly. The figure in the doorway appears hesitant and I think for one awful moment that Sarah is about to turn and leave, but instead she shrugs off her cream Macintosh and slides into the chair opposite me. She is wearing a pale blue cotton blouse with tiny white daisies printed on it. "Pauline, could we have another coffee, please?" I call towards the vexed-looking woman and sit down again, smiling shyly at Sarah. "Is it still white with one?"

"Good God, how on earth can you remember that? Yes, it is, as it goes, I guess I am a creature of habit." She looks around. "It's very quiet in here, where is everybody?"

"It's the weather," I reply, nodding out of the window and trying not to sound gloomy. "It keeps the visitors away. I think it's brightening, though; I'll show you around the grounds when it dries up. If you like, I mean." My phone starts to ring and I quickly switch it off. "Sorry about that, it's just my mate Tony, I'll call him back later."

I glance over at Sarah and see she is trying to hide a smile as a hunched Pauline painstakingly shuffles over with the coffee and plonks it down heavily on the table top, slopping a good deal into the saucer. She returns to the counter, rubbing her back and muttering to herself.

"Do you remember Mrs Overall?" Sarah whispers with a giggle, dabbing the underneath of her cup with a tissue. "We should order two soups for lunch!"

I grin. "Probably best put your Macintosh back on then." There is a short silence. We both take a sip of coffee and I fiddle with a teaspoon. "I wasn't sure you'd come."

"I nearly didn't." She looks at me earnestly then her lips twitch again. "But you looked so damned hot last time, I couldn't resist."

I give a snort of laughter. "Which trousers did it for you, the PVC cling film or the white ankle-grazers?"

"Neither, it was the 'Woodley Ladies Do It On The Grass' that swung it. I wanted to know exactly what sort of gardening you were into. Anyway, how's Virginia?"

"W-what?"

"I'm joking! Sorry, that wasn't funny." She takes another sip, her eyes turning serious. "Did you know that Cath came to see me?"

My stomach plunges. "I didn't. When was that?"

"She turned up at the hotel on Monday morning. Your nephew told her where I worked."

"I see. And, you spoke with her?"

"Yes. I didn't want to, but she wouldn't go away. She told me she'd lied about you seeing Virginia Parker, she said you weren't seeing anyone, it was just the first name that popped into her head. I asked her if she'd read my letters and she said she had."

I flinch. "Did she tell you why she'd done it?"

"Yes." Sarah looks at me searchingly and I can see she's considering how to phrase her words. "I told her that whilst I could understand she'd been though a traumatic time with your mum's death, it didn't explain why she kept quiet for the next thirty years." She shrugs. "Cath didn't really have an answer other than she couldn't face telling you. She's very sorry, you know." I can't respond. "It must have been an extremely difficult conversation you had with Cath."

"It was." I look down into my coffee cup, nauseous at the memory. "I'm not sure I'll ever speak to her again."

"Don't say that, Colin, she's your sister."

"I can't forgive her, I'll never forgive her."

"I know right now you feel like that, but give it time. Don't do anything you'll regret."

"She said some awful things. Told me wicked lies." I grip the teaspoon so hard it digs right into my palm but I don't care, it's deflecting the pain. I can't risk the tears returning. "Do you think what she said about Mum was true?"

"I think Cath has convinced herself it's true," Sarah says carefully. "However, it's hard to believe that someone so seemingly cheerful could do something like that out of the blue. There would have been warning signs, you'd have known."

I press the teaspoon further still. "That's just it - *seemingly* cheerful. What if it was all an act? What if Mum was genuinely suffering and we never knew?" I look down at the table top. "I can't find the death certificate."

"You don't need to see it, so stop looking." Sarah speaks quietly but firmly. "It's not true. Cath said it because she was under attack – people do that, say terrible things. They do it to fend off the guilt or blame or responsibility, whatever. My mother was masterful at it. She still is, actually. Nothing's ever her fault, always someone else's. But, what can I do, she's still my Mum, you know?"

I nod. "I do know, but I'm not ready to deal with Cath, it's too raw. And it was your letters she hid, she lied to your face; I don't know how you can feel anything other than bitterness."

"It's a wasted emotion, Colin," Sarah moves her cup around in its saucer, not meeting my eyes. "People tell lies all the time; some people lie so often they convince themselves they're telling the truth, that's why they're so believable."

I wonder if she's talking about Glen. "Are you still referring to your mother, or someone else?"

"Cath's son seems a very interesting young man," Sarah swiftly changes the subject. "Louie, isn't it? Cath talked a little about him and Sophie, they seem to have become pals. I'm hopeful Sophie might have found a kindred spirit at last, she's always struggled to make friends." As Sarah takes out her phone to show me some pictures of Sophie, the door to the tearooms opens and Mrs Winter enters, unwinding her wet head scarf and flapping it about irritably. She barks an order at Pauline then sits down at a table at the back of the tea room, removing a folder from a carrier bag. I lean on my right elbow, my hand partially covering my face fervently hoping not to be spotted. We didn't get official breaks, just a lunch hour and my buttocks clench at the thought of being told off in front of Sarah.

"You said Sophie wasn't getting on with her father very well," I prompt, feeling guilty because I know I'm hoping to hear something negative about Glen. "Is it a teenage thing?"

"I don't know." Sarah's face clouds over. "She really seems to hate him at the moment, I don't know what's going on between them. On the other hand, she's being extremely nice to me, so perhaps I shouldn't complain."

"Would we have had kids?" I blurt before I can stop myself, but fortunately Sarah laughs.

"Yes, I'd already named them in my head two days after I'd met you. Twin girls, Coco and Lori."

"Not Pepsi and Shirley?"

"Here, Colin!" We both jump as Wes bangs on the window. "Tony's texted me." He pressed his iPhone against the glass and I read 'tell Col daft bast switch phone on'.

I acknowledge the message by giving Wes the thumbs up, willing him to move on. As he walks away, Pauline calls from the counter: "Ask your mate to stop texting me, will you? I'm not a messenger service."

Shut up Pauline, shut up. "I think she's talking to you," Sarah grins, enjoying my squirming.

"He says to leave now for the ten thirty-nine," Pauline throws her hands up in exasperation. "I haven't a clue what he's on about, he's a complete imbecile, that lad, as if I didn't have enough to do without being used like a bleedin' carrier pigeon."

"Yep, thanks for that, Pauline," I call, sensing Mrs Winter's eyes raking the back of my head.

"Was that your mate Tony again?" Sarah asks. "Perhaps you'd better call him, it sounds urgent."

"It's not urgent," I half-whisper, conscious of Mrs Winter's bat-like hearing. "Tony's on a TV show this afternoon and he's desperate for me to be there. It's being filmed in Bristol and I've already told him I can't go, but he won't take no for an answer."

"That sounds exciting! What show?"

"Deal or No Deal."

"I didn't know they still made that." Sarah drains her coffee cup. "But how does he know he's going to be picked this afternoon? I thought it was random."

"Best you don't ask."

"You should be there for him," Sarah says firmly. I almost laugh out loud at her dogmatic sense of right and wrong, so familiar from the past. "It's a big day for him and he needs your support."

I look at my watch. "It's too late, I'll never make the 10.39, not on my, er, push bike." *Loser.* I feel my face burning up.

"I'll drive you."

"What? No, really, I can't ask you to."

"What is it, an hour to Bristol, tops? And I've nothing else on today." She is blushing now and my heart leaps – could it be possible that she wants to spend more time with me?

"I'll have to ask Mrs Winter," I jerk my head and Sarah looks over at the woman in the corner. She grins. "She does look terrifying. But I'm sure she's no match for the dandy highwayman."

I grimace. "You're about to see Adam Ant squashed under a pair of Hush Puppies."

"Don't tread on an ant, he's done nothing to you," I hear Sarah singing softly as I get up, heavy-legged. Mrs Winter watches me approaching, her table scattered with files, papers and a calculator. Oh God, she's doing the accounts; does that mean she's in a good mood, or a foul one?

"Um, Mrs Winter, I'm so sorry to trouble you. I appreciate this is dreadful timing–"

"What's happened now? Where's Ron, what's he done?"

"No, no, Ron's fine, he's with Nat, they're mucking out the stables. Look, I am sorry to ask, but would it be all right for me to leave? I mean, not permanently, just for the rest of the day, as in, take the time off. Now. Right away. I'm sorry, er, very sorry to ask."

The pale eyes narrow. "Tony's still off sick, isn't he? I can't cope without you both, Colin, not at this time of year. I'm surprised at you even asking."

"I know, sorry, I will put in extra hours to cover. It's just something's come up and it's really important to me."

Mrs Winter looks pointedly over at Sarah who holds her gaze, then back to me. I realise I'm not breathing. "Hmmm, well, I don't suppose you'd ask if it wasn't something urgent. All right, as it's just a one-off, and it's raining, you can go. But I want the hours made up next week."

"T-t-thank you!" Gratitude washes over me. "Thank you very much." I give a thumbs-up to Sarah and we make for the door.

"Oh, and Colin," Mrs Winter says lightly, her head back down in her figures.

"Yes?"

"Wish Tony luck from me."

The car journey had felt awkward at first, which I put down to our sudden close proximity in the car. The grind of the windscreen wipers jarred my nerves and when the sun finally burst through, I felt hot and uncomfortable in my waterproof clothing. It was a relief when Sarah opened her window and the long-forgotten smell of apple-blossom drifted across me as the breeze ruffled her hair. I tried not to look each time her hand grasped the gear stick, still freckly though I noted the lines and pronounced veins, finding myself taking in every detail. Our conversation had been stilted at first, not as easy as it had been in the tea room, but it became more free-flowing as we reminisced over our time in college: the grotty common room, the teachers' strike, our attempts to set up a debating society. The first topic was 'The Falkland Islands, not worth the loss of life' and Sarah's New Romantics had trounced The Tory Boys in front of a raucous and packed lecture theatre. These were safe memories, skirting around the fact that we were inseparable at college, and throughout that magical summer, when our friendship became so much more.

The drive to Bristol is quick once the rain has cleared and we finally find a space on the roof of the multi-storey close to the TV studios, having driven around in dizzying circles. We locate the studios in a large, sandy-coloured building, and as we walk through the four-pillared entrance into reception, a huge TV screen is showing the lunchtime news. We hover until one of the receptionists looks up with a smile. "Can I help you?"

"Hello, yes, one of the contestants on Deal or No Deal has put some tickets aside for us. Tony Chisholm."

"Ah yes." She glances at a clock on the wall. "I'll just give Sash a call, she'll come and get you."

We didn't have to wait long before a slim young woman with curly auburn hair appears. I recognise the hard green eyes from the Skype call. "You're just in the nick of time," she tells us, hurrying us through the turnstile. "The afternoon session's about to begin. It's earlier today because the morning session was over so quickly, which is a shame. It's always disappointing when a contestant chicken-shits it, hardly worth broadcasting. How's your dog, Colin?"

"Um, fine, thanks," I mumble as we speed-walk behind her along a corridor. It's lined with pictures of Noel, his arms wrapped around beaming contestants. Sasha reaches a door and beckons us through. We find ourselves at the back of a studio that is already full of people. We trot down the stairs after Sasha who directs us to our seats three rows from the front. "How many do you reckon are here?" I ask Sarah, glancing back behind us. "About a hundred and fifty? It's much smaller than I thought."

"It's to make Noel look bigger," she replies with a giggle.

A long, wooden counter rings the set in front of us and in the middle there is a white oval table, upon which a black dial-up telephone sits. Cameramen line the front of the set dressed top to toe in black and Sasha lurks at the side, headset on, clipboard in hand. There isn't much preamble; I guess that had all been done at the morning session, and applause breaks out as the contestants appear, each wearing a white name badge and carrying a red box with a number on the front. There are twenty-two in total. "Which one's Tony?" Sarah whispers.

"Second from the left. Next to the blonde girl."

"Oh! I didn't realise he was blind, poor thing."

"He's not, he's just got a problem with his eyes. Well, with his eyebrows, to be precise."

"How unusual, I've never heard of an eyebrow condition. Is there a name for it?"

"Eighth-pint syndrome."

Tony, peering over the top of his aviators, suddenly spots us and waves like crazy, his gleaming white teeth contrasting starkly with his deeply tanned face. We both wave back and then there is a huge burst of applause as Noel Edmonds is introduced. He bounces on dressed in a dark blue paisley shirt, his trademark bouffant silvery grey swept back hair. He paces along the row of contestants rubbing his little gingery beard and teasing us: "Who will it be? Who will it be?" before a white light begins to flicker over the contestants. "Where is it going to stop? Nobody knows..." *Oh yes they bloody well do.* "It's ... Tony!"

A shaft of neon light illuminates Tony as his name flashes up on the screen. The audience and contestants whoop and cheer as a delighted and over-astonished looking Tony takes the 'walk of wealth', placing his red box on the white table in front of Noel.

"So, we have Tony Chisholm from Devizes! I have to tell everyone straight away that Tony has not gone all rock star on us, he is suffering from an eye infection, hence the dark glasses." There is a collective 'Awww' from the audience although I notice some of the contestants exchanging knowing glances amongst themselves. "I went to Devizes once," Noel continues. "It's full of pubs, as I recall."

"Twenty-four," Tony confirms. "All of them shite. Oh, shit, sorry, I didn't mean to swear."

"That's ok," Noel nods at Sasha. "We'll edit that out. What do you do for a living, Tony?"

"I'm a horticulturist, Noel."

"Oooh, that sounds very grand! What does it involve?"

"Growing stuff." The audience roars with laughter.

"Of course." Noel pulls a 'we've got a right one here' face at the camera. "Well, I think everyone's ready. Tony, you chose box number two at random and, as always, all the boxes have been sealed by an independent adjudicator. Tony Chisholm from Devizes – good luck!"

Tony's name is replaced on the giant screen by two columns of numbers, the smaller values in blue on the left and the larger amounts of money in red on the right. Tony refused the proffered high chair, choosing instead to pace around the studio floor in front of the other contestants, enjoying his moment. He stops at the end of the line and addresses the blonde girl. "Jenny, please, number seven."

Jenny smiles and removes the seal from box number seven. She opens it slowly to reveal a blue label with £50 printed on it. Amidst the whoops and cheers, Tony punches the air and rushes over to give Jenny a massive hug that lasts a little too long to be comfortable. I notice Sasha's face souring. Another three blue labels follow in quick succession; Tanya £100, Rosie

£1 Shimla 1p. The audience is going wild and while Sarah's eyes are shiny with excitement, I shift awkwardly in my seat. This feels a bit too good, surely Sasha hasn't fixed the actual game? Is she the independent adjudicator, have they agreed the number sequence between them? Perhaps not; there is a loud groan as the first red number is revealed. Siobhan's box contains the £10,000 label.

The black telephone on the table rings and Noel lifts the receiver to talk to the banker. "He wants to know if you have a system for selecting your numbers." Tony taps his nose knowingly.

"I could tell you, Noel, but then I'd have to kill you."

"I see. Well then, are you ready for the question, Tony?"

"Born ready."

"The banker's offer is eight thousand pounds. Deal, or no deal?"

"Blimey!" I exclaim. "That's not bad for ten minutes' work!"

Tony slaps his left fist into the palm of his right hand like a prize fighter. "No deal!" he declares dramatically, sending the audience into raptures. The next round gets under way with another blue label, Charlotte with £500, but then two red labels in a row: £1,000 and £20,000. "It's ok," Sarah murmurs reassuringly. "He's doing really well, the big values are still left so it should be another decent offer." I am surprised she knows the game so well and she gives me an embarrassed smile, reading my thoughts. "Shift work. You get to see rather a lot of daytime telly." The telephone rings again and Noel has another chat with the banker. He replaces the receiver with a knowing smirk. "He's on to you!"

"W-what do you mean?" We can't see Tony's eyes but his head swivels in Sasha's direction.

"He's sussed your system." Noel wags a finger at Tony. "You're selecting all the women!"

"Has he only just worked that out?" Sarah chuckles. "Anyway, are you ready for the question, Tony?"

"Yep, bring it on."

"The offer is fourteen thousand pounds. Deal or no deal?"

Wow. There is a long, dramatic pause. I hold my breath. Tony turns to the crowd. "NO DEAL!" Everyone explodes into noisy applause, myself and Sarah included. *Come on, Tony, come on.*

Having run out of women to select, Tony turns to Jack, a young skinny lad who opens his box to reveal a blue £250, triggering thunderous cheers. The next two boxes contain red labels, but they are at the lower end of the red spectrum, £15,000 and £1,000.

"This is looking very bad for the banker!" Noel exclaims as the phone rings again. He listens without speaking then nods at Tony. "Just as I thought, you've put him in a really bad mood, a *really* bad mood. So, are you ready for the question, Tony?"

"I am Noel, yes."

"The offer is twenty thousand pounds. Deal or no deal?"

My goodness, surely Tony must be tempted? Clearly he is as the pause is much longer this time. He rubs his chin, cracks his knuckles and runs his hands through his hair. "No deal."

"YES!" The crowd are delighted and Tony's stoicism is rewarded by an absolutely brilliant next round, with three blue boxes in a row: 5p followed by 10p followed by £10, each one met with huge cheers. Some of the audience members are stamping their feet, egged on by a beaming Noel, who appears just as excited as everyone else. "This could be the perfect round of Deal or No Deal," he gushes as the phone rings. "It just got very interesting." He doesn't say anything as he listens to the banker, hanging up very serenely before turning to Tony. Long pause. I hold my breath. "The banker is offering... forty-four thousand pounds."

There are gasps around the studio. I doubt Tony can hear himself think above the hullaballoo that follows, everyone is shouting, 'Take it!' 'No Deal!' 'Don't do it!' 'Deal!'

Take the money Tone, take the bloody money.

There are only two blue values left on the board and six red. The odds favour Tony with the big numbers remaining, but 50p or £5 could just as easily be in Tony's box as the £250,000 jackpot. Noel manages to quieten the studio. "So, you can grow a lot of stuff with forty-four thousand pounds, Tony. Are you ready for the question?"

Tony appears to be looking in my direction but I can't read his expression behind those stupid glasses. Is he asking me what he should do? I nod at him encouragingly - *take the money, bloody take it!*

"I'm ready, Noel."

"Forty-four thousand pounds. Deal or no deal?"

Take it, Tone, for Christ's sake take it! "No deal," Tony states, his voice wobbling.

"Brave man," Noel acknowledges approvingly over the roar. "Very brave." Sarah and I look at each other – *what has he done?* Noel gets everyone to settle and the next round commences. Tony points to a white-haired elderly man. "Eddie, number six, please."

Eddie opens his box. It is red, £100,000. Huge groans of disappointment rumble around the studio. I look at the other people nearest to us in the audience. They are all wide-eyed, and some have their hands over their mouths. Tony shrugs off the groans, the £250,000 is still in play. The next box belongs to Sanjay, who removes the seal with a pained expression on his face; he also reveals a red label - £75,000.

I shoot a glance at Sarah. Her hands are over her eyes, she can't look. I can see damp patches appearing under Tony's armpits as he paces anxiously up and down the studio. He wipes his hand across his brow, unsure who to choose next. He finally stops in front of Pete, a huge bear of a man with a long bushy beard. "Good luck mate," he nods to Tony as he removes the seal and opens his box. It is the £250,000.

"Pete, you total and utter dickwad!" Tony explodes. "You useless great pile of blobby crap!" The audience is stunned into silence and Sasha runs on with her clipboard. "Don't worry, Noel, we'll cut that. Pete, can we do another take please?"

Pete, dark faced and fuming, has to open his box again, repeating "Good luck mate" through gritted teeth. The audience emits a loud fake "Nooo" as the £250,000 is revealed for the second time. My heart is on the floor. Tony's dream is in tatters but he still has the £50,000 left, there is still hope.

The telephone rings and Tony snatches up the receiver before Noel can reach it. "Who's this, the speaking cock? I know you're not real, Noel just pretends... oh, oh, right, yep, sorry." He hands it back to Noel. "It's for you." The audience laughs, Tony winning them back round after his outburst. Noel listens to the banker before hanging up. "Well, as you would expect, the banker is rather gleeful after that round." Noel is much more subdued. "Are you ready for this?"

"I guess so."

"The offer is now eleven thousand pounds. Deal or no deal?"

"That's not a bad offer, you know." Sarah is trying to be positive. "I mean, you can do a lot with that sort of money."

"Absolutely," I agree, nodding towards Tony. "To wake up tomorrow eleven grand richer, he's got to be happy with that."

"No deal," Tony says firmly. "Might as well see it through." There is encouraging applause. "Good on yer!" someone yells. "Come on Tony!" The shouts go up again. I glance at Sarah and find her anxious brown eyes gazing straight back into mine, taking my breath away. *It is exactly how she used to look at me.*

The next round begins and now there are only two boxes left to open; one contains the £50,000 and the other £3,000. Tony's box is sitting on the white table like an unexploded bomb. There is only one contestant Tony hasn't chosen and all eyes now turn to him.

"Jason," Noel says solemnly, putting his arm round Tony's shoulders. "It's all down to you."

Nattily dressed in a tweed waistcoat and yellow cravat, Jason appears on the verge of tears. As trembling fingers fumble to untie the seal, you could have heard a pin drop in the studio. Sarah takes my hand and grips it hard, making my pulse race even faster. Jason shakily opens the lid. It's the £50,000. It's gone.

In the horrified hush, Noel, looking genuinely upset, opens Tony's box. "We've got to do it," he says miserably. The label reads £3,000. "Oh, Tony, Tony, Tony..."

We can't see Tony's face, he's sitting head-bowed at the table, arms hanging limply from his sides. "Tony Chisholm, you are an extremely courageous man and you go back to Devizes with £3,000. Give him a big hand everyone."

As awkward silences go, this one is a humdinger. I'd read the hotel bar menu nine times and re-arranged the flower display ten, which was quite some feat given it was a single gerbera in a test tube. Sarah is looking at me over the rim of her coffee cup, nodding towards an ashen-faced Tony. She's urging me to say something consoling, reassuring, *cheering*, even. But how do you comfort someone who has just thrown away forty-one thousand pounds? The words don't exist. I have to try though, Sarah is expecting me to take control, to be the man. I clear my throat. "Three thousand pounds better off, Tone," I say brightly. "That's not bad for a day's work."

"Don't give me all that 'I came with nothing' crap," Tony mutters into his pint glass. "I can't hack it."

"But it's true, three grand is a lot of money."

"It won't change my bloody life though, will it?" Tony's voice cracks. "Jesus, I owe the bank nine hundred of it! Why couldn't I have had a bit of luck for a change? I don't ask for much, which is just as well, I never frigging get anything. Even as a kid all I wanted was a normal life like my friends had, you know, with loving parents who helped them with their homework and took them to Thorpe Park every once in a while. My Dad had me flogging knock-off laptops up and down the country, out in his van until all hours; I was so knackered during the day I couldn't focus in the classroom, I was either half asleep or waiting for the cops to show up and cart me off. I was so scared I was going to end up in one of those, what do you call them-"

"Borstals?"

"Documentaries. You know, grown men scarred for life by their experiences, weeping into the camera. I was convinced that was going to be me one day." He takes a sip of beer. "I got shoved into the dunces' class and there I bloody well stayed. I didn't get a single qualification, and the school wouldn't even give me a certificate of attendance because my absence record was so shit."

"What about your mum?" Sarah asks. "Didn't she help you study?"

"Mum? She's thicker than a whale omelette. She thought Mussolini was one of the Ninja Turtles."

"You've got a lot to be thankful for, Tone," I try. "You've got your health, a job, a roof over your head – it's more than many people have got. You're not your father, you've managed to rise above a life of crime, despite the rocky start. And you work really hard, there's a certain dignity in doing an honest day's work."

"Mate, there's no dignity in having your visa card declined in front of a tutting queue in Greggs, or trying to find a backstreet barber that still does a five pound haircut. And there's certainly no dignity in your mum borrowing condoms off you because she's getting more sex than you are."

I swallow a grin. "Well, why not use your winnings to pay for evening classes, get a qualification?"

"In what? I can't do anything."

"Of course you can!" I exclaim. "You're a bloody whiz on your phone and anything to do with social media and, er, that sort of thing. You could do wonders in the IT industry."

"That's true. Bill Gates is probably shitting himself right now."

"Your cup's half empty, Tony," Sarah gently scolds him. "It's understandable, you've just had a massive disappointment. But Colin's right, you've got to focus on the positives."

"Like what? I'm so done with being a minimum wage, shit-shovelling, bottom-feeder. What will tomorrow at Hogpits Shites bring, I wonder, fingering weeds out of the cracks in the crazy paving or scraping the droppings out of a rabbit's arsehole? Call me Mr Negative but I can't find the positive in any of that."

Sarah nods her head. "Yes, you can. You create a beautiful environment for people to enjoy, to marvel at, even. And if it wasn't for Hogpits you'd never have met Colin, would you? You found someone who's become your best friend and that's worth more than anything, Tony, because you can't buy friendship, not real friendship; it's the most valuable possession you'll ever have. Especially Colin's friendship," she blushes. "I should know, he was my best friend and I lost him. People like that don't come into your life very often. Trust me, they're not easy to replace."

"Yeah, well," Tony can't be consoled. "I know you're both trying to cheer me up, but I'm sick and tired of always getting the fuzzy end of the lollipop."

"Marilyn Monroe?" I ask.

"Bill Clinton."

"Think that was a cigar."

"Anyway," Tony drains his pint and rises heavily to his feet. "Let's get out of here. I'll go and get my stuff from my room and check out. And I'm bloody well emptying the mini-bar before I go; salvage something from this disastrous episode."

We watch him slope off to the lifts by reception. I fire what I hope is a cheeky-chappy grin at Sarah. "Irreplaceable, was I?"

"I didn't say that! I said you weren't easy to replace."

I'm crushed, the grin rapidly falling away.

"You said I was the love of your life when you came to the hotel." Sarah is examining her coffee cup. "Before you tried to drown yourself in champagne. Did you mean it?"

"No one's come close, ever." I pause. "When I saw you at The Waterboys I asked if you were happy with Glen. You didn't answer."

"No, I didn't." She taps her fingernails thoughtfully on the table. "I was happy, really very happy for a long time, but I'm pretty sure Glen isn't, not anymore. Like I told you, the eagerly awaited proposal never came and then we started to coast along, then drift, and now it does feel as if we're in free fall. He spends so long at work, at least, that's where he says he is, and when he is at home, his head's clearly not. I think he wants to be somewhere else."

"He's an idiot!" I blurt.

"Maybe," she shrugs, "but he can't help how he feels, can he? And anyway, I might be completely wrong, I have a tendency to be mistrusting."

"Haven't you had it out with him? The Sarah I remember, the one that took down the Tory Boys, would have thrown it all out in the open. You never let anyone off the hook."

She manages a sad smile. "You're right, but I've got a lot more to lose than a college debate. It's the kids, you see, I'm only their step-mum, well, technically I'm not even that, I have no rights at all. If Glen and I separate I might never see them again, and I couldn't bear that."

"But, they would choose to see you, they're old enough. Glen couldn't stop them."

"To use a favourite phrase of Sophie's, he can be a bit of a douche."

I warm to Sophie. "Do you think there's someone else?" I ask as gently as I can.

She sighs. "Possibly. I've been half-wondering if Sophie thinks it too. It might explain why she's so angry with him and why she's being so protective of me right now." She shakes her head in confusion. "But I don't know if I can trust my general mistrust, if you know what I mean."

"What are you going to do?"

She takes a deep breath. "I've been sitting here thinking about that. After witnessing Tony's brush with Lady Luck, I've decided it's about time to take control of my own destiny. I've let too many others interfere in mine – your father, my mother, Cath, now Glen. Tony took a chance. OK, it didn't pan out, but at least he tried, at least he did something, unlike me who's living in limbo-land. We all have the right to live our lives how we wish, haven't we? I'm going to speak to Glen. Tonight. Not accuse him of anything, but just try and get him to talk, to open up."

"Wow, that's really brave." I examine my empty pint glass. *The six million dollar question. Ask it, ask it.* "And, what about us?" I'm pushing my luck, I know it.

I hold my breath, silently pleading with her not to respond "What about us?"

"We'll see, shall we?" She takes a sip from her coffee cup,

but I know it's empty. She sets the cup down slowly, carefully, then finally her eyes lift to meet mine. We smile at each other, neither wanting to look away.

"Bollocks!" There is a commotion in reception. Tony's suitcase has burst open and we hurry over to gather up the tiny bottles of Jack Daniels, the miniature shampoos and the thirty-three packets of Highlands Shorties.

Chapter Fifteen

I know I'm in full view of passing neighbours as I hoover the lounge to 'Flashdance... what a feeling' but I don't care. I'm singing at the top of my lungs as I back into Dad's chair. I just manage to stop myself apologising to him. He's still here but his presence is not so strong, like a stain that's fading. It feels such a different room now, probably because I've raised the blinds for the first time in a decade and the sun is streaming in. It reminds me of another time, when Mum was here, and everything was so cheery and full of light. There's a new addition to the lounge, too; a twenty-one inch Acer computer screen sits proudly on the mahogany writing desk. A black and silver business card is propped up on the keyboard: 'S.O.S - Silver Onlining Services – later life computer and social media tuition. Friendly and simple, Tony Chisholm. Call me now 07885 629101.' As Tony's first client, I'd been extremely impressed with his PC prowess and online expertise. Admittedly, he had some work to do on his interpersonal skills: "No, no, not *that* fucking button, *that* one. No, no, no, for the love of Christ! I've shown you this fifty fucking times already…"

It is brilliant to be able to view the World Wide Web through a middle-aged-eyesight-sized screen and although Facebook can't convince me, I have become hooked on Twitter, enjoying the witty commentary on national events and relishing the apoplectic rants. I wish I'd joined it years ago. Louie and Sophie have launched their own YouTube channel, 'Grave Vloggers', attracting hundreds of followers with their intriguing and intensely dark series of short films. I don't always follow their meaning; for example, 'Wheelie-bin rebirth' which has them both emerging from wheelie-bins at various churchyard locations. Nonetheless, I've marvelled at the clever editing and haunting Clannad background music.

I turn the hoover off and wave to Derek as he jerks past the window, trying to get used to his new mobility scooter. I'd managed to get him a fantastic deal on Gumtree, although the wiring is a little dodgy; the hazard lights come on each time Derek rides through a puddle. The computer had, initially, been a twenty-one inch reminder that the truth surrounding Mum's death was only a few clicks away, but despite my finger poised over the mouse at the Register Office website several times, I hadn't gone any further. This morning, I made the momentous decision to stop searching. The relief is enormous. Mum shall stay forever joyful - laughing, happy, *alive.* It's what she'd want. She'd also want me to use my new-found computer skills for something positive and with that in mind, I'd spent all morning excitedly scrolling through properties for sale on Rightmove.com. I'm ready to move on. I don't want to stay here at number seven, held hostage by its memories; I'm getting out of Codger's Close for good. There have been happy times in this house as well as the sad ones, but even so, I won't miss this place. I've never lived anywhere else before; a little cottage would be wonderful, if we can afford one. It will need to have enough bedrooms so the kids can stay, and a garden is a must. It wouldn't have to be very big, just somewhere to sit and relax, enjoy a bottle of wine together... no, no, *stop!* I'm moving too fast, getting way ahead of myself. She's only coming round for a chat, 'just to talk', she said. But that meant there was something to talk about. It might mean nothing. But I have the feeling it's going to mean everything.

The shrill ring of the doorbell snaps me from my daydream. *Goodness, she's early.* I haven't put the coffee on yet and I wanted the house to smell all homely. Never mind, it's a good sign, she must be keen to see me. I dart to the hallway mirror and give my eyebrows a quick smoothing. "Wish me luck, Mum," I whisper to the silver frame. Gone is the picture of Cath's graduation; I've replaced it with a photograph of Tony and I standing in the doorway of The Hut, underneath a blue plaque. In honour of my thirty years of service to Hogpits, The Hut has been renamed and the plaque reads: Hectors' House. The misplaced apostrophe will irk me forever, but as I'd overheard Mr Winter snarl to his wife, "What do you expect for a freebie?"

Right, this is it. Eyebrows under control, Mum beaming encouragement, I turn eagerly to the front door. On the other side of the glass, a slim figure is waiting. I throw the door open, grinning like the Cheshire Cat. Ginny stands in front of me. My face instantly drops and I quickly fight to switch the smile back on. "Oh, Ginny, hello. This is a surprise, I mean, a nice surprise, of course."

"Can I come in?"

No, you bloody well can't! "Sure, sure," I reluctantly stand back to let her in to the house. My God, this is going to be hellish awkward. *Just take the bollocking, arsehole, you deserve it.* We stand uneasily in the hallway, Ginny staring at me expectantly, waiting for me to speak. "Can I get you anything, coffee, cup of tea?" *Please say no, please say no-*

"Do you have any peppermint tea?"

"No, sorry, I don't have any of that" *hippy shit* "sort of

thing. I could dissolve a Tic Tac in some Typhoo if you like?" My pathetic attempt at a joke, quite rightly, falls flat.

"I'll just have a hot water, then."

"OK." Who the hell drinks just hot water? Perhaps she's intending to put a pet rabbit in it... I lead the way apprehensively to the kitchen and offer Ginny a seat at the little oak table. I had scrubbed it clean and given it a fresh coat of varnish, with a vase of pink and white peonies from the garden the finishing touch. The kettle takes a lifetime to boil, and I add a good splash of cold water to the mug, hoping Ginny will drink it down quickly. I snap off the radio just as 'Total Eclipse of the Heart' comes on.

Ginny takes a small sip from her mug and considers me. "That's a nice shirt. Is it new?"

"Er, yes, yes it is." I sit up straight to ensure I don't put any more creases in my non-iron cream shirt and make a monumental effort not to glance at the clock. "I'm glad your hair's back to its normal colour." I tap my fingers impatiently on the table willing her to give me a piece of her mind and get it over with. "Look, I'm really sorry I've not been in touch, I've been a little preoccupied. It's no excuse, I know, I should have phoned you."

"It's ok." She twists the mug around in her hands. "Cath told me you'd fallen out."

I frown. "Has Cath sent you round here? She shouldn't have done that, it's not fair to involve you in our issues."

"No, that's not why I'm here." *Here it comes, the dressing down, the disappointment, the hurt. Brace yourself...* "I came because I have something to tell you." She takes a deep breath and looks straight across the table at me. "I'm pregnant."

I blink. "Gosh, I mean, congratulations, that's great."

"It's yours."

The kitchen shifts around me. "What?"

"The baby. It's yours."

Blood rushes in my ears. The kitchen clock is ticking, a fly buzzes at the windowpane. Is she joking? She must be. Search her face, she's not joking. This can't be happening, one night, one lousy night? My mouth opens, the words 'How do you know it's mine?' march insultingly on my lips; I bite them back, she's made, surely, a mistake.

She giggles. "You look like a goldfish!"

"I-I thought that–"

"I'm too old to get pregnant? It is a little risky, of course, but I'll be well monitored and I shall take good care of myself." She smiles reassuringly. "I've read all the books."

"But, it was just the one night–"

"I know, it's incredible that I happened to be ovulating on that night! What are the chances?" What *were* the chances? Why hadn't I taken precautions? I'd not even thought about doing so, not in the rush to get it over with. "Of course," Ginny continues, devastatingly well-informed, "your chances of conceiving drop dramatically after the age of thirty-five and not every egg is a winner as you get older, but I think avoiding caffeine and alcohol helped, although it was really difficult to give them up."

"Are you quite sure you're pregnant? I mean, it was only recently that we, er, we–"

"We created life! It is a miracle, isn't it? Yes, I'm quite sure. In fact..." Ginny shoots me a radiant smile as she fishes around in her handbag. She produces a small white envelope and removes a photograph, sliding it across the table to me. "Colin, I'd like you to meet our child."

I stare blindly at the photo. *It's just a white whirl, there's nothing there, she's got it wrong, she's mad, a fantasist.* "I can't see anything."

"That's because he's only about three millimetres. It might be a she, of course, but I keep saying he! Oh, I know they say you shouldn't, but I couldn't possibly wait for the twelve week scan, I had to see for myself, and it was only a couple of hundred pounds for the ultra sound. And there he is!"

"Where?"

"There, you see? He is difficult to make out at the moment because he's so tiny. He's currently just a gestation sac in my uterus."

Head reeling, I clutch at the edge of the table, nausea sweeping through me. Bile rises and I swallow hard. Ginny reaches across and pats my hand. "It's ok, Colin, I can see you're overwhelmed. It's quite a thunderbolt isn't it, but hopefully a good one, right? Can you believe it, we're going to be parents! And Louie will have a little cousin, so this is bound to bring you and Cath back together. It's the most perfect timing." *No, no, it's the most horrific timing*. "Did you ever think you'd be a Dad?" Not recently, not for years, I assumed it would never happen. I don't want a child with Ginny. I want Sarah. "You are with me on this, aren't you, Colin?" She is staring at me anxiously. "I can't do this on my own, a child needs its father. I don't want to be a single parent, it's too hard."

I have to say the right thing. The words won't come. *Say something*. "It's all so–"

"Wonderful, I know, I feel exactly the same! And I was thinking, as my place is so small, it might make sense for me to move in here. For us to move in here, I mean, I keep forgetting there's two of me now!" She laughs, looking out through the window. "Your garden's so lovely, I can imagine our little one running around out there; we could put a swing under the apple tree, get rid of that shed and dig out a sand-pit. We could add a conservatory as a playroom, or convert the attic to bedrooms, like your neighbours have done."

"I don't love you, Ginny."

"Do you think I've got a bump already?" She rubs a hand over her completely flat stomach. "I'm going to be enormous! No one will be able to look right through me now, I won't be Mrs Cellophane for much longer. I'll be someone of significance for once. I'll be a mother."

Hadn't she heard me? "Ginny, did you hear what I said?"

She picks up the photo and runs her forefinger softly over it. "We're bringing a new life into the world, Colin, what can be better than that? We'll grow to love one another. We'll grow together, the three of us, we won't need anybody else."

The doorbell rings. *The clanging chimes of doom.* "Aren't you going to get that?" Ginny asks, as I sit frozen to the chair. Another ring, longer, louder, like a scream in my head. I want to run, but instead I rise and walk zombie-like to the door. Sarah's here, smiling, expectant, the breeze ruffling her hair. She's clutching a handful of Caramac bars.

"Hiya! Remember these? We used to live on them at college!" She has a DVD in the other hand: Kevin Bacon, playing a guitar. "I thought we could watch Footloose this afternoon, it feels appropriate! Do you remember taking me to see it?" Her face falls. "Colin? What's wrong, has something happened?" She steps tentatively into number seven. "Are you ill, have you cut yourself? I can smell TCP."

I shake my head. From the kitchen, Ginny scrapes her chair back from the table and Sarah looks at me in surprise. "Is someone here?"

"I can explain," I mumble.

Sarah doesn't wait for the explanation, she's already moving down the hallway. I follow, leaden-legged. *This isn't real, it can't be real, it's a dream, a terrible dream, please let me wake up, I have to wake up.* Sarah stops in the kitchen doorway. "Oh, hello."

Ginny turns from the garden window. "Hello there. I'm Ginny."

Eyes wide, Sarah turns to stare at me. Her head moves slowly back round to Ginny again. "Ginny, as in, Virginia? Virginia Parker?"

"Good Lord, I can't remember the last time anyone called me Virginia! But yes, Parker's my maiden name. Have we met before? I'm so sorry, I don't remember you - I hope I haven't got baby brain already!"

Sarah's eyes fall to the photograph on the table, then to Ginny's hand placed protectively over her tummy. Ginny nods out across the garden. "I'm just trying to persuade Colin to make some alterations to this place, for when our baby comes. I think we should put in rooms upstairs, like next door have done. I met Derek in the street just now, he nearly ran me over! He's lethal on that scooter. This could be a really nice family home; we should definitely have an upstairs, like Derek's. What do you think?"

There's a deathly hush. No one moves. The fly buzzes in the window, and then a rush of red and gold as the Caramac bars tumble to the floor. They slide across the polished tiles towards Ginny's feet. "You're having a baby together?" Sarah whispers.

"That's right," Ginny beams. "We're so excited, neither of us thought this would ever happen."

Sarah puts her hand to her forehead. "You're... together? Oh my God, you've always been together, all this time! Cath wasn't lying."

I find my voice. "No, Cath *was* lying, you know she was, she told you that when she came to see you."

Her white face is in front of mine. "You made her come and tell me that! She said she'd do anything for you and so she did, didn't she? I should have known better, why did I believe you, *why*? When will I ever learn?"

"Sarah, please listen to me, you've got it all wrong! Ginny, tell her."

"Don't hide behind your girlfriend, it's pathetic. You did get my letters, I bet your whole family had a bloody good laugh at the *annoying fly* who kept writing to you, Virginia too, no doubt. So, what were you after, a quickie for old times' sake? 'Sarah Shaw put out at college, I'll give her another go.' Are you working through all your old flames before you settle down into fatherhood? You disgusting pig!"

"Just let me explain!" Kevin Bacon zooms towards me, slapping me full in the face. As I reel backwards I try to speak but my breath catches in my chest as a sharp bony knee jabs straight into my groin. I slide down the wall. "Sarah," I groan, one hand between my legs the other stretching out as I crawl after her along the hall. "Don't go! Sarah, please don't go. *Sarah!*" I get as far as the doorway to the lounge but the front door is wrenched open bathing me in sunlight before the whole house rattles from the slam. The blinds in the lounge fall down casting long shadowy bars across me.

"I think we're alone now," Ginny sings as she steps over me and into the lounge. "Thank goodness she's gone, we don't need that sort of drama in our lives. You can't waste your time on people like that, Colin, you've got us to look after now." She looks around the lounge, hands on hips. "I'm not being rude, but I probably earn a lot more than you do; we need to discuss parenting roles. Lots of men are househusbands these days, and it would make sense, wouldn't it? You cared for your father all that time, so you're used to dirty nappies and feeding schedules; aside from it being a slightly smaller person to look after, of course! Your life will be just as it was."

I look up but I can only see her shadow in the gloom. A black cloud has smothered the sun and the room is in darkness again. No, no, no, don't let this happen - get up Hector, get up and fight! For once in your sad, sorry little life, *fight for something.* I haul myself to my feet and stagger to the front door, tugging it open. Wincing in pain, I lurch down the path. Sarah is in the Golf, she's pulling away from number seven… I'm losing her again. Derek is pootling along the pavement on his mobility scooter.

"Derek! Stop that car!"

Derek looks up startled by my scream and immediately loses control of the scooter. As Sarah steps down on the accelerator, Derek veers into the middle of the road in front of the car, forcing it to screech to a halt. Sarah tries to manoeuvre the Volkswagen around Derek, but he judders backwards blocking her path. I hobble towards the Golf, reaching it as a distraught Sarah steps from the car. "Get out of my way."

"Sorry love." Derek jerks forwards again. "It's like a Tesco's trolley, got a mind of its own."

"Sarah, please," I grab the door of the Golf and hang on. "You must listen to me."

She turns on me, eyes brimming with tears. "No, Colin, I don't have to listen to you. I've wasted enough time on liars and cheats. I'm going."

"No, you're not!" I wedge myself between Sarah and the open door of the car. "You stay right where you are. You're not leaving until you've heard me out."

Sarah blinks in shock at my forcefulness. Derek lets go of his steering wheel and stares at me open-mouthed. I try to speak calmly but the excruciating pain in my groin raises my voice an octave. "I'm not with Ginny, I never have been. We had a one-night stand which shouldn't have happened. That's it. That's all there is to know about me and Ginny."

"Apart from the baby." Sarah angrily swipes a tear from her cheek.

"I only found out she was pregnant five minutes before you did." It's all I can do not to slump to the ground and I grip the door frame to stay upright. "Sarah, I'm not a liar, or a cheat. Everything I've said to you is true - you're the only one I've ever wanted, the only person I've ever loved. I know you feel the same, you said so in your letters, and that magic is still there between us, even after all this time. Feelings that strong don't just *dissolve.* We've got a second chance to be together;

please don't throw it away because of one pitiful mistake." I hear a whimper and cringe. I didn't hear her approach but I know Ginny is behind me. I turn, still clinging valiantly to the door. "I'm sorry, Ginny but I love Sarah; I always have and I always will. I need to be with her."

Ginny glares at Sarah and there's complete silence as the two stony-faced women study each other. I can't even hear Derek's raspy wheezing, he must be holding his breath. Ginny speaks first. "Sarah's not got much to say Colin, has she? It doesn't look to me as if she wants to be with you. I can't say I blame her, you're as bad as *him*, my ex." We all jump as Ginny's right arm shoots skywards. She pulls it back down under control. "So, our child was conceived out of pity?"

"No, don't twist things." I'm aware of curtains twitching around the close as neighbours wonder what is going on. "I spent the night with you to comfort you because you were in a bad place. I didn't want to make you feel even worse by turning you down. It *was* a mistake, but I'm not shirking my responsibilities. I can still be a good father, I won't be…" *Like mine* "Lacking in any way. I'll support our child."

"How? You earn a pittance."

"I'll get a second job," I say, defiantly.

"I need a gardener," Derek chips in. "So do lots of folk round here. It's about time you started getting paid for everything you do in this close, people take advantage." He clambers off the scooter. "Motor's cut out again, son. Give it another charge for me, would you, I've got to get back inside. That rhubarb gin won't shake itself." Derek hobbles away leaving us standing disconsolately in the middle of the road. Ginny is morose, Sarah crushed. I desperately need to sit down; the pinching ache from my groin is spreading. The sky is black overhead and a few fat rain drops begin to fall. The scooter's hazard lights come on.

Ginny rubs her arm and sniffs. "This is ridiculous. All this negative karma is extremely bad for the baby; they can sense things from a very early age. I'm going inside before those lights trigger a migraine. I'll leave you two to sort things out." She shoots a pleading look at Sarah before turning away. "Don't be long, Colin, we've lots to discuss."

I'm out of time. Sarah rubs a weary hand across her face. "Please move that piece of junk out of my way, Colin. I want to go home."

Defeated, I release my hold on the door frame and step away from the car, but she makes no attempt to get in. It's a tiny spark of hope and I edge a little closer to her. "Don't give up on us, Sarah, *please*. I can't lose you again, I couldn't bear it. I know the baby's the most dreadful timing-"

"That's quite some understatement!"

"But would it be so bad to have a child in our lives? And with Tom and Sophie, we could have that noisy, messy house of fun we used to dream of."

She stares at me. "I can't believe you remember that."

Encouraged, I give a little chuckle. "I remember everything we said! Although more kids are out of the question, I'm afraid. You've got a very sharp kneecap." My nervous laugh is not returned. She's not going to give in, she won't be persuaded. *Beg, that's the only thing left now.* "Don't go, Sarah. Don't leave me this way."

There is a sudden flicker of amusement behind the granite eyes. Her lips twitch. "I suppose it would be unfair to leave you trapped in the 1980s forever. That much is true."

A wave of joy engulfs me. "You do know I've been saving all my love for you?"

She nods down at my jeans. "I didn't really want to hurt you. How are your agadoos?"

I wince. "In need of some baggy trousers." The little splats of rain are becoming more persistent and Sarah hovers by the car door, ready to go. Over at number seven I make out

Ginny's figure behind the blinds in the lounge. She's watching us. I know I must go in and talk to her but I can't let Sarah drive away without knowing if I'll ever see her again. There is a sudden movement at next door's upstairs window as Derek appears, his hands pumping vigorously up and down.

Sarah's hands fly to her mouth. "Oh my God, is he-"

"Just shaking his gin jar," I quickly assure her. "You must remember doing that while we were house-sitting for him?"

"Gosh, yes." Sarah gives a shudder. "What was that wine we sneaked a glass of... dandelion? It stripped every nerve cell from my tongue; I couldn't taste a thing for three days, not even Space Dust." She pushes a damp strand of hair from her face as she gazes wistfully across at Derek's house. "We made a lot of plans up in that room. But it was a lifetime ago; we were so idealistic back then, a right pair of dreamers. Things are more *convoluted* now." She shoots a poignant glance at Ginny's silhouette before the earnest dark eyes refocus on me. "I've got so much to untangle with Glen, and you're going to be a father... The 1980s are long gone, Colin, we're not the New Romantics anymore. Our relationship is like synthesized pop music and shell suits – out-dated and in the past. What makes you think we stand a chance in the twenty-first century?"

"Because we're still us." I reach out and take her hand in mine. She doesn't pull away. "The way we feel about each other is very much in the present. And I'm on Twitter now and everything, I'm quite the modern man, not some tragic 80's throwback. Nothing's gonna stop us now." *D'oh!* "I mean, hell yeah, we're gonna make it, like, one hundred per cent. Hashtag no-brainer."

I'm holding hands with Sarah Shaw again. She's laughing. This is really happening. I'd better get rid of that shell suit.

✉

ACKNOWLEDGEMENTS

With grateful thanks to my readers for their kind words of support and encouragement. Thanks also to The Brickmakers posse for their ideas and suggestions, and for sharing their real-life experiences. I wish I could remember more of them.

ALSO BY JO EDWARDS

THE KATE KING TRILOGY - BOOK 1

WORK WIFE BALANCE

Kate King is flailing to keep afloat. As her team bicker, finger-point and cheat their way through rumours of sackings and site closures, her ill-tempered husband is becoming increasingly embittered and secretive. Kate knows she must address his petulant question: "Surely there's more to life than this?" but all her energies are required to dodge the corporate bullets constantly fired in her direction.

If things aren't bad enough, Kate also has to contend with a career-climbing attractive younger colleague and the sudden appearance of back fat. Beige knitwear has started calling to her from the shelves of M&S.

Something has to give, but will it be her marriage or her job? And which does she care about more?

"This is well-written, very funny and I raced through it, occasionally squealing in horror at the antics of Kate's colleagues. It's also a joy to read about a strong woman with a big job and fiery opinions, a nice antidote to the sugary sweet sort of chick lit." Daily Mail

"Best book in a long time! I have never read a book where I have laughed out loud before. Not the sort of book you can read quietly in bed next to a snoring husband! I felt that by the end of the book Kate was a friend, not a character from a book. Funny, funny book, can't wait to start on Pot-Bound."
Amazon Review

THE KATE KING TRILOGY – BOOK 2

POT-BOUND

The team from Perypils Insurance are back, primed to protect the things you value most in life... unless your locks are described incorrectly on your policy. Under the fraught leadership of Kate King, the team blunder their way through hopeless sales targets and mounting complaints. Mini-Cruella does her utmost to undermine Kate's authority. The Drain wants to snuff out the light at the end of the tunnel. The Snake drips her venomous gossip while The Rock attempts to limit the damage. A hostile press only serves to fuel the company's increasingly desperate attempts to mislead its customers and regulators.

Under intense pressure from her formidable boss and condemned to a one-incomed existence by her treacherous husband, Kate is forced to fight for the job she despises. Eager for someone to share her load, she dips a cautious toe back into the dating pool but stumbles into another swamp of pretence, exaggeration and downright lies.

Terrified of sliding into a homeless, vodka-fuelled oblivion, Kate's options are rapidly running out. She must determine the depth to which she is prepared to plummet in order to protect her livelihood. Will Kate be capable of spreading new roots amidst the harshness and turbulence of her life or will she forever be twisted into knots?

"Kate is a wonderful character, believable and likeable and with a nice line in funny put-downs." Daily Mail

"Having read 'Work Wife Balance' I could not wait to find out the next chapter in Kate's life - I was not disappointed! If you have ever worked in an office you will relate to the daily grind which, when added to Kate's chaotic personal life makes this a great read. I found myself laughing and cringing at the same time, it is so true to life!" Amazon Review

THE KATE KING TRILOGY - BOOK 3

MIXED RECEPTION

Kate King should be an extremely contented woman. Her new man is good with his hands, she has just embarked on a new career with the prestigious Hi! Hotels leisure chain, and she still fits a size twelve, albeit in elasticised sweatpants. But all is not well.

A long-term sufferer of agro-phobia (fear of parenthood), Kate struggles to forge a relationship with her new partner's child. Her attempts to bond with the little boy only serve to traumatise him, while her prospective in-laws do their best to thwart any progress Kate makes.

The team at Farzyk Hall provide little comfort, with Reception a hotbed of malicious gossip and extra-marital affairs, while the penny-pinching hotel directives drive guests to distraction. To make matters worse, a shapely love rival is lurking, perky bits primed and ready to fire the minute Kate trips up.

As her troubles multiply, Kate begins to wonder if any relationship is worth the constant torment.

"Perhaps the funniest writer I've read in many years. I'm running out of time now - almost finished the last book! Hoping there's plenty more on the horizon and soon. Marry me Kate! Fabulous stuff, but not to be read during the daily commute on public transport. People will think you odd if you wet yourself laughing." Amazon Review

"What an excellent read, so hard to put down! I didn't want it to end. Well written and extremely funny." Amazon Review

NOVELLAS BY JO EDWARDS

FOGGY'S BLOG

I am Morten Astley Fogarty, call centre worker and all-round entertainer. Although I have an extremely rewarding career answering the phones at Perypils Insurance (customers are always telling me what a total brick I am), my ambition is to perform on the stage. I am, after all, named after two of the greatest singers of the 1980's.

My girlfriend has a fantastic voice too and we often duet together. She has asked me to consider a three-way, so if I can find the right person to perform with us, we might even become the next Earth, Wind and Fire.

My colleagues are a wonderful bunch and are always doing little things to brighten my day. Only yesterday, I returned from lunch to find they'd re-arranged the letters O,K,N,B on my keyboard. We do have such fun!

"This was a great find. I read it almost in one sitting, needed to keep finding out what would happen to dear, innocent Foggy next! There are some wonderful characters: an unfortunate hero, a nymphomaniac mother, a Granny who stuffs sausage rolls up her sleeves....! There are many laugh out loud moments, if you don't know what 'speed-mincing' is you really need to read this. Very quirky, very entertaining and highly recommended."

Amazon Review

"Absolutely hilarious! I had tears streaming down my face I was laughing so much! If you've ever worked in a call centre or contact centre environment then this rings so true in many ways.
I've recommended this to several of my work colleagues and have now read Jo's other books. Brilliant!"

Amazon Review

A VERY FOGGY CHRISTMAS

I am Morten Astley Fogarty – insurance complaint handler, part-time barista and all-round entertainer. My career at the Perypils call centre has really taken off since my colleagues all voted for me to leave the team and transfer to complaints; I was chuffed to bits at being chosen! I love helping our customers resolve their concerns and as I've only received three death threats so far, I'm clearly doing something right.

On Sundays, I work with an extremely talented Chef, Joe, who trained under the calming influence of Gordon Ramsay. Joe's party-trick is to hurl his bread knife through the kitchen hatch towards my head. He always deliberately misses, of course; he's such a joker!

My girlfriend, Myra, is a wonderful actress and our director has tried her in lots of different positions. I know Myra is desperate to secure a leading part in our Christmas production, The Wizard of Oz and she has been scouring eBay for ruby slippers, size 9. Let's hope she can continue to satisfy the director!

"What can I say, I loved every word of this hilarious story. Rowan Atkinson or Jim Carey should star in a movie based on this wonderful, laugh every sentence tale. Now I have to read the rest of Jo Edwards' stories. Too bad the ratings only go to 5 stars as it deserves more."

Amazon review

That's all folks!

If you would like to know more about the author, please visit Jo's Amazon Author page or via her website at www.jo-edwards.com

Printed in Great Britain
by Amazon